SOUT

A Novel

Alice Barton

iUniverse, Inc.
New York Lincoln Shanghai

South Station
A Novel

iUniverse books may be ordered through booksellers or by contacting:

iUniverse
2021 Pine Lake Road, Suite 100
Lincoln, NE 68512
www.iuniverse.com
1-800-Authors (1-800-288-4677)

ISBN-13: 978-0-595-35918-9 (pbk)
ISBN-13: 978-0-595-67295-0 (cloth)
ISBN-13: 978-0-595-80372-9 (ebk)
ISBN-10: 0-595-35918-3 (pbk)
ISBN-10: 0-595-67295-7 (cloth)
ISBN-10: 0-595-80372-5 (ebk)

Printed in the United States of America

Acknowledgements

Many thanks to Jennifer and Chris who helped me give birth to Honey Lee, to my family for their patience as I worked through the story, to my Boston Writing group, especially Roz Rosenmeier, and to my endlessly patient husband, Millard.

CHAPTER 1

▼

1943

When Honey Lee Murphy was fourteen years old, she overheard a boy in the Immaculate Conception School yard call her the Belle of Belvedere. Puzzled, she turned the phrase around and around, first in her mouth and then in her head. She hadn't lived in the North long enough to know that both she and her mother, Savannah, were called Belles by all of her father's people and by everyone else in Lowell who knew or had heard about them. She knew the phrase "Southern Belle" but had certainly never thought about it in reference to herself. She also knew that Belvedere was the Irish Catholic section of this northern city where she now lived, and that *belle* in French meant beautiful. The boy's tone, however, didn't suggest approval of beauty. It suggested Lowell, the kind of small-town city where people lived in neighborhoods with their own kind and did not welcome strangers, especially strangers with odd names and strange accents.

That afternoon, she sat at the small mirror in her room at her grandmother's house in Catholic Belvedere and searched herself for beauty. She was almost six feet tall—way too tall for a fourteen-year-old and not happy about towering over just about everyone she knew. Her face, she decided, was too long despite her thick black bangs. And too much chin beneath her mouth. Her blue eyes—her father's eyes—didn't match her dark hair, and her skin was too white. Not at all beautiful.

"Nana says you better get down here fast," her cousin Peter yelled from downstairs.

Startled, Honey Lee jumped up. "Tell her I'm coming, will you Peter?"

She had only lived in her grandmother's house for two weeks, but already she knew that Sunday dinner was served at two o'clock on the dot and that she had better be on time. She stood up, pushed her hair back, and ran down the dark back stairs. She resisted the impulse to go into the kitchen to check on her mother and instead went directly to the dining room. Her grandmother, Nana Murphy, her father's sister Aunt Kitty, and her cousin Peter were already seated at the table. She sat down at her place beside her grandmother who kept tapping her fork on the table and looking at the clock, which had struck two at least five minutes earlier. Aunt Kitty coughed politely for the third time. And Peter, at the sound of a loud thud followed by an unmistakable curse, turned completely around in his chair to look into the kitchen. Honey Lee flushed and jumped up.

"Excuse me please, Nana, Aunt Kitty, Peter."

She went out to the kitchen to her mother. Savannah stood by the sink with an ice pick in her hand. On the floor at her feet lay a round chunk of ice from a pail that had been filled with water and put out on the back porch the night before to freeze.

"This damn kitchen! Just look what I have to do just to make iced tea."

Savannah's hair had come loose from the blue ribbon she always wore and hung limp against her flushed face. Her smart looking blue skirt and white blouse were hidden under an outsized apron that her mother-in-law had insisted Savannah wear if she were going to "cook in my kitchen."

"Do I look just awful, darlin?" She touched her hair with the back of a flour-dusted hand.

"No, Mama, you're beautiful," Honey Lee answered.

Smoke rose from the pot of boiling fat on the huge iron stove. The stove was unlike anything she or her mother had ever seen. It took up one whole side of the kitchen. Its black surface served as a source of heat for the kitchen, but two of the burners were hot enough for cooking. Bits of browned flour danced on the smoking oil. Spatters jumped from the pot, hit the hot stove, and popped.

"Mama, are you almost ready?"

"Yes, yes. Pick up that ice and chip some more into the glasses." Savannah pointed to the five glasses near the sink. At the bottom of two of them, a few ice chips were melting. While Honey Lee attacked the ice, her mother opened the oven door and pulled out a tin of brown muffins so dark that Honey Lee knew they were corn only because her mother had told Nana Murphy that she was making "a real Southern dinner" of fried chicken and sides. The kitchen table, at which they usually ate, was covered with flour, some of which had drifted onto the floor. An open box of corn meal and a tin of shortening sat near a mixing bowl. Honey Lee had never before seen disorder in her grandmother's kitchen.

Savannah turned the muffin tin over and tapped it, but the muffins stuck stubbornly to the pan.

"Did you grease it, Mama?"

"I do not need cooking tips from you, thank you very much."

Honey Lee continued to chip at the block of ice.

"Do see if you can budge these muffins while I see to the chicken, darlin'."

Savannah took a long handled fork and fished out pieces of chicken. Spots of browned batter oozing dark oil clung to them as she arranged them on a platter. Honey Lee had managed to pry about six of the muffins from the tin, their black bottoms remaining stubbornly in the pan.

"Now all I have to do is fix the tea and we can eat." Savannah picked up a large aluminum teakettle and poured hot water over tealeaves. She let the tea sit while she rearranged the chicken to better hide the bare spots. Then she poured the pale tea over the ice chips.

"Fine. Now isn't that just fine, darlin'?"

Savannah carried the platter of chicken to the dining room, came back for the muffins, and told Honey Lee to bring the tea. Honey Lee took another look at the floured, oily, wet kitchen. The fat still bubbled on the front of the stove. She wondered if she should move it away but decided not to risk irritating her mother. She went into the dining room with the tray of glasses, passed a glass to each of the diners and sat down.

Nana Murphy watched Savannah remove her apron, pat her hair, smooth her skirt, and sit down smiling in triumph.

"This is the way we eat in the South. Always in the dining room. Always fine Southern food."

Nana Murphy made the sign of the cross and prayed, "Bless us, oh Lord, and these Thy gifts which we are about to receive from Thy bounty through Christ Our Lord, Amen."

Savannah sighed her impatience, and almost before Nana Murphy finished praying, picked up the platter of chicken and passed it to Aunt Kitty. Nana passed the muffins.

"Honey Lee, darlin'," Savannah said. "I plum forgot the peas. Open the can and warm them will you?"

Honey Lee began to stand, but her grandmother put her hand on her arm.

"I'm thinking we should forget the peas," Nana said.

Half standing, Honey Lee wondered whose was the last word. Savannah sighed hugely, and Honey Lee sat down. Aunt Kitty cut into the piece of chicken on her plate. Chunks of batter fell off under the pressure of her knife and pink juice spurted onto the table. Peter laughed. Nana glared at him. She looked down at her own plate and picked up a muffin. When she bit it, the muffin cracked. Crumbs spilled onto the tablecloth. Peter laughed again. Savannah watched frowning. Then she picked up her glass, her fingers gracefully spread and sipped at the warm, watery tea. She put her glass down, burst into tears and ran out of the room sobbing. Honey Lee didn't know whether to stay at the table or follow her mother up the stairs. She longed to be back in Atlanta. She longed for her father.

*   *   *   *

She and Savannah had arrived in Lowell from Atlanta two weeks earlier, a week before her father's army unit was shipped overseas. Both of her parents had told their versions of how they met and married so often that Honey Lee felt she had been witness to their early lives. Savannah Burton insisted that she was a daughter of one of the oldest families in Atlanta, and that although she hadn't gone to Miss Melanie's School for Young Episcopal Ladies, she had acquired all the Southern graces she would have learned at that private school. She had gone instead to the public school near her home on Acorn Street. But she had learned to dance, to wear clean white gloves, to serve tea, to walk like a lady, to talk like a lady, to act always like a lady especially with gentlemen. Honey Lee heard in these stories a subtle criticism of her father, who was neither a Southerner, nor a gentleman, nor an Episcopalian.

When Savannah and Tommy Murphy met, Savannah, at sixteen, was exactly five feet tall. As she still did every night, she had wound strands of her black hair into tight flat circles, which she pinned to her scalp with bobby pins. When she combed her hair in the morning it fell in tight waves to her shoulders. She tied it back loosely with a thin ribbon, usually a blue one, in such a way that curled strands trailed down the side of her pale face. Her black eyes tilted up at the outside edges giving her a slightly Asian look. She favored bright lipstick. Passion Flower was her current favorite, but Honey Lee also remembered Fire and Ice, and Crimson Peony. Savannah liked the shape of her mouth with its full lower lip. She knew she had what fashion writers called good bones. She pinched her cheeks to give them color, a beauty trick she tried unsuccessfully to pass on to her daughter. She spent a lot of time looking at herself in mirrors. Tommy Murphy used to joke, "her bedroom mirror, hall mirrors, bathroom mirrors and just about every mirror and store window that she passes. But," he always added, "she was worth looking at."

Tommy Murphy, a tall redhead with deep blue eyes, was the son of an Irish Catholic widow from Lowell, Massachusetts. It was therefore surprising to some that he had met Savannah at a tea held at Saint Luke's Episcopal Church Hall in Atlanta. He had always laughed as he told the story to his daughter. A friend, he said, had suggested that they attend a tea sponsored every month by the church to welcome newcomers to the city. Tommy protested.

"A tea? With little old ladies? With little tiny cups? At a Protestant church? My mother would disown me!"

After twelve years of Catholic schools, his mother expected him to become a priest or to go to Boston College, "a good Jesuit school," and then think some more about becoming a priest. But he had wanted to work, and since there was no work in Lowell, he went south just as most of the mills in Lowell had. They quarreled bitterly before he left and had not seen each other since.

And so he went, and there met the beautiful Savannah.

Not allowed by her mother to date until she was sixteen, Savannah had very little experience of men when she met Tommy Murphy. She'd had mild crushes on boys before, but she'd never imagined how her stomach could lurch or that she'd forget to breathe in the presence of a boy, until Tommy Murphy walked into Saint. Luke's Episcopal Church Rectory.

She noticed him the minute he entered. She had to force herself not to follow his every move until at last he stood beside her waiting to be served tea. Back in Lowell, more than one girl had already succumbed to Tommy Murphy's gallant ways. So it was no surprise to him or to his friend that Savannah's hand shook when she handed him his tea. The cup and saucer rattled.

"Do y'all want sugar, Sir?" she whispered.

"I surely do love sugah." He laughed as she blushed.

In less than five seconds, Honey Lee's journey North was foreordained.

Within months, Savannah and Tommy were married at a private ceremony in the rectory of Christ the King Catholic Church. Savannah's dream of a big, white wedding at Saint Luke's Episcopal Church was dashed by Tommy's firm insistence that he would be married only by a priest of his own faith in a Catholic Church. He learned from a stern priest that he needed a special dispensation to marry a non-Catholic and that he could not be married in the church proper. So despite Savannah's tearful pleas, they were married in a simple ceremony only after Savannah swore that she would raise all children of the marriage Catholic. Neither of their parents approved; neither attended the wedding. The young couple moved to a small apartment in downtown Atlanta where Honey Lee was born and spent the first years of her life.

Honey Lee remembered with delight her father's love for her. During her early days in Lowell she often tried to make herself hear his laughter and his voice.

"How's my little Honey Bee? Here's a great big bear coming to get some Honey."

When she was still little she would squeal and run until he caught her up in his arms and lifted her almost to the ceiling. When she was older she told him how silly he was and that she was too old for such nonsense. But she loved being special to him.

"Who's the most beautiful girl in Atlanta?" he would ask.

"Mama," she would say.

"No, it's the Honey Bee. Everyone knows that."

Savannah would wait impatiently until Tommy had finished his "ridiculous games" so she could tell him about her day. More often than not the day had been "hideously difficult." Tommy, though often frustrated with his child bride, loved her. And Savannah was still drawn to the strong handsome man she had so quickly fallen in love with.

But two weeks before their arrival in Lowell, when Tommy came home to their apartment near the Army Base and told them that his unit was being shipped overseas, Honey Lee and Savannah were astounded even though they knew that soldiers and sailors were leaving almost daily for the Pacific and Europe. What shocked them even more was Tommy's announcement that he had called his mother and made arrangements for them to go to Lowell to live with her for the rest of the war or until he came home. Savannah was hysterical. She had never wanted to lay eyes on her Yankee mother-in-law, let alone live with her.

"I won't. I will not go," she announced tears streaming down her face.

"Yes, Savannah, you will," he said holding her by the shoulders.

"But why?"

"Because you need to be taken care of, dear," he said wiping a tear from her face, "and I can't do it from the other side of the world."

"My mother would help me. I could ask her again. I know she would." Savannah looked up at her husband opening her eyes wide and then lowering them.

"She's never even wanted to see us, Savannah. I won't do that to Honey."

"Honey Lee, Tommy, not Honey. And what about 'doing that' to me?"

"All right, all right, Honey Lee." Then more softly, he said, "My mother is a good woman. You'll both be fine."

"Your mother didn't want to see us any more than mine did, and you know it," she said placing her hands on her hips. "So why it's better to go there is beyond me."

"Because I want Honey Lee to be raised Catholic." Tommy's voice was quiet, firm.

"I'd make sure she went to Mass and Sunday School."

"Alone, all by herself? She needs more than that, Savannah. It's all arranged. That's the end of it." He turned away from her. But it wasn't the end of it. They argued up until the day he said good-bye to them at the station in Atlanta.

At the station, Honey Lee was alarmed at the masses of men in uniform and the crying women and children holding on to their men as if they could prevent separation. Sobbing, Savannah grasped Tommy's lapels so fiercely that Honey Lee thought she would rip his coat. He moved her backwards toward the train peeling her fingers from his coat.

When the train began to move Tommy lifted Savannah up and put her on the steps saying, "Please, dear, it's only for a little while. Be brave."

She pounded his chest and wept. "I hate you, Tommy Murphy. I hate you."

Tommy pulled away from her and kissed Honey Lee good-bye.

"Take care of your mother, Honey Bee, will you?" Honey Lee nodded, afraid to speak.

When the train began to move, she noticed that her father stood in a crowd of weeping women, and she and her weeping mother were alone on a train filled with men in uniform.

CHAPTER 2

▼

At first, Honey Lee was excited about a train ride to a place where it snowed real snow—snow that fell like confetti in the crystal ball her father had given her. He would turn it upside-down and say, "That's what it really looks like, Honey Bee. Some day I'll show you."

But entering the crowded coach car with her weeping mother dampened her spirits. Tommy had been lucky to get tickets because travel for non-military folks was forbidden. The train was so full of soldiers and sailors being shuffled from one place to another that there weren't seats enough to go around. But once on the overcrowded train, getting seats was easy. Soldiers and sailors were more than happy to give up their seats to a beautiful, weeping woman. After a while Savannah began to enjoy their attentions so much that she forgot how angry and sad she was. Although Honey Lee disliked seeing her mother respond to the attentions of men other than her father, she was relieved that Savannah had stopped sobbing and berating her father and his mother and all of the damn Yankees in Massachusetts.

When finally the train from Atlanta arrived at busy South Station in Boston, Savannah left Honey Lee under a large clock with their small suitcases telling her not to budge while she went, with two helpful soldiers, to see to their trunk. Honey Lee noticed that she was one of the only people in the station not in uniform. Soldiers and sailors rushed for trains or taxis. She focused on the hands of the clock inching from minute to minute until her mother returned with the two helpful soldiers; then they all went outside. When they felt the cold wind blowing off the water, both mother and daughter gasped. The two soldiers hailed a cab for them.

"Y'all are just the sweetest gentlemen I ever did meet. I truly do thank y'all for savin' me," Savannah said as the soldiers helped them into the cab. Honey Lee couldn't look either at her mother or the two helpers she was so embarrassed. Her father had told her that they would have to cross Boston and to get a train to Lowell. From South Station you could only go south or west. From the North Station you could only go north. Honey Lee's heart and her life broke in two as she left her mother's known, safe world in the South to enter her father's unknown world in the North. Savannah, having similar thoughts and no men to comfort her, began crying against Honey Lee's shoulder.

The train to Lowell was also crowded with men, some in uniform, some not, on their way to Fort Devens. The small, dingy station in Lowell had only one set of tracks for trains going either north to New Hampshire or south to Boston. Soldiers heading to Fort Devens in Ayer had to continue their journey by bus. Honey Lee tried to remember what her father had told her about his home, but she was so exhausted she could remember nothing.

When she and her mother stepped down from the train into the bitter cold of the mid-January late afternoon, only one woman waited on the platform steps. She wore a long black coat with a brownish fur collar, a black hat with a half veil, and black tie-shoes with oxford heels. She was so tiny she might have been mistaken for a child dressed in old woman's clothes. The woman did not smile as she approached, and for a moment Honey Lee was filled with dread. Then she noticed the old woman's startling blue eyes—her father's eyes, her own eyes— and felt somewhat reassured. When her grandmother finally stood before her and her mother, Honey Lee felt like an overgrown giant between the two little women.

"Might you be the Mairphies then?"

So that's what a brogue sounds like. Honey Lee knew her grandmother had come from Ireland as a young woman, but that she still sounded like Scarlet O'Hara's father in *Gone with the Wind* was a surprise.

"Yes. I am Savannah Burton Murphy, Thomas Murphy's wife, and this is my daughter, Honey Lee Murphy." Savannah took Honey Lee's hand in her own, the first sign of affection she had shown since the trip began.

"I am his mother," the old woman said. There was no warmth in her voice.

The two small women stiffened and didn't move toward each other. Honey Lee had no idea what to do or say. She didn't even know what she should feel. It seemed appropriate to embrace a grandmother, but the older woman did not invite it, and she knew her mother would not approve.

For want of anything else to say or do, Honey Lee spoke. "Thank you, ma'am, for meeting our train."

Her grandmother nodded, smiled tightly, and introduced the man with her as her brother Andrew, who would help with the luggage and drive them home. Home, Honey Lee thought, home. Where was home? Savannah went off with Andrew to collect their trunk leaving Honey Lee alone with her grandmother, who stared at her for several seconds.

"You've your father's height, haven't you? And his eyes as well."

Honey Lee nodded. "Yes, ma'am."

"Is this what they wear in winter in Georgia?" The grandmother touched the collar of the new coat Savannah had bought for the trip. The pale blue coat barely covered her knees, and her feet were cold in her thin black shoes.

"My mother bought it special for the trip."

"Sure and your mother will need to learn about winter in New England. We'll need to find a way to keep you warm." Her grandmother looked down at her shoes." Do you have overshoes?"

"Ovah shus?"

"To wear out in the snow."

"We all don't have much snow."

"Well, we do here, and we'll have to find overshoes for you."

"Yes, ma'am," Honey replied. She wondered what sort of shoes you put on over shoes.

Drawing closer to Honey Lee, Nana Murphy made an awkward gesture, something closer to a pat on her shoulder than a hug. "Could you call me Nana, then? I am your grandmother."

"Yes, ma'am."

Honey Lee and her grandmother waited together until the trunk was found and loaded into a borrowed, battered truck. Nana Murphy got into the truck on the driver's side leaving room for Andrew at the wheel. She directed her granddaughter to get in on the passenger side first so that her mother could sit on Honey Lee's lap, "since you're so much bigger than she is."

They drove off slowly in silence until Nana Murphy said, "Andrew, take a left then won't you so they can see the City Hall and the Library."

Andrew drove slowly by the two large Victorian stone buildings before turning around and heading down what appeared to be Lowell's main street.

"This is Kearney Square, named after one of our own," her grandmother said as they came to an intersection of two streets. Honey looked out and saw a huge clock in front of one of the stores.

"That tall building there is the Sun Building, where they publish our paper, *The Lowell Sun*." As they drove over a small bridge, Andrew spoke for the first time.

"That's one of our canals. Sure and we had so many they used to call us the Venice of America, that many canals we had. Built by the Irish they were."

When they reached a large stone church, her grandmother said, "That's our church, the Immaculate Conception. Stop, will you Andrew? Your father was baptized there, made his First Holy Communion there, and was confirmed there. Didn't I always think he would be married there too?" Honey Lee felt her mother stiffen in anger, but fortunately she said nothing.

Honey Lee had never been in a large Catholic church. She and her father had most recently been going to Mass at a chapel at the base. Her mother never went with them. She said that signing the paper promising to bring Honey Lee up Catholic was the last Catholic thing she would ever do.

Just beyond the church they took a right turn onto a street that backed up to the canal they had crossed. Mills lined the far side of the canal. Shabby brick and wood tenements that looked frozen and broken lined the street, the red brick and the wood darkened by years of mill smoke. As they drove further up the street, the houses improved some, and Honey Lee noticed that the street name had changed from Fayette to Concord. Her grandmother was quick to point out that her house was on Concord, not Fayette Street. Honey Lee wondered what line divided Concord and Fayette and who had drawn it and why. Although in better repair, the houses on Concord Street were crowded onto tiny lots almost touching each other.

The two-story house where her father had lived as a child was on the corner. It was larger than she had imagined and larger than the other houses nearby except for a multi-family tenement across the street. Nine steps led up to a small front porch. Andrew drove past the house and turned left on Sherman Street into a driveway at the side of the house. Two bare trees towered over the roofline. Andrew parked the car near the back door, and they climbed out—first Andrew from the driver's side, then Nana, and from the passenger side first Savannah from Honey Lee's lap, then Honey Lee. Nana Murphy led the way into the kitchen. Right away Honey Lee noticed the huge black stove on one side of the room. Its surface was bigger than a table and rising above it was a shelf decorated with gleaming chrome. Instinctively, she moved toward it. The warmth felt like balm on her cold face. Her cheeks reddened.

Nana bustled to the stove and poured water from a steaming kettle into a blue and white teapot. On a round oak table, six places were set with teacups and plates. Nana Murphy went into the pantry and came back with a pitcher of milk and a plate of pound cake.

"Sit you down now and have a cup of tea. A good cup of tea always makes things better."

A woman with red hair, older and much taller than her mother, came up to Honey Lee and kissed her on the cheek.

"I would know you as Tommy's child anywhere. You have his eyes. I'm your father's sister, Kitty." She turned to Savannah and said, "Welcome to Lowell, Anna."

Her mother bristled. "My name is Savannah."

"Let me take your coats," Kitty said and called her son Peter from the other room to hang their coats in the back hall. Peter was younger than Honey Lee and shorter. Aunt Kitty introduced him to the newcomers, and they all sat down. Honey Lee savored her first cup of Nana Murphy's tea—hot, sweet, and pale with milk. It was comforting, and as she sipped it things did begin to look a little better.

Afterward Nana led the way up the narrow back stairs and down the long hall to the front of the house. Honey Lee and her mother were to have the two front bedrooms.

"Your father's old room," she said to Honey at the door of the first room, "and now your room."

For the first few days on Concord Street, Honey Lee spent most of her time worrying about Savannah, who cried and ranted against her mother-in-law and Tommy and the North whenever she and Honey Lee were alone together. But she also had to spend time with Nana Murphy, who, on the first full day, quizzed her.

"Who made you, Honey Lee?" She waited while Honey Lee thought.

"My parents."

"No. God made you. And why did God make you?" Again Honey Lee thought and Nana Murphy waited.

"I don't know why," she answered confused.

"God made you to know Him, to love Him and to serve Him in this life and to be happy with Him in the next."

"Yes, ma'am."

"You don't know the catechism, do you child? What on earth did they teach you down there?" She shook her head, went to a bookcase in the living room, and pulled out a small blue book, which she handed to Honey Lee. "Well, old as you are, you'll have to start at the beginning then. By tomorrow, memorize the answers to all the questions in the first lesson. It's called 'The End of Man.' Word for word, mind you. That's the only way."

"Yes," Honey Lee said looking down at the small book in her hand. It was the first time she had ever seen *The Baltimore Catechism*. She felt ashamed of her ignorance and even more shy with her grandmother than when she had first met on the platform at the depot. Her grandmother said nothing more that day about her lack of religious training, but Honey Lee sensed that she blamed Savannah with whom she was distant and formal, disapproving. Honey Lee tried to convince Savannah to come out of her room and get to know her mother-in-law. But there was no truce between the two women. Honey Lee continued to be deferential and polite, never quite mastering the manner of address for the older woman, stuttering out something between ma'am and Nana.

"Nana, Nana, Nana. How many times must I tell you?" her grandmother chided.

CHAPTER 3

▼

Only one good thing, a wonderful thing, had happened during the week after their arrival. A winter storm, a blizzard it was called, transformed Concord Street. Honey Lee couldn't wait to go out. Her grandmother improvised proper winter clothes for her from Peter's closet. His stiff corduroy pants hit three inches above her ankles. Nana Murphy gave Honey Lee thick wool socks which she put on over her own shoes, then tucked the pants into the socks before putting on rubber overshoes with three buckles. Every step she took the buckles rattled and the corduroy pants produced a sound like a zipper opening. She would soon learn that all the boys at school zipped as they walked down the narrow aisles, that they all had the boy smell she now had, a not quite clean smell, like rubber and stale urine.

What had been magical from inside the house was miracle and blessing when she stepped out into the deep snow. The snow still fell heavily shrouding the trees and nearby houses in gauze. Honey Lee threw her head back and raised her face to the lacy flakes letting them fall onto her open eyes and into her mouth. She picked up a handful of snow and tasted, then ate it. Laughing out loud, she ate handful after handful. Then she rubbed it on her face.

"Oh, daddy, daddy," she cried out. "I wish you were here. It's too beautiful." She walked further into the yard and fell back onto a deep drift, her arms outstretched at her sides. She lay motionless in the still coldness.

"If you want to make angels, you have to move your arms." The voice startled her. She raised her head and saw Peter coming down the steps.

"What do you mean, make angels?"

"Watch," he said lying down near her and moving his outstretched hands up and down. Then he stood and pointed to where he had lain. She stood up to look.

"Angels, white angels with wings. How wonderful," she said lying down again and moving her arms.

"Want me to show you how to make snowballs? I can make them so hard they'd kill Japs and Nazis."

Honey was not at all sure she wanted to hit anyone with a lethal snowball especially someone who might carry a grudge against her father because of it. Despite Peter's ongoing teasing about her height, about the way she talked, and about her red-eyed mother, a great whoop of joy bubbled up and escaped. Content, she lay in the snow, opening her mouth wide to breathe in the white coldness. But as the snow melted on her clothes, she grew cold and knew she would have to go back into the house. Then she thought of the trees back home—the live oaks and evergreens and the magnolias, which even in winter, kept their waxy green leaves. She thought of her father's blue eyes and quick smile. She shivered and moved toward the door.

The day after the storm, Honey Lee ventured forth on her own. She had to get out of the house where the two older women still circled each other in silent anger. Heavy snow covered the grass in the yard and snow banks as tall as she lined the street. Dressed in Peter's clothes, she crossed Concord Street, walked a block to Perry Street, and turned right. A few yards down on her right, she saw several mammoth snow-covered hills. Too regular to be real hills, they resembled nothing she had ever seen before. Some boys stood on top of one of the mounds playing King of the Hill. They called out to her, "Hey kid, come on and play." She smiled to herself realizing they thought she was a boy. She took the ends of hair that still showed and tucked them up under her blue wool cap and walked slowly past, enjoying her disguise. She wondered what it would be like to really be a boy. Would it be easier? At least if she were a boy, her great height wouldn't be a problem.

She continued on down Perry Street to the end, then walked back to Concord and headed down Fayette. Again she noted the dreary brick buildings, some with shops on the first floor. One of the stores was a fish market, which held the lingering smell of the fried fish. Her aim on that cold Saturday was to take a look at the church and the school. She wanted to see them before she attended Mass the next day and went to school the following day. Her father and her grandmother had decided that she should repeat the second half of eighth grade at a Catholic school even though she had begun high school at home in Atlanta. They wanted her to study with the nuns. She hated the idea of starting at a new school where she would be a year older than most of her classmates and surely taller than any of them.

As she came to the end of the street, she saw the huge church with its two square-topped steeples—if they could be called steeples—with no spires. A high wrought iron fence surrounded the churchyard. She climbed up to the front door and tugged at the doorknob. The door didn't budge, so she went around the side of the church to another smaller door which opened easily. Inside, the church was dark and empty. At least at first it had seemed empty, but there was a woman dusting pews in the front of the church. When the woman heard Honey Lee, she looked up and called out.

"The upper church is closed during the week, young man. Take your hat off and go downstairs if you want to make a visit."

She left the church quickly and headed toward the school buildings, two old brick buildings with fire escapes down the sides. On a third building a sign announced *Convent of the Grey Nuns of the Sacred Heart.* Honey Lee stood for several minutes looking up at the convent hoping to catch a glimpse of a nun. But the shades were pulled and the convent house empty.

She walked away from the school buildings to seek out a less gloomy route home. The sun was going down and she began to feel the cold through Peter's corduroy trousers. Her feet in their thin shoes under the overshoes were aching. During the long walk home, her eyes filled with tears from the bitter wind and from loss and loneliness. She wondered if it was cold where her father was. Only his strong arms could have lifted her up at that moment.

When she got home it was almost dark. She could hear her grandmother in the kitchen and tried to slip up to her room without being seen, not because she was afraid of her grandmother but because she wanted to be alone. But her grandmother called out to her from the kitchen.

"Is it you then? Where in the name of the good Lord have you been all alone?"

"Just walking, Nana."

"Well your mother's crying again," she said, pointing to the ceiling. "See what you can do, will you? Sure as God is my witness, I try to make a home for her—for both of you—and what do I get but endless tears and a runaway. Wisha, Wisha."

Honey Lee went up to her crying mother who lay on her bed in a kimono, more suited to Atlanta than to the cold house where they now lived. Nana didn't believe in "overheated bedrooms."

"Mama, what is it?" Honey Lee went to the bed and put her hand on her mother's forehead.

"I hate this house, I hate it. I hate the North, I hate her, and I hate your father. I want to go home."

"Mama, it'll get better," Honey Lee whispered hoping to get her mother to talk more softly. "We'll get used to it, you'll see."

"Never, never, never," Savannah said, her voice rising on each word.

"Shhh. She'll hear you. Please, Mama."

Savannah's sobs wound down. Honey went to her mother's still unpacked suitcase and found a blue skirt and a pale pink sweater.

She handed her mother the clothes she had chosen saying, "You'll feel better if you dress, Mama. Pink is your color. Daddy loves you in pink."

"The first time he ever saw me I had the prettiest pink dress you've ever seen. I think he fell in love with my dress."

"Not just the dress, Mama. You are his 'Southern Rose,' the prettiest girl in all of Atlanta."

"Oh, Honey Lee, whatever will we do so far from home?"

"When daddy comes back, we'll go home. He promised." She tugged at her mother to get her to stand up and dress.

"If the damn war ever ends," Savannah said pulling the pink sweater over her head. She dressed slowly, smoothing the skirt over her flat stomach. "No one could ever tell I had a baby, could they?" she said and fluffed her hair. To Honey she was as beautiful, more beautiful even than Vivien Leigh. She wished she looked more like her mother and less like her father.

They went together to the kitchen and sat down. Aunt Kitty and Peter were already seated waiting for them. On Saturday night at the Murphy's, the menu was always the same, just as it was on Fridays. Fish on Fridays and beans and hot dogs on Saturdays. In the center of the round, oak kitchen table was the plate of hot dogs, the bowl of beans, bread and butter, and a pot of tea. Nana Murphy began the meal by making the sign of the cross.

"Bless us Oh Lord and these—" Honey had already learned the short prayer by heart. Just after the Amen, Nana said, "Now about tomorrow. The nine-fifteen is the children's Mass. Kitty and Peter and I always go to that Mass. Tomorrow, we'll all go." Savannah said nothing. Honey Lee said, "Yes, ma'am."

"Yes, Nana, Honey. Call me Nana. And I'll be calling you Honey," Nana announced. "No need for double names up here. I can't imagine your father giving you a name like that, not a Saint in either of two names. Father Finn would never have baptized you with that name."

"Yes, Nana. I'm sorry." Honey ignored her mother's foot kicking her under the table.

"Are you prepared for Communion?"

"I think so. You mean…"

"I mean, are you in the state of grace?" When Honey Lee looked puzzled, she continued. "How long has it been since your last confession?"

"I…maybe a month." She was unfamiliar with the term state of grace, and she couldn't remember when her father had last taken her to church on Saturday for confession.

"A month? You haven't confessed a sin for a month, and you think you're ready to receive Our Blessed Lord in Holy Communion? We'll go early to church and get Father Finn to listen to your sins."

"Yes, Nana."

When her grandmother also told her that she must keep "a strict fast from midnight" taking care not to swallow a drop of water when she brushed her teeth, Honey Lee realized that her education as a Catholic was even more deficient than she had thought.

Her mother had no intention of going to church with them. She had never gone with her and Tommy. Honey Lee had just not figured out how Savannah was going to tell her mother-in-law she wasn't going. On Sunday morning, she found out.

As she left the bathroom, she heard her mother cry out in a weak voice, "Honey Lee, darlin."

"Yes, Mama, I'm coming." Honey Lee was wearing a new school dress her grandmother had bought for her before they had even met. The dress almost fit except for the length. But Honey Lee had experience with clothes that were not long enough for her. She found her mother lying on the bed, not dressed for anything but sleep.

"Darlin', I have the most terrible headache." She placed the back of her hand against her forehead and lowered her head to the pillow. "Tell her for me, will you sugah?"

Nana Murphy did not for one second believe in Savannah's headache. "Heathen," she muttered.

Honey Lee followed the others on the long walk to church. She felt cold again. A coat, borrowed from her Aunt, was not long enough to cover her legs down to the boots she was wearing. She hunched down and walked as fast as she could without passing the others. They arrived at church by nine o'clock so Honey Lee could have a private confession with Father Finn in the darkened downstairs church. Nana Murphy led Honey Lee directly to Father Finn's confession box. What a strange phrase, confession box. At her old school they had Valentine Boxes and Suggestion Boxes and Ballot Boxes. The confession box wasn't at all like any box she had ever seen with its three entrances, a center door for the priest and two side entrances curtained in velvet. Her grandmother pushed her toward one of the curtains and told her to go in and wait. She entered and quickly began to speak the words she remembered, "Bless me Father, for I have sinned…" Then she fell silent. She couldn't remember the rest. Nor did she realize that the priest had not yet opened the window through which he could see and hear her. When he slid the panel aside, she jumped up and cried out. She held her breath hoping her grandmother hadn't heard.

"Is it the little Murphy girl?"

"Yes, sir." She knelt back down.

"Yes, Father Finn. OK, dearie?"

"Yes, Father Finn," She wondered if she would ever get titles straight.

"Well, now what would you like to say?"

"I don't know, Father Finn."

"Just Father will do. Are you settling in OK? Are they treating you right?"

"Yes, Father."

"Well, let's just wait a bit here and then you can go along. We'll do confession another time. And you needn't tell that to Mrs. Murphy. All right?"

"Oh yes, thank you, Sir."

She heard the old priest chuckle as he slid the window back. She pushed the curtain aside and walked toward her grandmother, who led the way to the upper church. It was a wonder to behold. Its Gothic arches shot up so high that the ceiling was in darkness. The brilliant windows, lit up by the cold January sunlight, were unlike anything she had ever seen before, two round windows on each side of the church and smaller ones down the length and behind the massive white carved altar. By the time Honey Lee and her grandmother got upstairs, all the pews in the front of the church on both sides were filled with children. At the end of every third or fourth row sat a nun with a black veil. From time to time one of the nuns stood up and touched the head or the shoulders of one of the children who was not sitting up straight or who was whispering to a seatmate.

The nuns were mysterious. Honey Lee had only the vaguest of notions about them. Her father had told her about going to "the Immaculate," as he always called it. He described the clothes the nuns wore—"long dresses, funny head coverings, and old-lady black shoes." He told her she would call the nuns Sister, "probably Mary something or other. Or Saint something or other." He also said that she better learn that in her grandmother's house the nun's word was always the last word. Many a time he had been twice punished for bad deeds, once by the nuns and again, more thoroughly, by his mother.

By counting Honey Lee found what she believed was the eighth grade class. The next day she would meet them and Sister Rose, the eighth grade teacher. Peter told her that Sister Rose was very strict and that she preferred boy students to girls. This school year for the first time she had a mixed class, and that she was not happy about it she made clear to the entire class. Honey Lee was somewhat comforted by the Mass, which followed the pattern she knew fairly well, but she left the church more worried than when she had entered. So much that was new, so many people looking at her, the fierce Sister Rose waiting for another unwanted girl student, and so many eighth grade students younger and smaller than she. If only she could, like her mother, just stay in bed.

CHAPTER 4

▼

On Monday morning, Nana Murphy woke Honey Lee at seven o'clock." Up with you, now, and say your prayers."

Honey Lee knelt beside her bed praying fervently for some excuse to keep her from school. Her grandmother held out a dress Honey Lee had not seen before. "This dress will make you look more like the others. Your own just won't do. Too Southern, not warm enough, not the way we dress."

"Yes, ma'am. I mean Nana." Honey Lee took the dress from her grandmother, working to keep her face expressionless. Cotton, like her own dresses, it had long sleeves, a high neck with a white collar. The brown, white and orange plaid was bold and over bright. She hated it. She also hated the brown knee socks Nana had given her to wear. But she put them on.

Her mother, when Honey Lee went to kiss her good-bye, stared at her. "Where on earth did that come from? For God's sake take it off."

"Nana says I have to wear it."

Savannah sighed deeply. "Of course she did, and of course you have to do it." She turned her head to the wall refusing Honey Lee's kiss.

Nana Murphy told Peter to take good care of his cousin, but Honey Lee could tell he was embarrassed to be seen walking with her down the long stretch of Concord and Fayette Street. She was wearing her aunt's coat and heavy rubber boots with buckles which clicked at every step. She asked Peter if they could please walk over two blocks to High Street and down that way because High Street was prettier, but Peter said that he always walked down Concord with friends he picked up along the way. She recognized one of his friends as one of the boys who had called out to her to come and play King of the Hill. She determined to walk alone the next day. The closer they came to the school, the more anxious Honey Lee became. Before the boys made the turn up East Merrimack toward the schoolyard, she stopped and let them go ahead. Peter turned and called out to her but shrugged when she stood still not answering and kept walking.

Walking on alone, she heard the high-pitched voices of children before she saw the schoolyard. Scores of children of all ages filled the yard, some huddling near the doors waiting to get out of the cold; others making snowmen; still others, boys, throwing snowballs at each other and at girls. Honey Lee could not see her cousin and was pretty sure that if she did, he would ignore her. She waited on the sidewalk outside the playground for the children to go in. The idea of walking through a bunch of strange children was intolerable.

Finally she heard a bell and the children raced to form silent lines apparently according to grade. A group at a time, they entered one or the other of the red brick buildings. When the last child had filed in, Honey Lee slowly walked to the nearer of the two buildings and entered through the door the children had used. The hallway was silent. Each of the several doors was labeled with a grade and a Sister's name. First Grade, Sister Mary Bernard, Fifth Grade, Sister Henrietta, Seventh Grade, Sister Mary of Charity. There was no discernible pattern to the arrangement. Honey Lee began to get angry at Peter for not seeing her to the principal's office as Nana Murphy had asked him to. There seemed to be no office on the first floor of the building so Honey Lee climbed to the second floor. It was identical to the first except it didn't have the door to the outside.

As there was no one to be seen in either the up or downstairs corridors, Honey Lee decided that she was in the wrong building. She walked through the schoolyard to the other building and entered the first floor corridor. It looked similar to the first floor of the other building. No visible office. She climbed the stairs to the second floor and saw at the end of the corridor a sign on a frosted glass door. She approached the door and read, Sister Mary Veronica, Principal. Relieved, she stood a slight distance from the door willing herself to knock. She could neither breathe nor move. Behind her, she heard someone stomping down the stairs from the third floor. One of the Sisters? Seeing no place to hide, she stood still then turned to see a boy about her own age on the landing above her.

"Are you the new kid?" he asked.

"Ah…I think so."

"What kind of talk is that?"

Honey Lee didn't answer. The boy stared at her without speaking for so long she was about to turn around and knock on the office door just to get rid of him.

"Well, if you are, you better hurry up and get upstairs. Sister Rose is looking for you."

Behind her, the office door opened, and the first nun Honey Lee had ever seen appeared.

"All right, William, I'll see to the new student. Go back to class."

"Yes, Sister," the boy said and began to back up the stairs. Honey Lee had not yet been instructed in the etiquette that required students to back out of rooms and up stairs when a nun was present.

Despite everything her mother had taught her about not staring, Honey Lee stared at the woman. The overall impression was of a person cut in two, the top black, the bottom beige. The shoulders and arms to the elbows were covered with a black cape that ended at the waist. From the waist down, a deeply pleated beige skirt fell to the floor. A semi-transparent, stiff black fabric that came to a point on the forehead and ended in a wide bow under the chin made a heart-like frame for the face. In those first moments Honey Lee didn't have time to register the silver crucifix that was so much a part of the dress of the Sisters and the black strip that hung from the waist almost to the hem of the skirt.

"Good Morning, dear. You must be the Murphy girl. And I am Sister Veronica. Come in and let's get acquainted." She led Honey Lee into the office and motioned for her to sit in the chair near the desk.

"When your father was a boy, I taught him in seventh grade. Later I taught your Aunt Kitty." Honey wanted to ask what her father had been like, but she didn't have to. Sister Veronica went on. "He was a handful, your father," she paused and smiled remembering, "but we loved him. I pray every day for him and all of our others gone off to this terrible war."

Honey Lee almost cried at this reminder of her father and the dangers he was facing. Sister Veronica changed the subject asking about her school in Atlanta and her religious training.

"Did you learn the catechism down there?"

"No, ma'am."

"No, Sister," the nun interrupted.

"Yes, Sister. I'm learning it now. My grandmother gave it to me to learn."

"And this is the first you've studied the Catechism?"

"Yes, ma'am. But I'm up to Lesson 12."

"I want you to finish the first book and come in to talk to me about it next week. Then we'll start you in on the second book. All of your classmates learned these books some years ago."

"Yes, ma'am."

"Yes, Sister." She smiled at Honey Lee and put her arm around her. "Have you heard from your father, dear?"

"Not yet, Sister." Sister Veronica smiled and patted her shoulder. She walked from the office beckoning to Honey Lee to follow her up the stairs to the eighth grade classroom. Sister Rose answered the soft knock and greeted them.

"Tall, just like her father, isn't she?" she said to Sister Veronica, then turned to the class. "Children, this is your new classmate," she paused, turned to Honey Lee and said, "Is it Honey Lee?"

"Yes, ma'am."

"Yes, Sister Rose."

Honey Lee thought she heard giggles from the students who sat with hands folded on their desks. Why are they laughing? Is it my name? The dress? My size?

"All right, Honey Lee, take the seat in the last row. Jimmy Jackson, take Miss Murphy's coat to the cloak room." A thin raggedy boy seated in the first row came and took her coat from her. Sister Rose pointed to the girls' side of the room. Honey Lee murmured excuses when she bumped desks in the narrow aisle. When she sat down at the small desk which did not allow room for her long legs, she heard more giggling. Both the desk and the chair were bolted to the rough wooden floor. Sister Rose rapped sharply on the teacher's desk with a ruler. Like the others, Honey Lee folded her hands and sat in silence until Sister Rose rang a small bell. Everyone stood up. Honey Lee looked at the girls in front of her hoping to see someone her height or at least close to it. Then she noticed that all of the students had their heads bowed and eyes closed. The prayers were long. Honey Lee knew the Our Father and the Hail Mary, but two of the others, the Apostles Creed and the Glory Be she didn't know by heart. At the end of the prayers the students turned to the large flag in the front corner of the room and said the Pledge of Allegiance.

As soon as they were seated, Sister Rose wrote an equation on the board and told the students to solve it. Then she walked toward Honey Lee with a pile of books and showed her how to open the desk to put the books away until they were needed. Honey Lee had no pen or pencil to work the equation. Next to her, a girl looked up from her paper.

"Here," the girl said tearing a page from her notebook and handing Honey Lee a pen.

"Ann, are you talking without permission?"

"Yes, Sister Rose, I'm sorry."

Honey Lee had begun algebra in her first year of high school and was able to solve the equation quickly. At least they wouldn't be ahead of her in math.

The rest of the day was a blur. She did remember two contests, called Bees: a math Bee and a grammar Bee. The students lined up on either side of the room, boys on one side, girls on the other. Sister fired questions to the first boy in the boys' line and then to the first girl in the girls' line and proceeded down the line. Students who failed to answer the questions correctly had to sit down until the Bee was over. Whichever student was the last one standing claimed a ribbon for the side, blue for the math and red for grammar. Honey went down on the first round in grammar having failed to recognize the indirect object in the sentence, "The boy in the dark blue suit with the red tie gave Mary a valentine." In both Bees the same boy, Jimmy Jackson, and the same girl, Ellen Flynn, were the last to go down and were rewarded with holy cards. Honey didn't know what the tiny cards were until she finally won a bee and was given a card with a picture of Jesus pointing to His Heart, bright red and visible on the front of His robe. Underneath was printed, *The Sacred Heart of Jesus.*

Sister Rose fostered learning by encouraging competition. Honey Lee swore to herself that she would one day beat Ellen Flynn. She did, on occasion, win the holy cards, Ellen coming in second, but by that time Honey Lee and Ellen Flynn had become friends. Ellen lived on High Street, closer to the school than Honey Lee, and the two often left school together and stopped at Ellen's house. Ellen had two brothers and a sister, a plump easy-going mother, and quiet gentle father who taught Latin at the high school. Honey treasured her visits at the Flynns' house, so different from her own quiet house. Ellen's family could not hear enough from Honey Lee about Atlanta and Savannah. They began to divide into North vs. South, Rebel vs. Yankee in their games even when they were just playing rummy. Honey was as often Yankee as Rebel.

Jack, Ellen's older brother, already in high school, often asked her to talk, just so he could listen. He said he loved her soft Southern voice. He also told her he loved seeing a girl who could look directly into his eyes without even tilting her head back. Honey was even a bit taller than he was. She didn't think much about Jack as a boy interested in her as a girl. She didn't yet think about any boys in that way.

Once Honey Lee had made friends with Ellen, the school year became less frightening, even pleasant. She learned that the gruff Sister Rose was in fact a kind woman and a wonderful teacher. Although she often felt sorry for the students who never could and never would win a bee, she loved the thrill of competition. At some point Sister, perhaps bored by having the same two or three winners, decided to set up mixed teams, boys and girls against boys and girls. Honey and Ellen were never on the same team, and both of them wanted to play against Jimmy Jackson, who was always the boy winner. Both Honey and Ellen could sometimes beat Jimmy, sometimes not.

Jimmy Jackson was a strange boy. His hair hung in clumps to the neck of his shirt. No one was taking clippers or a razor to that hair. Often he wore the same shirt and pants for days at a time. He seemed to have only one pair of shoes—jackboots that were too big for him and very worn. But he was studious, always reading, able to solve tough equations quickly, and always at the head of the class in grades. Honey Lee often wondered about him especially after she learned he lived on Fayette Street. That explained his grooming: he was poor, poorer than she and her mother. He had to wear hand-me-downs. She tried to talk to him several times, but without success. He was quiet, shy, and distant—except in class where he was quick to answer and to ask questions.

CHAPTER 5

▼

One day early in April, Sister Veronica came to the classroom looking very solemn. She whispered something to Sister Rose who stiffened, then walked down the aisle to Honey Lee's desk. She bent and whispered.

"Honey Lee, please go with Sister Veronica."

Honey got up and followed Sister Veronica out of the room, down the two flights of stairs, across the playground, and into the convent where she had never been before. Sister didn't say a word to her. Honey Lee was frightened. Had she done something wrong? Was she being expelled? She was even more alarmed when she entered a formal sitting room and saw her grandmother sitting in one of the two blue armchairs. When Honey Lee looked at Nana, her worry deepened. This was something terribly serious. Her grandmother slowly stood.

"Sit down, Honey, sit down so I can see you, dear." Nana Murphy pointed to the chair where she had been sitting. Her face looked rumpled, and her eyes were liquid. Honey's worry turned to terror. Her father, it must be about her father. She had imagined terrible things happening to him. The papers printed the names of the dead and missing every day. Nana leaned toward her, put her hands on Honey Lee's shoulders and then awkwardly embraced her, holding her head against her breast. Honey Lee was surprised at how soft her grandmother felt.

"Oh, Honey, he's gone."

"My father? My father!" She tried hope. "Missing?"

Nana shook her head. Tears fell from her eyes.

"Savannah? My mother. Where is she? Does she know? Where is she, Nana?"

Honey Lee tried to get up, but her grandmother pulled her even closer.

Finally she said, "Your mother—Your mother—She's—she left."

"Left? When? Where did she go?" She stopped struggling against her grandmother.

"I don't know, dear. Maybe she doesn't know herself. She read the telegram, she threw clothes into her suitcase and just ran and ran. I tried to stop her. I followed her all the way to the depot. She was crying. She wouldn't listen. The train came, and she just left."

Honey Lee wailed, "Without me? Leaving me here alone?"

"Honey, sweet child, she'll come back. She loves you. I know she will." Honey Lee couldn't breathe or speak. She couldn't move as if giant hands squeezed her chest and pushed down on her head forcing her down and down.

"Father Finn will help us, darlin'. Try—to—be—" Her grandmother's voice trembled and stopped.

Sister Veronica came in with a tea tray. She put it down and then folded Honey Lee in her arms.

"I am so sorry, Honey Lee. Have some tea, both of you. Father will be here in a few minutes. Let's pray together for your dear father."

She listened as Sister and Nana said a prayer that she had never heard before. "Eternal Rest grant unto him, oh Lord, and let the Perpetual Light Shine upon him. May his soul and the souls of all the faithful departed, through the mercy of God, rest in peace, Amen."

The heaviness of her body made it difficult to raise the cup to her mouth. Honey Lee couldn't swallow the warm milky tea. She became conscious of her grandmother's embrace, but she could not respond.

Father Finn entered and told them he would take them home. The trip up Fayette Street seemed as long as her trip from the South to the North just months before. She turned slightly away from her grandmother and stared out the window noticing nothing until she saw Jimmy Jackson entering one of the most derelict buildings on Fayette Street. He was alone and looked terribly sad; even in her own misery, she pitied him. She lapsed again into non-seeing until they finally reached the house on Concord Street, the house she had only just begun to call home. Without mother or father could there be a home? She dutifully thanked Father Finn, who gave her a long hug and promised prayers for her father and for her mother and for her. The feel of a man's body was strange to Honey Lee who had last been embraced by a man when her father had said good-bye to her.

She was sure, despite what her grandmother had told her, that she would find her mother at home. She ran to her mother's room. It was empty; the house was empty. Sure she would find a note, she ran to the dresser, then to the bed, then the dressing table. Nothing. She pulled out all of the drawers so hard that two of them went clattering to the floor. She wanted a note, a note asking her to follow her mother wherever she had gone, a note promising that her mother would return, a note that was at least an explanation. But there was nothing on the dressing table—no lipstick, no hairbrush, no perfume, nothing at all. The bureau drawers were empty and so was the closet except for her mother's kimono. Honey took the robe from the hook and held it to her face. Her mother's lavender scent was fresh. She closed the door, lay down on the bed, and put a pillow over her head.

"No. No. No." The word exploded from deep within her. Then she began to moan. She knew that Nana Murphy was standing outside the door, waiting. When at last her moans became sobs, Nana came into the room and sat on the edge of the bed. She talked quietly, in a voice that was new to Honey. She told stories about Tommy Murphy. She talked and talked, reliving his youth and giving it to his daughter. Tears filled the old woman's eyes again and again, and spilled unwiped onto her dress. She told Honey of Tommy's recklessness as a baby.

"He ran before he walked. Oh, you should have seen him. Such a scrawny little thing running to beat the wind." She talked about how the girls in high school had followed him home, how they called him on the telephone over and over.

"He was such a handsome one, and such a dancer. I wish you could have seen him." She gently rubbed Honey Lee's back as she spoke. She talked about the danger of loving too hard.

"He was my first baby and I loved him, more than anything in this world or out of it. More than I should have, I know, but I couldn't help it. Only children should love that way. They have to. Sure and you loved him even more than I did, I'm sure of it, and sorry for it. But Honey Lee, I cannot bear this cross alone. Will you help me? Please?"

Honey Lee nodded and forced herself to sit up. She put her arms around her grandmother and they sat in silence until the room darkened. Finally Honey Lee spoke.

"Nana, how did you find out?" Who told you?"

"There was a telegram for your mother. She opened it. Then she handed it to me. Didn't I know before she ever opened it what it said? 'We regret to inform you that your husband, Thomas Murphy, Sergeant U.S. Army, has been killed in action. He was a brave soldier, and the nation honors him for his sacrifice.'"

"Nothing for you? For me?"

"No. Only for the person closest to the one who dies, the "next of kin" is what they call it."

"Can I see it?"

Nana Murphy reached into the neck of her dress and pulled out the wrinkled yellow sheet. She smoothed it, and put it into Honey Lee's hand. Honey Lee studied it.

"But you and I are the closest."

"Your mother loved him. And she knew how much you loved him. You are so much like him. That's maybe why she had to leave. It was too hard for her to see you."

"I hate her. She only thinks of herself. Just herself. I hate her." Honey began to moan again. Her grandmother held her closer. When she could speak again, she asked, "Does anyone else know?"

"Father Finn and the Sisters. I called him and he brought me to you."

"Are you going to tell people?" Honey Lee pulled back to look at her grandmother, who bent her head slowly and shook it.

"Sure and I don't know what to do."

Honey Lee studied her grandmother, frightened to see her for the first time as old and weak.

"Nana, where is my grandfather? Your husband."

"Oh, Good God, darlin' sometimes it seems to me that all we do in life is lose things. He died when Tommy and Kitty were babies. I thought I would die too. I wanted to. And then I went and quarreled with your father and I lost him, too. I lost him for fifteen years because I was stubborn. I drove your mother away, too. Oh Honey Lee, I am so sorry. So sorry for everything." Again they sat in silence holding each other.

When the telephone rang, they went downstairs together. Nana Murphy picked up the receiver and told the speaker that Mrs. Thomas Murphy, Jr., was not in, and that she didn't know when to expect her. Yes, she had heard the terrible news. No, she did not want to talk about it. Yes, she would appreciate an obituary: the caller could contact Father Finn at the Immaculate Conception Rectory. And so the news would spread to everyone in Lowell. The handsome Tommy Murphy was dead.

Aunt Kitty knocked softly on the door and came in. She had heard the news and come home early. She went to her mother and kissed and held her. She turned to Honey Lee.

"Where is your poor mother, dear?" Honey Lee could find no words. Kitty embraced her and all three wept silently.

Suddenly, a door slammed and Peter walked in throwing his books on a chair. When he saw the three women, he stopped, at first puzzled, then frightened. "Mom, what's wrong?" He shouted and pulled at his mother's arm.

"It's Uncle Tommy," Kitty whispered.

"Wounded? Missing?" Like Honey Lee, Peter hoped.

"No, dear."

Terrified, he stared at his mother. "Oh, Mom." Then he hugged his grandmother and moved toward Honey Lee. He patted her shoulder awkwardly. "Gee, Honey. Gee whiz, I'm so sorry." Death is as new to him as it is to me, Honey Lee thought. His mother took him into the kitchen. Honey Lee could hear her talking to him. He had a father in the war, too. Aunt Kitty came back without her son. The three women were alone together, the widow, the sister, and the child.

The Lowell Sun was delivered to homes throughout the city early in the morning. By eight o'clock, the telephone began to ring. The doorbell rang, and neighbors carrying food and speaking in whispers came and went. Nana sat in her usual chair near the radio that her son-in-law had bought her. He claimed that when the new thing, television, came the radio could be converted to show pictures. Nana listened to the news off and on all day as if some new report might cancel out her son's death. Honey pulled the footstool up beside her grandmother's feet, craving her grandmother's touch on her head, her back, her hand.

Father Finn came back and talked to Nana about a memorial Mass.

"A memorial Mass? Don't you mean a funeral, Father?"

"Lizzie, we can't have a funeral without a body. You know that." Nana shook her head and started to cry again. No body to be honored. No laying her son to rest in Saint Patrick's Cemetery.

"I can't do it, Father."

"Lizzie, I need to tell the papers. So when should it be?"

"I don't know. Can you decide?"

"All right then, Lizzie. I'll arrange it." He took their hands in his and said, "God bless you, both of you."

The Mass was to be held the following Wednesday. Aunt Kitty planned a meal for family and friends after the Mass. Honey Lee and Nana quietly followed directions from Kitty and from Lizzie's brother Andrew who had come over from Billerica to be with his sister. As the days dragged on, other relatives, Nana's husband's family, came and went. Honey did not leave her grandmother's knee except when she retreated to her room to grieve alone, which she did more often as time passed. She lay still on her bed for hours at a time. Twice Ellen Flynn came by, but Honey wouldn't see her. Her grandmother worried. She came into Honey's room late one afternoon.

"That funny young Jackson boy, with his hair slicked back and his face clean for a change, is here to see you." She spoke in a crisp, cheerful voice.

Face buried in her mother's robe, Honey said, "Tell him I'm not home, will you please Nana?"

"It's tired I am of putting him and the others off. Won't you just see him?"

"I can't, Nana, I can't, Please." Nana Murphy shook her head slowly and left. Seeing anyone would take far more strength and resolve than Honey Lee could muster. She knew that gossip had already begun about her mother. People felt sorry for her, and they judged her mother. How was she ever going to be able to go back to school?

The day of the Memorial Service finally came. Nana Murphy came to Honey Lee's room to get her and to explain what she herself had so much difficulty accepting—that there could be no funeral without a body. A body, Honey Lee thought. Not Tommy, the tall, laughing man who would swoop her up and kiss her even when she had grown to her full height. Another flood of grief overcame her and she fell back onto the bed. When Nana told her that her father would want her to be at church and to be brave, she got up and went down to the car which took them to the church. She remembered nothing of the Mass for her father or the lunch Aunt Kitty served afterward. A few people still milled around in the house when she went back to her room. She lay very still staring at the ceiling. She could hear her cousin's voice and her grandmother's crying. After a while, she fell asleep. When she woke up she felt as if she were coming up from a deep black hole. She resisted returning to the world. She lay on the bed, completely still, even when she heard her grandmother open the door and look in at her.

I can't bear her sadness; the most I can do is bear my own, Honey Lee thought. She stayed in her room for the rest of the day and the night, denying her hunger.

CHAPTER 6

▼

The next morning Honey Lee got up and went to her closet and pulled out the clothes she had worn on her first days in Lowell, Peter's clothes. They still hung there after all this time. Three months had gone by while she and her mother waited for her father to come back and take them home. She pulled on the corduroy pants and the jacket. She found Peter's hat and jammed it onto her head, tucking all of her hair under it. She looked at herself in the mirror. She could hardly recognize herself except for her shoes. Overshoes in April didn't make much sense, but she pulled them on anyway, and went to the top of the stairs to listen for her grandmother. She heard cooking sounds from the kitchen. She went down the front stairs and left the house. Outside, the air was sweet and warm. A green mist hovered in the tall elms in the yard. Buds were beginning to form on the small pear tree. Nana had told her that the pears were as sweet as honey when ripe. She had shown Honey the rope marks from the swing that Tommy and Kitty had used when they were young. Nana even had a picture of her father standing under the tree next to the swing.

"When he was a wee lad, he would sit and swing for hours," she'd said.

Honey crossed the road and headed for Perry Street and the one place she knew she could be alone, Telephone Park. What had seemed great mounds of snow in January were great stacks of telephone poles held in place by thick metal cables and mounted on pallets high enough to allow children to crawl underneath. The piles were stacked high enough to challenge the more daring children, who had named the park. As she had hoped, no one was in sight. Children were at school, and workers at Fleming Paper Company were inside. She had never seen telephone workers in the park. Had someone forgotten that the poles were there? What were they for? She counted again the eight stacks and chose the second for her refuge. She lay flat on the ground and wiggled on her back until she was completely under the poles. She smelled the creosote coating and the dampness of the earth giving up frost. She inched along until she was hidden in the center of a personal cave.

She lay on her back and closed her eyes. What if she just stayed here until she died? Who would care? Not her mother. Not even her father. Maybe he was in heaven looking down on her as Nana had said, but she couldn't feel him and she didn't believe it. The world was empty, empty. She remembered other excursions to Telephone Park. She had never minded racing over the top of the poles, but she had always felt suffocated when she played hide-and-seek under them. That a cable might break and the poles shift crushing her to death had been too real to her. Today she did not fear that. She welcomed the thought. She fell asleep and woke to her name being called. It was Peter.

"Honey Lee, Nana says for you to come home." She did not answer. "Honey, are you there? Hon—neeee, Hon—neee."

She waited for him to give up, hoping he would not think to look under the poles. He knew how she hated to go under them. He gave one more try, and then she heard his corduroy pants zipping and his boots crushing the cinders as he headed home. After a while she heard other noises, a truck leaving the printing factory across the street, shouted farewells and then silence. It was beginning to get dark. She heard the sounds of cinders being scuffed again and thought that Peter was coming back to look for her, but he didn't cry out again. She tried to stop breathing so he would not find her. She heard a different voice.

"Are you all right under there?"

She froze. Who on earth knew she was there? She knew the voice, but could not place it.

"I know you're there, Honey Lee. Tell me you're all right."

Jimmy! Jimmy Jackson. What on earth was he doing and how did he know where to find her? She kept very still waiting for him to leave as Peter had earlier. Instead she heard the sound of cinders crunching near her. He was pushing himself under the pile to where she lay hidden. He moved slowly. She held her breath, outraged at his encroachment. When he was about three feet away, he stopped. For a long while he lay still. Then he moved to her side.

Without turning her head, she asked, "What are you doing here? Go away, please, go away." He said nothing. "How did you know where I was?"

"I saw you leave your house." He spoke softly.

"What were you doing at my house?" She hadn't seen him.

"I came to see you. I came three times before, but you wouldn't come out."

For several minutes she didn't speak, then abruptly, "Why?"

"I'm worried about you. I wanted to tell you how sorry I am."

"About my father or my run-away mother?" She enjoyed the bitterness in her voice.

"About your father." He paused. "I know what you're feeling."

"No, you don't! You don't. Leave me alone. Get out of here." She wiggled away from him, but he stretched out his arm so that his hand almost touched hers. She moved again.

"Everyone at school misses you,"

"Yeah. I'll bet they're having a grand time talking about my mother."

"They don't know about her, Honey Lee."

"And you do, right?" She intended sarcasm, but unused to it, failed.

"Yes, I asked Peter how you were doing. He told me."

"Big mouth!" Her voice was harsh with anger at her cousin. Then she cried, tears falling from her open eyes. Time stretched out over her misery. When he moved closer, she stayed where she was.

"How did you know it was me?" she asked.

"If you had a beard and glasses, I'd know you, Honey Lee Murphy."

In spite of herself, she laughed. "I don't look like a boy?"

He laughed too and said, "Like no boy I've ever seen."

After another long silence he spoke again. "Honey Lee, I do know about losing a mother. I know about people you love getting killed." When she heard the pain in his voice she remembered seeing him the day her father died, noticing how lonely and sad he seemed.

"Did your mother run away, too?"

"No. She died in December at the hospital." He grew angry. "I never even got to see her before she died."

"And your father?"

"I don't know where he is. He staggered out drunk a long time ago when my brothers were still home and my mother was alive. All he ever did was drink. I hate him."

"Well, who takes care of you?"

"I take care of myself. Until my brothers come home from the war—the ones who aren't already dead." He coughed to mask his grief.

"You mean you live alone?"

"Yeah."

"On Fayette Street, right?

"Uh huh."

"I saw you there once."

His voice was cold. "I'm not ashamed."

Honey was astounded both that someone her own age lived alone and that he had more cause to suffer than she did. She began to understand his silences at school and his unkempt look. Probably he read all the time with no one at home. That's why he's so smart. What would it be like to live alone? She tried to picture herself alone in her grandmother's house, in charge of everything. No, she couldn't do it. She couldn't. She could not see his face but his ragged breathing told her he was trying not to cry. After a while, he began to talk in his slow, deliberate way. "Never tell anyone I live alone. I promised my brothers I would stay until they came back. And I am not going to let anyone move me out."

"Who would try?"

"Father Finn, for one. And other busybodies who want to make a nice home for me." He became angry again. "They even tried it when my mother was alive."

"Tried to take you away from your own mother?"

"Yeah. When she got sick."

"Tell me about your brothers, Jimmy."

"Johnny went missing over a year ago. He was in the Navy. On a submarine. It went down." The movement was slight but she could tell he wiped his eyes.

"I was so wrong. You do know how I feel."

"They never said he was dead, just missing. My mother died believing, hoping I guess, that he was going to walk in the door good as new. My brother Frank is somewhere in Europe and Danny's on a ship in the Pacific."

They lay side-by-side for another long time, their hands now touching. They were so quiet they seemed to sleep, their even breathing matching until once again Peter began to call out. Honey Lee decided to ignore Peter until she realized that Nana Murphy was with him.

She heard her grandmother telling Peter that there was no use looking for Honey here; she wouldn't be here. "She must have gone somewhere else. But where? Where could the poor thing be?"

Honey melted when she heard the sadness and worry in her grandmother's voice. She whispered to Jimmy.

"I have to go, but not yet. I don't want her to find me here. Please be still."

"Yes, you have to go home." When Honey heard the words, "Go home," she started to cry again. Jimmy held her hand tight in his.

"Honey," he whispered after a long time. She didn't answer, and again he whispered, "Honey."

"Shh! Please, Shh!" He did. They listened to Peter and Nana Murphy walk away, their voices muffled. Finally Honey Lee took her hand back and wiped her eyes and her nose. Forgetting where she was she tried to sit up and bumped her head. Jimmy reached out and touched her head. "Poor Honey Lee."

"Home. Where is home, Jimmy? I want to go home, but I don't know where it is."

Jimmy slid away from her and began to pull at her feet. One of the rubber overshoes came off in his hand.

"What the heck?" he said.

Honey started to giggle, then she laughed until her sides hurt.

"Peter's overshoes. Aren't they ugly? How did I get so ugly? Don't pull the other one off, I'm coming." She began to inch forward until she finally emerged beside him. They looked up at the sky. The sun had set. She had to go back. It would be cruel to Nana to stay any longer.

"Jimmy, how do you eat? Who feeds you?"

"I feed myself, Honey. Frank and Danny send money and I pay rent and I buy food."

"What do you do all day, all alone?" Jimmy stood up and reached for her hand to pull her up.

"Mostly I read. Sometimes I talk to my mother, sometimes to my brothers."

"Do you think they hear you?"

"I don't know, Honey. God knows I don't. But I keep promising my two brothers they will come back to their own home."

"Nana talks out loud to God," Honey Lee said.

"Maybe it's the same thing, Honey Lee. It makes me feel better; it probably makes her feel better." He tried to start walking, but she held him by the sleeve of his jacket.

"I am not talking to my mother ever, ever again. Nana wants me to call her at my other grandmother's, but I won't." The spotlights blinked and came on.

"Let me take you back, now. It's late."

"No. Go home. I want to go alone."

"When are you coming back to school?"

"Nana says I have to go back on Monday."

"Do you want me to walk you to school?"

"No." She pulled her hand from his and walked off toward home thinking how what they had in common had separated them from their classmates.

When Honey Lee came in the back door, she called out. "Nana, Nana, I'm home."

Nana Murphy called quietly from the living room. "Honey Lee. Thanks be to God." She heard the sob her grandmother tried to cover and felt guilty. Her grandmother sat in her chair beside the radio her rosary in her hands. Honey sat on the stool at her feet and took her grandmother's hands in hers. She was ashamed of her selfishness.

"Nana, I'm so sorry. Forgive me. I didn't mean to worry you. I just needed to walk and think by myself. Sometimes I feel like I'm smothering. I can't breathe. I'd never worry you on purpose."

"Now, darlin', you are a grown girl and a good girl. I have no business worrying. It's just that I miss you."

"I miss you too, Nana. I love you."

"God Bless you, darlin', I love you too. Shall we have a cup of tea?"

Tea was still Nana Murphy's way of making things better. Honey noticed that her grandmother had been holding the small service flag when she had come in. Half sewed over her father's blue star was the gold star that announced his death. She wondered if Jimmy had changed the star on his mother's flag. Had he changed the Silver Star for his missing brother to gold after his mother died? Poor Jimmy. She picked up the small flag and asked her grandmother if she could finish sewing the star. Her grandmother said of course she could. Hadn't she lost as much and more than she herself had? Nana Murphy had begun to call her Honey Lee whenever she didn't call her darlin'. She was pleased and wished there were a way for her to show her grandmother how much her feelings had changed too. They sat together, Honey on the stool at her grandmother's feet making careful stitches around the gold star.

CHAPTER 7

▼

Honey Lee started out for school on the Monday after the funeral. She got as far as the end of Concord Street and stopped. Feeling nauseous, she bent her head to her knees. It's impossible. I can't do it, she said to herself. She turned back. Nana Murphy had told her, "sooner is better than later," but when Honey Lee came back after fifteen minutes Nana comforted her, suggesting that Honey Lee ask Ellen Flynn to come after school. Nana had never before suggested that Honey bring anyone home. That afternoon when she called Ellen, her friend ran the three long blocks from her house. Breathless, she held Honey Lee in her arms, but she found comforting words difficult. "I'm sorry," she said stiffly.

Honey also had trouble talking to her friend. Strangely what was so easy with Jimmy was hard with Ellen. "I saw you at the Mass," Honey Lee said. "Thank you for coming."

"You're welcome."

"Did they tell you about my mother?" Honey Lee's eyes filled.

"Yes, my mother told me." She reached out and took Honey's hand. "That's so awful. My mother wants you to come over. So does everyone in my family."

"I will, Ellen, soon." She rubbed her eyes with the back of her hand. "I'm afraid to go back to school. I tried today and I couldn't."

"We'll go together. I'll meet you at the corner and we'll just walk in big as life."

And so they did. On Tuesday morning Honey Lee and Ellen arrived at school late enough that they didn't have to go into the crowded school yard before class. Together, they walked into class.

"Keep your head up, Honey Lee," Ellen whispered. Honey nodded. Sister Rose welcomed Honey Lee back, opening her arms and holding her close against her soft bosom. The coolness of Sister's silver cross pressed on her cheek.

"We are all praying for you and your family," she said. "You are a brave girl and a blessing to your grandmother." Honey took her seat relieved; it hadn't been quite as bad as she feared. Ellen had moved to the seat across the aisle from her. From time to time she reached out and took Honey's hand. Honey Lee looked over to see if Jimmy was there. He gave her a small smile and a nod as if to say, "It's OK, I'm here."

As she was leaving the classroom at the end of the day, Sister Rose told her that Sister Veronica wanted to see her. Ellen said she'd wait downstairs. Honey Lee went down to the second floor, knocked on the office door, and entered when she was told to.

"Sit down, dear. We're all glad you're back. It must be difficult."

"Thank you, Sister."

"I know how hard it is to understand God's ways. We want to know why bad things happen, and we can't. We have to hold blindly to our belief in His goodness."

Honey didn't answer for fear she might cry.

"Last November, God tested me almost beyond what I could bear. The terrible fire..."

"Coconut Grove?" Sister nodded. "My grandmother told me that there were dead from almost every street in the parish."

"Yes, there were. My brother, his wife and their son, my whole family."

"Dead?"

"Yes. So I thought maybe if you ever need someone to talk to, you could come to me." She came toward Honey Lee and embraced her. I am so sorry, dear."

"Thank you, Sister." Honey Lee backed out quickly before tears fell.

She didn't remember much of the rest of eighth grade. She, Ellen and Jimmy continued to lead the class. In May she was chosen to crown the Blessed Mother on First Communion Day. In June, she graduated with the rest of her class. She got a scholarship to Notre Dame Academy, the private Catholic girls' school in nearby Tyngsboro. Nana was thrilled. Jimmy got one to Keith Academy, the Catholic boys' school on the other side of the city. Ellen, because her father taught at the public high school, was going to there. When Honey Lee announced that she didn't want to go to Notre Dame, Nana was at first shocked.

"I need to go where Ellen is going, Nana. I can't lose my two best friends and begin all over again at a strange school."

"Of course you can't," Nana said waving away the arguments of Father Finn and the sisters, who had wanted her to go to Notre Dame.

Honey Lee began high school with Ellen in September. The high school downtown drew students from all over the city. The long, three-storied building stretched for an entire block bordered at the end by the Merrimack River and on the side by one of Lowell's many unused canals. Honey Lee had spent almost all of her first eight months in Lowell in Belvedere. On occasion she had gone downtown to shop; she had gone to the library just beyond the city hall, but the rest of Lowell was still a mystery to her. She knew about the Greek section of the city with its own Greek Church and the French sections also with their own churches. She was aware of the Polish and the Lithuanian churches in Belvedere, but she knew only Irish Catholics from the Immaculate Conception. At the high school, students introduced themselves by telling what section of Lowell or what parish they had come from: the Grove, the Sacred Heart, Saint Michael's, Saint Patrick's, Belvedere, Centerville, the Highlands, the Acre, Christian Hill.

The big school felt comfortably small to Honey Lee because she took all of her classes with the same students, several of them from the Immaculate. She loved her classes and studied hard. She had to endure teasing about her height, her name, and her accent, but she wasn't much bothered by it anymore. It was good-natured. She kept in touch with Jimmy, but missed seeing him every day. They managed to talk on the phone, and they sometimes met on the way home from their different schools or at church.

Honey continued to attend the Immaculate Conception Church, which she had come to love. Often she went to daily Mass before school. She enrolled in the parish CYO, the Catholic Youth Organization, where she took Christian Doctrine classes, played basketball and took small parts in the annual minstrel show. For most young people, the best thing about the youth program at the Immaculate was the Friday night dance, the Hoodsie Hop. High school students from all over Lowell flocked to the dance at the Immaculate church hall. The priests hired a "big band," lowered the lights in the gym, and charged twenty-five cents admission. Ellen pleaded with Honey for two years before she finally agreed to go to the Friday dance.

Honey Lee frequently visited Sister Veronica. Once Sister had called her at home to ask if Honey Lee would be so kind as to go shopping with her. Sisters were required to have a companion whenever they went out. Usually the companion was another sister. But on this one day, Honey Lee was the companion. It was a hot summer day, and Sister handed Honey Lee a large black umbrella to hold over both of them as they walked downtown. Honey was sure that everyone in the city was downtown that day and that they all laughed to see her walking in the sunlight with a nun under a black umbrella.

Honey Lee spent more time alone than most girls of her age. She had learned from her time of grief how to escape. For one thing, she walked. For hours at a time she roamed Belvedere. She climbed up the hill from her house and wandered through the neighborhoods with big houses and elaborate gardens. She visited its parks, Shedd Park and Fort Hill Park, climbing to the top of the Fort Hill to look down on the city. She also knew how to lose herself in books, so much so that her grandmother often found it difficult to get Honey to come out of her room where she lay book in hand, oblivious. She loved and hated the end of novels. She couldn't wait to finish, but she hated the shutting down of the fictional world. Her grandmother often chided her for coming to a meal with a book in hand unable to put it down.

"Just one more page, Nana," she would say putting her finger on a line in the book.

"All right, dear, but just one page, mind you." Nana Murphy patiently waited for Honey to finish the page.

Her grandmother often tried to get Honey to go out more with friends. She was old enough and beautiful enough to have dates if she wanted to, but she didn't. Unlike Ellen, who lived for the next issue of *Seventeen*, Honey Lee was uninterested in fashions or makeup. Such things reminded her of her mother, and she had vowed to be as unlike Savannah Burton Murphy as she could.

Honey Lee and Jimmy sometimes went to the movies together and sometimes met at the Epicure where kids from all the high schools met after school. Whole groups of them sat in the big booths ordering a sticky, fresh fruit orange drink and English muffins. More than a few girls learned how to smoke at the Epicure. But Honey had no desire to smoke. Her father had smoked and so had her mother. She could remember once thinking how glamorous her mother looked when she smoked, the thin line of smoke rising slowly to the ceiling, her mother carefully picking at a stray bit of cigarette paper on her lip. She imagined how her father might have lit two cigarettes in his mouth and handed one to her mother as Charles Boyer had in a film she had recently seen.

One day at the Epicure, Honey and Ellen had a booth to themselves. Some of the other girls called to them and asked them to sit at their table, but Honey Lee put her hand on Ellen's sleeve telling her without words that she wanted to talk.

"Sorry, girls, we have big things to talk about." Ellen raised her eyebrows and laughed. "Secrets." Honey often talked to Ellen about things she might have talked about to her mother, things she couldn't talk to Nana Murphy about. This time they talked about religion, more specifically about whether or not Honey Lee had a religious vocation. Sister Veronica had asked Honey if she had ever thought about becoming a nun. Honey Lee had taken the question very seriously. Ellen was shocked.

"You can't be serious," she exploded. "You are definitely not the nun type." She laughed out loud.

"There's no type, Ellen. I'm serious. Very serious. I think maybe God took my parents so I could find my real home in a convent." Honey Lee had thought about this for weeks.

"That's the stupidest thing I ever heard you say. And you know it. Your father wasn't killed to send a message to you." With every word, Ellen shook her finger at her friend. And your mother didn't leave to set you free to become a nun."

"But maybe I do have a vocation. How are you supposed to know?"

"It's a call. If you get it you just know. I pray all the time that I won't be called. Now I have to pray for you too."

"Just imagine, praying all day except when you're teaching." She couldn't imagine it.

"Just imagine never getting married." Ellen crossed her eyes. "I'd hate it."

Honey reached across the table and pointed to Ellen's still crossed eyes, "Stop it. They'll get stuck. I'd hate it, too. But I should talk to Father Finn."

"Well, what do you think he's going to say?"

"He knows me. He'll help me decide." She laughed. "You certainly didn't."

Uncomfortable with the subject, Ellen asked Honey Lee about Jimmy Jackson. She had learned the hard way that Jimmy was special to Honey Lee. Once in eighth grade when she had teased Honey about being sweet on "poor, dirty Jimmy Jackson from Fayette Street," Honey Lee had flashed into anger.

"Don't you ever talk about him like that or I'll never speak to you again." Ellen had stared at her friend, speechless. She never again teased Honey about Jimmy.

CHAPTER 8

▼

On May 6, 1945, Ellen called Honey Lee. "Did you hear? Did you hear?" She cried, breathless with excitement.

"Hear what?" Honey Lee asked calmly, accustomed to Ellen's enthusiasms.

"It's over, Honey Lee. It's over at last." Relief and joy colored her voice.

"What are you talking about?" Honey Lee asked, drawn into Ellen's mood. "What's over?"

"The war, the war, silly. The war is over. It's on the radio and people are running out of their houses shouting. Everyone's going downtown. Let's go. Hurry. Hurry." The day Honey Lee had once longed for so desperately had finally come and so suddenly that she was speechless.

"Honey, did you hear me? Come on. Run. We've got to go downtown."

"Yes. Thanks be to God. I'm coming."

Five minutes later she was at Ellen's house. They joined a parade of rejoicing people all headed to Kearney Square. Church bells rang, people ran out of their houses crying, they hugged each other, and rushed, by instinct, to the heart of the city. Revelers stopped the girls several times on their way.

"It's over, Thank God. It's over."

"We did it! We won!"

More people than she had ever seen crowded into the square. They shouted and danced. They formed Conga lines that snaked through the streets. Men kissed women they had never seen before. Women hugged women, men hugged men, children were lifted high into the air. Honey Lee kissed and hugged, was kissed and hugged. She joined Conga lines, but her heart was in Africa where her father lay. Without saying good-bye to Ellen, she left and walked up Fayette

Street wishing Jimmy would appear. If she knew exactly where he lived, she'd have knocked on his door. He would understand why she couldn't rejoice, why she resented the raucous joy downtown.

On the way home, she smiled at people who called out to her but hurried on. When she got there she called out for her grandmother, but Nana wasn't there. If only she had been, Honey Lee wouldn't have thought about Savannah, about how she and her mother had once longed for the war to end. Savannah would know how she felt. She needed her mother. She went to the living room and sank down into her grandmother's chair. She reached for the telephone. Twice, she picked up the receiver and put it down. Then she took it up again, dialed operator, gave her maternal grandmother's name and address, and asked to be connected person-to-person to Savannah Murphy.

A woman answered on the second ring. Could it be her mother?

"Savannah Murphy has not lived at this address for many years." The voice was cold. The woman hung up before the operator finished asking for another number for Savannah Murphy.

Returning anger choked Honey Lee. "Stupid, stupid, stupid," she wailed. "If she wanted me she would have called me, ages ago." She ran to her room and fell onto the bed, berating herself for weakness. Then she wept for the first time in months.

The war in the Pacific ended in August, and little by little, soldiers who were lucky enough to be coming home, returned. In the beginning, parades honored the returning heroes, but as the days wore on and more men returned, people got on with the business of living. One of Jimmy's brothers, Frank, had finally come home to live with Jimmy; the other was in a hospital in the Philippines.

In late August, a doctor from a hospital in Maryland called Aunt Kitty to tell her that her husband was coming home. Honey Lee thought it odd that Uncle Peter didn't call himself, but Kitty was too thrilled to notice. And young Peter was beside himself. When Honey Lee had first met her cousin Peter, the ten-year-old bragged to anyone who'd listen about his hero-father "who would, single-handed, wipe out whole bunches of Nazis when he got to France." At twelve, the news of his father's return electrified him.

He and Aunt Kitty rushed out to find an apartment, and even though housing was scarce, they found a place on nearby Rodgers Street. It seemed like a good omen. When they returned with the news, Peter raced from room to room in Nana's house looking for things his father would need in the new apartment.

Nana promised the bed he had been using and a double bed for Kitty and her husband. Then they went shopping for a new couch, an easy chair, and a radio.

"We have to get Dad a radio so we can listen to the Braves games together. And a good lamp for beside his chair. He needs that to read the paper."

He kept running back and forth from his new home to Nana's house with urgent requests: extra sheets for the big bed "so mom won't have to be washing his sheets when he needs to rest," and "your old bean pot, Nana, so mom can make baked beans for him," and "the hassock for his legs while he's listening to the ball games."

Nana, amused by his excitement, teased him." Your father's a Red Sox fan, Peter." She winked at Honey Lee.

Peter exploded. "No sir. He's Braves all the way."

"Take the hassock, then, and be gone with you."

On the day Peter Rourke came home, they all walked down to the train station, an hour early at Peter's urging. He had made a sign, *Welcome Home Dad,* which he attached to two long sticks. He asked Honey Lee to carry it with him. While they waited for the train, he held the sign aloft and shifted his feet asking his mother at five-minute intervals what time it was. When the train finally arrived, several men in uniform got off. Some of them seemed healthy and happy. Others were on crutches or had slings or bandages. Some were missing limbs. As they alighted, squealing girls, puzzled young children, wives, and parents of boys who had become men far from home flocked around them. Uncle Peter was one of the last to get off.

"There he is," Aunt Kitty cried and ran toward a thin, white-faced man. Young Peter frowned unable to match his father to the man his mother was embracing. For a moment, he held back then flung himself at this father.

"Daddy, Dad, oh Dad." Startled, his father flinched and drew back. "It's me, Dad, Petey."

"Oh, Peter." His voice was flat. "You've grown." He put out his hand, but Peter either didn't see it or ignored it and threw his arms around his father.

"I missed you so much, Dad. I've got so much to tell you."

The father shook off the embraces of his tearful wife and son. He nodded to Nana Murphy and looked at Honey Lee.

"This is Tommy's girl," Nana Murphy said.

"I heard about Tommy. Sorry."

Honey Lee studied him. He bore no resemblance to Aunt Kitty's photographs of him, neither the one always on display in the living room, nor the other in Aunt Kitty's bedroom. In the pictures, although not handsome, his broad face and huge smile were engaging. She had thought she would like him. While they looked for his father's suitcase and a taxi, young Peter kept firing questions at his father, tugging at his sleeve.

"Did you get all the way to Germany?"

"What kind of gun did you use?"

"Did you get to go up in an airplane?'

Aunt Kitty put her hand on her son's arm. "Sweetie, let Dad rest a bit. I think he's tired." She turned to her husband. "Are you tired, darling?"

Her husband looked at her and the boy as if he didn't know who they were. When they got into the cab, young Peter began his machine gun chatter again. "Wait till you see our new place, dad. You're going to love it. It's right up the street from Nana's. We got you an easy chair and a radio. The Braves are playing tonight. Isn't that good luck?" Still the father said nothing. He turned away from his wife and stared out the window.

Nana and Aunt Kitty had planned a special meal for the return, but Aunt Kitty's brightness dimmed as her husband retreated further and further into silence. Peter was puzzled and hurt. He was close to tears. Halfway through the meal, Uncle Peter jumped up without saying a word and left the house. Apparently, he couldn't even bear to sit through a meal with his family. And things didn't improve in the weeks that followed. Battle Fatigue, they called it. In the old war, Nana told her, they called it Shell Shock. "But it was the same thing. Boys came home from that war too damaged to live anything like a normal life. And it's the same this time."

Honey Lee cried both for her father who would never return and for Uncle Peter whose return had been so pain-filled for him, his son, and his wife. As far as she knew, he hadn't been shot or physically injured. Unlike others she had seen and heard about, he had all four limbs yet he looked mortally wounded. Something in the way moved, as if all his parts were made of wood except for his slumped shoulders. His face was deeply lined. His deep-set eyes stared without blinking. Aunt Kitty beseeched him with words and gestures to respond to his son and to her. And young Peter had no better luck than Aunt Kitty in drawing him out. Poor Aunt Kitty, poor Peter.

Maybe it was better not to come home at all than to come home like that. Honey Lee was grateful that the Rourkes weren't living at Nana Murphy's house. It would have been too difficult for everyone.

Before long, a defeated Peter stopped trying to get his father's attention. He spent time away from his new home, a lot of it at Nana Murphy's. Whenever

Honey Lee asked him about his father, he said, "I wish he'd never come home. I hate him."

In the first few weeks, Honey Lee defended his father and urged patience, but then she stopped. She let him talk about his father when he wanted to. At first he was reluctant to complain to her. At least his father, unlike hers, had come back. And he was proud. But she encouraged him to talk when he wanted to, at least in part to spare his mother.

Honey wondered about Jimmy and Frank. She hoped Frank was really doing as well as Jimmy said. She hadn't seen much of Jimmy since his brother had returned, but they talked on the phone. At the first Christian Doctrine class in the church hall, she sat with him. They walked out of the classroom together discussing the Immaculate Conception, the topic of the class. Father had said it was time they heard more about the sacred mystery for which their church was named. Despite the lesson, they understood little more than they had before. They walked by the church and over to Fayette Street. The night was clear and bright. A full moon rose slowly directly in front of them as if from the far end of the street. Jimmy stopped in front of a three-story brick building near the fish market. She smelled fried fish and thought of children she had often seen standing on the sidewalk just to smell the fish their parents could not afford to buy. She imagined them crowded into the dingy tenements. More than once she had hurried by these buildings, especially the one they stood by.

"I'd like you to come up and meet Frank," Jimmy said. "He's home. I've told him all about us." When Honey Lee didn't respond, he said, "Please come in and meet him."

About us, what about us? Did he mean told him about you? Honey wanted to meet Frank, but she had never been in Jimmy's house. A few times, especially when he was living alone, she had thought about going to his house to help him, but he had never asked. Probably for the same reason she held back. Nana Murphy and the nuns had told her over and over that she should never be in a house alone with a boy. They had talked in hushed tones about appearances of evil and occasions of sin. But she held back not because she was afraid of being alone with Jimmy and his brother, but of the building. It was one of the worst on the street in front of which men gathered in warm weather. And an immense woman always sat on an old wooden chair beside the door. Folds of fat hung from her body. Her face melted into her huge bosom. And she smelled so bad. Signs forbidding loitering and expectorating hung over the doorway. But Jimmy's eyes begged her to go in with him. And so she did.

The front door was not locked. Jimmy pulled it open and they entered a dark hall. Honey tried not to wrinkle her nose, but rotting plaster, urine, and old cooking smells filled the air. Chunks of wall had fallen off exposing thin slats of wood underneath. How could anyone live here? She had been prepared for bad, but her imagination had failed her. Was Jimmy so used to the stench that he didn't notice it anymore? They climbed two flights of steep stairs. Some of the steps had remnants of rubber treads that had lifted up. Jimmy held her elbow, guiding her. From behind the doors, music blared, children cried, people shouted, coughed, and laughed.

"These stairs are killers," Jimmy said.

When they got to the top, Jimmy went to the door on the left and knocked.

"Frank? Are you here?"

"Yeah, Jimbo. You home already?"

"I brought company. Get yourself decent," Jimmy said.

When they entered, there was no sign of Frank. Honey looked at the home where Jimmy had spent so many months alone. It was hard to tell whether they had entered kitchen, dining room, or living room. A large black iron stove hunkered down against one wall. Heat poured from it. She recognized it as a cooking and a heating stove similar to the one in Nana's kitchen. A bushel basket of wood stood beside the stove. Honey tried to imagine Jimmy tending the stove by himself and cooking his meals on it. From two easy chairs, stuffing leaked and springs poked through. The biggest item of furniture other than the stove was a round oak table in the center of the room with six wooden chairs, one for each of the brothers, she thought, and one for Jimmy's mother. Could the other be the father's? A half-filled bottle of milk, two cups, a few *Lowell Suns*, and dishes with crumbs, bones, and orange rinds littered the tabletop. Linoleum from which design and color had long since worn off covered the floor. In places it had worn through to the wood. Honey thought about her grandmother's neat home, its shining wood floors covered in places by rugs braided by Nana Murphy herself.

"Sit down," Jimmy said.

She chose one of the wooden chairs and sat stiffly, trying not to touch the table. Frank, dressed in army pants and an undershirt, came in from a door at the far end of the room. He had the same thick brown hair and green eyes as Jimmy. Jimmy will look just like that when he's older, she thought. She smiled and stood up.

"Well now, who is this lovely giant?" Frank said.

"Stop it, Frank. This is Honey Lee Murphy. You know who it is. Go put a shirt on."

"He thinks he's old enough and big enough to boss me around. Honey Child, what do you think?"

"I think he's as brave as any soldier keeping things going here while you all were gone. I think he's old enough," she said, "and he's almost as big as you are."

Frank and Jimmy laughed, and so did Honey. Frank shook her hand and dipped his head.

"Jimmy didn't do you justice. I'm glad to meet you, glad Jimmy had a friend like you while we were gone." He sat down at the table and looked around at the room without saying anything. Honey looked at Jimmy asking with her eyes what she should say or do. The bizarre notion to ask if he had known her father crossed her mind. She had no idea how to talk to a man who had fought in a war, maybe killed other men, been wounded himself. Frank looked at his brother and then turned to Honey Lee.

"You're right. Jimmy was a home-front soldier. He kept this place for us to come back to. It's not much. It never was, but it's where we lived with our mother, God rest her soul. Believe it or not, this was the place I dreamed about all through the war. But now I see that with her gone..." He stopped. Then more lightly said, "As soon as Danny gets better and comes home, we're going to move out of here into a nice new house. Right, Jimbo?"

"Right, Frank. But this place wouldn't be half-bad if you picked up once in a while. What did they teach you in the Army anyway?"

"Nothing I ever want to use again in my life." He stared down at the table and, scowling, pushed one of the newspapers to the floor. He picked up a cup and stared into it without saying anything more. Noises from the other apartments made her conscious of Frank's long silence. Jimmy, strangely silent like his brother, was no help. When she couldn't bear not knowing what Frank was thinking, whether he was angry or sad, and what he would say next, she stood up.

"I think I'd better go." She put her hand out to Frank. "I'm glad to meet you Frank. I'm glad you came home safe."

"Come again, Honey Child. You light up the room." She was relieved. Everything would be all right.

Jimmy led the way down the stairs to the street. The fresh air was a blessing. She breathed in deep gulps of air. She couldn't think what to say to Jimmy. She couldn't say she liked his house and she didn't know what to say about Frank. It seemed best to say nothing. They walked silently up Fayette Street to Concord toward Honey Lee's home.

CHAPTER 9

▼

In September, Honey Lee entered her junior year at the high school and went to her first CYO dance. Ellen had been going to the dances for over a year, but until the second Friday in September, she hadn't been able to convince Honey Lee to go with her. Right after supper, as Ellen had insisted, Honey Lee walked over to her friend's house to finish getting ready. Ellen had insisted.

"You don't have any makeup or good hair stuff. We need to dress you up."

After a few silly arguments, Honey Lee agreed to lipstick and a little rouge but refused a hair bow and earrings. At 8:30, half an hour after the dance began, they entered the church hall. Father McGowan, the new young parish priest, sold tickets at the door. After they passed him, Ellen rolled her eyes and pretended to swoon. They climbed the stairs swaying to the music that drifted down. At the entrance, they paused until their eyes adjusted to the darkened hall.

"I can't believe this is our basketball court," Honey said. She smiled and tapped her foot. The music was irresistible.

Girls bunched together at the back of the hall trying to look indifferent to the boys who lined the sides.

"We just stand here and wait for someone to ask us to dance?" Honey Lee asked.

"Yes, but don't worry. You won't wait long with your looks." A husky red-head appeared out of nowhere beside Ellen.

"Want to dance, Ellen?" Ellen looked at Honey Lee and shrugged.

"Sure," she said and followed him onto the dance floor. Honey Lee watched them disappear into the crowd of dancers. Then she stared up at the stage, counting the musicians, twelve of them dressed in tuxes. She was amazed. Someone touched her shoulder. She jumped.

"May I have this dance?" A tall dark haired boy smiled at her.

She stiffened and stammered, "No thanks."

He smiled again and said, "Maybe later?"

"I don't think so." He walked away just as Ellen came off the dance floor.

"What's the matter with you? He's handsome and he's a good dancer." Ellen asked.

"I don't know. I was too surprised, I guess."

She didn't get asked again that night, but she enjoyed the music, both the slow, sad ballads and the fast swing numbers to which everyone jitterbugged.

Ellen asked her if she minded going home alone. The red-head had asked to walk her home, and she liked him. Honey Lee didn't mind because she'd had enough and wanted to leave. When she reached the bottom of the stairs and went out the door, Jimmy called out to her. He was standing alone near the door.

"Jimmy, I didn't see you upstairs. Where were you?"

"I was there. I saw you refuse big Gerry." They stood facing each other on the sidewalk outside the hall.

"I just like watching. I don't like to dance with people I don't know." Through the open windows of the hall they heard the band start a new set.

"Me either," Jimmy said. "Come on, I'll walk you home."

Arm in arm they walked the length of the street toward home. When they got to the house, Nana Murphy was standing on the porch waiting. Because it was well after her grandmother's bedtime, Honey was puzzled. When Nana Murphy noticed that Honey Lee wasn't alone, she looked closer and recognized Jimmy.

"Well, aren't you the nice young man to walk Honey Lee home?"

"Thank you Mrs. Murphy; it's my pleasure to go anywhere with Honey Lee." He sounded just like his brother with the sweet talk.

"Come in, Jimmy, and have a cup with us, won't you?"

"Thank you, I will, Mrs. Murphy," he said climbing the stairs to the front door. He and Honey Lee followed Nana into the kitchen. The kitchen table which was already set for tea for two. Nana motioned to Jimmy to sit.

"I heard that Frank is back," Nana said. "God be praised." She went to the cupboard to get a third cup and saucer. "And how is he then?"

"He's fine, Mrs. Murphy."

"And Danny?" Nana asked.

"He's not good, Mrs. Murphy. But good enough that he's coming back to the states to another hospital near Boston. Then at least we can see him."

"I'm sorry for him. This war was a terrible curse on us all. We'll not get over it in a hurry." She poured tea and passed cookies.

Honey Lee wondered what was going on with her grandmother. She never entertained Honey Lee's friends, and she was obviously nervous. When Jimmy left, Nana Murphy fussed and fidgeted in the kitchen with the teapot and the cups even though Honey had offered to wash up. When Nana finally came back to the living room to sit, Honey Lee was ready for bed, but knowing that her grandmother had something important to say, she sat on the footstool. Nana took one of Honey Lee's hands in hers.

"I've some news for you, dear."

"News?" Honey Lee straightened.

"A phone call." Nana turned the gold ring on her finger around and around avoiding Honey Lee's eyes.

"A phone call?" From school? From Father Finn?

"From your mother, from Georgia."

Honey Lee could hardly breathe. Nana Murphy leaned down from her chair and smoothed Honey Lee's hair. Honey put her head on her grandmother's knee. Neither spoke for several minutes. Finally Honey Lee spoke.

"You are my mother. The only mother I have or want."

"She wants you to come home to her. She has a husband and a house. You have a tiny sister. She wants you to meet her. She wants you very much."

"Is she crazy?" Honey Lee asked not expecting an answer. "How dare she call after all this time?"

After she had made the person-to-person call to Savannah's mother's house, Honey Lee had formally disowned her mother. From that day she willed away all memories of her life with her mother both in the South and in Lowell. She knew she was where she was supposed to be, with her father's people, with Nana who loved her and cared for her.

"I will never speak to her again, never."

Nana sighed and continued to smooth Honey Lee's hair.

Honey Lee worked hard at school and got good grades. In addition to being at the top or near the top of her class, she was also a star in the gym classes, which meant that she was likely to be made a girl officer at the end of the year. For three years, Honey Lee had been conscious of the girl officers. They helped the gym teachers with the younger students. They held military ranks, the highest, most coveted, was Colonel, followed by Lieutenant Colonel, Captains, First and Second Lieutenants. To be named Colonel was the dream of most girls in the junior class; not be chosen at all was a social disaster from which many girls never recovered. The officers wore their navy blue uniforms and black stockings for their entire senior year. On Field Day in late spring, the entire school paraded to the South Common where each class performed the routines they had worked on for the entire year. But girl officers starred both in their own complicated drill routines and in supervising and leading the other class drills.

Ellen, passionate to get a high rank, practiced the complicated drills with clubs for hours on end. Sometimes Honey practiced with her. The day on which the officers were chosen and named was a big day in Lowell. At seven o'clock in the evening, the local radio station began to announce the winners. Just about everyone in the city was glued to the radio. Ellen and Honey listened together. Ellen's brothers listened with them, laughing at Ellen's moans, as one name followed another. First the Second Lieutenants were named—neither girl was listed. Then the First Lieutenants—neither girl. By this time Ellen was crying.

"I didn't make it. We didn't make it, Honey. How can we ever go back?"

"Ellen, they haven't finished yet," Honey Lee said calmly. "There's still the Captains and the two Colonels to go."

"I won't get that high, I know I won't."

The announcer said, "Second Captain, Ellen Flynn."

Ellen jumped up and ran around hugging her parents, her brothers and Honey. She was practically out the door to run downtown when she remembered Honey Lee.

"Oh, Honey, you taught me everything."

The final announcement came after a dramatic delay by the announcer.

"And finally, the Colonel of the Girl Officers of Lowell, Massachusetts, for 1945–46, Honey Lee Murphy."

Again Ellen started jumping and hugging and pulling at Honey to hurry up.

"We've got to go. They take pictures for the paper. They might even interview us. Everyone's there already. They'll all be waiting, especially for you. Oh Honey, congratulations."

The rest of the family hugged Honey Lee; Mr. Flynn gave them each a dollar and told them to have a good time. The square was full of young girls crying and screaming and hugging one another. The *Sun* photographer asked Honey Lee to pose for a single shot and then for two or three group shots. Honey Lee was the star, and she was dismayed.

When the picture appeared on the front page, people would say, "Isn't that the Southern girl whose mother ran off?" But she smiled and smiled and wished she were somewhere else and then went with the others to Paige's for ice cream.

During the school year, Honey Lee and Jimmy went to the movies together once in a while and sometimes met at the Epicure after school. A few times, Frank took them out to eat. Aside from that, Jimmy and Honey Lee saw each other infrequently. Lately Frank had been too busy to take them anywhere. He was dating a girl he had gone to school with before the war. A WAC, she too had recently come home from the war.

"They might as well marry. They can't seem to stay away from each other. I never see him anymore," Jimmy complained.

"You like Mary, don't you?"

"Sure, I do. But I miss Frank. He's never around any more; it's almost like it was before he came home." She had never heard him complain about anything before.

One day in June, Frank asked Honey Lee and Jimmy to meet him at the Princeton Lounge, the nicest restaurant in Lowell. They both guessed what the occasion was, and weren't surprised to see Frank standing at the door with Mary Robinson. Both Frank and Mary were smiling, Frank holding Mary at her waist. She was lovely. Her silky blond hair hung to her shoulders where it turned under at the ends. She was wearing a deep blue dress with pearl buttons down the front and very high-heeled pumps with sling backs. She carried red roses. She came only to Frank's shoulder and had to look up at him, which she did for the entire evening. Honey Lee wondered what it was like to be so attracted to a man, what it was like to be so much shorter than a man.

As soon as they sat down, Frank said, "James Joseph Jackson and Honey Lee Murphy, I would like you to meet the future Mrs. Francis Xavier Jackson." Mary blushed when Jimmy hugged and kissed her. Frank asked the waiter to bring champagne.

"I can't serve those two," he said pointing to Honey Lee and Jimmy. "They're not old enough."

"This is a major celebration, sir. War Hero Chooses Bride and Celebrates with Family. Never mind how old they are."

The waiter smiled and brought the champagne and four glasses.

"What would Ma think, Jimmy, my boy, if she could see her boys sitting here drinking champagne?" He reached over and tousled Jimmy's hair.

"She'd probably worry that we were going to turn out like dad."

"Jimmy, my boy, you are too serious."

Frank and Mary hadn't made definite wedding plans, but they said the wedding would be small and soon. "No time to waste," Frank said.

When Honey Lee and Jimmy walked home, they talked about Frank's plans.

"Where will they live?" Honey Lee asked as they walked by his house. He looked up and laughed.

"I don't think she'll want to live with us, do you?"

"What will you do?" She was worried about him.

"Well, I guess just hang out here until Danny gets home."

"Not alone, again, Jimmy." She pulled at his sleeve. "You can't."

He shrugged and walked on.

After that, Honey Lee didn't see Frank and Mary for several weeks. She didn't see much of Jimmy either. One day at the Epicure, Ellen asked to sit in a small booth by themselves. When Honey Lee didn't speak for a few minutes, Ellen broke the silence.

"Are you thinking of becoming a nun again?"

"No, silly," Honey Lee said, but she took her time getting at what she needed to talk about. She played with her straw, sipped her fresh fruit orange, and traced circles on the shiny tabletop. Finally she spoke.

"Jimmy's leaving."

"Where? When?"

"To Billerica."

"Is he changing schools?"

"I don't know." Her eyes filled up. Ellen, I can't imagine him not being down the street from me. I hate it." Ellen took her hand. "Honey Lee, are you and Jimmy dating?"

"Of course not. He's my best friend."

"Thanks!"

"Oh, Ellen, after you," she lied. Jimmy had been her rock ever since that day they had lain together under the telephone poles when her father died and her mother ran off. She couldn't imagine her world without him, her neighborhood without him. "Frank and Mary are moving into her parents' house in North Billerica. And Frank says Jimmy can't stay alone." She was angry.

"Well of course, he can't." Honey Lee had never told Ellen or anyone else that Jimmy had been alone on Fayette Street for over a year. "What about the other brother? Isn't he coming home?"

"Some day, I guess."

Honey Lee stared into space. She hated change. She especially hated people going away. She swore to herself that when she finally had a home of her own, she would never, never leave it, even if it was nothing more than the terrible space in which Jimmy had lived for so long. She hadn't left Lowell once in almost four years. She belonged in Lowell. And so did Jimmy, but he was leaving.

"It's not that far away, Honey," Ellen tried to reason. "You can walk there for heaven's sake."

"I know, but you and Jimmy are my only friends. People should stay put." Ellen made comforting noises until Honey Lee calmed down.

Jimmy moved to Garden City, a small part of North Billerica separated from the rest of the town by the Concord River, which powered the woolen mills of North Billerica. During the war, the mills had been busy. Many women worked there including her Aunt Kitty. But as soon as Uncle Peter came home, she stopped working. Frank and Mary moved there because Mary's family owned a two family house where they planned to live until they could buy their own home. Their side of the duplex had a living room and kitchen and two tiny bedrooms, barely enough space for the newly married couple. Jimmy had argued that he should stay in Lowell until Danny came back.

"I promised you, and I promised him I would keep the house until you both got back." Frank wouldn't listen.

Jimmy continued at Keith Academy even though getting to and from school took three hours of his day.

As it turned out, Honey Lee's fears were exaggerated. She saw Jimmy often. Mary liked Honey Lee's company and encouraged Jimmy to bring her often.

In July, Danny Jackson arrived back in the States. Jimmy was ecstatic. He asked Honey Lee to meet him so he could tell her the great news.

"Honey Lee, he'll be coming home for good soon. I know he will. Then we can live together in Lowell. I can't wait." Jimmy's face was bright with happiness.

"Will he want to live with you?"

"Of course he will."

For the past year all Honey Lee heard about was how ill Danny was. But she knew little else about him. "What's he like, Jimmy?"

"Sort of like me, I guess."

His answer failed to give her any idea of what Danny Jackson was like.

CHAPTER 10

▼

For two years Ellen had tried to convince Honey Lee to come up to New Hampshire to visit for a week at her parents' home at the Weirs, New Hampshire. Ellen had often raved about the Weirs and beautiful Lake Winnepesauke. But Honey Lee feared leaving her home on Concord Street. Leaving Concord Street, even for a brief time, threatened that home. But finally, at her grandmother's urging, she agreed to go to the Weirs for one week, but only one.

"Honey, dear, it'll be fine. It's getting sick of you, that I am," Nana said as she smiled at her grandchild. "I'll be right here waiting for you." They were drinking tea at the kitchen table.

"But who'll help with the cleaning and cooking?"

"Dear heart, before you came, didn't I do it alone? Sure and it wasn't as nice, but I did it. Now go tell Mrs. Flynn, 'Thank you, I'd love to come.'"

Honey made plans for a Friday train departure, her first train trip since she had arrived in Lowell. She both dreaded and was excited by it. The train station was unchanged; there was still only the one track. When she stepped up onto the train and turned to wave good-bye to her grandmother, she couldn't stop her tears. Nana Murphy looked so little and old.

The trip took about two hours. Ellen's whole family came down to the station at the Weirs to meet her and greeted her as one of their own. Honey Lee had been shy of Mr. Flynn until she took her first Latin class with him. He was one of the most popular and most demanding of her teachers. Like her mother, he was not a Catholic. Honey Lee first heard the expression, 'mixed marriage,' to refer to a marriage like her parents' when Ellen told her about her parents' marriage in the rectory of the Immaculate. Mr. Flynn was the only person Honey Lee knew in Lowell who didn't go to church.

Noreen and Bobby clamored for her attention, promising to teach her how to dive, swim out to flat rock and canoe over to Spindle Point. And even Jack, a junior at Dartmouth now, was there looking more like a man than the boy she remembered. His voice had deepened and he had grown taller. When he greeted her with a bear hug, she remembered the embraces of her strong father and her breath caught in her throat. How long, she wondered, has it been since I thought of my father?

Jack said, "Honey Child, I had forgotten how beautiful you are."

Ellen pushed him away from Honey Lee. "Let her be, Jack. She's my friend. Pay no attention to him, Honey Lee. He's girl crazy."

Jack pointed to and then touched his sister's nose. "Listen, little one, if it weren't for me you wouldn't have so many guys to dance with." He turned to Honey Lee and said, "She likes my friends."

"I suppose I desperately need a brother to get dances for me."

"That's right," he said and picked her up and lifted her off the ground.

As the commotion of her arrival calmed down some, Honey looked around at the Weirs. The train station was right on the lake. Across the water she could see the blue-purple outlines of distant mountains and closer in green islands. Nearby was a long pier with a large white building at the end: *Irwin Pier and Ballroom*, a sign read.

When Bobby saw her looking at it, he pointed and said, "That's where we go to church."

"Where? There's no church there," she said.

"Yes, dear, unfortunately that is the church," said Mrs. Flynn, "and it's also a dance hall on Friday and Saturday nights. Ellen and Jack might just as well sleep there on Saturday nights and wait for Mass to begin."

"Gene Krupa played there last week," Ellen said. "I can't wait for you to see the inside. It makes the Hoodsie Hop seem like a sandbox. We're going tomorrow night."

Honey Lee barely heard Ellen she was so intent on taking in her surroundings. She had never seen such a beautiful place. As they walked past the bustle of the boardwalk and the pier-church-dance-hall to a quieter area, she breathed in the lake air and watched the sun on the water. They walked past a small diner, took a right down to the water and then a left to a narrow path that wound along the shore. Every few feet, trellises covered with wisteria marked property lines. The first house on the water was a huge white house with a wrap-around porch.

Ellen said, "Don Jones's grandmother lives there. Remember him? Algebra II?"

"I guess so," Honey Lee replied although she had no memory of Don Jones.

"Of course you do, he's the one whose mother got divorced and everybody talked about it for months. He and Jack are always out on his speedboat. Sometimes they take me."

They passed another few houses and finally stopped in front of a small green house with steps leading up to a front porch. Honey loved it: the white chairs on the porch, the roses near the steps, the small pier in front and the view of the mountains. Without going inside she knew that this was a happy home, a comfortable place with friendly ghosts watching over the family.

At six o'clock they sat down to eat at the large oval table near the front window. They all began talking at once of plans for the week and asking Honey Lee for details of her train trip and news of Lowell. Honey Lee sat beside Jack who directed most of his questions and comments to her. He was more handsome than Honey Lee remembered. His dark hair was wavy in spite of the short brush cut. His sun-darkened skin against his light blue open neck shirt was beautiful. Honey Lee began to feel warm; she was sure her face was flushed. She tried again and again to turn the conversation to Ellen and her mother by talking about girl things: what was Ellen going to buy for school clothes; how did Mrs. Flynn make the wonderful pot roast. Ellen, amused at Honey's unusual interest in domestic matters, laughed at her.

Mrs. Flynn excused Ellen from kitchen duty so she and Honey Lee could have time to catch up. Ellen wanted to show Honey Lee more of the Weirs so they started out in the opposite direction from the way they had come in. Ellen walked only as far as the dock next door to their house. She ran to the end, took off her shoes and sat on the edge and dangled her feet in the water.

"That feels so good," she said kicking at the water and splashing it up over the dock. Honey followed her example.

"I can't wait to go swimming," Honey Lee said.

"Why wait?" Ellen said and slipped off the edge of the dock. She bobbed up and said, "Come on in. It's great."

Honey Lee looked down at her new shorts and shirt, worried that she only had two pair of shorts for the week. She was also a little afraid. She could barely remember the last time she had been swimming. When she lived in Georgia, her father had taken her swimming often and had praised her strong strokes.

"You're Olympic material," he'd joke as she swam beside him trying to match her stroke to his. Since coming north she'd had little opportunity to swim.

Watching Ellen in the water, laughing and calling out to her was enough to over-come doubts. She dove in, and in a few quick strokes caught up with Ellen who was swimming straight out toward a distant island. The cool water felt like a blessing on her head.

"Where are you going?' she called.

"To table rock. Follow me."

She followed keeping her face in the water as much as she could. She loved the feeling of the water on her face. Once when she looked up, she saw Ellen stand-ing in water barely up to her waist. Honey Lee swam closer and saw the huge flat rock the Flynn's had talked about at dinner.

"It's like an island," she said. "How did you ever find it?"

"My father's father took him out to this rock when he was ten years old. My father takes each of us out on the year we turn ten. Some day I'll take my own kids out when they're ten."

Such unbroken continuity amazed Honey Lee. "Wow," was all she could say.

They stood on the rock looking out to Spindle Point and to the mountains beyond.

"Oh, Ellen, this is heaven."

"Well, it'll be hell in my house if we don't get out of the water before dark. I'll bet he's sitting there watching us right now," she said referring to her father.

As they swam back the sun disappeared and the mountains darkened and then disappeared. They walked barefoot back to the house. Mr. and Mrs. Flynn were sitting on the porch.

"Catherine, I do believe that two sea nymphs have come up out of the lake."

"Ellen, you have been swimming again without a bathing suit," said Mrs. Flynn.

"Mother, you know I don't skinny dip," Ellen replied laughing.

They climbed the narrow stairs up to the back bedroom. The inside of the house was unfinished. On the rough wood walls, pegs held hanging clothes. Honey Lee's suitcase was lying on top of one of the twin beds.

"We might as well get dressed for bed. I don't think we'll get out again tonight." Ellen pulled off her wet clothes and dropped them on the floor. She yanked the top of a pair of pajamas out from under the pillow and put it on. Then she raised up one foot and examined her toenails.

"Do you like this color? She asked Honey Lee, who was astonished at how casual Ellen was about being naked. Honey Lee had never even seen her mother naked and certainly not her grandmother. Neither had she ever taken her clothes off in front of another person. She went to her suitcase and pulled out her pajamas and asked Ellen where the bathroom was. Only when she was alone in the bathroom did she begin to remove her wet clothes.

Before going to sleep, she and Ellen talked, Ellen at length about Beau, whom she had danced with three times at the dance hall last Saturday. He was handsome, Ellen said, captain of the football team, and really interested in her. He was going to be at the dance the next night "to dance with me," and Ellen added smiling broadly, "maybe walk me home." She asked Honey if she had gone out at all during the summer, out on a date is what she meant. Honey Lee hadn't. She'd gone to the movies with Jimmy a few times and had gone with him to visit Frank and Mary.

"I wonder what it's like to be married," Ellen said.

"Me too. Mary and Frank seem to love it."

They were talking and not talking about sex. They had heard a lot from the nuns and priests about sins of the flesh and occasions of sin, but beyond kissing on the front steps of the house, they were ignorant. But when Ellen told her how she felt whenever she saw Beau, Honey recognized the feelings: breathlessness, a fluttery feeling in her chest, hands shaking so she couldn't hold on to a cup of coffee without spilling it. Honey Lee had felt something like that as Jack Flynn had continued to look at her and tease her during dinner. She'd had to use care in putting her glass down on the table lest her shaking hand spill milk on the tabletop. She never felt like that with Jimmy or with anyone else. She found fumbling attempts at kissing silly at best. But now she wondered how it would feel to kiss Jack Flynn. Again she felt a fluttery feeling in her chest.

Ellen finally mumbled, "Night, Honey Lee."

Honey Lee lay awake for a long time listening to the house whispers and sounds from outside the house: snatches of music from across the water, the quiet rumble of a power boat, the rise and fall of Mr. and Mrs. Flynn's voices from downstairs. She didn't want to sleep. She wanted to treasure the day.

"Make yourself at home," Mr. Flynn had said when he saw her.

She numbered the delights of the day: the family dinner—seven people crowded around a table, laughing, talking listening—the lake, the mountains, table rock, which she had claimed as an honorary Flynn, her long talk with Ellen, who slept peacefully across the room from her. This is what it would have been like to have a sister, Honey Lee thought. You'd share a room and secrets and problems. Eventually her eyes closed and she slept dreamlessly until she heard a loud pounding on the bedroom door.

"Polar Bear Club Meeting. Everybody up and out."

Ellen groaned, but sat up and pulled her bathing suit off the peg above her bed.

"Come on Honey Lee, it's a torture they wont let die. On their first day, every guest has to join the PBC at six o'clock in the morning."

Honey Lee pulled her new bathing suit out of her suitcase and, turning her back to Ellen, dropped her pajama bottoms, and pulled the suit up under her pajama jacket. She turned around. Ellen stared at her.

"Oh, Honey Lee, you're beautiful."

Honey Lee's face was pink with sleep and her dark hair hung down to her shoulders. The contrast between her fair skin and the sea foam green suit was striking. Her full breasts pushed at the top of her bathing suit. Ellen, almost a foot shorter and freckled, looked like a child in a navy tank suit that lay flat against her chest. Ellen dashed out of the room, down the stairs, across the porch to the dock where all of the Flynns except Mrs. Flynn stood waiting. All of them wore bathing suits. They chanted "Polar Bear, Polar Bear," as they took Honey by the elbows and marched her into the water. It was much colder than she remembered from the day before.

"Welcome to the club," they shouted as they dove in after her.

"Table rock?" Mr. Flynn said. They all started to swim furiously toward the rock. It was big enough to hold them all. After several dives, they headed back to where Mrs. Flynn had set the table on the porch for breakfast. The porch got the early morning sun and they dried off as they sat and ate blueberry pancakes.

CHAPTER 11

▼

After breakfast the girls walked to Endicott Rock, the public beach. They spread their towels on the sand and lay down near some of Ellen's friends, including Beau. He looked like a football player—tall and thick in a way that displeased Honey Lee. Jack Flynn was tall and thin. She had once heard someone describe Gary Cooper as rangy. That was the word for Jack. He had eaten breakfast with the family and gone off with friends. Beau and Ellen wanted to talk to each other. To give them time alone, Honey Lee decided to swim. She walked toward the water and stood watching the boats going through a channel to the right of the beach.

A few people waved from their boats and she waved back. Someone called out, "Hey, Colonel Murphy, want to water ski?"

She recognized Jack in the back of the boat with two girls. She felt stupid about being disappointed, but she laughed and called out, "Maybe in the next century."

She walked out to a line of buoys she thought marked the children's swimming area, dove under the ropes and began to swim. Again she relished the cool water on her head. Why do so many women wear bathing caps when the water feels so great in your hair? Swimming made her body feel alive and free. She heard the piercing sound of the lifeguard's whistle but ignored it thinking someone else was being summoned. When the sound persisted and was followed by shouting, she stopped and turned around to see the lifeguard waving frantically at her. She headed back embarrassed by the attention she had drawn. Several people had gathered on the shore to watch her swim in. When she got close enough to stand, the lifeguard rushed toward her.

"What in hell do you think you're doing? Ordinary buoy lines don't pertain to you?" he called out. When he got closer to Honey and saw how tall and how lovely she was, he stopped talking. Finally he was able to say, "You really scared me. You can't swim out that far."

"I'm so sorry. I didn't know," Honey Lee said shaking the water out of her hair and walking beside him to the sand and Ellen.

"Charley, this is my friend from Lowell you're yelling at. Honey Lee, this is Charley Franklin. His job goes to his head."

Once again, Honey Lee said how sorry she was and then acknowledged the introduction.

"Are you two going to Irwin's tonight?" Charley asked.

"Yes, Charlie, and no, I won't let you stomp on my feet again and call it dancing," Ellen said.

"Well I think your friend owes me a dance. How about it Judy Lee?"

"It's Honey Lee, and yes, I do owe you and would love to dance with you," Honey Lee said.

Ellen was ready to go, but waited until Honey Lee was dry enough to put on her shorts and shirt. They headed back to the Flynns' house stopping at Connors for Karmelkorn. Jack didn't come home for supper. He worked off-and-on at the big white hotel near the boardwalk both in the kitchen and in the bowling alley. Supper was easier for Honey Lee not having to worry about Jack and the effect he was having on her. After supper, the girls did the dishes and then were free to get ready for the dance. Honey had brought only one dress, a church dress, but it had to do for the dance. Like so many of her clothes, it had been chosen by Nana. Honey Lee's floral print dress had a v neckline with a white collar and a fitted bodice and waist. Ellen's dark blue sundress with white trim on the straps and across the top was more suited to a dance than Honey Lee's. They both wore flat, comfortable shoes—ballerina shoes.

Both girls loved dancing. They practiced the jitterbug together at home, in sessions that often ended up with the two of them on the floor collapsed in giggles. Honey Lee was so much taller than Ellen that any attempt to pass under Ellen's raised arm was impossible. When they swung away from each other and then back together they never quite connected. Before they came downstairs they danced through the hall and into the bedrooms. "I think we'll do just fine," Ellen said.

Even though Honey Lee had no Beau waiting for her, she was excited to be going to a real dance hall. They waited to start out until they heard the first music from the band. Ellen said it wouldn't look good to be too eager. Let Beau and whoever else wait for them. As they walked toward the boardwalk they sang the lyrics to the songs in high falsetto, giggling at their voices. They kept their feet moving in time with the music, their skirts flaring out around them. They paused on the boardwalk leading down to the dance hall to watch one of Ellen's friends call out bingo numbers at the Bingo Hall. Ellen stuck her tongue out and crossed her eyes trying to get him to laugh. He ignored her. At the entrance to the ballroom, they bought tickets. The ballroom was dim. A narrow spot played on a faceted, mirrored ball which slowly turned causing the lights like floating stars to play over the dancing figures. On one side the hall was the bandstand, on the other windows opened to the lake. At the end furthest from the entrance, a deck overlooked the lake. Couples wandered in and out. Honey Lee and Ellen walked slowly toward the open deck but stopped when Beau called out to them.

"I've been waiting for you. There was no beauty here until you two walked in. Let's dance, Ellen."

Honey watched them make their way to the dance floor, Beau's arm around Ellen's waist, Ellen's head leaning on his shoulder. Honey lost sight of them as they melted into the swaying crowd. Suddenly Honey Lee found herself guided toward the dance floor. She felt strong hands on her waist and heard Jack laugh when she sputtered,

"What's—"

"Aren't you here to dance, Honey Child?"

"Yes, but usually I'm asked, not pushed."

"I claim host rights to the first dance."

The band played the opening notes of *Ma'mselle*. Honey and Jack danced slowly. Jack held her tightly at the waist and put his face next to hers. His hair was damp and he smelled like Ivory Soap. Honey Lee's heart thumped. When he spoke to her, Honey Lee could feel his breath on her cheek. One song followed another without any breaks. When the set ended and the band took a break, Jack took Honey Lee's hand and led her to the open end of the pier. They stood at the railing looking out at the lake.

"Hey, Jack. Aren't you going to introduce us?"

Honey Lee recognized the boy and one of the girls she had seen with Jack on the boat.

"This is my little sister's friend, Miss Honey Lee Murphy of Atlanta and Lowell."

Honey Lee was so angry at the mention of Atlanta that she didn't immediately register "little sister's friend."

"Jack Flynn, I am not from Atlanta. I'm as much a Lowell person as you are."

"OK, OK. This is Bob and Alice. Bob owns the boat you are going to ski behind before you leave the Weirs."

As he spoke, the blond girl she had seen on the boat earlier in the day came up behind him.

"I've been looking for you, Jackie. Let's dance."

Jack introduced Beverly Winters and excused himself. Beverly took hold of his arm as if she owned him. "I heard Ellen had a friend up this week. I hope you're having fun," she said to Honey Lee before she and Jack moved off to the dance floor leaving Honey Lee alone.

She was irritated by the girl's possessive behavior, and she resented being called his little sister's friend. She did not feel like a little sister's friend to Jack, and he didn't, except with his friends, treat her like one. He had told her she was lovely, had held her firmly, had even, she thought, once kissed her cheek as they danced. Troubled, she stood looking out at the lake noticing the lights in houses on the nearby shore and listening to the gentle sound of water lapping at the pier until she became peaceful and dreamy.

"Haven't you danced at all?" It was Ellen and Beau.

"Yes, with Jack."

"Well Charley is looking for the dance he threatened," Ellen said.

Over Ellen's shoulder, she saw Charlie making his way toward them. He asked her to dance, and smiling she accepted. All the while she was dancing, she kept looking for Jack. At the end of the set, Charlie asked if she wanted a coke. They sat at a table and sipped at their cool drinks. Charlie was curious. He wanted a life history. How long had she lived in Lowell? Did she come from Alabama, Georgia, Louisiana? When? How many brothers and sisters? What did her father do? Honey Lee felt invaded. She denied being from the South at all and fudged on family while she tried to figure out how to get away from him. She was accustomed to the Flynns' tact. They never mentioned her mother. They asked kindly about Nana Murphy, but never mentioned her father.

Even Jimmy never talked about her parents unless she mentioned them first. Deeply troubled by Charlie's questions, she told him that she needed to go to the ladies' room and quickly left the hall. She walked slowly toward the public beach and the jetty near the channel. She sat down on a huge rock. Pulling her knees up to her chin, she drifted back in memory to that terrible day in April when Nana Murphy had come to school to take her home. She cried quietly and then sobbed. That she had survived that day amazed her. What kind of mother was Savannah? Ellen's mother would never leave one of her children. Suddenly she was angry and sad. Coming to the Weirs was a mistake. Too much family. Too many feelings. Savannah wasn't a mother, she was a monster. After two and a half years, she surfaces and asks me to join her new family. Tommy Murphy replaced as if he were a spare part, and she expects me to be part of her new life. What gall. She cried, then sobbed rocking back and forth on her stone perch. She picked up a child's shovel lying near the rocks and began to beat it against the rocks she was sitting on. With every stroke she cursed her mother. A few boats passed the jetty, but she was hidden by darkness. Finally, her anger spent, she lay down on a flat rock and was still. She heard the distant sound of the dance music—how sad these songs were—and the gentle lapping of the water. She fell asleep.

When the sound of a loud motor woke her, she had no idea how long she had slept. The music had stopped. The lights were out. It must be late. Mrs. Flynn would be worried. She jumped up and began to run. As she got close to the boardwalk she realized that it was not as late as she had thought. Couples were still wandering out of the dance hall. She walked toward them thinking she would get back exactly when she was expected. She tried to spot Ellen and Beau, but couldn't see them. Just as she made the turn toward the Flynn's house, Jack called out to her.

"Honey Lee, where did you get to? I wanted more than one dance with you. Where in the world did you go?"

"Jack, hi." She stopped to wait for him to catch up to her. "I took a walk. I needed some air."

Jack took her hand and led her back toward the dance hall. She followed, too tired to resist. They stopped under a light near the Bingo Hall. Jack turned her to face him and stared at her. He put his hand on her face.

"Oh, Honey Lee, what is it?"

"Nothing, nothing. I fell asleep on the beach."

He put his arms around her. She pressed her face into his chest. For a long time, Jack held her saying nothing. Honey Lee was embarrassed.

"I'm sorry, Jack. I don't know what's gotten into me," she said.

"Don't be sorry, Honey. I've always thought you were made of steel. But I worried about you. Ellen told me she's never seen you cry, and God knows, you had much to cry about."

"It's just being here with your family. Everything seems so connected, so right. I have Nana Murphy, and I love her, but…"

"I've always wanted to help you, but you wouldn't…" He searched for words. "Why are you so closed?"

"I hate pity." She pulled away from him and walked ahead.

"I'm not talking pity, damn it. I'm talking caring. I've always cared for you. Even before your father died I wanted to help you."

"Let's go home, Jack." Honey was ashamed and confused. Maybe he was just playing big brother and maybe he cared about her. She couldn't tell. She began to tremble and didn't know whether it was from crying, fatigue, cold, or some crazy thing about Jack. They turned around again and walked toward the street that led to the Flynns', but Jack walked past the street.

"Let's just walk for a while. I'll show you another way back."

They walked past the hotel to a dirt road with a sign, *Methodist Campgrounds, Weirs Beach, New Hampshire.* Tiny houses were tightly arranged in horseshoe fashion going down toward the lake.

Pointing to a large yellow building near the water, Jack said, "That's the Tabernacle."

"The Tabernacle?" Honey Lee's only idea of a tabernacle was the sacred, small gold box on the altar which held the Blessed Sacrament. This plain building was not a tabernacle.

"They use it for church during meeting week."

When they passed the Franklin House and the Tilton House as they made their way down to the water, Jack explained that the houses were named after towns in the Methodist District. "I used to play with some of the kids here when I was a kid, but as soon as I started to smoke and go dancing, that ended. They're really strict about stuff like that."

They walked past the Tabernacle and down to a short wharf that jutted out into the water. They sat down together on the dock. There were few lights anywhere on the lake, and it was so quiet Honey could hear her own breathing. Neither of them spoke. Jack held her. She looked out at the darkness. After a while she turned to him.

"Jack, what was it like to leave home?" She whispered.

"You mean to go to school? To college?"

"Yes. Were you afraid?"

"Of what?" He laughed, but noticing how serious she was asked again, "Afraid of what, Honey Lee?"

"Afraid that when you left everything would…I don't know…would change or something."

He thought for a minute then asked, "What was it like for you to leave home to come up here?"

"I was afraid. I still am. Nana's old. What if she fell or got sick or something?" Jack put his arms around her and pulled her close to him.

"Honey, Honey, the world is not as scary as you think. Your Nana is strong; she loves you; she's not going anywhere and neither are you if you don't want to."

"I don't want to. I want things and people to stay put."

"Honey Lee, your Nana would want you to grow up even if it meant going away."

"Where would I go?" she asked, astonished. "And why would I go?" The thought unnerved her.

"Well, you can't spend the rest of your life on Concord Street."

"I could if I wanted to," she said.

He laughed and said, "I suppose you could. You could just stay right there and not budge an inch until they come to carry you over to Saint Patrick's Cemetery." She giggled. "Seriously, Honey Lee. You need to begin practicing leaving home. To start out you go just like you did to come up here. Then you go back. And when you do, you find that your home is still there just as you left it and that your grandmother is just fine. Then sometime, you go off again, and come back."

Honey Lee suddenly knew that her grandmother and the Flynns had conspired to get her to leave Lowell. Jack had no doubt heard from his parents that she was afraid to leave home. She didn't have time to decide how she felt about this because Jack started talking again.

"I'd like to propose another practice trip for you," Jack said.

Honey laughed. "This is enough for me for now."

"I'm serious, Honey Lee. I want you to come up to Dartmouth for Homecoming in October."

"To Homecoming?" She had heard about college weekends at Dartmouth. She was surprised to find the idea appealing. "I'd have to...to think about it...to ask Nana."

"You do that," Jack said sensing her acceptance. "I think you're getting the hang of it already."

"We'd better go home, Jack. They'll be wondering what became of me."

"They'll be surprised when we show up together, he said, then added, "Pleased."

As they stood up to go, Jack leaned toward Honey and kissed her lightly on the lips. "You are a great beauty, Honey Lee Murphy, and I like you, I really like you."

She felt a flutter in her stomach. She could not speak. Holding hands they walked together along lakefront path to the Flynn's house.

The rest of the week went by too fast. They went as a family, except for Mr. Flynn, to Mass at the dance hall she had fled just hours before. She water skied with Jack and his friends, played Monopoly and Rummy one rainy day, and spent the good days at the beach or swimming from the Flynn dock. She and Jack had little time alone, but he asked her again to Homecoming and made her promise to ask her grandmother.

During the train ride back to Lowell, Honey Lee relived the week, one of the happiest in her life. She had a seat to herself, the only interruption to her thoughts being the conductor calling the stops: Tilton, Franklin, Concord, Manchester, Nashua, and finally Lowell. When the train pulled into the station, she saw her grandmother waiting on the platform, dressed in her Sunday best: the dark blue dress with white flowers, the black straw hat, and her black laced shoes. Honey Lee felt a surge of love. She rushed to her grandmother and bent to kiss her.

"Honey, darlin', I had forgotten how lovely you are. I missed you."

"I'm so glad to see you, Nana. You look wonderful."

It was good to be home.

CHAPTER 12

▼

Nana and Honey Lee talked all through supper and into the evening the night she got back from the Weirs. She bubbled over about everything except Jack's invitation to homecoming. She needed a little time to think about that herself. Nana told her several times to slow down and take a breath.

"But, Nana, it was so wonderful."

"Don't I know all about your gallivanting up there?"

"You do?" Honey Lee asked. "How?"

"Well of course I had to know that you were all right," Nana said.

Jack's lecture on practicing leaving home had apparently been part of a plan. Her unwillingness to leave Lowell had been discussed with the Flynns. They had all talked about her, and she didn't like it. She was not a child to be worried over; she was almost eighteen, old enough to take care of herself and certainly old enough that people should not be sharing worries about her without her knowledge. These things she thought, but didn't say to her grandmother.

Later in the evening, Jimmy called. He had called twice while she was gone. He wanted to come over to see her that night, but Honey said she was tired and wanted to spend time with her grandmother. While they were talking Honey heard Mary in the background saying, "Tell her she has to come to dinner tomorrow."

"Tell her I'd love to." They made plans for the next day and said good night.

When Honey Lee and Nana finally finished talking, Honey was happy to go to her room to think. She wished she had a picture of Jack. She was already beginning to forget his face.

The next day, Jimmy came by a little after noon. He wanted go to a movie before they went to Frank's for supper. They saw *A Tree Grows in Brooklyn*, which had just opened at the Strand. The story of a young girl growing up poor in a tenement distressed her. When the girl's father died, she wept. She was conscious that Jimmy beside her must have been thinking about his old home on Fayette Street. She had learned from her grandmother that the Jacksons were known as the poorest family in all of Lowell, poorer even than the family in the film. Afterward, neither of them spoke about the film.

It was a beautiful late summer day and they had plenty of time before they were due for dinner so they decided to walk the back way through South Lowell to Billerica. They walked slowly across the bridge into Belvedere, passing Fort Hill Park where she and Ellen and Jimmy had gone sledding several times during the snowy season. Their way past Fort Hill Park led to Shedd Park where the swimming pool was still open and children were splashing and laughing. Honey compared the pool in her mind to the beautiful lake in New Hampshire and laughed.

She started to tell Jimmy about her week with the same enthusiasm that she had when she told Nana about it. Jimmy listened without comment until she told him about Jack's invitation to Homecoming and her reluctance to ask Nana Murphy.

"Do you think she'll let me go?" she asked.

"How would I know? If I were her, I wouldn't. You shouldn't be up there with that bunch of drunks."

"What drunks? I've never seen Jack drink anything."

"The school has a reputation, that's all I know." Jimmy sounded angry. He started to walk a little ahead of her, kicking at small stones in the street. A bit later when they came to a large field he took her arm and led her through the high grass to the edge of a woods telling her he knew a short cut through the woods. "When we were kids, before my father started to drink, we had a car and we used to go out here for picnics. We were all together then, six of us." He stopped walking and leaned his head against a tree.

"Jimmy, what's wrong?" Honey Lee asked putting her hand on his shoulder.

"Nothing," he said and walked on. "I hate living in someone else's house. I wish Danny would get better and come home."

"How is he? Any better?"

"He looks a little better, but I know he'd be better still at home with me."

"You're the one I worry about. I want you to be happy."

"Thanks. But I want him home."

They were now deep into the woods. Tall trees arched over them filtering the sunlight. Honey Lee stopped and looked up at the leaves. "What will you do when he comes home?"

"Move back to Lowell. That's where I belong. And him, too." He was still gloomy." The woods was dark and cool.

"Jimmy, this is great. I love it," she said trying to cheer him. She wasn't sure what bothered him most, her visit to the Flynns' and Jack's invitation or his longing to get Danny and move back to Lowell. They came up out of the woods on Brentham Road just a short block from Frank's house.

"How did you ever find this route?"

"I just started walking one day trying to get lost for a while, and the next thing I knew I was almost in Lowell. I use it a lot now. Mary told me it's called McClain's Woods, but I've never seen or heard of a McClain."

"Just imagine owning a whole woods and never using it."

Mary met them at the door when they arrived. She and Honey Lee hugged and sat down to talk. A car horn started blaring. When Honey Lee jumped, Jimmy finally laughed and seemed more like himself.

"I forgot to tell you, Frank got a new car, a Plymouth. His baby. He won't stop until you go out to see it. He spends hours washing it and tinkering with the motor. Let's go out and let him show off." He laughed again and took her hand leading her out to the front of the house. The brand new Plymouth, shiny black with lots of chrome, was impressive, even to Honey who was not much interested in cars.

"Well, you're back from Paradise," Frank said. Have a good time?"

"Frank, it's beautiful."

"Just a lousy old car," he said laughing and rubbing a spot on the fender. The dinner with the Jacksons was the last celebration of Honey's summer. Labor Day came and went; the Flynns came back from New Hampshire, Honey Lee and Ellen began their senior year of high school. Every day, they wore the trim, dark blue Girl Officers' uniforms, which had been provided by the school complete with decorations indicating rank. As Colonel, Honey Lee was courted by boys and girls who wanted to claim special friendship with her. She liked the uniform well enough; she enjoyed working with younger girls in gym classes, but she didn't like special treatment, either from the teachers or from the other students. It embarrassed her as her height and her accent once had.

Mr. Flynn was her Latin teacher for the fourth year of Latin. He also acted unofficially as her guidance counselor giving her catalogues from Smith, Mount Holyoke, and Wellesley, all of which he felt were suitable. Honey Lee, however, knew that she would never leave Lowell to go to college, not even to a school as close as Wellesley. One alternative to these was Lowell Teachers' College, but Mr. Flynn discouraged her. Out of politeness she took the catalogues he gave her but never read them seriously. In any case, the colleges Mr. Flynn suggested displeased her grandmother, Sister Veronica, and Father Finn. All of them spoke of good Catholic boys and girls who had lost their faith at such places. Honey Lee had a vision of faith as a little suitcase one might put down somewhere on campus and forget all about it. In deference to them she looked at catalogues from Regis and Emmanuel, both Catholic colleges. But Mr. Flynn, since she insisted on commuting, had his heart set on Boston University for her. She read catalogues from Boston University, Simmons, and Emmanuel College.

Her school life and her social life continued on much as it had for her first three years. She and Ellen went to the CYO dances, Ellen more often than she. They studied together, went to Mass almost every day, and listened to the Hit Parade every week trying to guess which of their favorite songs would end up at the top of the list. Jack came home once and they went to a movie together. She continued to put off asking Nana Murphy if she could go to Homecoming. She kept working herself up to the point of asking and then backing off. One day in September when the weekend was less than three weeks away and Jack was pressing her for her answer, she forced herself to talk to Nana Murphy. They were sitting at the kitchen table after supper, as they often did to talk about the events of their days. Nana began to talk about young Peter's school troubles. Aunt Kitty was worried and wondering if she should pull him out of the high school and send him to Keith Academy to get him straightened out.

"It's at least three times this month that he's skipped school. Kitty can't do a thing with him, and his father's useless."

"Maybe he should walk to school with me, and I could see that he gets there."

"No dearie, that's no job for you, and he wouldn't agree anyway. It's not manly, you see."

"Poor Aunt Kitty."

They both meditated on Aunt Kitty's problems with Uncle Peter, who still suffered from whatever the war had done to him. At least her father wasn't suffering. Neither was Frank. He was so happy in his marriage that the past was like a bad dream he seemed to have forgotten. Jimmy told her he never talked about what he had done overseas. Jimmy said that Danny was also happy, getting well, and coming home soon. She hoped that Jimmy was right. She wondered how anyone who had been in a hospital for over a year could be happy.

"Honey Lee, where on earth are you?" Nana Murphy asked her voice breaking into Honey's sad thoughts.

"Oh, Nana," she said shaking her head, "I'm sorry. I was just thinking."

"T'was sad thinking, I'm guessing," Nana said putting her hand over Honey Lee's.

"Yes, it was," she said and then shifted back to the present. "Nana, I have to ask you something important, very important."

Nana looked worried. "And what is it, dearie?"

"Well, you know Jack Flynn, Ellen's brother?" Even as she spoke she saw how foolish her question was.

"I do indeed, and him up at that rich man's college."

"He got a scholarship, Nana." She felt a need to defend him. "He's very smart."

"Well then, what about this Jack Flynn?"

"Well, last summer he was kind to me. I really like him a lot."

"Yes?" If Nana was impatient at how long it took her to get to the question, she didn't show it.

"Well," she said. "Well, he invited me to Dartmouth for Homecoming Weekend. Can I go, please?" Honey Lee dashed through the sentence and then held her breath waiting for an answer.

"A whole weekend?" Just as she had feared, Nana was shocked. "Homecoming?"

"It's a big celebration they have every year. They have a football game, dances, concerts." She moved her chair closer to her grandmother as if to use her whole body to convince.

"And a young single girl still in high school would be going off to spend a whole weekend with a boy?" Nana shook her head from side to side disbelieving.

"Nana, they have special places for girls to stay. And if you and my father hadn't made me repeat eighth grade, I'd be in college myself." She hadn't realized how much she wanted to go.

"Oh my, oh dear. I've never heard of such a thing." Nana's hands worked together clasping and unclasping. "I have to think about this. I have to talk to Mrs. Flynn and maybe to Father Finn as well."

"Nana, I really want to go." It was so unlike Honey Lee to beg her grandmother for anything that even she was surprised by her own words.

"We'll see," Nana said. "If your poor father were only here it would be him that decided. But an old woman like myself needs some thinking time." She stood up and paced from the table to the stove.

Honey Lee knew exactly what was going through her grandmother's mind. Would such a thing be proper for a young girl? Nana Murphy had the same ideas as the nuns and priests about what was proper for young girls, that is to say what might or might not prove sinful. She remembered the time when she was in the eighth grade that Sister Rose had heard about a boy-girl party at which kissing games had been played. Honey had not gone. Nonetheless, when Sister solemnly separated the girls from the boys, she felt as guilty as any of the other girls. One by one, Sister questioned each girl, forcing the guilty to confess that they had been at the party and that they had participated in the kissing games. Some of the girls cried. Sister's message was clear. The girls had sinned and should go to confession as soon as possible lest they die with the sin on their souls.

"Boys," she said, "aren't like you. They have impure thoughts and they could lead you into even graver sin. Be very careful with boys." This was the first of many vague lectures Honey Lee had heard on sexual sin. Good girls remained pure. Good girls did not kiss boys. Good girls prayed often to the Virgin Mary. The voices of the nuns and priests had always become hushed as they warned of dangers never made explicit. Impure thoughts, words, and actions were forbidden. Occasions of sin were everywhere: in books, clothes, movies, dark places like parked cars, and even, if you were not in a Catholic school, in text books. For all of the many talks from the nuns and priests, Honey Lee had only the vaguest idea about sex. Honey Lee and Ellen had wondered together about what, beyond kissing, was impure and forbidden. She was now quite sure it had a lot to do with the somewhat alarming symptoms she had whenever Jack Flynn was near.

Happily, Nana Murphy's fears were dispelled by Mrs. Flynn and Father Finn because a few days later she told Honey Lee that she could go to Dartmouth for the weekend.

"In my day," she said, "such a thing would never have happened, I'll tell you. Maybe the war changed everything. But Mrs. Flynn says you'll be just fine. Her Jack is a good Catholic boy who knows how to treat a girl properly. And Father Finn says he knows of several girls from good families who have gone to Dartmouth for Homecoming and Winter Carnival. So I guess you can go."

"Thank you, Nana, thank you," she said and kissed her grandmother. "I'll be very good. I promise."

"Well then, you don't have a mother and father—I mean your mother isn't here," Nana was flustered, but she went on, "so I need to help you. I gave some rules to your Aunt Kitty when she was a girl, and I'm thinking I should give them to you. Don't stay in a parked car or wherever kissing away for hours. And never let a boy touch you more than to hold your hand or give you a quick kiss or a hug. Be sure that the clothes you wear and the way you act don't give a boy the wrong idea about you. Do you understand?"

"Yes, Nana," Honey Lee answered although she really understood very little.

CHAPTER 13

▼

Three weeks later, Honey Lee was at the Lowell train station again with her grandmother waiting for the train heading north. She imagined Savannah climbing up onto a train at this station. Her father had also taken a train from this place and never returned to Lowell, never saw his mother again. She shook her head and scolded herself for having gloomy thoughts when she should be thinking about Jack and Dartmouth.

Nana Murphy fussed over her, asking her if she had her ticket, if she was sure she had packed her new black shoes. Finally when the train came, she took Honey Lee's face in her hands and kissed her.

"Have yourself a grand time, but be good, mind you."

"Of course I will, Nana," she said folding her grandmother in her arms. "I'll miss you."

"Be gone with you. You won't have a minute to miss me."

Honey Lee entered a car already filled with young women heading for Dartmouth. She found a seat by herself and looked out at her grandmother who was waving a handkerchief. How tiny she looked in her navy blue dress. Honey watched her until the train picked up speed and she was gone. Most of the girls on the train seemed to know each other. They called back and forth to each other and wandered up and down the aisles to talk. They all wore similar clothes, saddle shoes, pleated skirts, matching sweater sets and pearls. Honey Lee began to feel uncomfortable. She didn't look like these girls. She pulled *The Sun Also Rises* out of her bag, a book she loved without completely understanding. She was drawn to it because Hemingway wrote about the other war in Europe. She was pretty sure Nana wouldn't like Hemingway, but she had often read books that

Nana wouldn't have approved going way back to Atlanta when she had read her mother's copy of *Gone with the Wind*. Nana had called that a trashy book.

She began reading where she had left off. Brett and Jake were complaining about Robert Cohn following them around and making everyone miserable. She was interrupted by a thin, dark girl who sat down beside her, sighed loudly, and lit a cigarette.

"Aren't they all just too damn much," she said waving her hands to include the whole car. "Thank God this is my last weekend. Mark graduates in January."

Honey Lee, who had marked her place on the page with her finger hoping to continue reading, closed the book and studied her seatmate. Her black hair was parted in the middle and drawn tightly back. Her skin looked golden against the black high-necked sweater she wore. She was so different from the others in the car that Honey Lee thought she might be older.

"I didn't know they had graduations in January."

"It's special for the returning veterans who want to finish early," the girl said flicking the ash from her cigarette onto the floor and exhaling slowly.

"Your boyfriend's a veteran?" Honey was intrigued.

"Uh huh. Is this your first Weekend?" she emphasized the word weekend in such a way that Honey could feel her contempt.

"Yes, it is." She tried to be casual not wanting this girl to know how excited she was, wanting this girl to like her. Honey Lee hoped she had chosen to sit with her because she, too, looked different.

"Are you Radcliffe?" The girl asked.

"No, Murphy."

The girl laughed quickly then apologized. I meant where do you go to school?"

"Oh, Lowell."

"They have schools in Lowell?" the girl laughed again. Honey Lee wasn't sure yet whether they were sharing a joke or she was the butt of one.

But when the girl smiled at her and said, "I'm Sophia Goldring, and you are Murphy? Just Murphy?" she felt better.

"Honey Lee Murphy." Honey was thinking that Sophia was as unusual a name in her experience as her double Southern name was in Lowell. Sophia leaned over and picked up Honey Lee's book.

"Are you taking American Lit?" Honey Lee nodded. "Depressing book, huh?"

"I like it. But I can't figure out why they all stay in Europe when they are so miserable there." She didn't say that she was also a bit confused by Jake and Brett.

"There's lots of guys not coming back this time either. My brother's best friend's still in France. Says he's not coming home."

"What about his family?" That real people outside of books might decide to stay in Europe rather than come home was incomprehensible to her. "He can't just forget his family."

"Read your book, Honey. Anyone in there worrying about Mom and Dad?"

"I guess not."

Honey Lee looked down at the book and wondered who might eventually tell the stories of her father's war.

Sophia began to talk again. "Mark, my boy friend, was Navy—fought in the Pacific and came back to finish up his last two years of college. He says the young kids drive him nuts. That's why I'm going up. He needs me to help him stick it out."

"Are there many veterans up there?"

"Sure, lots."

Honey Lee wanted to ask if Sophia had known Mark before the war. They would both have been very young. She also wondered if the war had changed him. Maybe it was more than just being older that made him so unhappy at Dartmouth. Her mind veered off into a daydream of what it could have been like if her father had come back. She and her mother would have lived with Nana until he came home. Then what? Her father had promised her mother that they would return to the South when he got back. But by then would she herself have wanted to leave Lowell? She had become accustomed to Lowell. No one ever commented anymore on her accent. Sophia hadn't asked, as people used to, where she had lived in the South. She thought, "So much for you, Savannah. I am a full-blooded Murphy, a Catholic, and a Yankee."

"Where are you staying in Hanover?" Sophia asked.

"In one of the dorms. I think."

"Yuck. I did that last year. All those girls squealing and running around. I'm staying at the Inn. At least that way, Mark and I can have our time together alone."

Honey Lee thought immediately about her grandmother's warnings. Sophia and Mark alone at the Inn. Staying together? No. Never. Honey Lee, to cover her embarrassment, took out a paper bag that Nana had packed for her: a sandwich, a piece of cake, and an apple. When Sophia looked at her as if to say, "You've got to be kidding," Honey Lee laughed.

"I live with a grandmother who mothers me to death." The minute she said it, she felt a pang of guilt. She offered Sophia half of her sandwich. Sophia said thanks and took the sandwich. When she saw that it was ham, she handed it back.

"Thanks anyway, but I don't eat ham. It's not a religious thing; it's a Jewish thing. Ever since I saw those pictures of the camps. God!"

"You're Jewish?"

"Yeah, probably the only Jew on this damn train going to visit one of the few Jews at Dartmouth."

Honey Lee had no experience of Jews, at least that she knew of, either in her early life in the South or in Lowell. She knew there was a small section in Lowell where some Jews lived. She also knew that there were places where Jews were not allowed to go. Hampton Beach, a favorite destination for Lowell vacationers, prided itself on preventing Jews from owning property. Like Sophia, she had been horrified by pictures of the camps. And here she was sitting beside someone who, had she lived in Europe, might very well be dead. It stunned her. She said nothing, waiting to see what more Sophia would say. She wanted to apologize to Sophia. But for what? For having heard people she knew call Jews names and brag about not letting Jews into Hampton Beach? Her father's death had made the war real to her. Sophia made the killing of Jews real. She couldn't think of a thing to say. Suddenly the scenes with Robert Cohn in *The Sun Also Rises* seemed to be written out in capital letters on the cover of her book. What did Sophia make of the book? How could Sophia be comfortable in this train full of non-Jews who were probably whispering in the nasty way that people did when they talked about people they didn't like.

"I will have some of that great looking cake, if you don't mind." Honey Lee handed her the cake and they both ate silently.

"What's it like at Radcliffe?" Honey asked.

"I love my major; great teachers, fabulous library, but I hated the dorm, so I moved out."

"My Latin teacher wants me to go to one of the sister schools."

"They're good. But I need to be in a city. I'm so used to New York that Boston feels like a town, but it's better than South Hadley or North Hampton."

The two girls talked comfortably as the train headed toward White River Junction. Sophia told Honey Lee about the fraternity parties and the drinking. Mark wasn't in a fraternity, but they had dropped into a couple of parties and hated them. She said the dance would be fun because a well-known swing band always played. They might even have one of the biggies like Miller, one of the Dorseys, or Artie Shaw. It's like being at one of the big clubs in New York. Sophia said she hated football and would skip the game that was, in theory, the purpose of the weekend. The one thing she was looking forward to was the veterans party.

"It will give me a chance to be with grownups at least for part of the weekend". Honey Lee wondered if she came close to being a grownup in Sofia's eyes. She didn't wonder long.

"I'd love it if you could come to the veterans' party. Would your date—what's his name anyway?"

"Jack Flynn."

"Would Jack bring you?"

Honey Lee suggested that they meet at the station and talk about getting together. She was sure that Jack would like Sophia, and if Sophia loved Mark, Honey was sure she would like him too.

Finally the conductor called out, "White River Junction, White River Junction, next stop." The car came alive. Girls stood up and pulled their suitcases down. They checked their faces in small mirrors and powdered their noses and added lipstick. Neither Honey Lee nor Sophia moved until the train stopped. There was much commotion as the car emptied out; girls called back and forth to each other about plans for meeting. Honey Lee began to feel nervous about seeing Jack in a new setting. She smoothed her hair, straightened her skirt and followed Sophia down the aisle to the exit. Mark reached up and grabbed Sophia by the waist. He kissed her deeply. He was short, at least by Honey's standards, and slight. He wore his dark curly hair longer than most of the boys on the platform. When he and Sophia had finished greeting each other, Sophia turned to Honey and introduced her to Mark.

"Honey Lee, Honey Lee, oh me, oh my, have we a Southern Belle here?"

Honey Lee laughed and said, "Ex-Southerner and never a belle. It's nice to meet you Mark."

"A pleasure for me as well." He had a beautiful smile. His dark eyes looked straight at her. She was being studied, then accepted. Honey almost forgot Jack until she heard him calling.

"Honey Lee. I've been looking for you." He put his arms around her and gave her a friendly hug, nothing like the hungry kiss between Mark and Sophia.

"You look gorgeous," Jack said.

Honey introduced her new friends to Jack and told him she hoped they could get together during the weekend. Honey Lee very much wanted to see Sophia and Mark again.

"Sure thing," Jack said and asked how to get in touch with Mark. Then he said, "We better get moving. I've got a ride for us."

"Call me at the Inn," Sophia called out to Honey Lee as she and Jack moved toward the parking lot.

The car was a new Ford. There were already two couples in the car. One in front and one in back. Honey and Jack climbed into the back seat laughing at being squeezed into the small space. Honey, half seated on Jack's lap, felt her head touch the car roof as they pulled out of the parking space.

"Oh, I saw you on the train. Why didn't you sit with us?" one of the girls said.

Honey Lee thought, how could I have when I didn't even know you.

"Honey Lee is something of a loner," Jack said.

"Well if she wanted privacy, she sat with the right person," the other girl said and giggled.

"Who are you talking about?" Jack asked.

"Sophia, the girl I just introduced you to." Honey Lee's tone was icy.

"Well it isn't that people don't like her, but she act so—you know—different," one of the girls said.

"Mark Stone's girl. They're both stand-offish," Bob, the driver of the car said.

Jack, sensing Honey Lee's discomfort with the conversation, asked her about Ellen.

"She's great," Honey Lee said, "but she's mad at you for not getting her a date for the weekend."

"I don't need my sister up here. You two would probably leave me by myself and run off somewhere to talk. You already found yourself a talking friend for the weekend."

Honey looked out the window. It was snowing lightly and snow already covered the ground. Lowell had not yet had snow, and Honey Lee felt the joy she always felt when it snowed.

"Winter comes early up here," she said.

"And lasts until June. You get sick of it soon enough." Bob said.

Jack reached for Honey Lee's hand and squeezed it. He knows I'm not comfortable, Honey Lee thought. She turned her head and looked at him. He leaned toward her and lightly kissed her. Jack explained that they were going to stop in at his fraternity house first so the brothers could meet her.

"They better watch out for your date, Jack. She's taller than most of them."

She was irritated as she always was when strangers commented on her height. But once again Jack smoothed things for her.

"And smarter and more strong-minded than most of them. They better treat her right."

By the time they pulled up in front of the large white fraternity house the sun had set and darkness had fallen. The house was ablaze with lights and music blared. When they got out of the car, Jack whispered, "They'll all love you. You're wonderful."

He stayed by her side as they moved from group to group sometimes holding her hand, sometimes putting his arm around her waist. Being with him for a whole weekend was more exciting than she had dreamed. She got used to feeling her heart skip a beat when he looked at her and having trouble breathing when he touched her. Nana would have been pleased at how little time they had alone, and so was she because whenever he kissed her she felt lightheaded and dizzy.

The welcome party at the fraternity house was the first event in a busy weekend. She cheered the team at the football game and danced half through the night. On Sunday after church, there was a brunch. Jack had planned so carefully that, though they tried, they couldn't connect with Sophia and Mark. Their schedules just didn't fit. She was sad to learn that Sophia would not be going back on the Sunday night train. Except for that disappointment the weekend was perfect.

CHAPTER 14

▼

One day in late November Jimmy called and asked her to meet him at the Epicure after school. He had news, great news. When she got to the restaurant, she saw him sitting alone at the back of the room. She paused to study him for a few seconds. His face was red from the cold and his hair wind-blown. He still wore it longer than most of the boys she knew and she loved the way it looked, even wind-whipped. A new looking jacket hung from the hook beside the booth. Honey thought about how he had looked when they first met. Her heart sang with joy for the new Jimmy. She treasured him as the first friend she had ever let into the secrets of her heart. He looked up, saw her and waved. When she approached, he stood up and awkwardly hugged her. Since they had grown older, it was difficult for both of them to know how to show affection. The best they could manage was the rough, friendly hug.

"Tell me your big news, Jimmy," she said as they sat down opposite each other.

"He's coming home." He didn't have to tell her who. "And he's going to live with me. Frank wanted him to live with them, God knows how or where he'd sleep. But anyway, Danny said no." He spoke in a rush and his face was bright with joy. "I'm going to take care of him!"

She stood up and so did he so they could hug each other again. "It's over," she sighed her relief. "Your war is finally over." When they sat down again, she asked, "Where? Where are you going to live?"

"We've already got a place. In the new veterans' housing. We jumped the line because of Danny's health." Housing was so scarce in Lowell that waiting lists were long. Families were doubled up waiting.

"Wonderful," she said. But then she started to worry about her friend. "How is he? I mean his health. Can you take care of him alone?"

"Sure. He's got to go back in every week, but he's ok. They wouldn't let him out if he was too sick."

"When is all this happening?"

"Next week. Isn't it great? Danny gave me money, and Frank and Mary went with me to pick out furniture. It's coming on Monday and he comes on Wednesday."

"Jimmy, I'm so happy for you. And for Danny." They held hands across the table until the waitress came with their drinks.

Danny's homecoming was like the last piece in a puzzle. It marked the end of the war for the Jacksons and for Honey Lee who had been hearing about Jimmy's brothers for four years. Although she was eager to meet him, she didn't press Jimmy about when she would. The meeting would happen when it happened. She could wait. The pictures Jimmy had shown her of his family showed Danny as different from his brothers, taller and darker. His thick hair was black. At least in the pictures it seemed so. She thought him more handsome than his bothers.

She had no idea what Danny's injuries were. Neither of the brothers had told her. Because he had been hospitalized for so long she had imagined terrible things. A man down the street from her had come home with a wooden leg. She often saw him lurching around the neighborhood. She had heard about others who came back without arms or legs, and some with arms and useless legs bound to wheelchairs. And others, like her Aunt Kitty's husband, so changed that his wife and son were afraid of him. She supposed there were others who would never come back home. A cousin of Nana's had told them that her son had written from France saying he wouldn't be back for a long while. And there were the thousands like her father, dead.

Honey Lee asked Jimmy if they needed help getting the house ready for Danny. She wanted to help, but she also wanted to see the new Jackson home. Jimmy said they would love help and gave her directions. He told her they'd be there by ten o'clock.

On Monday, Honey Lee woke early and ate her oatmeal with brown sugar, butter and cream. Nana had agreed that she could miss school for one day for a good cause. Honey decided to walk rather than take the bus as Jimmy had suggested. It was only two miles, much shorter than the walk to Frank and Mary's. She walked briskly down Concord to Fayette. New poor people had replaced old poor people in the decrepit houses. Jimmy told her that Danny had been against giving up the apartment when Frank married. He wanted to come home to it. It was hard for her to imagine that anyone would want to go back to that terrible place. But Jimmy told her often how full of life the home had been before the boys went away and his mother died.

Honey Lee decided to stop at church to say a prayer for Jimmy's family: the dead brother and mother, and Jimmy, Frank and Danny. The church was empty and dark except for the flickering vigil light candles, reminders to God of the people for whom prayers were needed. Honey Lee took a dime out of her pocket and put it in the small metal box at the bottom of the candle stand. She lit one candle for the Jackson family. Looking at the rows of tiny lights she wondered how many of them were for people lost or crippled by the war. Nana Murphy and she lit one every week for Tommy's soul. There weren't enough candles in all of the churches in Lowell to number the boys who had died.

But Danny was coming back to a brand new, better house. She knelt in prayer breathing in the wax-scented air, enjoying the stillness. After she had grown too big to find her private place under the telephone poles on Perry Street, she had begun to spend many hours in church where she was disturbed only by an occasional woman praying silently as she was. She loved the upstairs church, which was used only on Sundays and on special feasts, but she felt more tucked in and comfortable in the lower church with its low ceiling and dim lights. She finished praying and blessed herself, "In the name of the Father, the Son, and the Holy Ghost, Amen." Why was it called blessing oneself? Priests blessed things—candles, medals, statues, water. The things were made holy by the blessing. Ordinary people, even nuns, couldn't bless things. Priests also blessed people. But ordinary people could only bless themselves. Honey Lee liked the idea of blessing herself and wished she could bless everyone she loved: Nana, Jack and Ellen and their family, Jimmy and Frank, and Danny who was finally coming home. "I bless all of you in the name of the Father, the Son, and the Holy Ghost, Amen," she said out loud. Behind her she heard footsteps. She turned and saw Father Finn standing near the back of the church. He wore his long robe with the wide black belt that held a black and gold crucifix.

"Is that Honey Murphy talking out loud to God?"

She hoped he hadn't heard what she said. "Good morning, Father. I didn't hear you come in."

"Have you something special to pray about today?"

"Oh, yes, Father. Jimmy Jackson's brother Danny is coming home this week. At last."

"Bless his poor mother, who didn't live to see any of her boys come home. She had a hard life, Honey Lee."

"I didn't know her, Father."

"She was grand. You couldn't keep her down, no matter what happened, and the Lord knows she had bad times." Father Finn closed his eyes and shook his head slowly. She wondered if he was praying for Mrs. Jackson.

"You and Jimmy are fine friends, aren't you? I know he watched out for you."

"Oh, yes. I love Jimmy."

"Your boy friend, eh?"

"No. Father, my friend." Anxious to get started on her way, she told Father Finn where she was going.

"Just the two of you?"

"No, Father. Mary and Frank, too."

"Well that's fine then. It wouldn't do for you to be all alone with Jimmy. You know that, don't you?"

"Yes, Father," she said and began to walk toward the door.

"Good-bye, Honey Lee. God Bless you."

"And you too Father," she said giving him his blessing back. She smiled at her power to bless. She ran past the churchyard and the Lowell Memorial Auditorium, over the bridge and into the Square.

Being out of school while everyone else was in school made her feel free. By mid-afternoon, the Square would be full of high school students. Even those who lived on the other side of Lowell would come to the Square before heading home. You had to go to the square. It was a ritual not only for Lowell High School students, but for students from Keith Academy, Keith Hall, Saint Patrick's and even Notre Dame. Some just congregated in front of Kresge's or Woolworth's. Other went to Paige's ice cream store near the old clock. Still others, like Honey and Ellen, went to the Epicure. Honey Lee turned left onto Central Street, passing Barrows Bus Station where, during the war and for some time after, soldiers by the dozens poured out of busses from Fort Devens in Ayer to go to the USO or to the many bars on Moody Street. Often girls hung out at the station waiting for the soldiers to come. Nana Murphy had warned Honey Lee about "that kind of girl." But Honey loved watching the soldiers, dressed as her father had been dressed when she last saw him.

She left the downtown area and walked up a small hill. At the top, a courthouse and a big gray stone church, Saint Peter's, faced each other. Saint Peter's was one of the seven churches that she and Ellen and friends visited every Holy Thursday. It was as big as the Immaculate, but to Honey, nowhere near as beautiful. Behind the church was the Common, the large park where Field Day, in which Honey Lee would play a major part, was held every year in June. She paused to look at the empty field and the gray stone building beyond, Keith Academy, which looked more like a prison than a school. On field day the whole area would be alive with color and noise.

She hurried on up Gorham Street through the Grove toward the two Lowell cemeteries, Saint Patrick's—where Catholics, and only Catholics were buried— where her grandfather had been buried and where one day Nana Murphy would be. Her own mother, Savannah, even if she wanted to, couldn't be buried there. Beyond Saint Patrick's was Edson Cemetery—where non-Catholics were buried. Nana Murphy had told her that it was "unhallowed ground." No Catholic could ever be laid to rest there. Honey Lee wasn't sure whether the cemetery kept Catholics out or they didn't want to go in.

Not far beyond the cemeteries was the Veteran's housing where Jimmy and Danny would live. She saw the long, low buildings ahead. From a distance they looked like children's blocks arranged in neat rows. Each building had two doors. In front of some of the buildings, women tending babies in carriages sat on benches pushing the carriages back and forth. She smiled and greeted the women. They aren't much older than I am, and already they have babies, she thought. At building # 7, she stopped. Frank's car was out in front.

She knocked on the door and called, "Anyone home?"

Frank opened the door. "Hello, Honey Child. Are you ready to work?"

Mary, standing by the window across the room, waved to her. Jimmy came in from another room. "Hi, Honey Lee," he said. "Thanks for coming. We're waiting for the truck."

"This is great, Jimmy. Can I see the rest?" Jimmy led her into the small kitchen and showed her the brand-new stove and refrigerator. He turned the gas burners on and off, opened the refrigerator door, and turned on the hot and cold water.

"You're like a salesman," Honey said. They both laughed as he guided her to the other side of the living room to the two small bedrooms and the bath. One bedroom was much smaller than the other.

Pointing to the small one, Jimmy said, "The nursery. I sleep here."

Mary called from the living room asking Honey Lee to help her decide about the curtains. She had bought three pair of long lace curtains she planned to cut in half using one pair for the two windows in the living room and one for each of the bedrooms. When cut, the curtains came just below the windowsills. Honey said she liked them that length much better than all the way to the floor. She offered to help Mary hem the curtains while Frank and Jimmy put up the curtain rods. Frank had already put down rugs in each of the rooms, so they were ready when they heard the truck pull up. A slight man with fiery red hair jumped out of the truck and came to the door.

"My God, is it you Patrick?" Frank said. "What are you doing in Lowell driving a truck."

"Mary, this is the guy I told you about who was so good to Danny in the hospital. Patrick was at the hospital for the whole war."

"And I'll tell you, I saw more than anyone should of death and dying and wounds. I finally left last month," Patrick said before remembering Danny. He blushed and stammered. "We fixed most of them up as good as new. This place for Danny?"

"Yeah," Frank said, "he's coming home Wednesday."

"Great. You've got some great stuff here for him. I loaded it myself. How about helping us unload?"

Patrick's partner, a young boy, was still in the truck. Jimmy and Frank each carried in a brown and green plaid armchair. Patrick and his partner followed with a matching couch. They kept coming in with beds, tables, dressers and chairs. Mary directed the activity telling the men where to put the sofa and where the head of each of the beds should go. As they brought in the smaller pieces, she took them and placed them where she wanted them. Slowly it began to look like a home.

"We forgot lamps, and Jimmy will need his desk and bookcase from our house," Mary said.

When Patrick pulled away they all sat and admired their work. Honey Lee thought how excited some of the women she had seen outside must have been to be moving into their first home with their returning soldiers or sailors. Some day, she thought, I'll have my own new home with a husband and children.

"Well, I guess that's it," Frank said. "All we need now is Danny."

Mary went into the bedroom to get their coats, and they all went outside. Jimmy was going to stay in the new place until Wednesday, "just to get the feel of it," he said.

"Honey Child," Frank said, "we'll give you a ride home."

"No, no. I love to walk," Honey Lee said.

"I'll walk her home," Jimmy said taking Honey Lee's arm.

Mary and Frank drove off as Honey Lee and Jimmy walked toward the cemetery.

Jimmy said, "Let's go in. I'll show you my mother's grave." They walked slowly through the gates and followed the path to the right. Most of the gravestones had Irish names; some had small flags planted in the ground near them.

"For soldiers lost in the war," Jimmy said. He stopped in front of a grave. John Jackson 1888—.No date was given for John's death. Under his name was written "Mary Joanna Jackson, Beloved Mother, 1890–1942." A flag and a dead plant lay in front of the stone.

Pointing to the first name, Honey Lee asked, "Your father?"

"Yeah, when ma bought the plot, she insisted on two graves, one for him and one for her. Some day, if he turns up dead we'll put him in." He made the sign of the cross and bent his head. Honey Lee put her hand on his shoulder. For several minutes they stood in silence. He picked up the dead plant, and said, "Let's go out the back way."

Honey Lee followed him. They went downtown by a route new to Honey Lee. They stopped at the Epicure. School had just let out and the place was full. They saw Ellen in a booth with two friends and joined her.

"You weren't at school today," Ellen said.

"What did I miss? Anything?" Honey Lee said.

"No," Ellen said and laughed, "the same old stuff. I'm so ready to graduate, and it's only November."

"Me, too," Honey Lee said. "Do we have homework?"

Ellen took a notebook out of her green book bag, opened it, and handed it to Honey Lee, who started copying from it on to a napkin. They ordered fresh fruit orange and a toasted English muffin. The two girls with Ellen were smoking. They offered Honey Lee and Jimmy a cigarette. Honey Lee hated smoking and said no, but Jimmy accepted. The girl handed Jimmy a cigarette and then offered her own to Jimmy for a light. She held it in her hand and put it up to Jimmy's face putting her hand over Jimmy's as he inhaled. Honey Lee could tell that she was flirting. Jimmy didn't seem to notice.

When they were finished eating Honey Lee, Jimmy and Ellen left together and headed toward Belvedere. They passed by Fayette and went up High Street to pass by Ellen's house. When they got there, Ellen said, "Want to come in? My mother says she never sees you."

"Not today, Ellen. I've got all this to do," she said waving the napkin on which she written down her homework assignments. She and Jimmy walked on and turned down Sherman Street and over to Nana Murphy's house.

"Come in, Jimmy and have some tea with me and Nana."

Nana was full of questions about Danny, about the house and the furniture, about who would cook, and whether Danny would need nurses.

When Honey Lee went back to school on Tuesday she brought a neatly written excuse note to present to each of her teachers who initialed it and gave it back to her to show the next teacher. She had missed school only one other time in three and a half years. She had won several arguments with Nana Murphy, when Nana thought she was too sick to go to school and wanted her to stay home. But that Tuesday after helping Jimmy and Frank, she might as well have stayed at home. She revisited the apartment in her mind, thinking of more things that would make it homelike for Danny and Jimmy. She tried to picture them living together. Who would cook? Would Danny be neater than Frank who had been so messy living with Jimmy? She wondered how much care he would need. She knew he had come back from Manila on a hospital troop ship no doubt staffed by doctors and nurses. Honey admired women who served as nurses on ships and in hospitals overseas. In idle reverie, she had even imagined herself as an Army nurse near the battlefield where her father had died. In her dream story, she was the nurse on duty when her mortally wounded father was brought into the hospital tent. She had nursed him for days until he died with her name on his lips but without ever having recognized her. In her more practical moments she knew such dreams were ridiculous.

During Latin class, when Mr. Flynn called on her to translate the next lines from the *Aeneid*, she had no idea where the last translator had stopped. Mr. Flynn gently suggested that she try to stay in the room rather wandering throughout the world. The other students laughed. She smiled and told Mr. Flynn she would try to stay in the room.

She didn't expect to hear from Jimmy that night, but he called at seven o'clock. "Hi, Honey. They put our phone in this afternoon."

"Jimmy, hi. Are you staying there tonight?" She imagined him sitting on the green plaid couch.

"Sure I am. It's my home. It's where I live."

"I love it Jimmy. Danny will too."

"I sure hope so." He sounded so young.

"Did you go to school today?"

"No. I'll go back next week. Jack Shea's bringing me my assignments."

"Good luck tomorrow." She hoped for an invitation, but didn't get one.

"Thanks, Honey."

She hung up reluctantly. And then thought about how often Jimmy called her Honey instead of Honey Lee lately. Although she had grown accustomed to having people call her by the single name and had thought she wanted to be called by it, she realized that she didn't want to give up her full name. She found it especially troubling when a boy called her Honey. It might or might not be an endearment. Frank always called her Honey Child, and that was fine, but Jimmy's Honey made her uncomfortable. She liked to know where she stood with people and felt that his changing the way he named her might mean his feelings were changing.

When she began worrying about Jimmy being alone, she reminded herself of Fayette Street and laughed at herself. Jimmy could take care of himself, no doubt about that. On Wednesday night she waited and waited for a call from Jimmy. She fussed with her homework and put off taking a bath until almost midnight so she wouldn't miss the call. But no call came on Wednesday or Thursday either. Even though her grandmother and the nuns and even Ellen had told her repeatedly that girls should never call boys, even boys who were their friends, she almost called the new house. But what if Danny answered? What would she say? Finally on Friday she got a call, not from Jimmy, but from Mary asking her to a homecoming meal for Danny on Saturday.

"Jimmy wants you to be there. But so do I." she said. "I need another woman badly." She sounded worried.

"Is everything all right, Mary?" Urgent questions rose up in her mind and poured out. "Is Danny all right…? How is he?"

"Oh, Honey Lee he's so thin you want to feed him butter, steak and ice cream."

"But he can walk? I mean get out of bed and all?"

"Oh, sure, he's weak and tired, but I think he's going to be OK."

"You're sure?" Mary made an encouraging noise, and Honey Lee raced on. "Did he like the house?"

"Yeah, but he keeps talking about Fayette Street, just like Frank. He can't believe his mother and the house are gone. I don't know why they all love that old place so much. Well, anyway, two o'clock tomorrow. The boys will pick you up. Dress up. It's a party."

Honey hung the phone up and ran to tell her grandmother.

CHAPTER 15

▼

On Saturday morning, Honey Lee woke up early. She planned to wear her blue silk dress. She tried it on, smoothing the soft fabric over her hips as she looked in the mirror. Just like my mother, she thought, remembering how often she had seen her mother slide her hands over her hips and admire herself. She frowned and shook her head. She was about to pull the dress off when Nana Murphy knocked on the door and came in.

"Now don't you look a princess? It's a fine looking lass you are."

"I think it's too dressy, Nana," Honey Lee said.

"Well, you know best, dear" her grandmother said. "I'll be going downstairs to keep a look out for them, shall I?"

She left and closed the door. Not usually so nervous about how she looked, Honey Lee went to her small closet to look for something else to wear. Choosing and rejecting one dress after another, she finally settled on the long black skirt and white blouse she had bought when she and Ellen had shopped together for ballerina skirts. On Honey Lee the look was perfect; on tiny, freckled Ellen it was comical.

"I look like the wicked witch of the West," Ellen had said laughing, "and you look like Rosalind Russell. I'd give anything for five of your inches."

"And I'd give them willingly."

Remembering, Honey Lee smiled as she put on the blouse and tucked it in to the waistband of the soft full skirt. She tied a red velvet ribbon around her head to hold her long black hair, then studied her face and frowned. The ribbon also reminded her of her mother so she undid it and let her hair fall back to her shoulders. She rolled the front of it into a pompadour. Ridiculous she thought, and pulled her hair down and back fastening it with a barrette. She frowned again, then pulled a small strand of hair on each side of her head out of the barrette, wet her finger and wound the strands so that they fell, slightly curled, down each side of her face as if they had come loose by accident. That's it, she thought, I'm done. But she had forgotten lipstick. She didn't often wear lipstick, but she tried three before she chose Cherry Red. What's the use, she thought as she rubbed most of it off.

When she came downstairs, Nana Murphy smiled her approval. They sat together in the living room waiting for the Jackson brothers to arrive. But they weren't thinking about the Jacksons. They were thinking about their own soldier killed in the war four years before. Honey Lee could always tell when Nana Murphy was thinking about Tommy because she tipped her head down so that Honey Lee couldn't see her eyes. Honey Lee hated that because she wanted to know that her grandmother missed her father as much as she did. Soldiers and sailors returning from Europe and the Pacific for over a year had been constant reminders that he was never coming back. Every time she thought about him, her breath, knifelike, caught in her throat. The Westminster clock struck three fifteen-minute intervals as they sat silently together.

Finally the car pulled up in front of the house, and Jimmy came to the door just as Honey Lee opened it.

"Hi, Honey Lee," he said and whistled. "Wow, you look great."

"You're alone?" She was disappointed.

"Yeah, I already took Danny over." He took her coat and held it for her.

When he started down the stairs, Honey Lee called out, "I'll be back early, Nana. Don't worry."

When they got to the car, Honey Lee asked, "How's it going, Jimmy?" She worried about how Jimmy was managing, and her voice showed it. When he looked annoyed, she quickly said, "I mean, how is he?"

"Well, he's, I don't know, weak, different, sick. Maybe just tired." Jimmy sounded tired.

"You took him over to Frank's because he's not strong enough for a long ride?"

"Yeah, he's got to take things a little bit at a time." He started the car and pulled away from the curb.

"Jimmy, are you going to be able to do this?"

"Yes. Stop worrying. He's not helpless and I'm not either."

He drove in silence until they reached the house. When they arrived, Mary came to the door.

"Oh, here you are, Honey Lee," she whispered hugging Honey Lee and leading her into the kitchen. "Help! I'm a little nervous."

"Hey, you two, this isn't a hen party," Jimmy said guiding Honey Lee through the kitchen and into the small living room where Danny Jackson sat in the far corner in the blue armchair, his feet up on the ottoman. Frank stood by his side, his hand on Danny's shoulder to keep him from getting up.

"Honey Child," Frank said, "this is the other brother, the ugly one. Honey Lee Murphy, Danny Jackson."

She walked slowly toward Danny and stood in front of him.

"Hello, Danny. I'm so glad you're home at last. Jimmy's been waiting for you for so long." She couldn't take her eyes off him. Unlike his brothers, he had thick black hair. He wore a white shirt with the neck open and gray trousers. His face, pale around his eyes and forehead, was shadowed along his jaw as if he hadn't shaved recently. His dark eyes fixed on her.

"Jimmy told me you were beautiful," he finally said. "He lied. You're ravishing," She laughed nervously as Danny, shaking Frank off and ignoring Honey Lee's outstretched hand, stood, put his arms around her, and held her close. Embarrassed, she pulled away and was amazed to find herself having to look up into his eyes. She noted his face, heart shaped by a widow's peak, his dark eyebrows grown almost together, the lines on either side of his mouth, and the fine wrinkles around his deep-set eyes. He continued to stare at her while his strong hands resting on her shoulders prevented her from moving.

"OK, Danny, take it easy," Frank said taking Honey Lee's hand. "Honey Child, what are you doing to this invalid? He was half asleep until you showed up."

Honey Lee slowly dropped her eyes and moved away from Danny to Frank, who gave her a hug, very different from Danny's. Frank was inches shorter than Danny and much more muscular. Jimmy, still standing silently by the kitchen door, watched Honey Lee and his brothers.

Mary patted the seat on the couch next to her and said, "Sit down Honey Lee. And have something to drink. Frank, get Honey Lee some tonic. Root beer? Ginger ale?"

Danny and Frank were drinking beer. Jimmy was not.

"She's old enough to celebrate the occasion with a beer, Mary," Frank said.

"No beer. She doesn't drink," Jimmy said.

"Jimmy, Jimmy, a beer never hurt anyone." Frank went to the kitchen and returned with a bottle of Harvard Beer and a glass for her.

"A toast," Frank said, raising his glass. "To Danny, home at last, thank God."

When Honey Lee took her first sip of beer, she was so startled by the taste that she couldn't swallow. She held it in her mouth as long as she could and then swallowed and coughed.

"And to Johnny," Danny whispered, closing his eyes, "not coming back ever." They drank again and sat quietly. By her third sip of beer, Honey was able to swallow without choking.

But then Jimmy said, "And to Honey Lee's father, also not coming back."

Honey Lee gasped and again choked on the beer. Mary took the glass from her and led her into the kitchen.

"Are you OK, Honey?" Mary asked putting her arm around Honey Lee.

"Sure," Honey Lee said although her eyes stung. "The table looks beautiful, Mary."

"Someday I'll have a real dining room."

The table, covered with a white cloth, was set for five with multicolored din-nerware—a red, a yellow, a green, and two deep blue plates. Honey Lee guessed that the cut crystal vase in the center was a wedding gift.

"We're having Danny's favorite meal. At least that's what Franks says. I hope I made it like his mother used to." She went to the stove and lifted the lid from a large pot. Steam rose up.

"It's corned beef, isn't it? It smells wonderful."

"I've never cooked it before."

Honey laughed. "When I first came North and was still terrified of Nana Murphy, she was cooking corned beef one day and she kept asking me to go to the kitchen to see if it was all right. I had no idea what to look for so I just picked up the cover of the pot and looked in and then went back and said, 'It's fine.'" Mary laughed with her.

"What's it supposed to do, anyway?"

"Simmer, simmer, simmer." She pointed her finger at Mary on each syllable as if Mary were a child. They both laughed. "Never, never boil," she continued shaking her head slowly and wagging her finger back and forth.

Raising her hands in mock horror, Mary said, "Oh, Oh, this has been boiling for hours."

"When it's done, you have to press it," Honey Lee said and giggled.

"Press it?"

"Put something real heavy on it, like an iron or something."

"Why?"

Honey shrugged and laughed, "Because Nana Murphy says so."

"I'm afraid I didn't press it either. I'm a complete failure."

Honey Lee had learned to love corned beef and cabbage, although she had never even heard of it before she arrived in Lowell. Her mother had hated it. "Irish Peasant Food," she'd muttered. When Mary drained the vegetables, Honey Lee delighted in the familiar aroma. Mary arranged the cabbage, potatoes, parsnips, turnip, and carrots on a large blue platter around the sliced meat and took it to the table.

"Ready, boys, come and get it," she called.

Frank and Mary sat at either end of the table.

Jimmy took Honey Lee's arm, and said," Sit here by me."

Danny sat opposite them. He looked over at her, pointed to his blue plate and said, "Honey, look at this. We both have my favorite color, the color of your beautiful eyes."

Honey Lee blushed. Jimmy looked irritated.

"Easy Danny. This is no Moody Street pick-up joint. And Honey Lee's a high school kid," Frank said. "Behave yourself."

The others laughed nervously.

When Mary passed the platter to Danny first, he tried to decline but Mary said, "You are the honored guest today."

He filled his plate taking some of each vegetable and three slices of meat." Mary, now I know I'm home. This smells wonderful."

When they had all served themselves, they began to eat. Danny ate slowly and thoughtfully. He asked for seconds, and Mary was eager and grateful. Honey Lee also ate slowly, but her mind was busy. She was remembering reading *The Odyssey* in Mr. Flynn's class. Danny's delayed return from war reminded her of Ulysses' return. She felt grateful to be part of a celebration she had been denied by her father's death. Her grandmother had told her about a woman at church who had traveled the whole length of the center aisle on her knees in thanksgiving for her son's return from the war. Honey Lee wondered if she had cooked the welcome home meal first or afterward.

Mary had made a cake for dessert. In red and blue letters she had spelled out 'Welcome Home Danny.' They all clapped as Danny cut the cake and put thick slices on the plates Mary handed him.

Danny sighed and leaned back in his chair. "What a prize this woman is, Frank," Danny said reaching over to put his hand over Mary's. "I'm jealous. If I had come home first, you wouldn't have had a chance with her, right Mary?"

"Rubbish, Danny. Mary likes her men with a bit of meat on them and of manageable size, don't you sweetie?" Frank took Mary's other hand in his.

"I do love you, Frank, but I have to say Danny would have been a contender, and if Jimmy here hadn't been a baby," she took her hand from Danny and patted Jimmy's hand "you would never have won me,"

Honey Lee smiled as she watched the brothers tease each other. Frank looked older than the other two. He was heavily built and shorter than Danny. His face was fuller, more finished than Jimmy's. But he and Danny both looked like men who had gone to war. When they were not talking or listening, their eyes went away. She had seen eyes do that, the eyes of fathers and brothers of her friends. She always shivered when she saw that look on Frank's face and on her Uncle Peter's face and now on Danny's face. Thank God Jimmy had been too young to go off to war. He had told her about the long battle between mother and son when Danny turned eighteen and wanted to enlist. By then, Johnny had been missing in action for two years, and although his mother always said that she knew Johnny would walk in the door some day, she had to know that her son had died when his submarine went down. She had told Danny that she could not endure another loss. But he had begged and pleaded, even cried, until finally she had given in. She did not live to learn that he had at last come home safely.

Honey Lee saw the dead brother as a silent guest at the table. The others seemed to feel him too because from time to time all talk stopped so completely that Honey could hear chewing sounds. The dead were in those silences—the one Jackson she didn't know—but also the one that only she could see. Tommy Murphy and Johnny Jackson. Tommy and Johnny. Would they have come home to become Tom and John as they continued their passage into manhood? Jimmy, she supposed would one day become Jim as Frankie had become Frank. The others were buried in their childhood names.

When they finished eating they went back into the living room, comfortably full and content. Danny had been watching her so constantly that she was not surprised to look up and see his eyes fixed on her again. It was almost seven o'clock. Danny, looking tired and pale, turned to Jimmy and said," What do you say kid? Shall we get going?"

"Sure Danny, right away. I'll get our coats." Jimmy looked worried. He brought Danny's coat and tried to help him put it on.

"I can do it myself," Danny said sharply, "and I do not need help getting to the car."

Jimmy helped Honey Lee with her coat and they headed for the front door. Danny turned back and gave Mary a hug. "Thank you, Mary, this is the best day I've had in years. Everything was great."

Honey Lee also kissed Mary and gave Frank a hug. Jimmy jingled the car keys. When they got to the car, Danny got into the back seat.

"Let me sit in back, Danny," Honey Lee said. "You need the leg room."

"So do you Honey Child. I'm fine in back."

They drove off slowly. Jimmy was a careful driver, proud to be driving Frank's car. Still content and over-full from dinner, the boys said little during the drive to Concord Street. When they pulled up in front of the house, Jimmy got out and came around to Honey Lee's side to open the door for her. Danny also got out. Honey Lee gave Jimmy a quick kiss on the cheek and thanked him. Danny came to her and put his arms around her again holding her too long and too tight.

He kissed her on the cheek and said, "I am so glad you came today. You'll never know how glad. Thank you."

Honey pulled away and looked up at him. Then she lowered her eyes, frightened.

"OK, Danny. Let's get you home where you belong." When Danny didn't move, Jimmy called out, "Now, Danny." Then he said, "Honey Lee, I'll see you soon. OK?"

"Good bye Jimmy. Bye Danny." Honey said.

She went up the steps and turned to watch the car drive off. She wasn't at all tired; her gloomy thoughts had receded. The day had excited her in ways she didn't quite understand. She thought she saw Danny waving and she waved back. She stood on the porch leaning against the wooden railing. She could feel her heart beating and her face burning. She tried to slow her breathing and calm herself before going in. Nana Murphy would want a full report on her day. She tried to sort out her feelings, almost all of them about Danny. She hardly knew him yet all day she had felt his eyes on her. She touched her cheek where he had kissed it. It felt hot to her hand. She shook her head trying to put him out of her mind, telling herself that he wasn't a boy, but a grown man who had seen death up close and had probably even killed other men and she was a high school girl with no mother or father. She swore to herself that she would stay as far away from Danny Jackson as she could.

She went inside to her grandmother, who was sitting in her usual chair beside the radio. Turning the radio off, she motioned for Honey Lee to come and sit on the footstool near her. "Did you have a fine time, darlin'?" Her grandmother's hand on her head was gentle.

"Yes. Nana?" Honey Lee spoke very softly; her answer was a question she didn't know how to ask.

When Honey Lee didn't go on, Nana said, "Shall we have some tea?" She tilted Honey Lee's head up so she could see her face. "You're looking as if you could do with a cup."

"Yes, Nana. Let me get it."

She was glad to have an excuse for a few more minutes alone. She was worried that her face might tell more than she wanted to tell. When she brought the tea in and sat down, Nana began, as Honey Lee knew she would, to ask about the day. So she described the meal in great detail telling Nana about sharing the corned beef story with Mary. She described the cake, told what Frank and Jimmy had said and done, told her that Jimmy was driving the new car, mentioned everything except what was most on her mind. Finally Nana Murphy interrupted her.

"Honey Lee Murphy, I've never known you to talk so fast and so much. Slow down, dearie." She took Honey Lee's cup and put it down on the tray.

"Was I babbling?"

"Like a brook, darlin'."

"I'm done now, Nana."

Nana looked at her for several seconds before she said, "And the brother?"

For several seconds Honey Lee was silent. "You mean Danny?"

"Yes. Daniel. How is he? What is he like?" Nana said the words very slowly.

Honey Lee began to cry. "Oh, Nana."

Nana Murphy took her hand and led her to the couch so they could sit side by side. "What is it, dearie? What's the matter then?" Nana Murphy put her arms around her granddaughter. Honey Lee couldn't find the right words, couldn't even figure out what was the matter. She just held on to her grandmother, who patted her back and waited. Honey Lee's sobs came more slowly and finally she was able to speak.

"Danny is the tallest man I ever saw except for Daddy. He's so tall I had to look up to see his eyes just like I did when Daddy was..." She began to sob again. And again Nana Murphy waited silently for her to go on. "And he's thin, not slim but really skinny and pale. He can't stand up for long. He kept looking at me all the time. His eyes are so dark and so sad, and I got all mixed up about him and Daddy and I don't know, Nana. I got scared. I don't want to see him again."

She started to cry again. After a while Nana started to talk. "Darlin', I was worried about you all day, going to a homecoming celebration. I was sad knowing where you were and guessing how you might feel. Of course it was hard. You were happy for Danny and his brothers, but I knew you would think about your father. When you go mixing such big happy and big sad together it's a confusion that happens to you."

"I wish I hadn't gone, I didn't belong. I'm not family. Why did I go?"

"Hush, darlin', you need to rest now. It'll be better tomorrow. You'll see, it will be fine. Now let's just get you to your bed."

They climbed the stairs together and went to Honey Lee's room, her father's room.

"Just slip out of your skirt and blouse and get into bed," Nana said as she turned the bedspread and the blanket down. Honey Lee took off her skirt and blouse and stood in her white, lace-trimmed slip, her hands by her sides. She bent to her grandmother who kissed her good night.

"You're a dear good girl and I love you," her grandmother said smoothing Honey Lee's hair. "Now say your prayers. The good Lord in heaven loves you. He'll comfort you."

After her grandmother left, Honey Lee sat down on the side of the bed and looked at herself in the mirror. Why had he stared at her so? What had he seen in her? She sat until she began to feel chilled and then reached out to trace the crack in the mirror reminding herself again to replace it. For three years she had been planning to buy a new one.

CHAPTER 16

▼

On Monday, Honey Lee slipped back into her routine of classes and study. It felt good to be with people her own age at the Epicure after school ordering the usual fresh fruit orange and English muffin. Ellen asked her about Jimmy and the brothers but Honey Lee motioned for her to be quiet. Ellen understood that Honey Lee didn't want to talk in front of the others so she waited.

As soon as they left the square and were alone, Ellen asked, "Tell me. What's he like? The brother."

Honey Lee kept walking and didn't answer. When they came to the church, she said, "Let's just drop in for a quick visit."

They often made visits to the church and had both laughed about Honey's first attempt at a visit when the old lady had told her to take her hat off and leave. They didn't have hats so they fastened handkerchiefs to their heads with bobby pins before they went in. They dipped their fingers into the holy water, blessed themselves, walked to the front of the church, genuflected, and entered a pew. Honey Lee bent her head and prayed for her father's soul as she always did. Then she found herself praying that Danny would soon be well and strong. When she went to the altar to light a vigil candle as she had done countless times before for her father, she wasn't sure for whom she lit it, her father or Danny or herself.

They left the church and strolled up High Street. Children, just dismissed from school, were running and yelling. Honey Lee decided she would tell Ellen a stripped down version of the day saying as little as possible about Danny. Such withholding was unusual between her and Ellen. She held back, she realized, because of Jack. But what did Danny have to do with that?

A week later, Mary called her and asked her to come by for coffee, and she did. They hadn't talked since the dinner for Danny. Almost as soon as they sat down at the table, Mary began to talk about him.

"Did you ever see a more handsome man in your life?" She raised her eyes and sighed.

"Uh, no I guess not," Honey Lee said although she was very sure she had never seen a more handsome man in her life.

"He's gorgeous. When he starts getting around more, I tell you, he'll have a parade of sighing females following him. He's handsome and he looks like he needs caring for. Girls always go for that."

"Is he getting out at all?" Honey looked down into her coffee cup to avoid Mary's eyes.

"Oh, sure. He got himself a car, and he even went back to the hospital by himself for his check-up. Jimmy wanted to drive him in, but he went alone. It was pretty scary for everyone except him." Honey Lee shuddered. She couldn't imagine the pale sick man she had met driving himself into Boston and back.

After her visit with Mary Honey Lee got so caught up in Christmas preparations that she didn't think much about Danny and Jimmy. She still sang with the children's choir to help Sister Ruth with the children's music program. She had sung in the choir for the few months that she was in the eighth grade and had loved singing in church. When Sister had asked her to help out after she graduated, she agreed. The choir was preparing to sing the solemn High Mass at midnight on Christmas Eve.

Beside preparing for Christmas at church, Honey and Nana were busy making Christmas cookies and plum pudding for the Christmas meals. There was also shopping to be done for Nana and Aunt Kitty's family, Ellen and Jack, Jimmy, Frank, and Mary. She hated to shop except at Christmas. But she spent hours planning and looking for perfect gifts every year. To earn more for Christmas, she had also taken an after-school job in the toy department at Woolworth's, Nana didn't want her to work while she was in school, but Honey Lee, determined, prevailed. At first, she loved seeing the excited children in the store. She learned pretty quickly that the children weren't so lovable when they pulled toys off the shelves and knocked down displays.

A few days before Christmas, Jack came home from Dartmouth. He called and asked her to go to the Totem Pole Park on Friday, the day before Christmas Eve. She had heard wonderful things about the Totem Pole, a real night club where you sat at tables that had tiny lamps and danced to the music of a really big band, often a name band. She would miss the CYO dance on Friday, but the Hoodsie Hop could not compete with the glamour of Totem Pole.

Just after Jack called, Jimmy called. "Hi Honey Lee, I miss you. I haven't seen you for so long. Danny keeps me so darned busy. I feel like someone's wife."

"I can just see you in a little apron, setting the table, cooking up a storm, and doing up the dishes after." Honey Lee laughed and so did he, but then he became serious.

"I kind of keep the place up. I can't leave him alone much. He's still too sick and really moody."

"I was afraid of this, Jimmy," she said. "What do the doctors say?"

"They say be patient. Everything's going to be fine. Blah, blah, blah, but nothing changes." She hated to hear him so discouraged.

"Is he going to be able to work?"

"Who knows? Maybe in a while he'll get some kind of work. But he's got disability."

"Disability?"

"Yeah, disability. It means he gets money for getting wounded."

Honey Lee knew of money given to widows and children of men who had died in the war, but she had never thought about the government giving money for being wounded. All she could say was, "Oh."

"They give him a 50% disability for the loss of one kidney, nothing for part of the other one, and none for his messed up head." He changed the subject quickly. "Anyway, Honey, I've missed you. How about going to the dance with me on Friday or to a movie or something?"

"Oh, Jimmy," she said, "Jack Flynn called me just a while ago and asked me out on Friday." She hated to disappoint him. He needed a break; he needed her.

"Oh, well, I'll be seeing you…" He began to sing, "*I'll be seeing you in all the old familiar place which this heart embraces.*"

"Jimmy, stop it. I want to see you sometime this weekend."

"Yeah, sure. Whenever you can fit me in."

"Don't be like that," she pleaded. "Meet me at the Epicure tomorrow."

"OK, after school, around three," he said and hung up.

She sat by the phone thinking about Jimmy as the caregiver in his family although he was the youngest. She wished someone would care for him for a change. He had never had a childhood.

She got to the Epicure early. It was crowded and noisy, but she managed to get a small booth for them. She played with a straw while she waited looking up each time the door opened. When he finally walked in, his face was red from the cold. He stomped his feet and rubbed his hands together blowing on them. He had no hat and no gloves. She called out to him, and he came over and sat down.

"I'm freezing. I don't have the car today."

"You're getting spoiled. Where's your hat? Your gloves? And boots?"

"The car's not a bad thing." He took his coat off and hung it on the hook near hers.

"How are you, Jimmy?"

"I'm good I guess. But a little tied down." He sighed. "I thought it would be easier and more fun, but…."

"Is there anything I can do Jimmy?" She reached across the table for his hand.

"No, it'll get better. I'm just not cut out to be a nurse. And he's so sad all the time. He doesn't talk, but he thinks about bad stuff. He has nightmares."

Honey Lee couldn't think of what to say. She had never seen him so low "What are you doing about Christmas?"

"Frank and Mary's for dinner."

"Are you going to be at midnight Mass?" Although Jimmy no longer lived in the parish, he still came to church at the Immaculate.

"Danny doesn't go to church anymore. I'd like to go. I will if I can."

"Please do, and come back with me to Nana's for oyster stew." She invited him without thinking, but she knew Nana would welcome him. "She'd love to see you."

"I'll try, Honey."

When they finished, they walked together to the door. Jimmy gave her a quick hug and said, "See you later, kid."

The rest of the week was hectic. Most of the other students were so caught up by Christmas that the teachers might have been speaking Greek. Jimmy called to say he'd meet her at church and come back for Christmas supper. Between school, work, helping Nana decorate the house and wrapping presents, Honey Lee barely had time to eat. On Friday, school ended at noon, and a party was held in the gym. Honey worked until five o'clock, which barely gave her time to dress for her date with Jack. She had let Nana talk her into an early Christmas present, a dark green velvet dress. It was the first dress that Honey Lee had ever fallen in love with. She had admired herself in the dressing room before she came out to show her grandmother. The lush velvet shimmered when she made the slightest movement. When she came out to show Nana how beautifully it fit her, she turned around at least three times to show how the soft fabric flowed around her legs. At home she had put it on again and again.

At seven o'clock, when Jack rang the doorbell, she was still in her room smoothing the dress against her small waist. Nana called up to her. When she started down the stairs, Jack and Nana stood at the bottom waiting for her. She felt like a movie star as she slowly came down the stairs. In this dress she liked being tall. She liked how white her skin looked against the dark velvet. Jack said nothing until she stood in front of him. He put his hands on her shoulders and stared at her.

"Oh, Honey Lee…" he said and then kissed her.

"Merry Christmas, Jack," Honey Lee said.

"It's better than merry just seeing you." He stepped back and looked at her again. "You look just great."

"Thank you. You too, Jack,"

Jack, wearing a dark suit, white shirt, and red tie, looked as festive as she. Flushed with excitement, she kissed her grandmother good-bye and turned her back to Jack so he could help her on with her coat.

"You're a handsome couple if I ever saw one," Nana Murphy said.

They both thanked her and said good night. Two of Jack's friends with their dates were squeezed into the back seat. Jack introduced Honey Lee although they all knew each other slightly. All four had been two years ahead of her at Lowell High. The drive to Newton took about forty-five minutes. Jack drove with one hand on the wheel, his arm around her shoulder, which felt good, even though Honey Lee was not completely comfortable with him. It seemed like a long time since she had seen him at Homecoming. Her silence went unnoticed since the others were so busy catching up with each other. All of them were home from college for the holidays.

Jack turned the radio on for the last part of the ride. She wondered how many times she had heard Bing Crosby sing *White Christmas*. As song followed song, they all sang along or hummed if they didn't know the words. When they arrived, Jack parked the car and held Honey Lee's hand as they walked to the entrance. They entered the ballroom, and Honey Lee's eyes widened. The large room was dimly lit by small lamps on tables arranged in tiers in a semicircle around the dance floor. Dancers swayed slowly to soft music. They followed an usher down a sloping walkway to a table one tier up from the dance floor. Jack guided her to a seat on the cushioned bench behind the table reserved for them. Mesmerized, she sat down. Only in movies had she ever seen anything like the Totem Pole. She turned to Jack and smiled. A waiter came and took their orders for soft drinks. Then Jack led her to the dance floor. They danced well together, both the fast and the slow numbers during which Jack held her very close, telling her more than once how beautiful she looked and how happy he was to see her. They danced all of the early sets. Between sets when the orchestra took a break, they all returned to the table and talked about the music, about Christmas plans and about other friends. When the orchestra returned after one of the breaks, Honey Lee rose from her seat. Jack put his hand on her arm.

"Let's sit this one out, Honey Lee."

They sat quietly for a few minutes after the others had left. Jack had something serious to say. That was clear. Excited by the setting, the music, and how great she and Jack looked, Honey Lee hadn't been thinking seriously about anything.

Jack took both of her hands in his. "Honey Lee, do you think about me much when I'm away?" She recognized this as a very serious question, and she didn't know how to answer.

"Of course I do," she said quickly.

"I think about you all the time. I want you with me all the time."

Uncomfortable with his intensity, she laughed. "That doesn't make sense, does it?"

"Be serious, Honey Lee." He moved closer and took her face into his hands. "I'm trying to say that I love you. I don't want to see anyone else. I want to go steady with you. I want you to go steady with me."

She was alarmed. Going steady was a serious thing. "Go steady? Be your girl friend?"

"Yes, and some day, marry me." He reached into his pocket, pulled out a small velvet box, and handed it to her. She held it without opening it.

"Open it," he said. She did and saw his fraternity pin. "I want you to wear this until we can plan to marry."

She was astonished. "I'm still in high school," she sputtered. "Marriage? I can't, Jack. I'm not ready." She handed the box back to him.

"I'm not talking marriage now, dear. Just let's be pinned. We don't have to think beyond that. Please, take it." When she shook her head, he said, "Think about it. You don't have to say yes now. You don't have to wear it. Just think about it. Please." He leaned toward her, closed her hand around the box, and kissed her. When the others returned to the table, Jack and Honey Lee joined in the general talk. During the last set of the evening, Jack held Honey Lee close and from time to time kissed her. She let herself get lost in the slow pulse of the music and the unconscious movements of the dance putting off thinking about the velvet box in her purse.

Jack dropped his friends off in downtown Lowell, where they had left their cars, and drove across the bridge heading for Concord Street. He pulled up in front of the house but made no move to get out of the car. He pulled Honey Lee close and kissed her.

"Promise me you'll think seriously about us."

"I will, Jack, of course I will." She put her hand on his face.

"I want to go to midnight Mass with you."

"No, Jack." Instead of mentioning Jimmy, she said, "I have to go early to rehearse with the choir."

"How about afterwards?"

Nana has a big family thing. I have to be there."

"Christmas Night, then," he pleaded.

"Yes, but not until eight o'clock. More family stuff."

"I'll be here on the dot. I love you, Honey Lee Murphy. I think I always have."

She kissed him again and then reached for the door handle. "I'd better get in. She'll be waiting."

Jack opened his door, got out, and came around to open Honey's door. They held hands as they climbed the steps of the porch.

"Jack, it was a lovely evening. Thank you, so much."

"I'll see you Sunday. I love you." He kissed her again.

"Good night, Jack." She couldn't bring herself to say she loved him too.

Nana Murphy was in bed when Honey Lee got home, but she had left the Christmas tree lights on. Honey walked into the living room and sat down. The red, blue, green and yellow lights that she and Nana had hung on the tree that morning glowed softly. As they unwrapped each ornament for the tree, Nana told her again the stories of how and when ornaments came into the family. Nana was particularly fond of the small white Celtic cross that she had carried across the ocean from Ireland. The small rocking horse was bought "the year that your father was born." And the star for the top of the tree was "the first thing we bought for Christmas, your grandfather and I." A tiny doll marked Aunt Kitty's birth. Honey Lee's favorite ornament was a giraffe.

"I bought that the year you came to me. I couldn't tell you then, dearie, but when I saw that baby giraffe, I thought of you—so tall and awkward with your height. I loved it without knowing that I had begun to love you as much and more than I had ever loved anyone," her grandmother said.

Honey Lee took the giraffe from its branch and held it to her lips as she sat down in her grandmother's chair for a long time lost in tree magic.

The next morning she and Nana Murphy walked downtown together to Brockleman's to food shop. Brockleman's was Nana's favorite food store. She used markets closer to home for ordinary meals but for special meals, she insisted that they shop where the "best meat and fish in all of Lowell are found." Mr. Connors, the butcher, showed her five turkeys, each of which she poked with her fingers, asking to see the back and front of each before choosing the perfect one. They bought day-old bread for the stuffing, potatoes—which Nana Murphy selected one by one putting back those that had too many eyes or a sprouted eye—and the other vegetables for Christmas dinner.

Then Nana led her to the fish counter where she inquired about the freshness of the oysters. "When did they come in, young man? From where?" Looking at the price, she said, "Is Brockleman serious about this?" But she ended up buying two pints of oysters and cream, milk, oyster crackers and butter for oyster stew. Honey remembered the rich taste from the years before. Christmas Eve supper was her favorite meal of the year. Home at last, she helped Nana Murphy set the table for eleven people, Aunt Kitty and the two Peters, Nana's brother from Billerica, Grandfather Murphy's two sisters with their husbands, and Jimmy. She and Nana prepared the custard and stale cake for the tipsy pudding which, they would put together just before they went to church. The plum pudding for the next day, they had made weeks ago. At four o'clock Nana said, "It's a very long day we'll be having, and I'm thinking we should both take a long nap."

By ten o'clock, the relatives arrived. Honey left soon after to be on time for the brief rehearsal before the choir began to sing carols at eleven thirty. She walked down Concord and Fayette to the church, music playing in her head. Sister Ruth greeted her with a hug, "Merry Christmas, Honey Lee. Thank you for coming."

The children were in their places in the choir loft. The church was still dark except for the sanctuary light and a few dim overhead lights. Mrs. Field was playing Silent Night softly. Honey Lee went to the front of the choir and knelt to pray before taking her place beside the organ. Soon three altar boys in red cassocks and white surpluses came out to light the candles on the three altars. Suddenly, lights throughout the church blazed. The organist played a few bars of *Oh Little Town of Bethlehem*. Sister raised her baton and the children began to sing. The sound thrilled Honey Lee as it had the first time she heard the children sing. They sang most of the famous Christmas carols before the Mass began.

They also sang the solemn high Mass in Latin: the solemn *Kyrie*, asking for God's mercy and forgiveness; the joyful *Gloria*, using the angels' words to the shepherds on the first Christmas; the *Credo*, listing all of the beliefs of the church; the *Sanctus*, marking the beginning of the most solemn part of the Mass; and the

Angus Dei, another plea for God's mercy and peace. The priest said all of these prayers at every Mass, but quietly in Latin with his back to the congregation. But on great feasts, three priests presided. The main celebrant chanted, "Gloria in Excelsis Deo" and later "Credo in Unum Dominum," and as the choir sang the prayer, the three priests sat down.

Honey loved Solemn High Masses. She breathed in deeply when the priest lit the charcoal in the censor, put incense on the coals, and raised the censor three times to bless the altar; then raised it again to bless the congregation three times. Honey loved the rich symbolism of the Mass, and she knew by heart all of the common prayers both in English and in Latin.

After the closing hymn, *Joy to the World*, Honey Lee and the children went down the narrow stairs to meet with family and friends. Nana Murphy had already found Jimmy, who was waiting with the relatives. She kissed her grandmother and her aunts and cousins. She and Jimmy hugged each other. "Merry Christmas, Merry Christmas." The words could be heard throughout the church and out into the street. Honey Lee was happy.

CHAPTER 17

▼

On Christmas morning, Honey Lee got up early to make sure she and her grand-mother would have time alone together before the others came for Christmas dinner. She prepared a tray with cups and saucers and sweet rolls she and her grandmother had made. After preparing the tea, she carried the tray into the living room and set it on a table near the Christmas tree, plugged in the Christmas tree lights, and sat on the stool in front of her grandmother's chair. When she heard Nana Murphy coming down the stairs, she went to the tree and removed two small packages wrapped in silver paper and sat down to wait. At last Nana Murphy came into the living room dressed in her bathrobe.

"I never thought I'd see you up so early," Nana said leaning down to kiss her granddaughter.

"Merry Christmas, Nana. I made tea for us to have here by the tree."

"That's lovely, darlin'," her grandmother said as she settled into her chair.

"Isn't it beautiful?" Honey Lee said looking at the tree.

"The best we've ever had."

Honey Lee was still holding the two packages. "Will you open mine first?" she asked.

"I certainly will." Honey Lee handed the first package to her grandmother who said, "I hope you didn't go and spend a lot of money on me."

Honey laughed and told her grandmother to open it. The present was a scarf that Honey Lee had seen her grandmother admire when they had shopped together at Cherry and Webb, a silk scarf with deep red and white roses on a black background.

"Oh, and isn't this the most beautiful thing in the world? Thank you," Nana said putting it over her shoulders and touching it to her face. "And so soft, like baby's skin."

Honey smiled and handed her the second package, a Yardley's Lavender boxed set of toilet water, bath powder and soap.

As Nana opened it, Honey Lee said, "I always think of you when I smell lavender. It was one of the first things I noticed about you. If someone were to have asked me then what you were like I would have said, 'She smells like lavender.'"

"You are a dear girl. Thank you." Nana's eyes had filled with tears. "And I have something special for you."

"But you already gave me my new dress."

"Just one little thing more," Nana said handing Honey a small box. When Honey opened the box, she saw a small gold locket on the chain that she had often seen in her grandmother's jewelry box. She looked up at her grandmother.

"Open it up, dear." Honey opened the locket and saw that it contained two pictures, both of her father, one when he was a baby and one taken when he was seventeen, just before he left home.

"Nana, I love it. I never dreamed you would part with it."

"Who else should have it but you, his daughter?"

They sat together holding hands, Honey on the stool at her grandmother's feet and Nana Murphy sitting straight in her rocker. Nothing in the rest of the day came close to giving them as much joy as they shared in that quiet hour.

When Jack arrived as promised at eight, some of the company had left and the dishes were done. Uncle Peter and Aunt Kitty sat near the tree listening to Christmas carols on the radio. Jack came into the room and greeted the family, but remained standing while Honey went to get her coat and boots. As soon as Honey returned, Jack took her hand and started for the door. He had left the car running, "to keep it nice and warm for you," he said. The temperature had fallen and a brisk wind whipped snow into flurries.

"I can still remember seeing my first snow," Honey Lee said. "It was like a fairyland."

"How do you feel about it now?" He kissed her forehead.

"The same. It always feels like magic." He opened the car door for her and went around to the driver's side.

When he got in he asked, "Shall we go to the movies? Out for coffee? Back to my house to see the family? Your wish is my command."

"I'd love to go to your house. I haven't seen your mother for ages."

"Great, they'd all love to see you. My father tells me you are the star scholar. Ellen disagrees."

She laughed. "We still keep going back and forth getting the highest grade. One time me, one time her."

They drove over Sherman to the Flynn house and parked on the street. Stamping snow from their feet, they went in. The family was sitting in the living room with only the tree lights on.

Ellen jumped up and said, "I'm so glad you came. I told him not to monopolize you. Wait until you see what I got." She started to pull Honey toward the door to the stairs.

"Talk about monopolizing someone," Ellen's father said. "Let her say hello."

Honey laughed and went to Mrs. Flynn and kissed her. She shook hands with Mr. Flynn. "Merry Christmas, Mr. and Mrs. Flynn."

"How about us?" Noreen and Bobby said.

"You too," she said, putting her arms around them. "Merry Christmas."

Mrs. Flynn asked about the Murphy Christmas, and when Honey Lee told her that there had been twelve for dinner she groaned. "Your poor grandmother feeding all those people."

"She loves it, and so do I. I love to cook, and I love having that big house full of people. It seems like such a waste having that much room for two of us."

Noreen and Bobby tugged at Honey Lee to get her to look at their presents. Mr. and Mrs. Flynn's piles were small: a shirt, a tie, socks, and two books for him; a fox fur piece, nylon stockings, a blouse, and a pin for her. Bobby picked up the fox piece, which had a complete head with beady glass eyes, and a shiny black nose. Little fox feet dangled from the body which ended in a bush tail. Under the fox chin was a clip fastener designed to link head and tail when the animal was draped over the shoulders. Holding the fox in his hands Bobby kept snapping the clip under Honey Lee's nose and making what he imagined were fox-like noises. Honey Lee laughed and pretended to be frightened. The younger Flynns had books, skates, and a sled.

"And this," Noreen said twirling around to show her new red dress, "and these," she said tapping her feet loudly on the wood floor.

"Tap shoes! Can you tap dance?"

"No, but I'm going to learn." She tapped her feet again and turned in circles.

She and Bobby pulled at Honey Lee to lead her through the kitchen and out to the back porch to see the family gift, a full size toboggan.

"We're going to Fort Hill tomorrow. The slide's up and there's plenty of snow. Are you coming?"

"Who's going?"

"Everyone, except Mom and Dad," they answered.

"Will I fit?" She stood up on her toes to make herself look even taller than she was. "How many can it seat?"

"Sure, plenty of room, even for you."

When they went back to the living room, Mrs. Flynn handed Honey Lee a cup of eggnog. Honey Lee loved this rich yellow Christmas treat. She knew that there were two batches, one for children and one for grownups. Once she and Ellen had sampled the adult drink, and neither of them could imagine spoiling eggnog by adding brandy.

"Honey, you've got to see my best gift. Come on up." Ellen said. She led Honey Lee to the stairs and up to her bedroom. They passed by Jack's room, which Honey Lee recognized from the banner on the wall and the picture of herself on the dresser. She wondered if Jack carried it back and forth from school.

"Come on, come on," Ellen said pulling Honey toward her room and closing the door. Where is it? Where is it?"

"What?" Honey Lee held both hands up. She couldn't think what Ellen meant.

"The pin. The pin, silly."

"Oh, the pin," Honey Lee said, "I'm not wearing it…yet."

"Not wearing it? Why on earth not?"

"Can we talk about this later?" Honey Lee begged.

"Promise," Ellen said raising her right hand.

"Promise," Honey Lee answered crossing her heart.

Ellen pointed to a record player on the small table against the far wall.

"Wow!"

"Isn't it fabulous? Wait until you hear the sound," Ellen said picking up a stack of records from the floor beside the player. "What do you want to hear?"

"Have you got *White Christmas*?"

"Of course I do." Ellen slipped the record out of its hard cardboard sleeve, lifted the arm of the player, and put the record on. The mellow instrumental opening filled the room. Bing Crosby began softly, "*I'm dreaming of…*" Both girls sighed and lay down on the bed and closed their eyes.

"Why does that song make me want to cry?" Ellen asked.

"Me, too. Frank Jackson told me that soldiers listened to it over and over. Lots of them cried. There's so much longing in it. So much false hope."

"Yeah," Ellen said.

They began to sift through the pile of records, four Sinatras, two Benny Goodmans, and one Harry James.

Jack pounded on the door. "Hey, you two is this an all girl thing or can I come in?"

"Oh, Jack, can't you leave her alone for a minute," Ellen said, "Come in if you have to. Come in."

"As a matter of fact, I can't leave her alone," Jack said sitting on the chair near the player. "How about something a little faster?" He looked through the records and chose Glenn Miller's *In the Mood* holding it up for approval. The girls nodded and when the last notes of Sinatra's *Mamselle* died out, he lifted the record, put the Miller on the turntable and asked Honey Lee to dance. The first time he let one of her hands go to swing her out, she bumped into the lamp which almost fell over before Jack grabbed it. He let go of Honey and began dancing with the lamp.

Noreen called up the stairs for Jack and Ellen to bring Honey Lee down to play Monopoly. Ellen turned the record player off and the three trooped down the stairs. Noreen and Bobby already had the board set up on the dining room table.

"What do you want to be, Honey Lee?"

"A princess."

"Come on, what piece do you want?" Noreen held the pieces in her hand.

"I'll take the iron." Honey Lee said. "I have an iron will to win."

Mr. Flynn agreed to sit in to make the number even, and Mrs. Flynn offered to be the bank. Jack insisted on a time limit to the game "or else Honey Lee will have to sleep here. Ten o'clock. OK?"

"No, Jack that's not enough time," Noreen wailed. "Eleven-thirty."

"Eleven. And that's final," Jack said.

At eleven o'clock they counted up their currency and real estate holdings. Jack and Bobby had the best holdings, Jack having bought Park Avenue and Bobby all four railroads.

"It's not fair," Noreen cried, "Boys always win."

"Not always. We'll play partners next time, and we will win. I promise you that." Honey Lee said.

Jack left the room to get Honey Lee's coat. When he came back and held it for her, Honey made her good-byes and thanked them all. She hugged Noreen and Bobby, and she and Jack went out together into the crisp night air. Honey took a deep breath humming her contentment as she breathed out.

"Jack, let's just walk a bit. It's so beautiful," Honey Lee said looking up at the black sky. She began counting quietly naming stars for people she loved. First of course, her father, then Jimmy's brother, Johnny, then Frank, Danny and Uncle Peter. She was praying for the dead and wounded.

"A penny for your thoughts," Jack said.

"I was thinking about my father—about people killed in the war, naming stars for them."

"I suppose there are enough stars for all of them," Jack answered looking up at the sky.

He held her close to him as they walked down High Street. Every house had a lighted Christmas tree. Reds, greens, blues were reflected n the snow. Honey Lee began to hum *White Christmas*. Jack sang the lyrics while Honey Lee hummed alto harmony beneath his tenor.

When they finished, Jack said, "Merry Christmas, dear, dear Honey Lee." And kissed her. She fitted herself even more closely against his side, her left leg against his right so that they walked hip to hip. Jack slipped on a piece of ice and they both went down laughing.

They lay on the ground side by side until Jack pulled Honey Lee toward him and kissed her saying, "Oh, Honey Lee, I do love you."

"And I love you, Jack."

"Don't. Don't say that unless you mean it."

"I do mean it, Jack." She was almost sure she did.

"Then wear my pin."

"No, Jack, not yet." She leaned her elbow on his chest and looked down at him. "Don't rush me, please," she pleaded.

They headed slowly back to the car and drove out Andover Street to the Monastery to see the light display. Going to see the lights at Christmas was a favorite date in Lowell. The abbey parking lot was full even this late and couples wandered through the lighted trees and bushes ending up at the life-size crèche. Spotlights played on a kneeling Mary in dazzling blue and white bending down to the infant resting on straw. The infant, arms stretched out and lifted, was rosy and pink. Joseph, dressed simply in brown, stood behind mother and child and out of the light. Carols played over the loudspeaker and Honey Lee found herself humming out loud: *Silent Night* and then *The First Noel*. When she felt Jack's hand tighten on her waist, she turned her face away and blinked back tears, embarrassed. Jack turned her to face him; then kissed one eye and then the other.

"Your tears taste like wine," he said.

"I'm sorry," she said. "I always cry at Christmas."

"Don't be sorry."

They walked on toward the car both singing with the music from the speakers. When they arrived back toward Lowell, Jack turned left on Nesmith Street, but drove by Sherman Street. She knew then that he was heading to Fort Hill Park and would drive up the narrow road to the top of the hill, a favorite romantic parking spot for couples. When they got to the top where two other cars were parked, Jack stopped the car and turned out the lights. It was very dark and still. Jack kissed her, at first lightly, then more deeply. She felt at first warm and then hot and breathless. She gasped and pulled away in part because she remembered her grandmother's warnings.

"Honey Lee, Honey Lee, don't be afraid."

"Oh Jack," she was breathless. "I...I...could we just go now?"

"Only if you kiss me one more time."

She did and once again felt as if all the blood in her body were pounding. She pulled back again. Jack held her face between his hands and studied it.

"How am I going to go back to school without you?" He shook his head and drove down the hill and back to Concord Street.

They saw each other a few more times before Jack went back after the New Year. Honey was almost sure that she loved Jack, but not sure enough to wear his pin as he had again asked her to. But she went up to Dartmouth again, this time for Winter Carnival. She hoped to see Sophia again because she had seen *Gentleman's Agreement* and she wanted to ask Sophia about the movie, but then she remembered that Sophia's friend, Mark, had graduated at the end of the first semester. She felt more comfortable on the train this time but still found that she had little in common with the college girls on the train from Boston. She sat alone and read during the long trip. She loved the clicking sound of the tracks and the swaying of the car. They lulled her into another world which she peopled with those she loved. In the dream she was hostess at a big house into which she welcomed her grandmother, "I have such a beautiful room for you, Nana;" her father, "I knew you'd come back. I bought this house for you, for us;" Jimmy, Frank, Danny and the lost brother, "This is the home you lost when your mother died. Come in and rest." The dream did not include Jack. Maybe because the house was theirs, and she and Jack were welcoming guests together. She set the house on Fairmont Street, on the hill above the city, a house she had seen perhaps on one of her walks. She smiled to herself and returned to *Look Homeward, Angel*, the big heavy book she was reading for English class.

Winter Carnival was so busy that she and Jack spent little time alone together. They went from one party or event to another getting little if any sleep.

"You have two more of these to go," Jack told her as he helped her up on to the train at the end of the weekend.

"I'm glad. It's wonderful," she replied.

CHAPTER 18

▼

Throughout the rest of the school year, Honey Lee saw Jimmy from time to time. When she visited Mary and Frank, Jimmy often came to drive her home. He loved having the use of Danny's car whenever Danny wasn't using it, which was most of the time.

Honey Lee always asked about Danny: "Is he getting stronger?" "Does he go out at all?" "Is he going to work?" "Has he put on any weight?"

Jimmy gave brief answers: "No, not any stronger." "No, he doesn't go out." "I don't know about work." "No, he is not gaining weight." Once he said, "What is it with you? Are you training to be a reporter or a gossip columnist for *The Sun*?"

One day when they were driving from Frank's house, she said, "Maybe we should ask him to go to the movies with us."

"Yeah, and maybe he'll just say no or just stare at me and say nothing," Jimmy said glancing over at her. His tone was bitter.

"Or you could get one of his friends to call him," she continued ignoring his mood.

"What friends? He says they're all dead." Jimmy shook his head slowly. "It's no use. A couple of guys called him. He's just not interested in anything. All he wants to do is sit at the window and stare into space. The only thing that gets him out is his check-up at the hospital."

"What do the doctors say?"

"They say he's good," Jimmy said and paused. "At least that's what he says. He doesn't tell us anything."

"I'm really sorry, Jimmy," Honey Lee said putting her hand on his arm.

Jimmy was increasingly gloomy about his brother. Things had not turned out to be the exciting adventure he had hoped for. He was more and more anxious to go off to school. He had said it would be like getting out from under heavy weight, that it might even be better for Danny. "Then he'll have to go out, even if it's just to the market," he once said.

"Like Uncle Peter. He doesn't work yet either."

"Damned war! Crazy damn vets." He pounded his fist on the steering wheel. "I can't believe that I was dying to be old enough to enlist, old enough to become a hero. More likely old enough to die."

"A lot of dead heroes. That's for sure." She was thinking of her father. "But what does anyone know about how they died?"

"Some of the others should have died. There's a guy at our place that will be in a wheel chair for the rest of his life. And he's got a wife and two kids."

"He's a hero just going on living," she said quietly.

"Yeah. But, hey, he's happier than Danny. I don't get it."

Honey Lee was surprised to find herself sounding as bitter as Jimmy. She thought she had been healed of the war.

One day, irritated at Jimmy's hopelessness, she said, "Jimmy, at least try. Ask him to go on Saturday with us to see Bob Hope in *The Road to Rio*. If that doesn't make him laugh nothing will."

"I'll try, but don't bet on it."

Danny agreed. He and Jimmy picked Honey Lee up an hour before the movie began. Danny was driving. Jimmy got out of the passenger seat and helped Honey Lee into the front seat. Danny smiled and kissed her cheek. She had forgotten how handsome he was. His hair had grown longer so that it curled at the back of his neck. She was nervous sitting so close to him, conscious of his leg touching hers when he shifted gears. Uncomfortable with the long silence as they drove, she filled the spaces with meaningless chatter.

"You look great, Danny." "Are you doing OK?" "This movie is supposed to be really funny." She babbled on and on preventing the unnerving silent spaces.

Finally Jimmy punched at her shoulder and said, "Chatter box, calm down."

Honey Lee blushed and stopped talking.

After another silence, Danny finally spoke. "Honey Child, I am just fine. Better than ever now that I see you again." Again Honey Lee blushed.

"Knock it off, Danny. You're embarrassing her," Jimmy said.

"It's OK, Jimmy. I know he's kidding."

"Not me, Honey Child, I'm serious," Danny said patting her hand and then squeezing it.

When they reached downtown, Jimmy said, "I'll go buy tickets while you look for a parking spot. Come on, Honey Lee."

They got out of the car and stood in a short line in front to the theater. Just as they bought tickets, Danny arrived. They went into the darkened theater where a newsreel was playing. *General MacArthur Reviewing Troops at Okinawa.*

"The war's over," Danny shouted. "Can't we just quit this stuff?" There was a ripple of noise in the theater.

"Shut up, Danny," Jimmy said.

When the feature began to run, Honey Lee was drawn in almost at once. The three of them laughed out loud all through the film. Honey Lee had never seen a movie she hadn't liked. From the opening credits through to the end of every film she had ever seen, she was completely engrossed, sometimes having to remind herself to breathe. During *Rio*, her breathing problems related to laughing so hard.

After the movie they went to the Epicure. Fortunately for Danny the crowd on weekends was not as young as the weekday afternoon crowd. Danny had wanted to drive out to the Blue Moon. Jimmy objected strongly. Honey Lee was glad because her grandmother had forbidden her to go to bars. She was puzzled at Jimmy's sharp refusal. She looked at him in surprise, but said nothing.

Danny treated them to club sandwiches and hot fudge sundaes, the kind of food they never had when they hung out after school. Danny seemed more relaxed. A few people knew him and came up to say hello and to ask how he was doing. Some offered sympathy and prayers for his mother and brother. Neither Jimmy nor Danny was comfortable when people talked about their dead. Their faces tightened into frowns as they tried to stem the talk with a hurried thank you or a question for the questioner.

Honey Lee did not see the Jacksons again until Field Day, the last Saturday in May. Starting in early spring, Honey Lee and the other officers had been seriously preparing for Field Day, a major city event. Honey Lee continued to believe that she was colonel only because she was so much taller than anyone else. Ellen insisted that was colonel because of her looks "a beauty contest is what it was." Jack claimed it was her natural grace and poise. Whatever the reason, Honey Lee took her position seriously and worked hard on the Field Day exercises. As Colonel, she was responsible for much of the preparation.

The day began with the induction of the newly appointed Girl and Boy Officers, and continued with a parade through downtown Lowell. Except for the Girl Officers, all the girls wore carefully ironed white gym suits. Different colored sashes and different drill accessories distinguished one class from the other. The school band led the parade, followed by the boys marching to the commands of the Boy Officers, then the girls. Crowds lined the streets and made a broad tail to the parade as it drew close to the Common. Honey Lee had told her grandmother where to stand during the parade so Honey Lee would be sure to see her. She had also told her cousin Peter get to the Common early to hold seats in the stands for her grandmother and aunt.

Despite the crowd following the parade, the common was crowded with spectators when the students marched in. The day was clear and warm, too warm for the heavy blue wool officers' uniforms. Honey Lee felt drops of sweat dripping down her back. She led the girls into the parade ground to the sound of loud applause. So concerned was she that the exhibition go well that she was unconscious of the noise around her. When the entire student body stood in formation on the field, the band played a final number, and the students left the field in order to sit until it was time for their class to perform. Honey Lee heard her name called out from the crowd several times, but until she was seated, she did not look at the crowd.

She was amazed, as she had been each year, by the crowd that filled the park. She looked towards the seats she had told Peter to hold and saw Nana Murphy and Aunt Kitty. At first she didn't recognize her Uncle Peter. That he had come amazed her. He waved and raised his hands in mock applause. Then she saw Jimmy sitting near them. With him was Danny, who neither waved nor smiled but stared at her. He was out of place in the crowd, too old to be a student from one of the other high schools and not old enough to be a parent. Yet she was pleased that he had come. That he showed enough interest in anything to get out of the house was a good sign. The display of student skills went on for almost two hours. After the last event, Honey Lee and the others left their groups and joined family and friends. Several people congratulated her, some she knew, some she didn't. When she finally found her grandmother, Nana Murphy was overcome with pride.

"Darlin', I had no idea how much work you'd done. You were wonderful." She reached up to smooth Honey Lee's hair, then pulled her head down and kissed her. "I'm so proud of you. Your father would have loved to see this day."

Before Honey Lee could reply, Jimmy and Danny came up to the group. Jimmy put his hand on Honey Lee's arm, and she turned to him.

"Wonderful, Honey Lee." He smiled and gave her a hug. "You were great."

"Jimmy, thanks for coming." She turned from him to her family. "You all know Jimmy Jackson, don't you?" They nodded.

"I wouldn't think of missing your big day," Jimmy said. At first Honey Lee didn't see Danny standing beside his brother. Danny said nothing.

"Danny, how nice to see you." She hadn't seen him since they had gone to the movies in March. He looked better, more relaxed, more fit.

"Honey Child, you were the star, the sun, the moon," Danny said.

When she looked more closely, she noticed that Danny was flushed, his eyes bloodshot. When he put his arms around her, she smelled alcohol. It was barely past lunch. Honey Lee knew that Jimmy and Danny argued regularly about Danny's drinking. Once in an unusual outburst, Jimmy had described his father's rapid descent from respected father to drunken street bum. He couldn't forgive his father, he had said, for what he'd done to his mother. He tolerated Frank's drinking, which was limited to an occasional beer, but would not allow liquor in the home he shared with Danny.

Honey Lee introduced Danny to her grandmother and aunt. Danny handed Jimmy money and told him to go "buy lemonade for the ladies."

After Jimmy had moved toward the refreshment stand, he said, "He watches over me like a mother hen, follows me everywhere. Drives me crazy." He continued to look at his brother's back.

"From what I know, he loves you. He couldn't wait for you to come home. He's a good, good boy." Nana Murphy spoke quietly, but the rebuke was clear.

"Yes a good, good boy," Danny said and laughed a little too loud.

Honey Lee was uncomfortable. She tried to distract Danny by tugging gently at his sleeve to get him to move.

He turned toward her and smiled. "The general is marshaling me away. OK, Honey Child, let's go." He took her hand. She resisted as much as she could, trying to keep calm. Jimmy came toward them carrying drinks.

"Jimmy, you're a lifesaver," Honey Lee whispered as she pulled her hand from Danny's strong grip.

Jimmy passed the drinks to Nana, Aunt Kitty and Honey Lee. To Danny, he said, "That's it Danny. We're leaving. Right now." Danny looked from his brother to Honey Lee, then shrugged, and unsteady on his feet, followed Jimmy into the crowd. Nana Murphy stared after them shaking her head.

Graduation came within a week of Field Day. Honey Lee went both to her own graduation at the Lowell Memorial Auditorium and to Jimmy's at Saint Peter's Church across the park from Keith Academy. Jack came home from college in time to take her to her senior prom. Jimmy, who was not dating anyone, took Ellen, who was also not dating, both to her own prom and to his. He had asked Honey Lee, but she, nervous that Jack would not understand, had said no and suggested Ellen. She had tried before to get her two best friends together. Ellen was more agreeable than Jimmy, but nothing much came of their dates.

For the summer, Honey Lee had gotten a job at Bon Marche, one of Lowell's three department stores. She needed to save money for school, for train fare and clothes and books. She was determined to pay her own way. She and Mr. Flynn had finally agreed that she would go to Boston University. He had arranged a scholarship for her and guided her through the admissions process.

"I'm putting my reputation on the line for you as the best of the best. So study hard, and do me proud."

Ellen was going to Wellesley; Jimmy had had been offered scholarships both at Notre Dame and Boston College. He was leaning toward Boston College for reasons similar to hers, but he hadn't decided. His brothers were thrilled that he would be the one to carry out their mother's dream of having a college-educated son.

The summer was busy; she worked five days and saw Jack at least three times a week. Once Jimmy came into the store to talk. He waited for her to finish work so they could eat together at Paige's. He didn't want to go to the Epicure.

"Too noisy, too many people we know."

After ordering at the counter, they sat on small wrought iron chairs at a round table eating sandwiches and drinking ice tea. Jimmy stared down into his drink for a long time without talking. Honey Lee was patient. She never minded silences with Jimmy. They always gave each other time to think, remember, brood. At last, Jimmy took a deep breath and started.

"I decided on BC. When I talked about Notre Dame, it was always a pipe dream. I can't leave Danny. He's not ready to be alone."

"Oh, Jimmy, you need to get away." She watched him play with his spoon twirling it around on the hard surface of the table. "You can't spend your life looking after him."

"Yeah, but right now I can't leave. I'm going to live in the dorm, but I'll be home weekends."

"What does he need you for? He's a grown man." She emphasized each word by hitting the tabletop with her fists.

"Honey Lee, he's drinking. I can't let him drink himself to death."

"You can't stop him, either. How can you stop him?"

"By not letting him get too lonely, too isolated." His tone was flat. He was clearly resigned.

"Why can't Frank look out for him?"

"Frank threw him out of their place a couple of weeks ago. After dinner he got weepy, then so angry Mary was frightened. It was bad."

Honey Lee looked at her friend. He still looked like the boy she first met. In spite of his newly cut hair and carefully chosen clothes, she still saw the shaggy child whose great sorrow had matched her own. He still looked sad and worried, still carrying burdens too big for his age.

CHAPTER 19

▼

Honey Lee left her job a week before Labor Day to go back to the Wiers to spend time with the Flynns. The boardwalk, the lake and the Flynn's house were as she had remembered. What was different and not quite so comfortable was being in the same house with Jack now that their relationship had changed. He didn't press her again for an answer about his fraternity pin, but he did ask her to Homecoming, and he suggested in subtle ways that they were seriously a couple. Sometimes she daydreamed about marrying Jack, but in such fantasies her thoughts were more about becoming part of the Flynn family than about Jack. Her children, like all of the other Flynns, would be taken out to Table Rock when they turned ten; Mr. and Mrs. Flynn would be their grandparents, Ellen their aunt. She would spend summers at the lake. Such dreams and the full week of wonderful days with Jack did nothing to make her decide to wear his pin as a pledge to marry him.

School began right after Labor Day. Honey Lee had registered for four classes, Freshman Composition, Western Civilization, Algebra II, and Advanced French. She scheduled her classes so that she only had to go in to Boston four days a week. The fifth, she planned to spend at the library in Lowell. She quickly became aware that four college courses were very different from four high school classes. She read and studied on the train every day, spent at least two hours at night and a full day at the library studying. Her advanced French literature class became her favorite even though she found it difficult. The assigned texts included readings from Moliere, Maupasant, Racine, and Flaubert. She loved the sound of the names especially when pronounced by the professor, Doctor Martine, a Parisian on exchange from the Sorbonne. He hung prints of Paris scenes on the wall of the classroom and often talked about Paris. Although she didn't understand everything he said, she was fascinated when he described the city as it had been before and during the war and then after. His description of the liberation when American troops marched down the Champs Elysee thrilled her. She wished her father had lived to see that day.

Her first assignment in Freshman Composition class was to write "a detailed description of a meaningful experience." She quickly chose to describe her train trip from Atlanta to Boston. *Four days a week, I take the train from Lowell to Boston and then back from Boston to Lowell. Every time I get on the train in Boston, I think about the very first time I took that train in 1943.* She wrote about the arrival in Boston on that cold January day and the slow cab ride across the city from the South Station to the North Station. As she described this turning point in her life, she softened the picture of Nana Murphy as she had been on that day. Instead she described the Nana Murphy she had come to love as a mother. Even with omissions and her many revisions, Honey Lee was unhappy about having written so much about herself. Well, she thought, it's bland enough. So a Southern girl comes north and begins a new life. At least she hadn't written about losing in one day everything and everyone she knew and loved. But after that assignment, she avoided writing about herself.

She adapted quickly to college life—to the commute, the long walk to and from the train station in Lowell, the forty-five minute train ride, and to schoolwork. One day in October as she walked down Merrimack Street to the Square, a car pulled up beside her and someone called her name. She bent down and looked in the window. It was Danny Jackson. She hadn't recognized him or the car. When she did, she became self-conscious, wondering how she looked, what he wanted, how he had happened to recognize her.

"Those books look mighty heavy," he said. "Hop in, and I'll give you a lift."

"No, thanks," she said holding the books to her chest. "I'm fine."

Smiling broadly, he leaned across the seat and opened the passenger door for her. "Come on. You look tired."

"Well, OK. Thanks." She opened the door, put her books on the back seat and turned to Danny. "How are you Danny?" He didn't pull out from the curb right away. He stared at her for so long that she became uncomfortable and remembered how she had felt the first time they had met. His dark eyes seemed to look too deep inside her. What did he see that made him look at her that way? She was out of breath, and she knew that her face was flushed. She hoped he would think it was from walking with the heavy books.

At last he smiled, first with his eyes, then his lips. "You do keep growing up, Honey Child."

"Honey Lee, Danny, please." She never minded when Frank called her Honey Child, but she didn't like the way it sounded when Danny said it.

"OK. OK. Honey Lee. How's college?"

"I like it. It's a lot of work, but I like it."

Taking his eyes from her, he checked the rearview mirror and pulled out into traffic. "Do you always walk all the way from the station to your house?" he asked.

They moved slowly down Merrimack Street. When he turned on to Central, she almost objected, but didn't. Instead she answered his question. "Sure. I love to walk. Sometimes I even take a longer way home just for the walk. Is that what you're doing?"

"No, I'm just driving around," he said looking over at her and smiling.

"Oh." She noticed how different he looked, more filled out, happier.

"Your sidekick seems to like college, too. He's only been home once this month."

"Jimmy? I haven't seen him since school started." She realized how much she missed Jimmy. "You must miss him a lot."

"Who, me? Hell, no. I'm getting a life going here. I'm working at Sullivan's in the print shop as an apprentice."

"Danny, that's wonderful. Are you finished at the hospital?"

"Nope. Not yet. I have to go in once a month." For a moment he was serious, but then he smiled again and said, "Hey, maybe when I do, I could drive you in."

"I don't mind the train at all." She couldn't imagine driving all the way in to Boston with him. "I get a lot of work done on the train."

"Well I'll call you the next time I'm going in, just in case."

She didn't answer. He drove with one hand on the steering wheel, the other resting on the back of the passenger seat. Conscious of his arm behind her, she moved closer to the door. Danny seemed not to notice. Twice he started to say something, then stopped.

"Are you in a hurry to get home?" he finally asked.

"I should be there for supper by five o'clock."

"Let's just have a cup of coffee." When she was about to refuse, he said, "Please."

"OK, but not for long."

He turned off Central Street back toward the train station to a diner she had been to once before, after a dance. He parked in front of the diner and helped her out of the car. At four o'clock in the afternoon, there weren't many people in the diner. Two bus drivers at the counter, their hats sitting beside their coffee cups, turned to look as she and Danny walked in. An old couple sat in the last booth staring out the window. Danny ordered coffee and asked Honey if she wanted anything else. He offered her a cigarette, which she refused, and lit one for himself. She wished she did smoke so that she would have something to do with her hands. He drew on the cigarette as if he hadn't had one in years. He put his head back and breathed the smoke out slowly. She watched it curl and waver as it rose to the ceiling.

"Umm, that's good. You know it was the simple things I missed on the ship. A comfortable place to have a cup of coffee, my Camels instead of whatever cigarettes they had in the ship store." He paused for a long time. "You have no idea what it feels like to have a moving floor under you all the time and to be herded together with hundreds of guys you don't know and some of the ones you do know you can't even stand. God, that was bad enough, but when I think of Johnny on a sub. At least I could go up and get some air and look up and see stars, but him...cooped up for months on end. Then hit. He must've known right off he was done for. At least we had a chance to jump. God."

His eyes filmed over and he held his spoon so tight Honey Lee thought it might break or at the very least bend. She reached out and put her hand over his. The spoon, suddenly released, dropped to the table with a clatter as he turned his hand over to take hers holding it so tight she thought of the spoon he had dropped. She held back a cry.

"We had nothing to come back to anyway. Neither of us even got home for ma's funeral. I knew about it, but there was no way to get home. They gave me free time on board the ship. Big deal. Free time to sit and know that my life at home was over."

Honey Lee was still. She had imagined scenes of war many times. But hearing Danny speak overwhelmed her. She felt a tightness in her throat and her eyes stung. Danny, still holding her hand, was staring at the past, unaware of her. When he pulled himself back from the other side of the world, he looked at her and said, "Oh sweetie, I'm sorry. Sometimes it just comes over me. I didn't mean to scare you."

"I'm all right," she managed to whisper, "but some day, I'm going to find my father's grave. I need to see the place where they buried him. And I will." The idea had just blossomed in her mind.

"Poor Honey Lee."

She jumped up before tears started, ashamed. "I've got to go now."

"Honey Lee, please don't go." He tried to stop her by holding her arm. She shook him off and said, "I'm going now. Alone."

"Don't go. Please don't go. It's all right to talk about him."

He tried to prevent her, but she pushed past him out of the diner and began to walk as fast as she could toward home. She felt safe looking back only after walking three blocks, fearing that Danny might follow her. She hated herself for crying and for what she had said to him. *It's amazing that I didn't go all weepy and tell him about my mother. What's gotten into me?* All the way home she scolded herself and decided that she would avoid Danny Jackson from now on. *If I can't trust myself not to go all soft and crazy around him, then I just won't see him again.* True to her promise Honey kept finding different ways to walk home just in case Danny might be looking for her.

When Jimmy called the following weekend to say that he was home and ask if she wanted to meet him for coffee after church on Sunday, she asked, "Just you?"

"Who else would there be?"

"Sorry, I don't know what I'm talking about. Too much studying."

They met at Paige's after Mass to compare notes about classes and professors. Honey talked about Professor Martine and Paris, Jimmy about his course in church history. As he talked about the early church fathers, he was excited in a way she hadn't seen before. And he looked wonderful. Being away apparently suited him. *He is really handsome,* she thought. *I never realized just how good-looking he was.* She asked how he felt about being on an all-male campus, and he told her that was the one thing he didn't like but he was so busy studying and working in the library that he didn't have much time to think about it.

"How about a movie?" Jimmy asked during a pause.

"What's up?" Honey Lee asked wanting to know what was playing.

"*Easter Parade* at the Strand and *The Best Years of Our Lives* at Keith."

Jimmy had clearly intended to ask her to go to the movies. He knew exactly what was playing where and at what time. Honey Lee, amused at his indirection, wondered why he hadn't asked her when he had phoned.

"Let's see *Easter Parade.* I heard the other one is depressing."

After the movie they walked slowly toward Concord Street. As they turned on to Fayette, Jimmy became very quiet. When they got to the building where he had lived, he stopped and stared up at the third floor window. For a few minutes he said nothing.

"It seems like a lifetime ago. I honestly thought that when they came home it would feel like a home again. Never happened. Just Danny and me playing house. He's been miserable. Every time I come home I feel guilty about having left him; then I can't wait to go back, and I start to feel guilty about that." She waited for him to go on. "I don't know, maybe I should have gone to South Bend. At least I'd only leave him twice a year."

Honey Lee said nothing until he turned and started to walk again." Things should be better now that he's working," she said.

He stopped suddenly and turned to her. "How do you know he's working?"

Honey Lee hadn't mentioned seeing Danny. She didn't want to and hoped that Danny hadn't told Jimmy. Obviously he hadn't. She had done it herself. "He told me a couple of weeks ago." She started to walk but he grabbed her wrist and turned her toward him.

"Where did you see him?" He was angry.

"He happened to see me walking home from the station and gave me a ride." She didn't want to tell him about going for coffee.

Still holding her wrist, he said, "So he just happened to see you and just happened to ask if you wanted a ride home?"

"Yes." She tried to pull her wrist from his grasp. "Jimmy, let go. You're hurting me."

"An unexpected meeting." His voice was thick with irony.

"Of course, Jimmy. What's wrong?"

He let go of her wrist and walked ahead of her. Then he turned. "Stay away from him. He's bad news, Honey Lee. Do you hear me?"

Now as angry as he, she said, "I didn't go near him. He happened to see me and offered me a ride, and I said yes. All right?"

"Yeah, sure." He continued to walk up the street ahead of her.

She tried to get him to talk about school or the movie, but he was darkly silent until they reached home. He refused her invitation to come in saying he had to go. Danny was driving him back to school.

First semester classes ended in mid-December. Honey Lee was busy writing final papers and studying for exams. In November as her workload increased, she had started to spend even more time at school. She found that the university library was a better place for studying than the Lowell Library. She had found a carrel deep in the stacks that was always empty, her own study space. With a French dictionary she would read from whatever text had been assigned. She pronounced in her head the sounds the words made hoping she sounded like Doctor

Martine, hoping that if he could hear her, he would admire her accent. Her lips formed the unspoken syllables, sometimes pursed for words like *vous* and *jolie*, sometimes tightened for *tres* and *midi*. Some words she held in the back of her mouth tightening her throat. *Mon cher professeur, vous etes tres charmant. Je voudrais voir votre Paris, voir les lumieres de Paris, votre Paris des lumieres.* When her mind wandered away from the story or play she was reading, she would scold herself and force her mind back to the text.

The last novel for the semester was *Madame Bovary.* Honey Lee followed Emma's progress, sometimes sympathizing with the great beauty doomed to life among peasants, sometimes despising her as she manipulated her husband and her young lover. In the end she pitied Emma, who moved inexorably toward her terrible end. She tested marriages she knew about against Emma's marriage, Aunt Kitty and Uncle Peter's for one. Since his return after the war, Aunt Kitty had changed. She had stopped working, but it wasn't just that. The animated young wife praising her husband to anyone who would listen and longing for his return was gone. Her returned husband was not what she expected. Like Emma, she must be disillusioned and also lonely.

Maybe that's what happened in lots of marriages. What if she married Jack? What would that be like? Might she, like Emma, get bored? How bad does a marriage get before a woman takes lovers? She pulled back from that kind of thinking quickly imagining what Father Finn, the sisters, and Nana Murphy would say about her even thinking of such a thing. They would certainly all hate the novel, that is, if they would read it at all, not only for the seduction and adultery, but for its descriptions of the clergy and the church. Was *Madame Bovary* on the Index? She knew *Les Miserables* was, but she didn't even want to know if *Madame Bovary* was. She loved the book. Emma may have been too carried away by romantic ideas about love, but Honey Lee believed in true love and expected to experience it.

CHAPTER 20

▼

Because she spent so much time in the library, she often got back to Lowell well after dark. The walk home seemed longer, and Nana would usually have eaten by the time she got home. As soon as Nana heard her at he door, she began to warm Honey's dinner. They sat together and talked about their day. Other than her grandmother, Honey Lee talked to very few people. Most of her friends were away at school. Jack came home rarely. But she was too busy to think about missing friends.

One evening when she got off the train and walked through the waiting room, she heard someone call her name just as she opened the door to the street and was just about to walk out. She knew the voice instantly. There he was standing near the bench by the closed ticket window.

"Danny, are you taking the train?" When she spoke, he walked toward her.

"Nope." He stood so close she could feel his breath on her face.

"Then what—?"

"I wanted to see you," he said quickly. "Ask you to go for coffee."

"Danny, it's late. I need to get home."

She stepped away from him and moved toward the door. "Please, Honey Lee, just for a few minutes." The urgency in his voice stopped her.

"Why? Is something wrong, Danny?"

"No." He shook his head. "Yes." He nodded slowly, then firmly said, "No."

She put her hand out and touched his sleeve. "Are you sick again?"

"No."

"Is it Jimmy?"

He sighed. "No. I just wanted to see you. Please have coffee with me."

Reluctantly, she agreed to coffee but said she had to call Nana Murphy to tell her she would be late. Worried, her grandmother said that since it would be late she should take a cab. Honey Lee told her she had a ride.

"I'll keep your supper warm for you," Nana said.

"Thank you, Nana. I won't be long."

Danny suggested they go across the river to the Blue Moon and have something to eat, but Honey refused. They ended up going to the same diner they had gone to before. At this time of day the diner was busier. There were no booths open so Honey Lee moved toward the counter.

"Let's wait for a booth." He held her arm firmly. "See, there's someone getting a check over there. They'll leave soon."

But the couple sat for some time over their coffee. The man was dressed in work clothes. His lunch box sat on the floor near his feet. The woman wore a dark dress with a small collar, pearls and high-heeled black shoes. The man leaned toward the woman and from time to time touched her face with his fingertips. She smiled and put her hand over his. Danny was impatient for them to leave, but Honey Lee was fascinated. She doubted that they were husband and wife. Their intimacy completely closed out the world around them. A husband and wife would have such moments at home not in a cheap diner. Besides if they were married they wouldn't be dressed so differently from each other. Could these two, like Emma and Leon, be stealing time away from their real lives? Finally they got up to leave. They walked by her and Danny and out the door seeing nothing but each other. Honey turned to look out the window just in time to see them kiss and walk away in opposite directions.

The waitress cleaned the table and motioned them to sit.

"Danny Jackson?" she asked.

"Yeah," he said studying her face.

"Mary Sheehan. We were at school together at the Moody."

"Mary Sheehan. Well I'll be darned. How are you?" Danny's smile was strained.

"Married with two kids. Working nights to pay the bills," she answered. "So tired, is how I am."

"Married to?"

"Johnny Rodgers. Remember him? He was two years ahead of us. We married in '42 before he was drafted." She was in no hurry to take their order.

"Oh, my God, Johnny Rodgers. How is he?"

"OK, I guess. We're doing all right now," she said and sighed as if hoping to tell more. Danny said nothing.

She finished wiping the table and asked, "Coffee?"

"Yes, two and two pieces of apple pie with ice cream." He turned to Honey Lee. "That OK with you, Honey Lee?"

"Do I have a choice?" She laughed, nervous, then turned to the waitress and said, "What can I say?"

After they had been served, neither of them spoke until they had finished eating.

"So what did you want to talk about, Danny?" she said making tiny circles with her spoon in the melted ice cream.

"I just wanted to see you, Honey Lee. I was worried about the last time, wanted to see if you and I were still OK," he said.

"We'll always be OK, Danny. You're Jimmy's brother."

"Yes, I am." He paused. "But Jimmy's not here. He's not around. And Ellen Flynn is in Wellesley, and her brother's way up in Hanover. I thought maybe you needed a friend who's around."

It was true. Ellen rarely came home. Jimmy didn't always call when he came home. And she hadn't made friends at BU. She wasn't exactly lonely, but she missed doing things with friends. Once she had gone to the movies alone but a strange man bothered her. She had been slow to realize what the man had in mind until he took her hand in his and moved it onto his leg. She jumped up and left the theater. She did miss sitting with people her own age over coffee, but Danny wasn't the kind of friend you had coffee with or went to the movies with. For one thing, he was much older than she was; for another, Jimmy had told her to stay away from him." He's bad news," Jimmy had said. She didn't know what Jimmy meant, but she had heard what he said and it stayed with her. She was afraid of her feelings for Danny. She knew instinctively that Jack would see him as an older, handsome rival.

"I have other friends, Danny," she said looking directly at him for the first time.

"And when did you last go anywhere with one of these other friends?"

Irritated by the question, Honey Lee said nothing.

Danny reached across the table and took her hand. "I'm sorry, Honey Lee," he said. "It's really more that I'm lonely. I had good friends who didn't come back and others who married or moved away. I guess I thought that maybe you and I...I don't know, could just do something together once in a while."

Honey Lee still said nothing, but her mind was racing. There were reasons why she shouldn't see Danny, several of them; but maybe it did make sense for them to do things together. But Jack would surely object, and Jimmy's reaction worried her even more. She sipped her coffee. It had grown cold.

"How could it hurt if we had coffee like this from time to time? Or went to a movie when you had time? Wouldn't it be good for both of us to get out once in a while?"

Danny pleaded.

"Danny, I don't know. When I told Jimmy you had given me a ride home he was upset. He thinks that you planned to meet me."

"What claim does Jimmy have on you? What right does he have to tell you who to see and who not to see?" His eyes blazed. "He can't have you, and he doesn't want anyone else to either?"

"That's not fair," she said hotly. "Jimmy doesn't think about me that way, Danny. But Jack Flynn does. You know that. I go up to see him at school. I see him all the time when he's home. I write to him every week. He wouldn't like it."

"What about you? What do you want, Honey Lee? You have to live your own life."

"I do live my own life. I've been doing it for years. And I don't need anyone."

"Of course you do," he said reaching for her hand. "We all do, Honey Lee."

"Yes, it's just that…" She didn't know what it was. She was confused.

"Can't I meet you once in a while? Wouldn't you like that?"

It was true that she hadn't talked to anyone but Nana Murphy in the past months, and there were lots of things she didn't talk to her grandmother about. Writing to Jack and Ellen wasn't the same as talking to them. Maybe she was lonely. She wanted to agree with him that it would be a fine thing if they saw each other once in a while. But the arguments against seeing Danny were strong.

"I don't know. I just don't know."

"Think about it, Honey Lee. Think about what you want, what would be good for you." He was leaning across the table using his whole body to convince her.

"Danny could we just go, please."

"OK, but I'm going to meet you once more. Next week. Just once. If you say you don't want to see me, I'll accept that and never meet your train again."

They walked to the car in silence. When Danny opened the door and put his hand on her back as she climbed in, she could feel the strength in his hand. She liked it. On the way to the house he asked about her grandmother and her aunt and uncle and how she liked school. He commented on what she said and asked questions. She was sorry when they pulled up in front of her house. Before he got out to open the door for her he reached over, and with the back of his hand, brushed her cheek. Then he went around to open her door. When she turned to say good night, he bent and kissed her forehead.

"Good night, Honey Lee. I'll see you next week."

She pulled the door open and stepped inside. For several seconds she stood with her back to the door breathing through her mouth as if she had just run the length of Concord Street.

"Is it you, darlin'?" her grandmother called from the living room.

Honey Lee tried to slow her breathing before calling back. "Yes, Nana, I'll be there in a second."

She ran up the stairs to the bathroom. She splashed her face with cold water and looked at her face in the mirror as if she had never seen it before. A woman's face? A girl's face? A man, six years and a war older than she was, was courting her. Mary, the waitress, a woman his age was already married and had two children. She was excited and frightened. Well, she would have to decide whether to see him or not. She looked again at her still-flushed face and breathed out the air trapped in her body. Finally she went down to greet her grandmother.

"It's good to be home, Nana."

"And where on earth have you been?"

"Well, when I got off the train I found Danny Jackson in the waiting room. He asked me to have coffee with him."

"Danny Jackson? And you just found him, did you?" Nana Murphy sniffed. "I should think it was he that found you."

"No, Nana. He just happened to be there."

"A real coincidence, then?" Her grandmother was too quick to see the truth.

"Yes," she said trying to convince herself.

"So now you have two Jacksons following you around like puppies."

"Oh, Nana."

"Honey, Honey, dear. Danny Jackson is a grown man made hard by fighting. It would be better if he didn't just happen to meet you again. Better for you to be friends with young Jimmy, I'm thinking. But right now, you need to eat. I've a lovely Irish stew."

"My favorite. Thank you, Nana," Honey Lee said as she moved toward the kitchen welcoming the opportunity to get Nana off the subject of Danny. She sat at the table opposite Nana Murphy eating slowly, hoping the subject was closed.

"You know darlin', a boy who goes off to war, either dies—God Rest the Souls of the dead—or he comes back a man with a mark on him. Peter and your father were grown men when they went off. Your father didn't come back. Your uncle did, and even though he was a grown man, he came back marked." She paused thinking about her daughter and Uncle Peter. "It's a terrible thing that war does. I saw it in Danny Jackson's eyes when I met him at Field Day. I've spent time praying for that boy. There's grief and anger carved in his face."

"But Nana," Honey Lee said, "he just asked me if I would have coffee sometime, maybe go to a movie. As a friend." She hadn't eaten a bite from the plate Nana Murphy had put in front of her.

"Well darlin', he's taken great pains to find you to ask such a thing. Why is it he didn't just use the telephone? And why is it that you're so troubled?" Nana poured herself a cup of tea.

"I'm not, Nana."

"Honey Lee Murphy, why was it you needed to run up to the bathroom before you would see me? I've always loved it that you come to me as soon as you come in. And isn't your face still flushed and your hair a bit damp from the water you splashed on yourself?" She knew her granddaughter very well.

"Oh, Nana, why is everything so complicated? Why can't people just say what they want? You think Danny wants to date me, don't you?"

"That's what I'm thinking, darlin'. And I'm after asking you to be very careful with him. He knows a lot more about the world than you do. He knows things you'll never need to know, God willing."

"You know what else Nana? He thinks Jimmy loves me too."

"And maybe he's right."

"At least with Jack I know what he wants. Oh Nana, I don't even know what I want."

Honey Lee began to cry softly. She moved her chair closer to her grandmother's.

Nana Murphy stroked her hair slowly. "Growing up isn't easy, is it then?"

"But what should I do, Nana?"

"Just what you always do, darlin'. You pray and you think, and then you pray some more. You have a good head and a good heart. But as you grow, it gets harder to choose, and the things you have to choose between get more complicated." She stood up and put her arms around Honey Lee. "I've watched you grow and I know you'll always make good choices. But for now, let's listen to George and Gracie, shall we? You can pray and think later."

George and Gracie's domestic mishaps always made Honey Lee laugh. She and Nana listened faithfully to them and to Fibber McGee and Molly. Nana didn't like the afternoon soaps, *The Inner Sanctum, Superman* or any other other serious shows. "Enough trouble in the world without borrowing theirs," she'd say.

They always chatted before and after a show. But on this night Honey Lee got up after the show ended, kissed Nana, and went to her room hoping to study for an hour before she went to bed.

She pulled her notebook out of her green book bag and looked at the exam schedule she had pasted there. She studied it thinking about Danny's plan to meet her during the next week. She had exams on Tuesday, Thursday and Friday, and the last, French, on Monday of the following week. She hoped Danny would choose to look for her on Monday or Wednesday so she could put off worrying and choosing. But just in case he might be at the station on Tuesday, Thursday or Friday, she decided to come back on the earliest possible train when she hoped Danny would be working.

Two of her exams would not require much study. Either you knew how to solve equations or you didn't. If not, it was too late to learn. Anyway, she was good in math, so she knew she could handle whatever was given. Her English professor had told the class that the best preparation for a comp exam was a good night's rest. She did have a final paper due for composition. She had decided to write on the canals in Lowell. She knew quite a bit about the canal system, but she also knew that before writing she needed to walk the canals, which she was looking forward to doing over the weekend.

As she hoped, the next week went by without Danny finding her at the station. Over the weekend she walked the canal system, a longer walk than she imagined taking all day Saturday and most of Sunday afternoon. The walk had taken her to parts of the city she'd never seen before. At one stop, she had been approached by school boys who gently teased her asking if she were a basketball player. Even though she said no, they dubbed her "Lady Giant" and asked if she would play on their team. They asked her what she was doing and when she told them they decided to follow her and give her directions and information. She felt as if she were the pied piper leading the group of five or six ten-year-olds around the city.

With help from the librarian she had found information on the building of the canals, had learned which mills used which canals. She took some time trying to decide how she would write the paper, whether to do straight exposition, which she certainly had enough information to do, or a more personal piece in which she described her walks and spoke of what canals were still producing power and which were no longer in use, or a more personal family history about her family's connection to mills. She knew from experience that the way to write the paper would come to her if she didn't think too hard about it. And it did. By

Monday morning she was ready to write and the words flowed. She had a rough copy by late afternoon, which she planned to read to Nana.

Her math exam was more or less what she expected and she was sure that she had done well. The exam ended at noon after which she hurried to North Station to get the one o'clock train home. Danny, as she hoped, was nowhere in sight. She felt a pang of disappointment.

That night she read her paper on the canals to Nana. She had made a rough map of the canals, which Nana held as she read. In her paper, the canals served as background for the history of her father's family. She used stories that Nana had told her that located family homes on or near canals. Although she wasn't going to use pictures in the paper, she had looked at the old photos of her grandmother's parents taken just after they had arrived in Lowell with their children, including six-year-old Nana. She had written about one canal in Billerica because her great-grandfather had worked at the Faulkner Mills there; she wrote descriptions of the Boot Mills where her grandmother's brothers had worked; she included descriptions Nana had given her of romantic canal walks she and her husband had taken when they were courting. She even wrote a brief section telling how her father had worked one summer at the Boot. She ended by describing her own walk of the system commenting on the few remaining mills. Nana, of course, loved the paper and was certain Honey Lee would get an A.

"You are missing one very big family story, and you are old enough to know it," Nana said after listening to the paper and praising it. Your grandfather, Thomas Patrick Flynn, also worked for seven years at the Boot. He died in that horrible place. Caught up in a belt. When they came to me with the news, I ran to the mill thinking I could do something. They tried to stop me before I saw him, but they couldn't. I never sleep without seeing his ruined body. It was about working in that body-destoying place that your father and I quarreled. He couldn't understand why I forbade him to do it; he disobeyed me, lied to me, and it was then that I said words that couldn't be unsaid, and he left."

"Oh, Nana. I shouldn't have written this paper. I'm sorry."

"Darlin', it's a lovely paper, but you needed the whole story, not just for the paper, but for yourself. It's the strong link between you and me, and you should have it."

With a heavy heart, Honey Lee went back to her room to rewrite sad sections of her paper. But she couldn't unwrite what was written any more than she could undo what had been done. She finished the paper before she went to bed.

CHAPTER 21

▼

Honey Lee had learned over the years how to keep herself from thinking about things she didn't want to think about. Studying worked just as well as a movie or a good book. On the Thursday before her history exam, she reviewed whole sections of her European History book comparing class notes with the text. She found material in the text and not the notes and vice versa. She studied both. She made lists of dates, places and people in case there was a short answer section and thought about causes and effects of larger events. By Thursday night she was ready. The exam on Friday was, as she had expected, long and difficult. She was relieved when it was over. Just one more to go.

She was late getting home on Friday. When her train pulled into the station at four o'clock, she was so busy thinking about the exam and wondering how she had done that she hadn't thought about Danny. When she walked through the waiting room at the depot, she sensed his presence even before he spoke. He came up so close behind her that when she turned, her face brushed his coat collar.

"Oh, Danny. You startled me." She stepped back and looked up at him.

"I've been watching for you all week. Every day."

"I've been taking exams and studying." She almost apologized to him.

"Are you finished?" His voice was cool.

"Almost." She was tongue-tied in his presence. Underneath her brief responses, her heart, huge within her reached out to him. "I like to study."

"I never did. So noisy at home I couldn't. I almost didn't finish high school. All I wanted was to join the Navy."

"You could go back," she said brightly. "Lots of students in my classes are veterans, a lot of them older than you."

"I could, I guess. But it seems silly to me. I lost three, four years of my life. I need to get started living the rest of it."

"But you could finish in two and a half years."

"That's two and a half years I don't have to waste." He spoke with such intensity and stared at her with such longing that she knew that wasted time meant time without her. She became afraid. They walked together out of the station to the parking lot. Without asking, Danny guided her to the car and opened the door for her. She went with him without comment.

"It's Friday. No school and no work tomorrow. You need a break. I need a break. Let me take you out for a real meal."

"But, my grandmother…"

"Just call her, Honey Lee. You owe me an answer."

"All right. I'll call her."

She went back into the station to use the pay phone. As she expected, Nana Murphy was not happy.

"Are you sure you should do this?" Nana asked. Honey wasn't sure, but she told Nana that she was. When she got back to the car and got in, Danny leaned toward her and kissed her forehead.

"Good. Now let's go to the Blue Moon."

Nana Murphy had very set ideas about what places were proper for young girls. She had forbidden Honey Lee to go to the Commodore Ballroom, and Honey Lee was quite sure she would have forbidden the Blue Moon if she had thought Honey Lee would go there. It was out of town, and it had a bar. As a matter of fact, people thought of it as a bar. Honey Lee wasn't sure what to expect. As Danny drove through downtown and over the bridge, he hummed to the music playing on the radio and tapped out the beat on the steering wheel. They both laughed out loud when *Bongo, Bongo Bongo* played, Honey Lee clapping and Danny singing and pounding out the rhythm on the dash with his fist.

Almost Like Being in Love played next. Whenever the title was repeated, Danny sang along as if he were talking to her. She listened carefully to the lyrics of the songs as they played. Falling in love. Being in love. Almost like being in love. She wondered if she had ever really been in love. How were you supposed to know? With Jack, was it almost like being in love? Shouldn't she love him in the way love was described in songs she listened to and books she read. Shouldn't she feel the heartache of the singer in *Full Moon and Empty Arms* when she wasn't with Jack? She didn't, and though she looked forward to seeing him, she didn't daydream about him. Why was she even thinking about Jack, questioning her love for him? Because of Danny.

"A penny for your thoughts, Honey Child."

"Danny, don't call me that." In his mouth the name made her feel cheapened.

"I'm sorry Honey Lee. It's a foolishness I came up with when I first heard your name. It drives Jimmy crazy when I do it too. I won't anymore."

"Thank you," she said, and then answered his question. "I wasn't thinking at all. I was just listening to the music."

As they drove along the river, the lights from the city on the other side of the river looked miles away. There were almost no lights where they were driving until the blue sign for the restaurant appeared.

"There it is. *Blue Moon, I saw you standing alone,*" Danny crooned as they drove into the parking lot and parked beside a pre-war Plymouth.

"Look at that," Danny said looking at the car. "It looks brand new. I'll bet it was up on blocks for most of the war." He opened the door for Honey and stood with her beside the Plymouth.

"No one drove during the war, well almost no one," she said walking to the front of the car. "Did you ever see how we had to paint car headlights with black paint? Just half, down to the middle. In day time, the cars looked half a sleep." She stooped to look at the headlights. "I don't think this one was ever painted. It was probably off the road until last year."

"I never had a car before the war," he said admiring the shiny, black car.

As they walked to the entrance, Danny put his hand on her back guiding her. Inside, a woman in a neat black dress met them and led them into the dimly lit dining room. She stopped at a table for two right next to another table where two couples were studying menus. Danny asked for another table, a nice quiet one, "so we can talk." The woman smiled, said she understood and led them to a table in the corner. She put menus in front of them.

On the table, a small lamp gave just enough light to make the glasses gleam. Honey watched Danny shake his fan-folded napkin out and place it on his lap. She did the same, then opened the menu and looked down at it, not so much to read it as to find some place to look. Sitting across from Danny in this quiet, dark place made her nervous. When the waitress asked if they would have drinks before dinner, Danny looked at Honey Lee.

"I'll have a coke," she said.

"One coke, and one rum and coke, please," Danny said.

She felt a ripple of panic remembering how Danny had behaved on Field Day. She wanted to ask him not to drink, but she couldn't.

While they waited for drinks, Honey Lee looked at the menu pretending to read until Danny said, "Sooner or later, you'll have to look at me."

She raised her eyes and smiled. "I'm sorry. I'm nervous. The restaurant. You."

He smiled at her and took the menu out of her hands and put it down on the table. "I'll tell you the three best things on the menu, and you can chose one, OK?"

Honey Lee folded her hands on the table and looked at him. Half smiling, he looked at her and said, "That's better. You look beautiful, Honey Lee."

She touched her hair, which she hadn't combed since morning and then her lips, which were bare of lipstick. "I haven't looked in a mirror for hours. I must look as dusty as an old library book."

"You look perfect. I hope you don't have a comb or lipstick. I don't want you to change anything."

"I wish you wouldn't talk like that."

"I know. I won't."

When the waitress came, Danny told Honey Lee to choose steak or shrimp. She laughed and said, "That's all they have?"

He handed her a menu telling the waitress they needed a few more minutes and ordered another round of drinks. When the waitress came back they ordered. Shrimp for Honey Lee. Steak for Danny. The last time she'd had shrimp was over four years ago in Atlanta with her father and mother.

"Can we talk now?" Although uncomfortable, she nodded slowly. "I want to see you, he said. "I want to see you often, for movies, walks, maybe just to sit and talk, maybe dance sometime. I care for you. I have for a long time. You must know that."

She tried to make light of his words. "I am seeing you. Right now. For dinner."

"Don't do that. I'm serious. I'm very seriously asking you to let me see you."

"I know you are. But I don't know what to do. So much would change."

"Yes, it would. That's why I asked you to think about it. Things will change or they won't."

Somewhere inside her, she knew she wouldn't be sitting across the table from him if she hadn't already decided to make whatever changes she had to make. She couldn't say no to him. She stared across the table at him, mesmerized by his darkness, his hair, his eyes, his grave intensity, whatever dark secrets were buried in his heart. Something deep within stirred. There was nothing frivolous about what was between them. And she knew that it meant the end of whatever she had with Jack. It probably meant losing Jimmy as well. Nana Murphy would oppose her as strongly as she could. She was dumb as she thought about the upheavals to come. She wanted to cry.

"Honey Lee, Honey, don't look so sad. After dinner, I'll take you home. That will be the end of it."

"It's late for that, Danny. You know it is. I've already said yes. Even if I wanted to I couldn't change that." She recognized the truth of the words only in saying them. She had given herself to him, and she feared him. Now she knew what love felt like. It was not the girl-foolishness of trembling hands and short-ness of breath. This love uprooted her from her life. Danny reached across the table for her offering hands. He bent his head and kissed her fingers. She looked at her hands, resting in his thinking how small they were compared to his. She turned her hands so that she held his hands in hers. She raised them to her mouth and kissed them. Looking directly into his eyes, she nodded her head.

They released each other's hands only when the waitress brought bread and salad, but their eyes held. Even if she had wanted to, Honey could not take her eyes from him. She began to memorize him so she could call him up whenever she wanted to see him. She wanted to take her fingers and trace the sharp widow's peak on his forehead, to move her fingers over his darkly arched brows, then to touch his lips and the cleft in his chin. How incredibly beautiful he was! She wished and didn't wish that he would smile so she could see his teeth. She wanted and didn't want him to say something so she could hear his voice. When the waitress came to refill their water glasses, they looked away from each other and thanked her.

Honey Lee picked up her fork and put it down again. She wasn't hungry. But suddenly it was so important to her that he eat that she began to eat. She moved the plate of rolls toward him wanting him to eat all of them, to get well and strong. She managed to eat half of her salad and nodded when the waitress asked if she were through. She ate even less of her dinner, happy to watch the way he cut his meat, the way he held his fork, the movement of the small muscles in his face as he chewed, the way he was able to do all these things without ever looking away from her.

When Danny finished, he lit a cigarette. The waitress came back to the table. She looked at Honey Lee's plate and said, "Are you all done, honey?"

Both she and Danny laughed.

"Well, Honey Lee Murphy, are you all done?" Danny said.

"Oops," the waitress said. "I guess I should have said sweetie or dearie." They all laughed.

"Those are both perfect for this woman, and I could add at least a thousand more," Danny said.

Honey Lee blushed and said, "I am finished, thank you."

"Coffee, dessert?"

Honey shook her head.

"No thanks. Just the check, please," Danny said.

They left the restaurant holding hands. Before opening the car door for Honey, Danny pulled her toward him and kissed her. She put her arms around him, one hand on his back and one on the back of his head keeping him as close to her as she could.

"Oh, Danny…" she finally said.

"I have wanted to hold you like this for so long, he whispered. "It feels like coming home at last. You are a miracle."

A couple came out of the restaurant and walked toward them. As they came closer, Honey Lee stepped away from Danny. They stopped at the Plymouth parked beside Danny's car.

Still holding Honey Lee's hand, Danny looked at the couple, pointed to the Plymouth and said, "Is this yours? We were admiring it before we went in."

"Yep. I took it out of storage the day I got back from Germany, and she started up as if I'd left her the night before. I'm Jack Williams and this is my girl, Miriam, just as beautiful tonight as she was the day I left her in '43."

"I'm Danny Jackson and this is Honey Lee Murphy. Glad to meet you," Danny said extending his hand. When Jack put out his hand they noticed that it was shrunken and stiff. Another war sign.

"Miriam and I are getting married tomorrow at the Sacred Heart at ten o'clock. This is our very last date." He put his arms around Miriam, who looked up and smiled at him.

"Wonderful," Danny said. "I envy you. All the best."

They all shook hands and got into their cars. Danny waited for the other couple to pull out. They watched the taillights until they disappeared in the distance. Then they both turned to study each other's face as if the faces were strange new paintings. Danny's fingertips traced her face in exactly the same way she had imagined tracing his.

She put one hand on either side of his face and said, "Danny, you are so beautiful."

"Handsome?"

"No. Beautiful. I could look at your face forever."

He kissed her slowly. "I'm crazy about you, Honey."

"Does that mean you love me?"

"God, yes. I think I've always loved you. Even before I knew you existed. You are why I came back."

"How wonderful. How really, really wonderful," Honey Lee said, her eyes filling with tears. She let herself really cry as she had never done with anyone before. She cried tears that washed away old sorrows.

Danny was alarmed. "Don't be sad, dear. Don't cry." He wiped at her tears and kissed her face.

"I'm not sad. You know I'm not. I am truly happy for the first time in so long. It's like coming home."

"Then I love your tears. I love you. I want to care for you forever."

Just then loud laughter erupted as two couples came out of the restaurant. With one hand, Danny started the car and pulled out of the parking lot. He drove slowly for a few hundred yards and then pulled off the road and parked beside the river.

He bent his head and put his forehead on the steering wheel. "What am I doing? This is too fast for you, isn't it? I don't want to scare you."

"I'm not scared, but I can't think with you here beside me. I don't know what any of this means. Just hold me, just hold me tight."

They sat for a while holding fast to each other preventing for a time thoughts of anything else. Then at last Honey Lee asked, "What are we going to do, Danny?"

"I don't know, darling. I thought we would date or something for a while and see where it goes." He stopped, apparently as amazed as she was at the strength of their feelings. "Now I don't know. I just don't know."

"I think I need to go home."

"But when will we...?" He started the car, but waited for her to answer.

"Tomorrow, tomorrow, of course. In the morning."

"Where? When?"

Honey Lee couldn't think of any place she knew where she wanted to see him. She needed a new place for this new thing. "At the Sacred Heart Church. At ten."

"Jack and Miriam," he said smiling. He pulled out on to the road slowly.

"Yes. We'll just sit at the back and watch." She liked the idea.

They reached Concord Street too quickly. When they got there she asked Danny to drive around the block. "Just for a few more minutes. I don't want to say good night just yet," Honey Lee said.

Danny drove up Sherman to the top of the hill and turned left toward Andover Street. For a minute Honey Lee had thought that he was going to Fort Hill Park. She couldn't go there with Danny. That was the parking place for high school kids, no longer a place for her. He drove out Andover Street past the expensive homes to the country-like roads near Andover.

She watched Danny's face as he drove. He looked serious, almost sad. She began to worry. Was he having second thoughts? Had she been too eager? Had he decided that she was too young? He stopped the car on the side of the road.

"Is everything all right, Danny?"

"It will be, Honey Lee. It will be. But for tonight I am taking you home. In the morning, we'll talk. I love you. Everything will work out."

He kissed her and put the car in gear. When he parked the car outside the house on Concord Street, Honey saw Nana Murphy at the window. "She's waiting for me, Danny. Kiss me here and I'll run in. Don't come to the door, please."

"Tomorrow at ten," he said.

"I'll be there. I love you."

She opened the car door and ran up the stairs wondering how much her grandmother would be able to tell from her face. Surely she looked different, but maybe Nana wouldn't notice. She opened the front door and called out, "Nana, I'm home."

"I was worried, dear." Nana came into the hall. "What took so long?"

"We had dinner and got to talking and forgot the time. Did you have a good day?"

She tried to avoid talking about Danny. It worked for a bit.

"Yes, darlin'. How was the exam?"

"Good, I think. It was hard, but I think I did all right."

"Of course you did. Have yourself a nice warm bath and I'll make tea for us."

Honey went upstairs and ran the hot water until the bathroom steamed up. She stooped to take off her stockings and skirt and dropped them to the floor. Then she reached over her head and took off her sweater and her slip. When she stood in her panties and bra, she took a towel and rubbed at the mirror so she could see herself. He thinks I'm beautiful. How wonderful. How incredible. She studied her face remembering the way he had touched it; she touched her lips which still tingled from his kiss. When the tub was half full, she added cold water until it was just the right temperature. She took off her bra and pants and slid into the water relaxing her strong, healthy body. As she sat relaxing, she worried about Danny's body, about his health. Nana Murphy's concern had infected her. He felt strong when he held her, but he was going to the hospital every month and Jimmy had told her he had terrible nightmares. But she would help him, nurse his body if need be. But what could she do about whatever it was that troubled his sleep? Could she help him forget? Yes, she could and she would. He would be fine. She would make him heal.

When she came back downstairs in her bathrobe, Nana was waiting in the living room. She had brought a whole pot of tea into the living room instead of the usual two cups and had pulled a chair close to Honey's.

"Sit down, darlin'. You've had a long day, haven't you then?"

"Yes, Nana. I'm tired, but I'm almost finished. I'm pretty much ready for French on Monday. Then it's over, the end of my first semester." She was happy to be talking about school.

"So where did you and Jimmy Jackson's brother go to do all this eating and talking?" Nana was unwilling to use Danny's name. A bad sign. She didn't approve. Honey Lee's habit of honesty with her grandmother forced her to tell Nana that they had eaten at the Blue Moon. Nana said nothing. She waited for Honey Lee to say more.

"It's not a bad place, Nana. Just a restaurant. I mean it's a better place to talk than the Epicure or Paige's."

Nana still didn't speak.

"You don't like Danny, do you?"

"I couldn't say that, dearie. I don't even know him, do I?" Conversation between then had never been so difficult. "Honey Lee, darlin', I'm thinking that Daniel Jackson is a grown man, too old to be taking a young girl like you out for fancy dinners and bringing you home so late."

"He's not so old, Nana. And I'm not that young."

"And what would his young brother think about it, I'd like to know."

With difficulty, she held to the truth. "Jimmy told Danny to stay away from me. He told me to stay away from Danny. I don't know why."

"And maybe he's right darlin'. Maybe he knows some things you don't know. Daniel Jackson has had a war. He's been sick. You don't need such problems."

"If you knew him, Nana, I know you'd like him."

"And I'm sure I would if you say so." She paused and shook her head. "But I wouldn't like him to be bothering you."

"Nana, it's too late. I love him. I didn't want to. I didn't think I would. But I do."

Nana's voice trembled as she said, "Please listen to an old woman who knows about men who come home from war. They're broken in one way or another. It's not the body wounds that are dangerous. It's the ones you don't see. Did your friend Jimmy ever tell you about his da'?"

Honey nodded.

"Did Daniel tell you?"

"We haven't gotten that far yet, Nana. Everything happened so quick."

"It's well known that Mr. Jackson came back from France after the last war a ruined man. And his wife suffered dearly for his wounds."

"Did you know her, Nana?" Honey Lee wanted to hear about Danny's mother.

"To speak to in a casual way, yes. But everyone knew about the troubles in that poor family."

"You think Danny is like his father, don't you?"

"Your grandfather wasn't unlike Mr. Jackson, ruined by the war. He was never the same after he came back. He'd not be dead if he hadn't stopped caring about living. He couldn't help it, you know. I suppose Mr. Jackson couldn't either."

"But Danny's well now, Nana. He's working. He's fine. He loves me."

"Maybe if he loved you enough, he would have left you alone, safe and happy with the likes of Jack Flynn and his own brother who's so taken with you."

"Nana, he didn't choose to love me any more than I chose to love him"

"I so want to keep you safe and happy. And Daniel Jackson, I'm thinking, will bring you no lasting joy."

"But you can't change the way I feel, Nana. I'm happy, happier than I've felt in years. Don't you want that?"

"God help us all. Falling in love is a terrible thing. It strikes before a body knows the person she loves."

"But I really love him. I feel like I've known him forever."

"Yes, you would feel like that." Nana stood up slowly. "We should go off to bed now. Tomorrow, things might look different." She bent down to Honey Lee in very much the way she had bent to her five years before when she told Honey Lee that her parents were gone. Both times her eyes filled with tears of pity and love. They kissed each other and said a quiet good night.

CHAPTER 22

▼

Honey Lee knew that her grandmother was not finished objecting, but at least they had begun to talk. When she went to her room, she relived her time with Danny from his very first words at the depot to the last kiss before she got out of the car. How was it possible that she hadn't known that she would love him the very first time she had seen him? He was the reason she had refused Jack's fraternity pin. It had been naïve to think that her love for Jack would grow until she knew she should marry him. Real love was different. It would have its way with her no matter that it caused Nana Murphy pain, no matter that it cost her her best friends, no matter that she hurt Jack Flynn. No Winter Carnival at Dartmouth this year. No more vacations at the lake with the Flynns. Suddenly she wanted to slow things down, to call Danny and tell him that she couldn't meet him in the morning. She had never even heard his voice on the telephone. She really didn't know anything about him. She would tell him that they needed to take a week or two to think about what they had said to each other. It was too rushed. Nana was right. But her heart rebelled. She would see him as she promised.

She slept until eight o'clock then lay still in her bed remembering. She wrapped her arms around herself smiling. In less than two hours, she would see him. She got up and went to her closet to look for something special to wear, wishing she had said yes more often when Nana Murphy had told her to buy a new dress or sweater or skirt. She needed something warm for the long walk to the Sacred Heart Church half way across the city. Her long black skirt would do. If only she had a blue sweater to match her eyes. Danny loved the color of her eyes. She chose a white sweater with a high collar. She would need boots, a warm scarf and gloves. At least she had listened to Nana and agreed to buy a lightweight camel hair coat for college. She loved it. She dressed quickly and ran downstairs to where Nana Murphy was sitting at the kitchen table drinking her morning tea.

"You're up and dressed early. I was hoping you'd sleep a bit."

"I'm going..." Honey Lee started to lie to her grandmother for the first time. She caught herself. "I'm meeting Danny."

"I see." Nana Murphy's voice was low. She didn't meet Honey Lee's eyes.

"Nana, I have to talk to him. You're right. I don't know him. I have to get to know him," Honey Lee said begging her grandmother to understand.

"If you are going to keep seeing him, I would like him to come to the door to get you and to drop you off. That's the right way."

"He would have come here, but I told him to meet me at the Sacred Heart."

"At the Sacred Heart? Why on earth would you be doing a thing like that? It's not even your own parish, child."

"Last night we met a couple who are getting married there this morning. They were so happy and so nice." She began to feel how foolish her plan was. "I thought we'd just sit in the back and watch them get married."

"Did they ask you to do that?"

"No, Nana. The idea just popped into my head."

"It's a strange idea that popped into your head, going to a wedding you're not asked to." Nana was not making it easy for her.

"I can't undo it now. Maybe we won't go into the church."

Honey Lee saw worry lines on Nana's forehead, longed to smooth them out, hated causing them. "Nana, I love you so much. I hate to worry you. If I lost your love..."

"It's I, isn't it, who should worry about losing love. Look what I did with your father. I would never do that again."

"You won't ever lose me, Nana."

Nana Murphy stood up to embrace her granddaughter. Honey Lee was surprised again at how tiny and frail her grandmother felt. She put on her coat and boots and set out for Gorham Street. The rest of the walk was a straight line to the side street where the church was. She had just turned the corner when she saw him pacing back and forth on the sidewalk across the street from the church checking his watch every few seconds. She stood still and watched him. He didn't wear a hat. His heavy dark hair fell onto his forehead. His long legs carried him the full length of the block in five strides. He was wonderful. As tall as her father had been and as strong and handsome as she remembered him to be. Thank God he had come back!

Before she called out to him she said a prayer. "Jesus, let him be well, heal him and look on us with favor. Amen." She hurried toward him calling out, "Danny."

He turned abruptly and hurried toward her. The lines on his face softened into a smile. "Thank God. Honey, I was afraid you wouldn't come."

She took his hand in hers and pressed her fingers against the back of his hand. "I'm here," she said.

Across the street, the last guests were entering the old red brick church. A car sat at the curb idling. The driver, dressed in black, got out and opened the rear door. Miriam. It had to be Miriam, but so different in full sunlight in her long white dress and veil.

"Danny, isn't she beautiful?"

Miriam walked up the stairs with an older man, probably her father. She was followed by two girls in long satin dresses. After they went into the church, Danny and Honey Lee walked across to the church and entered. The organ played a slow march as Miriam and her father, preceded by the two girls and two young men in dark suits, walked down the aisle. Standing at the altar, Jack, in a dark suit with a white carnation in his buttonhole, stared at Miriam. Honey turned to Danny, her eyes bright with tears. He looked down at her and whispered, "Some day, some day. Maybe."

Miriam's father kissed his daughter and walked to the front pew. Miriam and Jack were alone before the priest, who spoke quietly to them and gestured to them to kneel. He then went up the altar steps and began the Mass. "Introibo al altare Dei." "I will go unto the altar of my God," Honey Lee silently translated and added her own words, "and pledge myself to this man forever." She usually loved the slow progress of the Mass with its prayerful gestures, the sign of the cross, the outstretched arms of the priest at prayer, the bowing before the altar, the kneeling at the most sacred moments, but today she was eager for the wedding ritual to begin.

Finally after the Lord's prayer, the priest came down from the altar to the couple.

"Do you, Jack Williams, take this woman, Miriam, to be your lawful wife to love and to honor in sickness or in health, for richer or for poorer until death do you part," the priest asked.

Jack answered, "I do," in a voice that could be heard clearly at the back of the church.

Miriam's response was softer. The rest of the service went quickly and soon Miriam and Jack were walking down the aisle in triumph. When they reached the pew where Honey Lee and Danny were sitting, they stopped.

"You? Here?" Miriam said. "How wonderful. A good omen for us."

"Congratulations!" both Honey Lee and Danny said.

"Call us sometime, "Jack said, and then they were gone.

Honey Lee and Danny waited as the wedding guests filed out of the church. The organ stopped playing. On the altar, a young boy in a black cassock and a white surplice snuffed out the six candles on either side of the altar. The overhead lights and the smaller lights in the sanctuary of the church went out in pairs. In the dim church, Honey Lee and Danny sat without talking. Honey turned to look at Danny. His eyes were closed. She wondered whether he was praying or remembering the things that kept him awake at night. His face was not peaceful. She closed her own eyes and bent her head placing her fingertips on her forehead. Again she prayed for Danny—for his health, for his happiness, then, without any thought, for a day like this when Danny would wait for her at the front of a church. Danny finally opened his eyes and nodded a quick question to Honey Lee. She blessed herself and together they rose and walked out of the church.

"Let's walk for a while, "Danny said. "My car's right down the street, but I'd like to walk a bit."

Honey nodded and took Danny's hand. Neither had yet put their gloves on. Danny placed his left hand over Honey's right hand and slid both hands into his coat pocket.

"That's the first wedding I've ever been to." Honey Lee said.

"You didn't go to Frank's?"

"No, their wedding was like a war wedding. Just a priest and Jimmy and Mary's sister."

"Frank is the only married Jackson. Just Jimmy and me left single."

Embarrassed to remember the prayer she uttered for a Murphy-Jackson wedding, she changed the subject. "Is Jimmy finished exams?"

"Yeah, he came home last night."

That Jimmy was home and hadn't called her worried Honey Lee. They walked toward Gorham Street and turned left heading toward the cemetery and the Veterans' Housing. Honey Lee fretted. What if they should meet Jimmy?

"You didn't say anything to Jimmy did you?"

"Not yet," he said.

"What if we run into him? We should go back to the car."

Danny stopped and put his hands on her shoulders. "We are not going to hide, Honey Lee. Not from Jimmy, not from anyone." He was angry.

"It feels wrong. Too quick. Too secret. We don't even know each other. I couldn't explain myself to Jimmy. Not yet."

"You don't have to justify yourself to anyone, and certainly not to Jimmy. What happened between us is not based on dinner last night, not for me and not for you either." They were still standing on Gorham Street near the railroad overpass.

"I'm confused, Danny. What am I supposed to do? Jack and his family all but have me married into their family. And Jimmy had a fit because we had coffee together. And Nana Murphy's upset."

"Honey, Honey, Honey. Let's talk about me and you. Let's make things right for us before you worry about others."

"That's why I don't want to run into Jimmy. Let's go back to my house and talk."

"No. Not yet. Your grandmother would overshadow everything we say."

"She would never listen in on us. Never."

"I believe that. But I also believe that we need another place to talk."

"We're so busy trying to find out where to talk that we never get to talk." She was cold now and impatient.

"Let's just go back to the diner," he said. "It will be slow now and we can sit as long as we want if we keep buying coffee."

They turned back toward the church to get the car and drove to the diner. They parked across the street just as they had the first time Danny met her on her way home from the depot.

When they were seated in the nearly empty diner, she asked him about that first day. "Remember the first time we came here?"

"Of course I do," he said taking her hands in his.

"Did you really just happen to see me walking home that day?"

"I am a patient man. I wanted to see you alone from that first day I met you When you were still in high school. And I waited and waited. Then I couldn't wait any longer."

"But you didn't know me."

"I know you better than you imagine. Jimmy talked about you a lot." They continued to hold hands across the table. She felt the oiliness of the worn plastic surface on the backs of her hands. She stared at Danny's face loving how intensely his gaze was focused on her.

"Just the look of you that day at Frank's house," he continued, "the way you were with all of us. I think I fell in love with you that day. No. It wasn't an accident that I found you that day. I planned it and I was crazy thinking you might say no, and that would be the end of it."

"I almost did three times," she said.

"I know. That's why I," he paused and thought, "why I was more nervous than I've ever been in my life."

More nervous than he had ever been before in his life after all he's been through? Danny read her thoughts. "Honey Lee, by the time I got to the Pacific, I had already lost my brother and my mother. I didn't care whether I came back or not. After I was hurt, I cared less. Then I met you, and I began to care again."

Honey Lee's eyes filled with tears. She imagined his despair and was overwhelmed by his claim that she had the frightening power to make him want to live. How could she ever live up to what he was claiming for her?

"I don't know what to say, Danny."

"Shh…" he put his finger to her lips, "don't say anything."

She didn't and they sat in silence sipping coffee that had grown cool. After a while Danny said, "Tell me about you and Jack Flynn. I need to know. I'm not the kind of guy who goes after someone else's girl. But when I heard that you started college, I thought, I hoped, that you and he hadn't made plans. I mean, I thought if you were planning to marry, you wouldn't start college."

She thought about how to answer him. "I love the Flynns. At first it was Ellen. But I came to love the whole family. Then two years ago, I went up to New Hampshire to visit them, and I started to date Jack. Then I got him all mixed up with how I felt about the family. He says he loves me, wants to marry me some day. He asked me to take his fraternity pin. I said no, but I still dated him and thought that one day I would marry him."

Again neither of them spoke for some time.

"And?" Danny asked.

"And I'm supposed to go up for Winter Carnival next month, and I thought I would be saying yes to the pin."

Danny pursed his lips and blew out a long breath shaking his head. "And?"

"And now I have to write him. I can't go up there until I know what's going on with us."

"No, you can't. Even if we didn't work out, you couldn't go until you were certain."

"Danny?"

"What, Honey Lee?"

"How are you really?" She didn't know how to ask what she wanted to know. "What happened to you? I mean—"

"I'm fine Honey Lee. I was in bad shape for a while. Now I'm not."

"But you still have to go to the hospital."

"Just for a check-up. That's all. I'm OK Honey, really."

She wanted to know more but something in his voice warned her that he wasn't ready. She was satisfied for now. They had begun a long conversation that would go on for years and years. For now she would not press him for more. She could wait. The next day she would write to Jack and study for her last exam on Monday.

They sat for another hour each telling the other the things that lovers tell each other. Then, reluctantly left. When they got to Concord Street, Danny agreed to go into the house with her to say hello to Nana Murphy so he parked the car at the side of the house and walked with her to the back door. Honey Lee opened the door and called out to her grandmother.

"Nana, I'm home. Danny's here."

Her grandmother came from the sitting room into the kitchen where Honey Lee and Danny were standing next to the black iron stove warming themselves.

"Nana, this is Danny Jackson. You met him on Field Day."

"I well remember that I did," she said coming close to Danny and putting out her hand.

"I'd just as soon you forgot that day and let this be our first meeting, Mrs. Murphy. I'm glad to meet Honey Lee's grandmother." He took Mrs. Murphy's hand and bent down to better meet her gaze. Honey Lee watched her grand-mother closely to see how she was reacting. She noticed first of all how tiny her grandmother looked standing side Danny. She also noticed that Nana Murphy was stiff and formal in her greeting.

"Well then," she said, "how do you do, Daniel Jackson."

"I'm well, ma'am, and I hope you are too. I've brought your granddaughter home safe. I'd better be going."

Honey Lee had expected her grandmother to ask them to take off their coats, sit for a little while, maybe even have tea, but she didn't. Danny turned to Honey Lee and said he would call her the next day. She walked him to the door. He squeezed her hand and went out into the cold. Honey Lee watched at the door. She heard the thunk of the car door, the whirr of the engine, and the crunch of the tires on the icy road.

"I'm sorry, Nana. He wanted to go to the diner for coffee. A neutral place to talk."

"Yes, I suppose that felt better to him. His brother called twice looking for you. He's coming here. Soon. It's better that Danny is not here for that, isn't it?"

Honey Lee was stunned. No wonder Nana hadn't offered tea. "He's coming here?"

"Yes. He's determined to see you."

"Now?"

"The last call was just a wee bit ago, maybe a half hour."

"I've got to change." She ran from the room. Maybe Jimmy just wanted to tell her he was home and wanted to make plans with her. But if it was only that, why would he say he was coming to the house without being asked. She changed quickly into her navy blue school skirt and a gray sweater. She sat on the side of the bed trying to figure out what, if anything, she would say about Danny. If she saw Jimmy, she would have to tell him. She had never been secretive about anything with him. She crossed herself begging God for the right words, asking that Jimmy not be too angry. When she heard the front door bell ring, she called to her grandmother, "I'll get it," and ran quickly to the door. Jimmy stood on the porch.

Before she could say anything, he said, "Have you been seeing my brother?"

"Jimmy, come in." She reached out to him.

"Just yes or no, Honey Lee." He stood firm outside the door.

"Please, Jimmy."

"Then it's yes."

"How—?"

"Never mind how. I don't want an explanation." His voice was harsh. "I should never have introduced you to him. I could kill him."

He turned and ran down the stairs. Honey went out on to the porch and watched him run down the street. He'll never speak to me again she thought. She hugged herself as the wind chilled her.

CHAPTER 23

▼

Honey Lee went to her bedroom and closed the door. If only she could have told Jimmy that she would never stop being his friend. But his anger was icy, worse than she had imagined. Suddenly a terrible thought came to her with the force of truth. Jimmy Jackson is jealous of his brother. He wasn't protecting her from Danny. He was in love with her himself. How stupid, how really, really stupid she was. He had always been protective of her, sometimes possessive. He had tolerated Jack Flynn, often teasing her about her crush on her friend's big brother. He asked her out all the time she dated Jack, acting as if she weren't dating. If she was right about Jimmy, and she was now sure she was, mending her friendship with him would not happen soon if it happened at all. Jimmy would feel betrayed by Danny. "How stupid, stupid, stupid I have been," she groaned.

Dark with these thoughts, she sat on her bed until all light went from the sky. Her grandmother's soft knock pulled her out of herself. She rose slowly and went to the mirror to straighten her hair and wipe her eyes.

"Come in, Nana," she said without going to the door. Her grandmother came in and pushed some books on the bed out of the way.

She sat down and said, "Come sit by me, dear." Honey Lee stood still by the mirror, her head bowed. "He's gone off, then, hasn't he, the poor lad?"

"He loves me, Nana. How could I not have seen it?"

"Well, you haven't much experience of the difference between loving someone and being in love, have you?"

"But I should have known." She raised her head and looked at her grandmother. "Did you know, Nana?"

"I'd thought as much darlin'. But I couldn't be sure."

"He'll never forgive me or his brother."

Her grandmother patted the bed beside her so that Honey would sit down. "You don't know that, dear. Life is long, and unimaginable things happen. The good Lord has His ways of caring for all of us, for Jimmy, and for you and Daniel."

Honey Lee came across the room and sat on the bed beside her grandmother. "How do I know what God wants for me? How does anyone know?"

"Well, it seems to me that after you twist and turn, wonder and worry, there comes a quiet time when you know God's way for you." She pulled Honey Lee toward her and held her close.

After they had sat together in the darkness until Honey Lee stopped crying, Nana persuaded Honey Lee to come downstairs with her to eat. Although Honey Lee wasn't hungry, she agreed. The fragrance of her grandmother's beans did not entice her as it usually did. In fact her stomach lurched at the thought of eating. But she managed to eat enough to please her grandmother. After they washed and dried the dishes, Nana said, "Why not get your books darlin' and try to study a bit. It's well to get your mind off the Jacksons for now. Do you think you can?"

Anxious to be alone with her thoughts, Honey Lee nodded and went to get her books. She tried to study, but her mind raced. She kept listening for the telephone. Surely Jimmy would have arrived home by now. Would Danny call? She read the same page three times and remembered nothing. At ten o'clock, Nana Murphy came in to say good night. She kissed Honey Lee and said, "May God bless and keep you through this night." The familiar words felt more appropriate than ever before.

"And you too, Nana." Honey Lee waited up until eleven o'clock. Danny would not call later than that. She gathered up her books and climbed the stairs to her room.

At six o'clock the next morning, Honey Lee woke up and went downstairs to put water on for tea. She wasn't sure how early Danny would call, and she wanted to get the phone when it rang. The night had been long. She woke up several times thinking she had heard the phone. She had dreamed. In one dream, she was hiding from everyone under one of the piles of telephone poles on Perry Street. One by one, people came to find her. First her grandmother came and called. Then Jimmy, then Ellen, then Danny, Frank and Mary. She answered no one and they all left. She had covered her ears against all of the calls, but she heard a rumbling noise that got stronger and louder by the minute. A cable had snapped and the whole weight of the poles was coming down on her. Just as the bottom poles touched her chest threatening to crush her, she woke up.

Her grandmother came down at six-thirty, and seeing the teapot and cups, said, "Honey Lee Murphy. You know we do not have tea before Mass."

Honey Lee had forgotten all about morning fast before communion. She moved the kettle to the back of the stove and put away the cups she had taken out. At seven o'clock, the doorbell rang. Honey Lee looked at her grandmother. Was Aunt Kitty coming to go to Mass with them? Nana shook her head and shrugged. Honey Lee ran to the front of the house to open the door. Danny stood on the steps. He had not shaved, and he had an angry bruise on his jaw and a swelling near his left eye.

"Danny. You saw him, didn't you? And you fought." She didn't want to believe that such a thing could happen.

"I didn't fight. I would never raise my hand against Jimmy."

"Come in, come in, and get warm. I'll get ice for your eye."

She led him into the kitchen where Nana sat in her rocking chair.

When she looked at Danny and saw Honey Lee go to the icebox for ice, she got a towel and took the ice from Honey Lee. "Hold this against your eye. It looks worse than your jaw," she said. Danny thanked her and held the ice to his eye. She left the kitchen without saying anything.

"Can you talk about it?" She stood stiffly beside him, barely able to get the words out.

"I can tell you what you can guess by looking. He was crying, shouting terrible things, and swinging at me. I couldn't stop him. I tried to hold his arms, but he's strong, and he had been drinking." Honey Lee gasped.

"Drinking? Jimmy?"

"Yes, and a furious drunken man is an awesome sight, especially when it's your kid brother."

"I can't believe this, Danny," she said. "I can't."

"He wouldn't let me talk. When he finally calmed down, he stood in front of me and said, 'Lousy bastard, you lousy bastard.' And then he left." Danny spoke without looking at her. He stared straight ahead.

"Are you hurt anywhere else?" Honey Lee stood in front of him searching his face. When he didn't answer, she led him to her grandmother's rocker. He sat down, still holding the ice to his eye. Honey waited some more. Then she put the water for tea back on the front of the stove and took cups from the cupboard. She would drink comforting tea with him and skip communion for once. She poured the water over the leaves she had prepared earlier. Steam rose from the pot and sent tea fragrance into the room. After the tea had steeped she poured two cups and took one to Danny.

"Nana says tea makes everything better."

He took the cup with one hand, gave her the towel and ice, and bent his head over the tea. He breathed in deeply as if to find the promised comfort. He held the cup in two hands, but didn't drink.

"He's right, Honey Lee. I am a lousy bastard. And I'm ashamed, so ashamed."

She knelt on the floor beside his chair and put her hand on his arm. "You have nothing to be ashamed of. I'm sorry about Jimmy. I'm really sorry. But he'll forgive us in time. I know him, Danny."

"No. Never." He shook his head slowly from side to side. "He'll never forgive me. You won't either. Damn, damn, damn." He put his cup on the floor and bent forward, elbows on his knees and head in his hands.

"Forgive you for what? What are you talking about?" She tried to pry his hands from his face. She needed to see him. When he resisted, she sat back on her heels and said, "Danny, talk to me. Right now. What are you thinking?" She parsed the events of the weekend, trying to understand what had happened and how she could fix it.

When Nana Murphy came into the kitchen to see if they were going to nine o'clock Mass, they both stood up quickly like children caught doing wrong. Nana looked at the two teacups and at Honey Lee.

Nana said, "I'll be going off now. I'm thinking maybe you should go together to the late Mass. You seem to need the Lord's help today—both of you, and your brother, too, Daniel Jackson."

"Yes, Nana. The eleven o'clock."

Honey Lee was relieved when her grandmother left. She needed Danny to tell her that he still loved her, that he didn't regret loving her. They now stood facing each other.

"Danny, what are you thinking? What is it?" Her voice rose in panic. "Tell me."

"Jimmy loves you. He wanted to protect you. He failed." The three flat statements fell like hammer blows.

"You're not making sense, Danny."

"He was right. I should have left you alone. I should never have started with you. Jimmy knows that and he hates me. I hate myself. Damn. Damn." He turned away from her.

"What are you talking about?" She grabbed his sleeve and pulled at it to turn him towards her.

He faced her and said, "About the fact that I was married."

She could not take in his words. "Married?" He turned from her. She pulled on his sleeve again and forced him to face her. "Married? You?" She pounded on his chest with her fists. "Married? And you didn't tell me?"

He did nothing to stop her from hitting him again and again. "Yes, God forgive me. Yes."

Her heart stopped. She paced to the other side of the room moaning softly. She heard him behind her. "Don't. Don't come near me." She whirled around. "How could you do this? How could you?"

"Oh, my God. I can't explain. I hardly knew her. A month after I went to sea, she met someone else. She divorced me. And I didn't tell you, God forgive me."

"Go."

As if he hadn't heard her, he put his arms around her. She could feel his lips brush her hair. She trembled but refused to face him. She knew that the only person in the world who could comfort her was the one who had wounded her. When she turned, he looked down at her and took her face in his hands and kissed her. "I'm so sorry. I'll go."

As he turned from her, her heart rose up. She loved him. God help her. She loved him. How could she let him go? She could survive anything as long as he loved her. She took his hand and walked unsteadily from the kitchen into the living room to the couch. "Just sit here with me. Just for a minute."

The sun streamed through the window and spilled on to the couch turning the dull maroon fabric deep red. The cushions were warm from the sun. She turned her face to the sun and closed her eyes. Danny leaned toward her and kissed her forehead telling her again how sorry he was. She could hardly breathe. Her heart was so large in her chest that she thought it would break out like a strong bird.

"Can you feel my heart?" she asked putting his hand on her breast. "Can you feel how fast it's beating?"

He took her hand and moved it to his chest. She felt his heart keeping time with hers. Her breath stopped inside her until she finally gasped and released it. She wanted both of his hands on her breasts, both of his hands on her bare skin.

"No. I can't do this." She pulled away, frightened by how much she wanted him even as the voices of nuns and priests and her grandmother, especially the voice of her grandmother, drummed in her ears. "Why did you ever even speak to me?"

She ran from the room up the stairs to her bedroom. When she heard his car start, she almost ran to the window to call out to him. She could not tell whether she cried from rage or from grief. At eleven o'clock when Nana Murphy came back from church, she was still lying on her bed crying. She had missed the last Mass of the day. She didn't need to see her grandmother's face to know how gravely she had sinned. She knew her catechism. The first law of the Church compelled her, under the pain of mortal sin, "To assist at Mass on all Sundays and Holy Days of Obligation." Breaking that Church law was deeply serious, but it could be forgiven if she repented and resolved never to miss Mass again. But marrying Danny would cause her to break another Church law, the sixth Church commandment, "A Catholic can contract a true marriage only in the presence of an authorized priest and two witnesses." No priest would ever marry her and Danny because, according to the Church law, "the Sacrament of marriage lasts until the death of the husband or wife." Any marriage to him would be adulterous. It would keep her from the sacraments forever.

Nana knocked on her door and came in. "It's a bad beginning, if that's what it is, to miss Mass on a Sunday. You know better than that, Honey Lee."

"I'm sorry, Nana." She stood up so quickly that she felt dizzy.

"It isn't me that you should be saying I'm sorry to. It's your Father in Heaven, who asks so little of us, that you need to tell you're sorry."

"I know. I need to talk to Father Finn, Nana."

CHAPTER 24

▼

Her grandmother's disapproval weighed heavily on Honey Lee. She and her grandmother had always talked at the end of the day about school, about her friends, her worries, her joys. But they would never talk about Danny. To avoid time alone with her grandmother, in which his name would surely come up, she went to the closet to get her boots and coat, called to Nana that she was going out, and left. At the sight of the telephone poles on Perry Street, she shuddered remembering her dream and the time shortly after she came to Lowell, when she accepted a dare to crawl the full length of one of the piles. The smothering smell of creosote, the damp darkness, the bugs, and the sense of tons of weight above her held in place by two thin cables had terrified her. The long belly crawl caused panic in her such as she had never felt anywhere else until the night before, when it had surfaced in a dream while she slept safe in her own bed.

She needed to talk to Father Finn. About missing Mass, but more important about her and Danny. Father Finn would help her to find a way to be with Danny. There must be a way. She hurried down the street to the Church. The upstairs church was locked, so she went around to the entrance to the dark, empty lower church. At the front of the church, she knelt, blessed herself and raced through the ritual prayers, the *Our Father*, the *Hail Mary* and the *Glory Be*, paying no more attention to the words than she had to her French textbook earlier. She needed to slow down. Usually when she said these prayers, she meditated. She began to say the *Lord's Prayer* slowly. When she came to the phrase "Forgive us our trespasses," she stopped to number her trespasses. She had sinned terribly. She had abandoned God for a man, stayed with him rather than go to church. She had let him touch her impurely. Had she really put his hand on her breast after all she had been told about chastity? And worse still, she had done it knowing that he was a married man. She prayed the phrase again and again. Then she went on, "Lead us not into temptation, but deliver us from evil." Part of her resisted the words. If Danny was temptation and being with him was evil, did she really want to be delivered? Of course she did. "Holy Mary Mother of God, Pray for us sinners." She begged Mary to pray for her, to make her strong to do the right thing. When she had finished the ritual prayers, she began to pray passionately in her own words for Danny, for herself, for a solution for them. She then said what she hoped was a perfect Act of Contrition, sufficient for forgiveness if anything should happen to her before she was able to confess on the following Saturday.

She raised her head when she heard footsteps. Miraculously, Father Finn appeared. His long black cassock made a swishing sound as he came down the altar steps. At the bottom step, he knelt and bowed his head. When he turned toward her, his hand rested on the large crucifix tucked into the belt of his cassock. She was frightened. She was relieved.

"Well, Honey Murphy, what are you doing here alone on a Sunday afternoon?"

She stood up and said, "Father Finn, I was so hoping I'd see you. But I didn't think I really would."

He looked closely at her before he said, "It sounds serious, Honey Lee."

"Oh, Father, it is. Will you hear my confession? I need to confess. Right now."

"I will. I'll go get my stole. Go in and wait for me."

She went to the confessional, pushed the heavy green velvet curtain aside, entered and knelt waiting for him to come. She heard him open the door and close it behind him. He settled himself in the chair and opened the small window. She bent her head and began to say the familiar words, "Bless me father, for I have sinned. It has been one week and one day since my last confession." She had not only missed Mass but also her regular Saturday confession. Father Finn bowed his head and put his hand on his forehead.

When Honey Lee said nothing further, he spoke. "Well, what is it, dear?"

She began by telling him she had missed Mass that morning. He asked her to repeat what she had said. "What on earth kept a good girl like you from Holy Mass?"

"It's very long and complicated, Father." She had no idea how to begin.

"I'm in no hurry."

"I'm in love, Father." She tried not to cry.

"In love. Lots of people fall in love. But it makes most happy, and here you are crying."

"But it's all wrong, Father. I love him and he needs me, and I want to marry him but I can't."

"Can we slow down just a bit," he said gently. You're thinking of marriage?"

"Yes, Father, I was, but now I'm not, but I want to."

"What's the problem?" He was confused. "How can I help you?"

"I don't know, Father. I've known him for a long time, but I just found out today that I can't marry him."

"You can't marry him. And why is that?"

"He's married, Father, and divorced." She sobbed.

"And you just found that out today?"

"Yes, Father, this morning. That's why I didn't go to church."

"What a terrible thing for him to do to you, Honey Lee. He doesn't know you very well," he paused. "Or maybe he knows you too well."

"He knows me, Father. He's a good man. He respects me. He wants me to marry him and I want to. I really do, Father."

"This is very serious, Honey Lee."

"I know, Father."

"You have to stop seeing him. Now. You know that."

"Is it true that he can never marry again?"

"Not without committing such grave sin that he would be excommunicated."

"That's hard, Father. Unfair."

"God expects us to do hard things, to take up our crosses and follow Him. This man's marriage is his cross."

"And mine, too."

"Yes, maybe so."

There was a long pause as if Father Finn were waiting for her to say something more.

"Should I make my act of contrition now?"

"Yes, and for your penance say your rosary every night and ask God to help you fight temptation."

"Thank you, Father," Honey Lee said and rose quickly so she could leave before he came out of the confessional.

She went over to High Street, which she always did when she needed cheering. Fayette Street still frightened and depressed her. Tonight it would be even worse. She would pass by Danny's old home. But after walking the first long block on High Street, she turned back toward Fayette because she knew that continuing on High Street would take her by the Flynns' house. She wasn't ready to meet the Flynns just yet. It was over between her and Jack. She walked slowly toward home.

Nana Murphy's home, her own home, was no longer the place of refuge and comfort it always had been. She had always brought her troubles to her grandmother and been comforted. But if Nana Murphy learned that Danny had been married, she would be hard set against him. How she had longed to tell her grandmother about the great love that grew in her. How she had wanted to celebrate with her. At the wedding on Saturday, she had pictured Nana watching her get married. But Nana would never celebrate and rejoice at a wedding for her and Danny. She began to cry again and walk as slowly as she could to delay arriving home. When she finally reached the house she hesitated and tried to go quietly in and up to her room.

"I'm in the kitchen, darlin'. Come in."

Honey Lee shrugged and went toward the kitchen slightly sickened by the smell of Sunday dinner—pot roast with potatoes and onions and carrots, one of her favorite meals. Before she reached the kitchen, she realized that Nana was not alone. At first she didn't get the other voice, but then she recognized it as Aunt Kitty's. She and Nana were speaking in hushed tones. Honey Lee went in and greeted her aunt and her grandmother.

"I thought it would be nice to have Aunt Kitty to dinner with us, dear" her grandmother said. It wasn't at all nice, but Honey Lee smiled and asked her aunt if Cousin Peter and Uncle Peter were coming.

"No, they're busy with men things today." Aunt Kitty said.

Aunt Kitty rarely came to dinner anymore and never without her husband and her son. If Uncle Peter didn't want to come, which mostly he didn't, Aunt Kitty didn't come. Aunt Kitty was there for a reason—to talk to Honey Lee about Danny Jackson, and she would have to listen. Uncle Peter was to serve as an object lesson on why Honey Lee should abandon Danny. Her aunt's face showed the stress her husband's return had caused. She looked older and sadder than when she had lived with Nana Murphy. Honey Lee had only seen Uncle Peter a few times since he had come home. Twice when she had seen him coming out of Terry's, the bar on lower Concord Street, she had been about to greet him until she saw that he had no idea who she was. He had looked sullen and angry. She had hurried past him her nose wrinkling at the smell of stale beer and cigarettes that followed him out of the bar. Young Peter wished his father had never come home because he made his mother so sad. Yes, Aunt Kitty had been summoned to warn Honey Lee about marriage to a veteran.

The table was already set so they sat down as soon as Honey Lee had embraced her aunt and grandmother. The meal tasted dry. Honey Lee talked and talked trying to avoid what was coming. She described in detail each of her exams and how she felt she had done on each; she talked about how much more studying she had to do for French; she talked about the weather and the food.

"Honey, darlin'. Shh," her grandmother finally said putting her finger to her lips. "Your tongue is racing away with you."

"I'm sorry. How is Uncle Peter, Aunt Kitty?"

"Much the same. He's not his old self at all."

"I'm so sorry, Aunt Kitty."

"Hospitals are filled with soldiers much like him. Some will never come home. Sometimes I worry that your uncle will have to go back to such a place." It was news to Honey Lee that her uncle had been in a hospital before he came home. "He will, if he gets any worse."

"Aunt Kitty, I—"

Her grandmother spoke sharply. "Honey Lee, listen. Don't interrupt."

"But I—" Nana shook her head in warning.

Kitty raised her voice and talked on. "He wakes from terrible dreams, sometimes with his hands around my neck swearing that he will kill me. He thinks I'm a German soldier. You would not believe the language he carries in him. Then he cries like a baby. One night young Peter came into our room and hit his father. Can you imagine it? I was terrified that his father would kill him. He can't understand. And what I'm telling you is only the once-in-a-while part of it. Your uncle was a fine laughing man before. I loved him for the joy in him. He always had a joke or a long tale to tell or a song to sing. And how he'd dance. I couldn't keep up with him. I was so thrilled when Peter Rourke asked me to marry him. We were so happy." Aunt Kitty wiped tears from her eyes.

Honey Lee had never heard her aunt speak so much. She had also never seen her cry. She went to her aunt put her arms around her. "I'm sorry, Aunt Kitty. I'm so sorry."

Kitty wiped at the tears of her face then sat quietly with her hands in her lap. "Honey," she finally said, "my mother asked me to tell you this because she thinks you are being reckless about poor Danny Jackson. It's not for us to say that Danny is like your uncle, but there are stories about him. He was half dead when they found him tied to a damaged lifeboat somewhere in the Pacific, not one of his shipmates near him. He couldn't talk, he didn't even know who he was. He had been alone in that terrible way for almost a week."

Shocked, Honey Lee saw Danny—alone, terrified, nearly dead. She wanted run to him. She wanted now more than ever to be with Danny. But her Aunt wasn't finished.

"You need to think seriously about what that can do to a man. We both love you, and we don't want you to go through the pain of trying to fix something that can't be fixed. You can't erase that kind of suffering."

Honey sat quietly. When her aunt had finished, she swallowed twice and wiped her eyes with the backs of her hands. Anger and grief struggled for expression. "How well you've made me see his suffering and imagine his pain. My heart is heavy with the knowledge. But I didn't need the lesson. Danny is gone. He won't be back."

She left the kitchen and went to her room. She would not answer their questions.

When she was alone, vivid images of the Danny her aunt had described ran like film through her head. Even before his ship had been hit, he hadn't cared whether he lived or died. Now she knew that he had even more reasons to despair than she had known—his mother dead, his brother gone, his wife's betrayal. And yet he had survived. He had clung to a diminished life. How could she abandon him? She had given him reason to live again. She couldn't take that away. What would he do? She had responded to his desperation without understanding. She was now the lifeboat he was clinging to. But his church, the church she loved, denied him happiness with her. She lay for a long time on her bed, grieving for Danny at one moment, furious with him the next, hoping never to lay eyes on him again one minute and wanting desperately to call him the next.

She resolved to put her mind to work on something else. The French Exam. She would try again to study for the exam. But when she went to her desk she realized that her books were in the kitchen. She didn't want to go down to get them. No doubt Aunt Kitty and Nana were still sitting there over tea, She would have to find something else. She looked down at the desk and saw a version of the letter she had tried to write to Jack Flynn. In the wastebasket near the desk were others. She pulled the wrinkled papers out of the basket and smoothed them out. It seemed like years had gone by since she had agonized over writing them. How stupid her attempts seemed now:

"Dear Jack"

"Jack, I feel terrible"

"Jack, I cannot come to Winter Carnival"

"Dear Jack, I was right not to take your fraternity pin. I only realized this"

"Dear Jack, Just this week I realized that I was right not to take your fraternity pin. I also know that I cannot come up to Winter Carnival. You must believe that I am as surprised as you will be that I have come to love someone else. I promise you that I did not look for this to happen"

She tore them all up. Writing to Jack Flynn had been daunting. She had tried to find the words she needed, wondering if any words could do such difficult work. She imagined his kind face—puzzled by a letter written one way, stunned by another, or hurt, or angry. Finally it hadn't mattered at all what she wrote or how she worded it. There was no right way to tell him in a letter. During the war people called such letters "Dear John" letters. She had always considered the girls who wrote them cruel and selfish. War or no war, the letter she had been trying to write was a "Dear John" letter. Writing it made her feel small and guilty. She had decided that the decent thing to do was to see Jack and tell him face-to-face. In a funny way, the last few hours made telling Jack about Danny unnecessary. She could, peacefully, go on as she had before as if Danny had never happened. That way she would at least keep some friends. But she knew that was nonsense. Even with Danny out of the picture, she couldn't go back. Loving Danny had shown her that as much as she loved Jack she had never been in love with him. Yet she had agonized for days over telling Jack Flynn that she would not see him anymore. How odd that she had sent Danny away with a few harsh words. Poor Danny.

She went downstairs to get her books. Her grandmother and Aunt Kitty were washing up the dinner dishes. Honey Lee picked up her books and excused herself quickly. Back in her room she disciplined herself to study. On Tuesday she would do whatever had to be done about her life. She sat on the bed and opened the French conversation book. At ten o'clock, she went to bed without saying good night to her grandmother.

CHAPTER 25

▼

On Monday morning, Honey Lee woke up at six o'clock exhausted from a restless sleep. She dressed quickly, had a cup of tea with her grandmother, who said nothing about the night before, and walked to the depot. Her grandmother had been tactful. As she walked to the station, she conjugated French verbs, memorized the gender of as many nouns as she could think of, and recalled story lines and character names from the French books she had read. When she arrived at the depot, Danny was standing on the sidewalk, still magnificent, even in his work clothes. She wanted to reach up and brush his hair back from his forehead.

"I was hoping you'd get this train. I had just time enough before work. We need to talk. We can't just—" His voice broke.

"I know." She leaned toward him but did not take the hand he held out to her.

"When are you coming back?" He brushed his hair back just as she had wanted to do.

"Two o'clock. I think."

"I'll be here. Wait for me if I'm not. I have to see you." He turned and walked away.

For four days they had seen each other every day. She had hoped to keep that pattern forever. And he had led her to believe that she could. Or did he? She tried to remember every word Danny had said to her, wondering if she had missed clues. Maybe he had tried to tell her and she had made it impossible. After failing to get her mind back on French grammar, her thoughts turned to Jimmy and then to Jack. She and Danny were alike. She, too, should have been more careful. She thought of Jack's gentleness and patience. How careful you had to be with people who loved you. She knew this, yet she was carelessly dealing hurt to the people she loved and who loved her. And so had Danny. How could he have kept such a secret?

When her train pulled into North Station, she gathered up her books and went through the station to the T stop across the street. The car, when it came, was crowded with other commuters. After Park Street she would easily find a seat. Several men in Navy uniforms got on the train at Scollay Square. They had probably been out all night, Honey Lee thought, remembering all she had heard about Scollay Square.

One of them smiled at her and said, "Hey beautiful, can I go with you wherever you're going?"

She moved away. When the car emptied, she found a single seat. The car filled up quickly and the train passed out of the station. She arrived at school early for her exam, but she went directly to the assigned room. A few students she recognized from class nodded and waved. She jumped when she heard a voice behind her say,

"Es que vous etes prete?"

She turned to see a student she had noticed a few times in class. He was older than most of the other students. She laughed and answered in French that she hoped she was. He sat down beside her and asked why she always ran off after class. She told him that she commuted and had to rush for a train.

"You are very good in French." She shook her head refusing the compliment. "Professor Martine obviously thinks so."

"I had a great high school teacher. I was going to…I'm thinking of majoring in French."

"Me too," he said taking the seat beside hers. "I want to go back to France and really see it. All I ever saw was ruined villages and torn up farm land."

"You were in France? During the war?"

"Yeah, there and Germany."

"And still you want to go back?"

"I didn't see Paris. They say there is nothing like it in the world."

More students filed in just ahead of Monsieur, who went to the front of the room and told them to put away all books and papers. He passed out blue books and the two-page exam. Honey Lee read through the exam quickly and smiled. She would have no trouble with this one. She began to write quickly and confidently finishing well before the hour and a half was up. She reread what she had written, and satisfied, went to the desk at the front of the room with her blue book.

Professor Martine looked up and smiled at her. "That easy, was it?"

"I studied all the right things." She handed him her exam.

"I'll be looking for you next semester."

"Thank you. It was a great course."

She left the room and started down the corridor. She heard running steps behind her and a voice called out. "Hey there. Wait up."

She turned and saw the student who had sat near her in the exam room. He was a tall thin man, too thin like Danny, but blond and blue-eyed with close-cropped hair. Just under his right eye, she noticed a scar, a fairly recent scar. Still pink and puckered, clearly not the result of a childhood fall from a bike or a swing.

"Do you have time today for a cup of coffee or something?"

"No," she said. "I have to get back." He walked beside her out of the building toward the trolley stop.

"Back to?"

"Lowell."

"North Station?" She nodded. "Then I'll just ride with you to Copley. If you don't mind. I'm going to the library."

They waited for about ten minutes for the train to come. He introduced himself and told her he was in his second year on the GI Bill, "The only good thing that came out of the war." When they got on the train and were almost to Copley Square, he asked her for her phone number. "Maybe we could go out to a nice French restaurant and taste some of that fine French cuisine Martine talks about all the time."

Honey Lee laughed, and said she couldn't.

"Someone else, huh?" He looked disappointed.

"Yes, also a veteran." The words caught in her throat.

"Are you OK?" He reached out to touch her, but she moved closer to the window.

"Yes. I'm fine," she said, trying to smile.

When he got off at Copley, she watched him walk down the platform. He turned and waved. She waved back. When the train pulled into Park Street, she got off. She had plenty of time before the two o'clock train, and she didn't want to sit in the waiting room. She took the Red Line to South Station to see how well she remembered it. When she came up from the subway stop into the main waiting room, she saw a man with no legs sitting in a wheel chair. He held a sign, *Wounded Vet* and an army cap into which people were dropping coins. Honey

Lee fumbled in her pocket to find a quarter. He smiled mockingly. "How about a dance, sweetie."

She rushed past him into the hall. The big clock she had sat under four years before was still there. The station was busier and bigger than North Station, but not as busy as it had been four years before. There were very few men in uniform. She wandered around looking at the times of departure and the destinations posted at the track gates. Any of the trains going to New York or Washington could be headed for Georgia, via Virginia and the Carolinas. What if I just got on a train like she did and went south? It would be much easier than going back to Lowell to clean up her messes. She still had to see Jack. She needed to find Jimmy and tell him she and Danny were finished.

There was also mending to do with Nana. Her brusque responses had hurt and puzzled her grandmother. That her grandmother had not even come in to say good night to her, told Honey Lee how hurt and troubled she was. And then there was Danny, who was waiting for her at the station. She had to greet him somehow. But how? You don't shake hands with a man you were thinking about marrying only a day or two before. You don't dare to let him touch you or all your resolve will crumble. She could pretend that he was no more to her than the veteran who spoke to her after the exam. It would be so much easier to hop a train and head south.

She wondered how often her mother thought about her. Probably as little as she thought about her mother. She shook her head and hurried out of the station to walk to North Station. It couldn't be much of a walk; the cab ride with her mother had been very short. She arrived for the two o'clock train with time to spare. She sat alone trying not to think, but when the train stopped in North Billerica, she thought again about getting off and running away. With no French exam to distract her, she thought about Danny, and she shook with anger. He had lied to her without using words. Even Jimmy had only hinted at what he should have told her. What good was it saying, "Stay away from him. He's bad news."? He should have told her that Danny was married.

Anger was hard for Honey Lee to sustain. When Danny's face rose up in her mind, she saw sorrow in his eyes. She thought about what her aunt had told her about his days alone on a dangerous sea. Surely he had been in pain for a long time. The Navy doesn't keep a person in the hospital for almost a year for no reason. She could have helped heal his wounds from battle. But not from a wife, not from a divorce. Before Danny, she had never met a divorced person. She used to think that such a person would look different, that divorce would leave a mark of some kind. Obviously, it didn't. She wondered about the wife. How could she have left him for someone else? Danny must have loved her.

She questioned herself about why she had given her love so freely. One reason was her response to his suffering. But it was much more than that. She loved everything about him. The way he talked, the way he pushed his hair back from his forehead, his long thin fingers resting on the steering wheel, the way he looked at her. She loved walking with him, her own long legs almost matching his stride. She hadn't felt so safe and happy since she had walked with her father. And she had to let him go. The train approached the station. He would be there waiting.

"We have to talk," he had said. But there was nothing to talk about, nothing would change what she had to do. She was crazy to have agreed to meet him. She listened to the chuff of the train slowing down. From her window she saw him standing on the platform, hands in his pockets, eyes scanning the train windows looking for her. She pulled back into the aisle so he wouldn't see her. She prayed for strength to do the right thing.

When he saw her at the door of the train, he rushed forward and grasped her elbow as she came down the stairs. Seeing him and feeling his hands on her made her tremble. She stared at him and said, "Thank you."

"How are you?"

"I'm fine," she said. But she wasn't.

"Oh Honey Lee, don't. Don't cry," he said trying to lead her away from the platform where a few other passengers were still standing. She couldn't move. Finally she whispered. Danny leaned closer to better hear her.

"I need to go home."

"Yes, yes. All right. We'll go right now." He guided her to his car as one guides a blind person. Her movements were jerky. "Talk to me. Please, Honey, talk to me." He opened the door for her and smoothed her coat over her legs so he could close the door. He drove carefully. She neither looked at him nor spoke all the way home, and not when he helped her out of the car and up the stairs. He rang the bell.

Nana Murphy came to the door. Alarmed at her granddaughter's appearance, she said, "What in God's name is wrong? Come in, dear, come in."

Honey Lee began to cry. Danny looked on helplessly as Nana led her to a chair taking her coat and scarf.

"I'll be getting her some tea. Stay with her, Daniel." He knelt on the floor beside her chair. When her whole body jerked, he leaned back but stayed by the chair.

"Go. Now," she said.

"Not until your grandmother comes back."

From the kitchen, they heard the chatter of cups against saucers and the thump of the kettle as Nana put it back on the iron stove. She wanted her grandmother to hurry, wondered why she was so slow. When she finally looked at Danny, she saw pain in his eyes and pleading as well. If she kept looking at him, she would get up and follow him wherever he wanted her to go. She turned toward the kitchen willing her grandmother to come back. At last she came with three cups and saucers and the tea. She set it down on the table near Honey Lee.

"Sit down, Danny Jackson, and tell me what's going on."

Honey Lee made a soft moaning sound. Danny waited for her to look at him, but she wouldn't. He stood up and said, "Thank you Mrs. Murphy, I'd better go. Good-bye Honey Lee. Good-by Mrs. Murphy."

At the door, he waited for some sign from Honey Lee. When he got none, he opened the door and left. Danny was gone, really gone.

"Oh, darlin', I never meant for you to be like this. I should never have asked Kitty to come. You've as much sense as she does. If you really love him…"

"No, Nana. It's over. I am not going to see him ever again. I can't."

"Because of me and Kitty?" Nana's voice was full of regret and worry.

"It doesn't matter why. I can't talk about it. I'm tired, Nana. I'm so tired."

Honey Lee sipped at her tea then put the cup down and rested her head against the back of the chair. They sat together as the room darkened. When the phone rang, both of them jumped. Honey Lee begged her grandmother to tell whoever it was that she wasn't at home. She couldn't think of anyone in the world she wanted to talk to. She listened to her grandmother tell the caller that Honey wasn't home and wouldn't be back early. Honey didn't even ask her grandmother who it was. Instead she asked if it would be all right if she went to bed and didn't eat supper.

"Of course, darlin'. Let me help you get tucked in. In the morning things will be better."

They climbed the stairs together. While her grandmother turned down the bed and plumped the pillows, Honey Lee undressed and put on her warm pajamas. When she was settled in bed, Nana Murphy brushed her hair back from her face and kissed her. She sat down on the side of the bed.

"I'll just sit here a bit with you."

Honey put out her hand. Nana Murphy took it in both of hers.

"It's all right dear. Go to sleep. I'll be asking the good Lord to bless you. You're a dear good girl."

Eventually she slept. She slept through the evening, through the night, and into morning.

CHAPTER 26

▼

When she woke up in the morning, her eyes were swollen almost shut. Her body felt as if lead had been pumped into her veins. She pulled the covers up over her head and tried to go back to sleep. She heard her grandmother come quietly to the door. She tried not to breathe so Nana Murphy wouldn't know she was awake. She wasn't ready to talk until she figured out how she could go on as if nothing had happened, how she could prepare a face and a story for her grand-mother. She needed time. She lay still on her back with the covers pulled over her face. Tears gathered in her eyes and fell as if they would never stop. When Nana Murphy came back again and knocked softly, she wanted to ignore her but she couldn't.

"Yes?"

"Won't you have a bite to eat?" Her grandmother pleaded.

She didn't want to speak or to move, but she said, "I'll be down in a little while, Nana."

"Will I bring you up a cup of tea?"

"No, Nana. I'll come down after I take a bath." She had to get up. Nana wouldn't stop worrying and fussing until she did.

She pushed the covers back, wiped her eyes with the sleeve of her pajama top, and stood up. She walked slowly down the long hall to the bathroom. The wood floor was cold on her bare feet. She was cold all over. She turned the hot water on full and stood near the tub in the steam trying to get warm, but even when she climbed into the hot water she shivered with cold. She leaned her head against the cold white porcelain and closed her eyes.

"I've lost the only man in the world I will ever love." She spoke out loud hoping to begin the long process of renunciation. As the water cooled, she shivered again and added more hot water, but there was not enough water in the world to warm her. So she got out of the tub and rubbed herself with the thick white towel, stiff from laundering. It made her skin sting. She scolded herself. "All right, all right. Now I'll get dressed. I'll eat. I'll smile. I'll go for a long walk. Then I'll be able to sleep again."

She dressed in a warm sweater and wool pants. In the kitchen, her grandmother had set a breakfast place for her. She had trouble swallowing the soft-boiled egg and toast but managed to finish it. Her grandmother's face spoke her concern. Apparently she was willing to wait until Honey Lee chose to talk. Honey Lee was not ready. She told her grandmother she was going out for a long walk to clear her head and promised to be home for supper.

"Your friend Ellen called again this morning, dear. Wouldn't it make you feel better to talk to her?"

"Not now, Nana. I'll call her later."

Honey Lee stepped out into the frigid morning air. She breathed in deeply. The moisture on the inside of her nose froze. She planned her walk carefully so she wouldn't run into anyone she knew. She climbed the hill to Nesmith Street and went over to Andover. Andover Street as it headed out of town was a broad street lined with large homes. Two girls she knew from school lived on the street, but she didn't know where. The big houses had always intrigued her. Mill owners had built and lived in these houses years before. Her grandmother's people had worked for their owners both in the mills and in their houses as servants.

Trying to keep her mind centered on the houses and their owners failed. She couldn't keep Danny out of her thoughts anymore than she could cut him out of her heart. She cut across Wentworth Avenue to Shedd Park. Her face felt stiff with cold, but she was walking so briskly that her body was comfortable. When she heard a car slow down behind, she ignored it until the driver beeped the horn. Then she jumped. Her first thought and strong hope was that Danny had found her, but when she turned she saw that it was Ellen. Her heart sank.

"Hello, hello, Greta Garbo," Ellen called reaching over the passenger seat to roll the window down. "I've been calling you."

"I know. I'm sorry. I was going to call you when I got back."

"Hop in. It's freezing out." She opened the car door. "Let's go get some hot chocolate."

Honey Lee couldn't refuse. She unwound her long red scarf and took off her hat and mittens. The car was warm. She turned to Ellen and asked, "When did you get home?"

"Yesterday. I called you as soon as I got in." Ellen bubbled over with news and questions as she drove to the Epicure. The lunch hour was over and the high school crowd hadn't arrived yet, so the restaurant was more quiet than usual. They sat in a booth near the back. Honey Lee looked at Ellen's familiar face and thought how wonderful it would be if she could only talk to her as a best friend without a brother, talk about Danny, about how sad she was. But she felt guilty and ill at ease with Ellen knowing that soon she would be telling Jack, Ellen's favorite brother, that she was breaking up with him. Ellen was so glad to see her friend that she seemed not to notice how quiet and subdued Honey Lee was. She told Honey Lee about her exams, about a new boy she was dating, and about her new dorm mates for the next semester.

The shift to Jack in Ellen's monologue was sudden. "Jack's coming home on Friday. I'll bet you can't wait. We should do something together. I'll find a loose male, maybe my old stand-by, Jimmy."

Honey Lee didn't know what to say. She asked what time Jack was coming and asked Ellen to have him call her.

Ellen laughed. "As if I had to tell him to call you. But I just hope you are there when he calls. And if you're not that you'll call him back."

"I will, Ellen. I will."

The next few days dragged by. Honey Lee had nothing to help her pass the time except reading. Her exams were over, she had no reading lists for second semester, she had no job. She dreaded hearing from Jack so much that she avoided Ellen even refusing an invitation to the Flynns' for dinner. Aunt Kitty called to apologize for being so blunt and pessimistic about Danny. Apparently, Nana Murphy had spoken to her. She didn't hear from any of the Jacksons. She wondered about Jimmy. Where would he be? Maybe at Frank and Mary's, but surely not with Danny.

She was so lonely that she invited her cousin Peter to go to the movies with her on Thursday after school. He was delighted telling her she was absolutely the best date he ever had. They went to the Epicure after the movies. When Honey Lee asked Peter about his father, the boy cursed softly.

"I hate him. I wish he'd go away. I hate it when he makes my mother cry. I hate him."

Honey Lee pitied him. He had lost a father as much as she had. Maybe it was even worse for him. When they got up to leave and went to the door, Jimmy Jackson was just coming in with two boys she didn't know. Her heart pounded.

"Hi," she said unable to find more words.

For a few seconds he didn't speak. He looked at her as if she were someone else, someone he didn't recognize.

"How are you?" he asked in a stranger's voice. He pulled his cap off and shifted it from hand to hand.

"OK."

He turned to his friends and said, "Hey fellows, give me a second here, will you? I'll catch up."

The two friends went on into the restaurant, and Peter walked a few paces down Central Street to wait for Honey Lee. She studied Jimmy's face to find some sign of affection. There was none. She became angry. "You should have told me. He should have told me. How could you not tell me?" She swallowed hard three times.

"I warned you, Honey, but you went ahead and did what you wanted." She could see how unhappy he was. Suddenly she wasn't angry anymore.

"It's not your fault. Maybe not his either."

"It is his fault." He paused, then added. "And mine too. But he had no right to date you."

"He's paying for it, Jimmy."

"And so are you. I can't forgive him for hurting you."

"I'll be all right."

He reached out and hugged her close to him. Relief flooded through her. He was still her friend. "How is he Jimmy?"

Whatever warmth there had been died. Jimmy's voice rose and he stabbed the air with his finger with each word. "Forget him, Honey Lee. Just erase him. End. Done. Gone. Finished."

Without saying good-bye, he stormed into the restaurant.

"What's the matter with him?" Peter asked when she caught up to him.

"Just a disagreement," she said walking quickly away from the restaurant.

"Mom said you were seeing his brother."

"I was. Now I'm not." She was impatient. "Hurry up, Peter."

"I think you and Jimmy should be together."

"We're friends, Peter. Just friends."

"Like Jack Flynn?" She felt as if he were accusing her of all the things she blamed herself for.

"Enough questions," she snapped. "What are you, a detective? Mind your own business."

She walked faster wanting to be home alone in her room. When she got home, she called out, "Nana, I'm home." Nana told her that supper would be ready in ten minutes and that Jack Flynn had called. Jack must have come home a day early. He would want to see her as soon as he could, and she couldn't think of a way to put him off. Well, sooner was better than later, she thought and planned to call him after dinner. But when Nana and she were only half way through eating, the doorbell rang.

"I'll get it," Honey Lee said. She went to the door half hoping it would be Danny. Her heart raced. When she opened the door, Jack rushed in, put his arms around her, and picked her up. "Am I ever glad to see you!"

"Jack, put me down. I'm too old for this."

"But not for this," he said leaning forward for a kiss. She put her hands against his chest to prevent the kiss.

"Come on in. We're almost finished eating."

He followed her into the kitchen, shook hands with Nana Murphy, asked how she was and sat down in the chair Honey Lee pulled out for him. His face was bright with happiness. She couldn't bear to look at it. She busied herself with clearing the table and bringing back bread pudding with three plates.

"Honey Lee, you're as quiet as a grave," Jack said laughing at his choice of words.

"I'm sorry," she said. "Let's eat and then talk."

Jack looked surprised at Honey Lee's tone but said nothing. Nana Murphy was also quiet. Honey Lee could hear them both chewing. She wished he hadn't come before she'd had time to prepare him. When he finally put his spoon down, she asked her grandmother to excuse them, and led Jack into the living room where she sat in her grandmother's chair instead of on the couch where she usually sat with him. She had sat with Danny on the couch just days before. Was it really only four days ago?

"A penny for—"

She interrupted him. "Jack, I'm sorry."

Puzzled, he said, "What on earth for?"

"I don't want to see you anymore. It's over."

In one swift minute he was at her side. "What in hell are you talking about?"

She put up her hands warning him not to touch her. "I'm trying to tell you that it's over between us." She could hardly bear the look on his face. "It's over."

"For God's sake, Honey, why?"

"Don't ask," she begged. "Please, Jack."

"Great, Honey Lee. The girl I've loved for years and who I thought loved me says she can't see me anymore. So I'm supposed to just pick up my hat and walk out the door without an explanation?"

"Don't Jack," she said putting her hands over her face.

"Don't what? I'm not going until I understand. You owe me that."

"I owe you so much more than that." She glanced up at him but immediately looked away. His face hurt her heart.

"Is it someone else?"

"No. Yes. No."

"That's helpful. But I'll take it for a yes. But I want answers. Let me get this right. I go off to school. I write to you every week. You write back every week. But you're going out on the town with some one else. Is that it?" His voice rose in anger. Honey Lee flinched. He turned away from her then wheeled around and barked, "Who is it, Honey? Jimmy Jackson? He's been mooning over you for years. Did you finally notice?" Anger was making him cruel.

"It doesn't matter who, Jack." She wanted to be any place but in this room with him.

"Damn it all, Honey, I was so sure we would get engaged this winter. I had everything planned—engagement, wedding, house, kids." He stopped genuinely puzzled. "How could I have been so wrong?"

"You weren't wrong. That's what I thought too. It was what I wanted. Then everything changed." She told herself that she deserved whatever anger he wanted to express.

"What changed everything, Honey Lee? Do tell."

"Danny Jackson." She whispered his name.

"Danny Jackson. The war hero. The big brother?"

"Yes."

"What's the no part of no-yes-no?"

"I'm not seeing him anymore. He's divorced." She looked down at her hands in her lap. "I didn't know when I fell in love with him."

"You fell in love."

"Isn't this enough talk, Jack?" She wanted him to leave "More won't change anything."

"So this big war hero courts you and you fall in love with him. Then he tells you he was married. What a prince." He shook his head. "Unbelievable."

"You don't choose falling in love. It just happens. It was the first time I was ever in love." The moment she spoke the words she wanted to take them back.

"Thanks."

"I've always loved you. I still do, but I'm not in love with you. I didn't know that until Danny. Please try to forgive me."

"Maybe some day. Not now. Are you sure about this? I'll never ask again."

"I'm sure."

"I loved you so much," he said and left.

Honey Lee sat down and reached up to put out the lamp beside her. She heard his car pull away. She had just lost her second family. It would take them a long time, maybe forever, to forgive her for hurting Jack. And she knew too well how much Jack hurt, crushed as she was by her own grief.

Once again the world had become a dark and miserable place. Except for her grandmother she was alone in the world. She went up the front stairs to her bedroom and closed the door. Without undressing, she got into the bed and pulled the covers over her head. She didn't answer when Nana Murphy came. She wanted only to sleep for a long, long time. But she couldn't close out faces of the people she loved: Jack's face, surprised, angry, and sad; Jimmy's furious face and stabbing finger; and Danny's eyes so full of grief it almost broke her heart. She lay still, her eyes open listening to the chimes of the Windsor clock. She had no idea how many hours and quarter hours passed before she slept.

CHAPTER 27

$$\blacktriangledown$$

When she woke up on Friday morning, she thought about the two weeks she had to get through before classes started and knew she had to find something to do to pass the time. She decided to look for work. She could work for the two weeks and then keep a part time job after school started. But jobs in Lowell were scarce. After the Christmas rush many workers in the downtown stores had been laid off. Remington and General Electric had closed down after the war and most of the mills were still closed. She was too old for baby-sitting. There was nothing for her in Lowell. She decided she would go into Boston to the student affairs office and see if they had any jobs on campus. Even if she found nothing, going into Boston would use up one day when she wouldn't have to sit around wondering what to do with herself. She got out of bed and dressed. Just in case she would get an interview, she decided to wear her best plaid skirt and white sweater. She would need her long coat and boots. Having a purpose gave her energy. When she came downstairs, Nana looked at her and smiled.

"You're feeling better then, are you?"

"Yes, Nana." She kissed her grandmother good morning and said, "I'm going to Boston to look for a job."

Nana bent her head to one side and said, "All the way to Boston for a job?"

"I want to work part time when I go back to school."

"You've no need to darlin'."

"I know. But I want to help out."

They ate breakfast together almost as comfortably as they used to. Honey Lee rushed to catch the nine o'clock train. It was less crowded than the earlier train she usually took. She found a seat alone and settled in listening to the rhythmic sound of metal wheels on metal track. She let her mind go blank as the train sped through the small towns on the way to Boston. Once in Boston, she walked from the North Station to BU, a long walk through streets she didn't know well, but it used up time. She passed through Scollay Square with its many bars and night-clubs and then up the back of Beacon Hill to the Boston Common.

The snow banks had melted a little, but she had lived in the area long enough to know that the back of winter would not easily be broken. The dome of the State House gleamed in the sunlight against the deep blue sky. For four years, the dome had been painted dull black to protect it from German bombers that never came. She walked down Beacon Street past the Common and the Public Gardens and crossed over to Commonwealth Avenue, a broad street with a center island, designed to be a continuation of the Public Gardens. Bare trees and an occasional patch of brown grass gave only a hint of parkland. The seats of the benches along the path were almost buried in snow. She made a promise to walk the route in spring, to spend more time in Boston during the next semester, maybe try to get to know some students.

The campus, like the parks, was dead. Several of the buildings were closed and there were no students on the walkways. She was lucky in her job search. The library needed full time help for two weeks setting up reserve shelves and cata-loguing books. The librarian promised to keep her on part time when classes began if she was a good worker. She could begin on Monday.

On Saturday afternoon, Honey Lee went as usual to Church for Confession. Four priests were on duty and some of them had much longer waiting lines than others. Honey Lee wanted to confess to Father Finn, whose line was fairly long. But the wait gave her time to think about what she wanted to say. She had to confess that her heart rebelled against the church law on marriage and that she still harbored strong desires for Danny Murphy. She wished without hope that Father Finn might have thought of something to help her and Danny. When she finally pushed the velvet curtain aside and entered the confessional and Father Finn opened the window, she felt less hopeful. He recognized her at once.

As soon as she had finished saying the ritual words, "Bless me Father for I have sinned," he asked, "Have you seen this man again?"

"No, Father, but—"

He interrupted, "There is no room in this matter for *but*. You must not see him again."

"Father, it isn't fair. I can't understand. Why would the church deprive a man of a home and children forever when he's done nothing wrong?"

"Honey Lee, you must pray very hard for a humble and obedient heart. No good will come of questioning fixed laws made by people far wiser than you and sanctioned by God himself."

"But I don't know how to stop thinking about him, Father."

"Pray to Mary. She will help you accept God's will." After he gave her absolution and a blessing, he told her gently that he knew this was a hard time for her and he promised to pray for her. She thanked him, but left sadder than she had been before. She had always loved leaving church after going to confession. She felt light and free, confident of God's love and forgiveness. But not this time.

She left the church and headed downtown to Brockleman's to shop for her grandmother. Nana Murphy insisted that there wasn't as good a butcher anywhere in Lowell than Mr. Connors in Brockleman's meat section. Honey Lee had a list and instructions: a good chunk of chuck for the Sunday pot roast, a pound of sweet butter, and two pounds of potatoes. Honey Lee had learned early on that there were potatoes and potatoes: you had to examine each potato carefully, count the number of eyes, be very sure that no eye had begun to sprout. While Honey Lee was examining potatoes one by one, she became conscious of someone standing too close to her. Instinctively she moved back and turned. The two potatoes she was holding fell from her hands and rolled onto the floor. Danny Jackson bent to pick them up.

"Danny. What are you doing here?"

"I'm sorry. I'm shopping for Mary. She asked me to dinner."

When Honey Lee took the two potatoes Danny held, her hand touched his. She pulled back quickly and the potatoes fell to the floor again. Both Honey Lee and Danny bent to pick them up. Their faces almost touched.

"Oh, Honey Lee, I miss you so."

"Don't."

They stood up and faced one another. Honey Lee's eyes stung.

"Can we just have coffee? I need to explain...apologize. I just need to talk."

Honey Lee wanted to say no. Father Finn had just told her she mustn't see Danny. But Danny's face before her stilled church voices. His dark eyes beseeched her. Just this once, she thought, just this once. She nodded, put the potatoes back and followed him out to the Square. They stood at the corner close to each other but not touching. The question of where to go to talk was even more difficult. She felt that now they needed to go somewhere where they wouldn't be seen by anyone who knew them. They walked to Danny's car, which he had parked behind Woolworth's. Without asking, Danny drove over the bridge and turned left heading out of the city on the same road they had traveled the night they had first spoken their love. Danny pulled into the parking lot of a diner, another diner more remote than their earlier meeting place. Honey Lee sat very still beside him, her hands folded in her lap. When he stopped the car and started to get out, Honey Lee spoke for the first time.

"I can't go in, Danny."

He closed the door and sat back. For minutes neither of them spoke. Honey Lee's throat was tight. If she spoke, she would cry.

"I never wanted to hurt you," Danny said. "I tried so hard to stay away from you. Even as I waited that first day for you to walk by, I was saying to myself, 'Don't do this.' But I felt I had to see you, that maybe seeing you might break the hold you had over me. I know that's crazy, but I felt crazy, obsessed. And then I saw you and you were so incredibly beautiful I—I lost my will."

"Tell me about her." She kept clasping and unclasping her hands.

"I ran into her in a bar on Moody Street when I was home after Johnny died. I had known her from high school. I went back after two days. She followed me, to Virginia. I guess I encouraged her. I thought, 'What the hell. Why not?' and we married. Two months later, I shipped out. Within a month, I got my Dear John. I didn't care. I have no idea where she is. I know she married again because they stopped taking money out of my pay for her, and they gave me the divorce papers."

"Who married you?"

"The chaplain. A priest."

"Father Finn says I can't see you. I shouldn't be here, Danny." She began to cry. "I loved you so much. I gave you my heart. What am I supposed to do? You should have let me be."

"I know, I know. That's why I wanted to see you to tell you how sorry I am and that I'm going away. It's the only way I can stop seeing you."

"Where?" She cried out. "Where are you going?"

"It doesn't matter. I'm going."

"No!" She reached out toward him. He groaned and took her in his arms. She pressed her face against his neck.

When she found her voice, she asked, "When?"

"As soon as I can. After I give notice at work. It shouldn't take long."

"And you won't be back?" She ran her fingers over his face.

"Not for a long time."

"No. You can't just go." She tightened her hands against the sides of his face.

"I can do whatever I have to do for you." He smoothed her hair with his hands and then put his hands over hers.

"For me? For me? I stay here all alone and you go."

"Yes."

"No. I can't bear it. I will always wonder where you are, how you are. You can't go, Danny."

She moved her face close to his offering it to him. With his index finger, he wiped the tears from under her eyes. She covered his hands with hers and held them against her face.

"I can't let you go. I can't," she cried. She put her mouth to his. He pulled back to resist her, but she leaned into him until with another groan, he returned her kiss. She felt a hunger deep in her that grew stronger and stronger. An overwhelming sorrow like that she had felt when her father died swept over her. She had thought never to feel such grief again. She could not do it. She would not. The war had taken her father. It had almost destroyed this man she loved so much. She would not let him go anywhere without her. She could not survive another such loss.

"Honey, Honey, you have to let me go."

"No. Never." The words came from a place so deep inside her that she hadn't known it existed.

"I should never have come back. Do you know what it means if I stay?"

"Yes. I know."

"No, you don't." He put his hands on her shoulders and talked to her as if she were a child. "You will lose your church, your family, your friends. Your grandmother will never accept our marriage. Our children will be bastards in her eyes and in the eyes of everyone you know. Do you really think you can live with that?"

"Nana loves me. She'll understand. I can make her understand."

"Did she understand your father when he married your mother? And he married in the church, Honey."

"I can make her understand," she protested. "I know I can."

"Can you make Father Finn understand?"

Honey Lee thought of Father Finn who had been so kind to her from her very first days in Lowell. She knew she had a special place in his heart. And because she did, he would be all the more opposed. Danny's words echoed her thoughts.

"He can't approve. He will have to tell you that you are choosing to live in sin and can never be reconciled to the church unless we separate. I know this. I've already asked a priest."

"But how can I send you off. Just tell me how I can do that, send you off to God knows what kind of life and what kind of life can I have without you?"

"Oh, God, I wish—"

"Shh, Danny Jackson." She put her finger to his lips. "No more wishes. No more apologies. I know what I want. Do you want me?"

"How can you ask me that?" He kissed her. "I have never wanted anything more."

"Then what are we going to do, Danny?"

Headlights from another car flared into their darkness. Honey Lee jumped and Danny held her making soothing sounds, "It's all right. Don't be afraid." When she became calm, he said, "If we—"

"Not if," she said calmly. "When."

"Then what we have to do is marry. Soon. I don't know how without a priest. We'll have to find out."

"How?" Having decided, she was impatient. "When?" She would have married him that minute.

"On Monday I'll go to City Hall and find out."

"Not Lowell City Hall. Someone there will surely know one of us. Lowell's too small."

"Then I'll go to Boston."

"I'll go with you. I got a job at the library at school. I need to tell them I don't want it."

"No. We have to go slow. Don't give up the job. Not yet. Take time. Think. I can't think with you here beside me. I'm still not sure I can let you do this."

"But you will go to Boston. You will find out how we can marry."

"Yes, and you will go to your job. I'll come there to find you."

"I hope we don't have to wait too long. I'll hate acting out lies until we are married." Her words reminded her of Nana and the undone shopping. "What time is it?"

"Seven-thirty."

"I haven't shopped yet. What time does Brockleman's close?"

"I'm not sure. We'll hurry." He kissed her one last time. Then he drove her back to the store, which was still open. Before she got out of the car, he took her hand and kissed it.

"Monday," he said.

"Yes, at the library." She went quickly to the meat counter.

"Well, girlie, I had just about given up on you," Mr. Connors said handing her the meat he had wrapped for her earlier. "Only ten minutes to closing. Lizzie Murphy would not like to miss her Sunday roast."

Honey Lee thanked him and rushed to pick up the carrots and potatoes. As she left, the lights went off, and a boy she didn't know was waiting to lock the door after her.

CHAPTER 28

▼

She was out of breath when she ran into the kitchen and called out to her grandmother. There was no answer. Feeling guilty, she was alarmed until she remembered that on Saturday night her grandmother and Aunt Kitty always went together to church for confession. Relieved, she put the groceries away and served herself from the bean pot on the stove. She had never eaten baked beans until she had come north. Her father had tried to explain to her mother how he thought they were cooked, but Savannah had never made anything close to the fragrant beans Honey Lee had come to love. Tonight she hardly tasted them at all. Her plans with Danny excited and frightened her. She had wandered into unknown territory. But she knew she was going to marry Danny Jackson as soon as she could. When or where they would marry, where they would live, and how she could bring her grandmother around to accepting Danny as her husband she couldn't tell.

She was finishing the last of the beans on her plate when the phone rang. She didn't want to answer it. It wouldn't be Danny. Maybe Ellen or even Jack or one of Nana's friends. She didn't want to talk to anyone. She let the phone ring hoping whoever it was would hang up, but it continued to ring. Disturbed by the caller's persistence, she went to the living room and picked up the phone.

"Hello."

"Honey Lee. Thank God you're there." Aunt Kitty's voice was shrill with panic.

Honey Lee clenched the receiver. "What's the matter? Are you all right?"

"Honey, it's Nana. She had a spell in church. They took her to the hospital."

Kitty's words cut into her heart. She cried out, "Oh God. I'm coming." She hung up and grabbed her coat from the hook in the hall. She ran the length of the street past the church to the hospital. Blood pounded in her forehead. "Sweet Jesus, have mercy, Holy Mary Mother of God, pray for us," she said over and over until she got to the hospital. When she entered the lobby, a woman at the desk told her that visiting hours were over.

"My grandmother was just brought in," Honey Lee said gasping for breath. "I have to see her."

"Oh, of course. You're the Murphy girl. Your grandmother's still in the emergency room." Pointing, she said, "Go right to the end of the hall. You'll have to wait."

Honey Lee ran down the hall. Aunt Kitty sat on a bench near the door to the emergency room twisting her gloves in her hands. When she saw Honey, she got up and said, "Thank God you're here." They hugged each other.

"Aunt Kitty, how is she?"

"I don't know, dear. No one's come out yet. Sit with me." They sat down on the hard bench and stared at the frosted glass on the doors.

"What happened?"

"She was just sitting beside me waiting to go to confession. Then without a word or a sound she slumped and fell into the aisle. I couldn't get her to open her eyes or talk to me. Father Finn came out. He called the hospital."

Three times the door swung open and nurses in rubber soled shoes padded past without stopping. Each time both women stood up. Aunt Kitty had put her gloves in her pocket and was now twisting her wedding band around and around. Honey sat rigid. Father Finn appeared at the end of the hall and walked toward them. They both stood.

"Any news, Kitty?"

"No, Father."

He turned to Honey Lee and said, "Hello, dear, how are you?"

"Fine, Father." Her automatic response belied the turmoil she felt. She had made a connection between what she had done and what had happened to her grandmother.

Father Finn patted her arm and said, "Lizzie Murphy is a strong woman. She will not be taken down like this. Not her. Not yet. She'll be fine."

"We're praying, Father," Aunt Kitty said.

"I'll go in to her now. When I come out we'll talk." He took a white stole from his pocket and put it around his neck as he went through the double doors into the emergency room. Honey Lee tried to see into the room but could see only heavy white curtains hanging from hooks on a metal rod.

Terrified, Honey Lee asked, "Is he giving her Extreme Unction?"

"No. No. She's not that sick, dear. He always puts that on when he comes into the hospital." Aunt Kitty was convincing herself as much as Honey Lee.

Five minutes went by before Father Finn came out with Doctor O'Leary, Nana's own doctor. Thank God it wasn't some stranger.

"Well, Mrs. Rourke and Miss Murphy, I'm not surprised by this. Your mother has had a heart condition for some time. Today for the first time it acted up, but she'll be fine. We'll keep her for a few days, teach her to make some changes, and send her home as good as new."

"She never told me she had a heart problems," Aunt Kitty said.

"No, she wouldn't. She's stubborn. Made me promise not to tell anyone."

Although somewhat relieved, Honey Lee was heartsick. "Can we see her, Doctor?"

"Yes. They're expecting you. Soon they'll move her upstairs. So just a short visit until tomorrow."

Aunt Kitty and Honey Lee walked through the door arm in arm. One of the heavy white curtains had been pulled aside. Nana was lying flat on a narrow bed, her eyes closed. Her clothes were neatly folded at the foot of her bed, her black hat on top of the pile tilted at the exact angle that Nana wore it.

"Mother," Kitty said softly. "Mother."

Nana Murphy opened her eyes. "Kitty, dear, and Honey Lee," she said reaching out for their hands. "Aren't I the fool then nodding off in church like that and scaring everyone."

Bending down to look closely at her grandmother, Honey Lee said, "Are you really all right?"

"Darlin' I'm fine." She looked over at Kitty who was blowing her nose. "Kitty, I won't have that sniffling around me. I'm going to rest now. Be off with you. Both of you. I'll see you tomorrow."

Honey Lee bent to kiss her grandmother, who looked tiny in the narrow bed. Aunt Kitty kissed her mother and said good-bye. At the door, they turned to look back and wave, but the old woman's eyes were closed. Aunt Kitty asked the woman at the desk to call a cab for them.

"It's too cold and dark to walk," she said to Honey Lee. While they waited for the cab, Aunt Kitty told Honey Lee that they would stop at Concord Street to get clothes for Honey Lee. "You can't stay in that big old house alone."

"Please, Aunt Kitty, I want to be at home. I'll be fine."

Aunt Kitty shrugged and said, "I suppose you're old enough."

"Thank you," Honey Lee said. A few minutes later, she asked, "How long do you think Nana has known about her heart?"

"I wish I knew, dear. I have no idea."

When they got into the cab, Aunt Kitty directed the driver to Concord Street and then turned to Honey Lee. "You can stay there, but I'm sending your cousin over to be with you."

"Are you frightened, Aunt Kitty?"

"No. And don't you be. The doctor said she's fine."

When the driver stopped in front of the house Aunt Kitty asked again if Honey Lee was sure she wanted to stay there. Honey Lee nodded. She went directly to the living room without turning on any lights. She settled into her grandmother's chair and put her head back. She became conscious of house noises she had never noticed before—the low rumbling of the furnace, the rattle of a loose pane in the window near her. She began to imagine others. A creaking sound became the footfall of an intruder. She got up and put on the lights in the living room, then making as much noise as she could with her feet and singing out loud, she went to the kitchen, the dining room, and both halls turning on lights as she went.

In the kitchen her dinner plate and fork lay on the table where she had left them, the liquid from the beans dark and hardened. She took them to the sink and ran water over them. Then she moved the bean pot to the side of the stove to cool so she could put it away later. When there was nothing left for her to do, she went back to sit in her grandmother's chair.

Nana and Danny fought for space in her head, both laying claim to her love and loyalty. She had chosen Danny over her grandmother. Doing so with Danny at her side, while difficult, was possible, and she had believed her choice was final. Nothing, no one, she had told him, could keep her from being with him. But alone in her grandmother's house, she lost that certainty. For years the nuns and priests had drilled into her the horror of mortal sin, sin so grave it caused spiritual death. If a person died with such a sin on her soul, she could go to hell. Over the years, she wondered how it was possible for anyone to commit a mortal sin. Now she knew. For a sin to be mortal, three things are necessary. The action had to be grave. Planning to marry a previously married man was surely grave matter. The sinner must have full knowledge that what she is doing is wrong. She knew what she had promised to do was wrong, not only from Father Finn, but from the sisters and her grandmother. Everyone she knew disapproved of divorce. The sinner must give full consent of the will. She had given full consent when she agreed to marry Danny. She had made a dreadful choice. Even though she had not actually married Danny, she had sinned. If a sinner deliberately plans to do something wrong and is prevented for some reason out of her control, she is still guilty. If for example she had been on the way to the judge to marry Danny and had died before they married, she would have sinned. And Nana Murphy's heart had begun to fail her at the very time that she was agreeing to marry Danny. Nana's illness was the finger of God warning her to step back.

Loud knocking at the door startled her until she remembered that Peter was coming to spend the night with her. She went to the door. "Are you trying to break the door down?" She was short tempered.

"Well I knocked twice before and you didn't answer."

"I'm sorry, Peter." She knew he was upset and was sorry she had snapped at him. "I didn't hear you. Come on in."

"Do you think Nana is going to be all right?"

"Yes. Doctor O'Leary told us she would be." She tried to sound convinced.

"That's what Mom says, but what do you think?"

"I think she's fine, Peter. Now take off your coat and come in." He handed her his coat and his books while he took off his boots. "Are you hungry?"

"No, we ate," he said, "but are you any good at Algebra? I'm having trouble with my homework. Do you think you can help me?"

"Yes. I won't do it for you. But I'll help."

She was glad he was there. They spent an hour on the Algebra problems. Then Peter began to talk about school, about his new girlfriend, and then about his father. Honey Lee was only half listening until he began to talk about his father.

"Did you know he was on Omaha Beach on D Day?"

"No, I didn't." She was surprised. "Did he tell you that?"

"Yeah, but nothing else. Just that he was with a bunch of frightened kids screaming their heads off."

"Is he any better?"

"I guess so. He doesn't wake up so much at night any more. But he never laughs. Heck, he never even smiles. Mom says, 'Be patient.' But I'll bet a nickel I'll be out of the house and married before he cracks a smile."

"Don't exaggerate, Peter."

"I'm not, honest to God, Honey."

Peter had stopped trying to get his father's attention a long time ago. These days, he spent more time at school, at the CYO hall, and at the homes of friends. From time to time Honey Lee had tried to help him by letting him talk about his father at least in part for his mother's sake.

But tonight, with Nana Murphy in the hospital and her own problems on her mind, Honey Lee cut short talk about his father by leading him to the kitchen for cookies and milk and a game of checkers. After he had beaten her twice, she was happy when he yawned and said he was ready for bed. He followed her from room to room as she turned off the lights. They went up together, she to her own room and he to his grandmother's. Honey Lee was exhausted, and sleep came quickly, but she woke up very early and couldn't get back to sleep. She went down to the cold empty kitchen, put the kettle on for tea and made toast for herself. She was breaking communion fast for the second time in less than two weeks. This time because she couldn't go to communion anyway, not with a mortal sin on her soul. She woke Peter at seven o'clock and told him to go home to get ready to go to Mass with his mother.

"Tell your mother that I'm going to the late Mass. I'll see her at the hospital at noon."

"I wish you had let me sleep in," he whined. "I would have gone to late Mass with you."

"Your mother needs you. Get going."

"Yes, Ma'am," he said and kissed her good-bye.

She planned to attend Mass at the Lithuanian church at the other end of the street from the Immaculate. Few people and none of the priests there knew her, so no one would wonder why she didn't go to communion. After Peter left she sat at the kitchen table staring into her empty teacup like a fortuneteller. She jumped when the phone rang, dreading to answer it. Her first thought was a call from the hospital. On the fourth ring, she picked up the phone.

"Hello."

"Honey Lee. My cousin just called and told me your grandmother went into Saint John's last night." Honey Lee could not place the voice. "Is she all right? Are you all right?"

"Yes, thank you," Honey Lee said vaguely still not recognizing the voice.

"Honey, it's Mary, Mary Jackson."

"Oh, Mary. I didn't recognize your voice." How fast news spread, she thought.

"Have you seen her yet?"

"Yes, for a few minutes last night," Honey paused. "Mary, she knew she had a heart problem and she never told us."

"Didn't want you to worry, I suppose."

"How are you, Mary? It's been ages." In spite of Mary's Jackson-connection, Honey was happy to talk to her.

"We're fine. Jimmy's here. Some kind of row with Danny. He's leaving for South Bend tomorrow."

"Tomorrow?" She was stunned. "To Notre Dame?"

"Yes. He didn't tell you?" Apparently neither Jimmy nor Danny had confided in Mary. "He says he's sick of looking after Danny."

It didn't surprise her that Jimmy was leaving without telling her or saying good-bye. What hurt was to hear the news so casually from someone else, news that Jimmy would once have shared with her before he told anyone else. "I haven't seen much of him lately," she said.

"We just want you to know that we're all thinking about you and praying for your grandmother."

"Thanks, Mary."

Honey Lee put the phone down. She wished she could talk to Mary. The impulse to call her back was strong, but she resisted. She wished she could ask her how sick she thought Nana Murphy was and tell her about Danny and Jimmy. She went upstairs to finish getting ready for church.

At twelve o'clock, she was waiting in the lobby of the hospital for her aunt. When one of the hospital nuns passed her, she said, "Good morning, Sister." She marveled, as she always had, that the Sisters were able to keep their large, winged head coverings on straight and wondered how much starch and bleach it took to keep them so stiff and white. She had always been a little afraid to get too close to one of these sisters for fear that she would knock the headdress off. How did they get close to patients without dislodging their hats? Once when she and Ellen had been practicing posture by walking with books on their heads, they put pillows on top of the books and dissolved in laughter as they bowed to each other saying, "Good morning Sister Mary of Charity."

"Oh, Honey, there you are. I came in the other door." She jumped at the sound of her aunt's voice. "We missed you at breakfast."

"Hello, Aunt Kitty. Where's Peter?"

"I told him to come back later. He wouldn't be good at a long visit."

At the desk when they asked for Mrs. Murphy, they were directed to the third floor. When they got off the elevator, a nurse led them down the hall to Nana Murphy's room.

"Company, Mrs. Murphy. Are you receiving today?"

"Sure and I couldn't say no to either of them. They'd just run right over you to get to me."

"Oh, Mother." Aunt Kitty was relieved. "You're feeling better, aren't you?"

"Yes, and I'm wanting to get back to my own bed."

"That's up to Dr. O'Leary," the nurse said.

"Well, I just might have something to say about that when I see him. It's nonsense keeping me here."

Honey Lee hadn't realized how worried she was until relief flooded into her. "Oh, Nana, I'm so glad you're all right."

"Thanks be to God, I am. And thank you for coming, both of you."

Peter came about a half-hour after they had arrived and they all stayed until the nurses asked them to leave. When Aunt Kitty tried to get some report on her mother's condition, she was told that they would have to wait until Dr. O'Leary came in the next afternoon.

CHAPTER 29

▼

Honey Lee convinced her aunt to let Peter go back home so he could leave for school from his own house. Her aunt fretted about "poor Honey Lee alone in that big house," but in the end agreed. Honey Lee needed to be alone to get ready to do what she had to do, call Danny and tell him she could never marry him. If she didn't see him, she could do it, and he would agree. He had to. After all, he had been prepared to leave Lowell for her sake. But he didn't have to go. They could live in the same city. Lowell wasn't that small. They could avoid each other. She rehearsed the conversation. It didn't go well. She had told him that her love was strong enough to risk anything. How could she take back such a promise? What a mess she had made. Like her mother, she had fallen in love with a man she barely knew. And like her father too. He hadn't been much better falling in love with a childish woman incapable of caring for a daughter. She should have learned something from their mistakes. She knew her grandmother had suffered because of her parents' love. And here she was ready to inflict a similar, if not worse, grief on Nana Murphy.

But could she snatch from Danny the hope she had given him? Choosing Danny yesterday had seemed irrevocable. But seeing her grandmother in a hospital bed changed that. She was afraid to call Danny, afraid that the sound of his voice could move her to change her mind again. Maybe she could wait until the next day and tell him then. But then he would spend the whole morning on a fool's errand. She looked his number up in the phone book. How odd to have planned to marry a man whose telephone number she didn't even know. She dialed hoping he wouldn't answer. But he did. Her breath caught in her throat when she heard his voice.

"Hello." She could not speak. "Hello. Who is it? Hello."

"Danny, it's me." She tried to control her voice but it betrayed her.

"Honey, what's wrong?" Panic made his voice high. "Are you all right?"

She wound the cord to the telephone around and around her finger. "It's my grandmother. She's in the hospital."

"What happened?"

"She was in church and she just…It's her heart."

"I'm coming right over."

"No," she said. "You can't. I'm alone."

"But—"

She cut him off quickly and said what she had to say. "Don't do anything."

"Don't do anything?" She could tell he didn't understand. She had hoped he would.

"About tomorrow, I mean," she explained, "about going in to Boston. I can't. Not now. I just can't."

"Of course you can't right now." He was patient and kind. "We'll wait."

"Danny, I can't do it. Not ever. I know I promised, and I thought I could. I wanted to, but I can't do it. I've got to go now," she said and put the phone down as if she were closing a book she had finished. It was done. She would no longer feel like a rag doll, her grandmother pulling her one way and Danny the other. But she felt neither peaceful nor relieved.

Restless, she walked from the living room to the dining room, and then into the kitchen. The bean pot was still on the stove and the dishes she had used the night before and in the morning were still in the sink. When she opened the refrigerator to put the beans away, she saw the roast she had bought for Sunday dinner. If she didn't cook it, it would go to waste. She had watched her grandmother prepare a roast so often that she could do it easily. Cooking would help pass the time. She found a piece of fat salt pork carefully wrapped in waxed paper. Half of it had gone as usual into the Saturday baked beans, the remainder was for browning the roast. She carefully sliced and diced the pork and put it into the heavy black pan. She watched it become translucent and then begin to brown and yield fat. She stirred it until the browned pieces were crisped. She had rolled the meat in flour seasoned with salt and pepper. She removed the pieces of pork and set them on a newspaper to drain. The fat sputtered and jumped up from the pan when she put the roast in. She felt the sting of hot fat on her forearms. When the phone rang, she was so intent on cooking that she didn't stop to think who might be calling. She pushed the pan off the hot burner and ran to the phone.

"Hello."

"Honey Lee, it's Ellen. What on earth's going on with you and Jack? He's like a bear and won't say anything except, 'It's over.' I'll kill him if he's hurt you."

"Ellen, hi. I'm sorry. I'm really—I can't talk about it."

"Listen, you're my friend, and he's my brother. You have to talk to me. You sound awful. I'm coming over."

"Please don't, Ellen. Things are all mixed up." She rubbed at the small burns on her arm. "My grandmother's in the hospital."

Ellen was all concern. "Oh, Honey. What's the matter with her?"

"Something about her heart. She's going to be all right."

"Are you all alone in that big house? I'm coming. Five minutes." She hung up before Honey Lee could say anything. Well, she couldn't avoid everyone forever. She went back to the kitchen to finish cooking the meat and to wait for Ellen. By the time the roast had browned enough, and she had added water and covered it, she heard Ellen at the back door. When Honey Lee answered the door, Ellen put her arms around her and held her.

"I'm so sorry. You must be scared to death." Ellen's warmth broke through Honey Lee's calm. She held on to Ellen hoping her tears would stop before Ellen saw she was crying.

"Tell me about it. What happened?"

Between sobs, Honey Lee told her about Aunt Kitty's call, Nana's collapse, the rush to the hospital, Nana's secret heart sickness, and how tiny and frail she looked in the hospital bed. "Doctor O'Leary says she's going to be all right. But I don't believe him. What would I do if anything happened to her, Ellen? I feel so guilty."

Putting her arm around Honey Lee's waist, Ellen led the way into the living room to the couch.

"Guilty? Honey Lee, that's plain silly, and you know it. Did you see her today?"

"Uh huh. She wants to come home."

"So stop worrying right now." She sniffed and said, "What smells so good?"

"Sunday pot roast." Honey Lee started to cry again. "I had to cook it so it wouldn't go bad."

"And she'll be home to eat it in a day or two."

"I hope so." The subject of Jack hung in the silence between them. She would have to talk, but the delicious comfort of having a friend to talk to about Nana Murphy was so great she would have done anything not to. Ellen was tactful. She waited, but Honey knew she wouldn't leave until she learned about Jack. Then

Honey Lee would have to tell her why. It was so like him not to have told the family that she was responsible.

"Ellen, about Jack," she finally said. "It's my fault."

"Seems like everything's your fault tonight—your grandmother, Jack. What other terrible things have you done?" Ellen crossed her eyes, trying to make Honey Lee laugh.

"Don't joke, Ellen. I'm serious. It was me." She pointed her index finger toward herself and jabbed it into her chest with each word she said. "I broke up with Jack."

"Why?"

"I fell in love with somebody else." She tried not to look at Ellen's face.

"Just like that. Bang. You're in love."

Honey Lee looked straight at her friend, ignored her sarcasm, and said quietly, "Yes. That's the way it happened."

The doorbell shrilled startling both girls. She knew it was Danny but desperately hoped it wasn't. She went to the door, and there he was standing on the porch. He walked past her into the hall saying nothing. She tried to stop him by tugging on his coat, but he pulled free and said, "I need to talk to you right now." She followed him into the living room. He saw Ellen and stopped, confused. "I'm sorry to interrupt."

Honey Lee stood between them and said, "Ellen, this is Danny Jackson, Jimmy's brother. Danny this is Ellen Flynn."

"Jack Flynn's sister," Ellen said strongly inflecting her brother's name. She looked at Honey Lee and said, "Now I get it. I'll leave you two alone." Honey Lee followed Ellen to the back door.

"Ellen, you don't understand. I didn't expect him. Really I didn't."

"I think I do understand, Honey Lee." She put on her coat and threw her scarf over her shoulder. "I can see why. He's really handsome. Congratulations. Have fun."

"Ellen, don't go. I'll send him away."

"Good-bye, Honey Lee," Ellen said and slammed the door. Honey Lee hadn't noticed that Danny had followed them until he spoke.

"What rotten timing. I'm really sorry."

"You shouldn't be here anyway."

"I know, I know. The neighbors will talk. Let's go out then."

"Oh, Danny, we keep doing that and look where it gets us."

"I thought," he said with ice in his voice, "we had finally gotten to the right place, and so did you. You owe me more than, 'I can't do it to her.' Don't I get a chance to say anything?"

"Like what, Danny? What is there to say?"

"Like you can't do this. You can't."

They stood near the door that Ellen had slammed shut. She had guessed about Danny immediately, and she had not believed that he was unexpected. She thought Honey Lee and Danny were taking advantage of Nana's absence to be alone in the empty house for as long as they wanted, to do whatever they wanted. How could you protect your reputation from neighbors if a friend believed you capable of such plotting?

"Never mind the neighbors," she said. "Come on in and sit." She sat in her grandmother's chair so he couldn't sit beside her. She needed distance to keep her resolve. She looked across at him. He sat forward on the couch, his hands clasped in front of him.

He stared at her for a long time and then took a deep breath and began.

"I want to be very sure that—I want you to be very sure that what you say to me today is final. We're not teenagers, Honey, going steady one day and breaking up the next. Last night you were a woman choosing a difficult path. Where is the woman who wanted to be my wife?"

"Saying no to you is harder. Much harder."

"No. That's not true. Saying no to me allows you to stay in your comfortable life." He spread his hands out to include the whole room. "No rules broken, everyone still loving you, maybe later, a good safe marriage to Jack or Jimmy or someone suitable."

"I built this comfortable life after I had lost everything." Her anger briefly energized her. "Then you come along and make me choose between two things, both of which I need to survive. Jimmy was right. You should have left me alone." Her anger drained away leaving her bereft. "No matter what I do, I lose." Danny got up to come to her. "No, Don't touch me."

He sat down again and waited for her to speak. "Nana Murphy has a weak heart. This craziness caused her heart attack. I know it did. She's more than a mother to me. She kept me alive when all I wanted to do was die. What do you think would happen to her if I married you?"

"You do not know what caused her heart attack."

"I did. And I won't risk hurting her again."

"You're so sure that your grandmother's health turns on what you do?"

"Danny, there'll be someone else for you."

"No thanks. I already tried marriage without love." He stood up. "I'm going now. I hope you—I don't know what I hope. I wanted you so much. You made me believe—"

He walked to the door. She sat still and watched him go.

CHAPTER 30

▼

The hours after Danny and Ellen left were as lonely as any she could remember, and the following weeks a desert. A week after she had entered the hospital, Nana Murphy came home and Honey Lee began working full time at the library. Danny was a closed chapter in her life. Honey Lee mechanically followed the same plan day after day: up at seven o'clock, train at eight-thirty, work until four-thirty, dinner at seven-thirty, bed at nine-thirty. To keep her mind from wandering she had developed a habit of counting: the number of steps from her door to the door of the train station; the number of men in uniform she passed; the number of times the head librarian pushed his glasses up on his nose during each encounter they had; the number of books on a given shelf. Counting helped pass the time on the days she worked, but the slow moving weekend days were less easy.

On the Saturday following her grandmother's return from the hospital she went to Father Finn to confess. Needing time to decide what to say, she waited until the line at his confessional had dwindled. After the last person had entered one side of the box, she pushed aside the curtain on the other side and went in. Whoever was talking to Father Finn before her also had a lot to say. Finally she heard the small door slide open. Through the screen she could see Father Finn, head bowed to his hands.

"Bless me Father for I have sinned." She paused. He waited. "It's been three weeks since my last confession."

"Three weeks?" She flinched at the shock in his voice.

"Yes, Father." She thought briefly about leaving. It would be so much easier to confess to a priest she didn't know. Father Finn knew immediately who she was. "Father, I have committed a mortal sin. I need to confess, but—"

He interrupted her. "A mortal sin is a serious matter." He paused rubbing his hand over his head. "Are you sure?"

"Yes, Father. In spite of what you told me, I promised the man—I promised Danny Jackson—that I would marry him." She spoke rapidly, her eyes lowered so she didn't have to look at him.

He straightened in his chair and put his face close to the screen. She heard his head touch it. "Are you now married?"

"No. But I made plans to. I decided I would do it."

"You changed your mind when you realized how serious a sin you were choosing to commit?"

"No, Father. I changed my mind when my grandmother became sick. If she hadn't gotten sick, I would be married now. I wanted it more than anything."

"You are right, Honey Lee. This is a serious sin."

"It didn't feel sinful, Father." She pictured Danny the night she had promised to marry him. She spoke boldly. "I still can't believe marrying him would be wrong."

"You would be excommunicated. You know that don't you?"

"Yes, Father, but still it seemed the right thing to do."

"It was not. Your heart is not right with God. You must pray day and night for a right heart in this matter. Danny Jackson is a grave occasion of sin for you. You must never see him again. Do you understand?"

"But I cannot see the rightness of the thing, I mean the wrongness of it. What I felt for Danny did—does not feel wrong." She was persuaded in this belief by Danny's sad eyes and his past.

"I will not give you absolution today, and not a minute before you accept the truth that harboring this love is sinful." He raised his voice in command. "Think. Pray. Your soul is in danger."

"Yes, Father," she said and left without a blessing.

She thought and she prayed, but in her thinking she never got beyond her grandmother's health as her reason for rejecting Danny. She could not believe the passion and tenderness she felt for Danny was wrong. He wasn't guilty of any sin in the matter. He had nothing to do with the divorce. Forbidding him to marry was wrong. He deserved happiness, and she wanted to give it to him.

Nana Murphy had not mentioned Danny since she had come home, but she was worried. Honey Lee could tell. She asked several times if Honey Lee were sick, whether the work at the library was too much for her. She kept suggesting activities that might "perk you up a bit." Honey kept insisting that she was fine, just resting up for school. Honey Lee also worried about her grandmother. She watched for signs of a relapse. She ran up and down stairs several times a day on errands for her. She anticipated her grandmother's needs in that and in other ways. She insisted on washing and sweeping the kitchen floor, putting the dishes up on the shelves too high for her grandmother, carrying groceries and changing beds. At first Nana Murphy had let Honey Lee wait on her, but gradually and firmly she insisted that she wanted to run her own house and let Honey lee worry about school and work. So life settled back into its normal patterns except that now Honey Lee had to work at looking happy and content. She had to mask her restlessness. Sometimes that meant resuming her long walks through the city. One day as she was walking down Merrimack Street she heard someone call her name, a female voice speaking her name as a question. When she turned around, she saw an attractive woman her own age. "You are Honey Lee, aren't you?" the woman asked.

Honey Lee could not place her, but she said, "Yes, Honey Lee Murphy."

The other woman laughed out loud. "You came to my wedding and you don't even remember me, Miriam Smith, Williams now. We met outside the Blue Moon the night before my wedding."

"Oh, Miriam, hello." Honey Lee was delighted. "You were so beautiful that day. How could I ever forget?" They embraced.

How are you and that handsome Danny?" Miriam fell in step beside her needing two quick steps for each of Honey Lee's.

Honey Lee's smile faded. "I don't see him any more."

"Why on earth not? You seemed so together."

"It's a long story." A story Honey Lee was eager to tell someone beside Father Flynn. She was sick from holding so much inside her.

"And a sad one, I guess," Miriam said. "Let's have coffee. I'm done shopping."

She carried two Cherry and Web shopping bags and a small brown bag from Woolworth's. Delighted at the offer of friendship, Honey Lee anticipated unburdening herself. They agreed on the Dutch Tea Room. When they were comfortably seated in a quiet booth and had ordered hot chocolate and English muffins, Honey Lee asked, "How are you and Jack?"

"Great." She was radiant and wanting, like Honey Lee, to share her feelings. "I love being married. It's wonderful. He's wonderful."

"I'm glad. You looked so happy that day. I prayed that you would always be."

"And you too, both of you, looked happy too. I was sure that you'd be married by now."

"That's what I thought too." Honey Lee spoke slowly. She took a long, deep breath. "It's hard for me to talk about it, Miriam. I don't think I can." Her voice cracked.

"Oh, Honey, I'm sorry. I'm so dumb sometimes." She reached across the table for Honey's hand. The simple gesture and the look of concern on Miriam's face caused tears that had been dammed up for weeks to flow. Miriam quickly moved from her side of the booth to Honey and put her arms around her. Honey Lee allowed her head to rest on Miriam's shoulder.

When she was able to talk, she said, "I loved him so much. I promised to marry him and I wanted to more than anything in the world."

"That's the way it seemed to me," Miriam said. "But?"

"There were problems. I was going steady with someone else when we met. Also Danny's brother, my best friend, was dead set against it. So was my grandmother."

She delayed telling the real reason.

"But, why?"

"At first I thought his brother objected because he was in love with me himself. My grandmother didn't like that he was older, a wounded veteran, and still sick."

"It does sound complicated." Miriam handed Honey Lee her handkerchief. "But I was going to do it anyway. But then. Then—" She stopped. Miriam held her hand and waited. "He was married during the war. She left him while he was overseas and got a divorce," Honey Lee whispered. She hadn't realized how hard it would be to say the words out loud.

"And he can't marry again."

Honey Lee shook her head and wiped her eyes. "Not if he and his wife want to be Catholic."

"That's terrible."

"But still I agreed to marry him. I couldn't stop myself." She looked at Miriam begging for the right answer to the question she was about to ask. "Can you understand that?"

"I know I can't imagine my life without Jack. But I'm not sure what I would have done if he had been married." Of course she couldn't imagine it. She and Jack were childhood sweethearts.

"Well, then I changed my mind. My grandmother—she's really my mother, my folks are dead—had a heart attack and that changed everything." The lie about her mother came easily. "I told him I changed my mind."

In the telling of her story Honey Lee had become angry again. "How could he have done that to me? Let me fall in love knowing full well that we couldn't marry."

"Oh, Honey, it was the war. It did awful things to people. Jack was lucky. He's got a bad arm, but he's OK. Some of his buddies and old friends are all messed up. Maybe Danny needed you so much he couldn't help himself."

"Nana Murphy was right. She told me he was dangerous. But I wouldn't listen He had a terrible time in the war."

"What are you going to do?" Miriam asked, taking her hand.

"Go back to school. Try to forget." She had said as much as she could about Danny. "Let's talk about something else. Where are you living?"

"We have a small house on Christian Hill in Centerville. I love it. You have to come see us some time." She took a pencil and a small pad out of her pocketbook and wrote her address and phone number on it.

"I'd love to," Honey Lee folded and refolded the paper into tiny squares.

"Look, Jack is working nights next week. Do you want to go to a movie some night?"

"Sure. What night?"

"Tuesday?" Honey Lee nodded. "I'll see what's playing and call you."

Honey Lee gave her the phone number. They paid the check and walked out to the Square.

"I'm so glad I saw you," Honey Lee said as Miriam hugged her." I've been lonely,"

"Of course you have. Let's be good friends."

Honey Lee no longer went to Mass with her grandmother. Ever since she had promised to marry Danny and had been refused absolution by Father Finn, she stopped going to communion. Even though she no longer planned to marry Danny, she couldn't arrive at what Father Finn called true contrition. She had refused to marry Danny, not because it was sinful, but because of her grandmother's heart. Except for her grandmother's heart, she would marry Danny. She had to use several excuses for going to church without her grandmother. She needed to sleep in. She was going with a friend to another Mass. She didn't want to run into Ellen's family.

"I'm missing your company, dear. Haven't we always gone together?"

Each time, Honey said she was sorry and promised to go with her the next time.

She hated adding lies to her other sins. And to think she used to have difficulty finding anything to confess.

CHAPTER 31

▼

When classes began in mid-January, Honey Lee had more to keep her busy. She was back for second semester French with Professor Martine, who had gone back to Paris during semester break and returned with wonderful stories about France's continuing recovery. The new reading list contained novels by Maupassant, Balzac, Zola, and an interesting new writer, Albert Camus. Nana Murphy still worried out loud about Honey Lee losing her faith in "that non-Catholic school." Her grandmother and the nuns still worried about losing one's faith as if it were a bundle you could put down somewhere and forget. Honey Lee wished it were that simple. Nana told her to check with Father Finn to see if any of the books on her list were on the *Index of Forbidden Books*. Honey Lee hadn't asked Father Finn last semester and didn't plan to ask second semester. She trusted Mr. Flynn who had told her not to worry about the *Index*. Anyway, Boston University was a Methodist school certainly not in the business of assigning books dangerous to religion. Jack had told her that Methodists were more strict than Catholics.

On the first day of French class, the veteran who had spoken to her during exams and asked her out greeted her warmly and took a seat beside her. He asked how she had enjoyed semester break and what other classes she was taking. When he asked her to have coffee with him, she was happy to be able to tell him truthfully that she had to work in the library right after class. He continued to sit by her and talk to her before class, asking once in a while if she were free for coffee or for a movie after she finished work. She liked him and would have enjoyed seeing him. But she knew that seeing him would get complicated, so she politely refused. She would also have enjoyed talking to other students outside of class.

Often the class discussions, in which she sometimes participated, were heated. She knew that even more interesting discussions were held in the cafeteria after classes. The presence of veterans was what made the classes exciting. One instructor told the class how much he loved having them in his class because they had lived a little. But she didn't have time for coffee after class. If she wasn't working, she was running off to another class.

Because work took up so much of the time she had used for studying first semester, she spent long hours at the kitchen table after Nana Murphy had gone to bed. She thought less about Danny as the days went by. She heard nothing from Ellen, Jack or Jimmy. She was not surprised, but she missed them. Miriam had become a good friend. They talked often on the phone and met for a movie when Jack worked late. Once she had gone to dinner at the Williams' when Jack was home. The couple's joy in each other and in their new home caused an ache in her heart. Their life was what she had pictured for herself and Danny.

One night at ten-thirty, the phone rang, a late call at the Murphy's. "I'll get it Nana," Honey Lee said running down the stairs. She had just finished brushing her hair before climbing into bed.

"Honey Lee. I know it's late, but I had to call you." It was Miriam.

"Darlin' who is it?" Nana called from upstairs.

"It's all right Nana. It's for me," she called back.

"Is something wrong?" Honey Lee asked.

"Not with me or Jack."

"Then what?"

"Jack was out with the boys. One of them who knows Danny Jackson said that Danny was rushed to Saint John's and then taken back to Chelsea Naval Hospital."

Honey Lee drew in a sharp breath, then spoke quickly. "Did he say what was wrong?"

"No. Just what I told you. I thought you'd want to know."

"Thanks, Miriam. I've got to go. I've got to go."

When she hung up the phone her hands were shaking. She went to the drawer of a chest for the phone book, and looked up Frank's number. She dialed once and got a wrong number, a man very unhappy to be roused from sleep. She dialed again and waited and waited as the phone rang on and on. She tried twice more and still got no answer. She called information to get the number of the Naval Hospital, dialed it, and asked about Danny Jackson's condition. The hospital operator asked if she were a relative. When she said no, she was told that all hospital information was private except for immediate family. Frustrated and certain that the refusal to give Danny's condition meant that something terrible was wrong, she sat by the phone for almost an hour then called Frank's house again. Still there was no answer.

In the morning by six o'clock she was frantic. Unable to wait another minute she dialed Frank's number. After four rings, Mary, her voice blurred with sleep, answered.

"Mary. What happened? How is he?"

Shocked at the panic in the voice, Mary asked, "Honey Lee?"

"Yes. Yes. Tell me," she insisted"

"But how did you—?" Mary was confused, still half asleep.

"Mary, is he alive? Tell me." It was a command, not a request.

"Yes. What's wrong with you anyway?"

"Please," Honey Lee begged, "just tell me what you know."

"We hadn't seen him or talked to him for over a week, and Frank got nervous. We went to his place and found him on the floor. We couldn't wake him. I thought he was dead, Honey."

"Sweet Jesus, help us." The words were a prayer.

"Honey Lee, what's this all about?"

"Just tell me." Again the words were a command.

"Honey?" Mary wanted to ask again why Honey Lee had called, but she went on, "Well, it was awful. They took him to Saint John's in an ambulance. They got him stabilized then sent him to Chelsea and—"

"Did you see him?"

"We were there until two-thirty this morning."

"Was he awake?"

"Yes. He was awake, but—"

"But what?" Mary couldn't keep up with the urgent questions, and Honey Lee could barely wait for the answers.

"He wouldn't talk to us. Told us to go."

"Oh, God. What did the doctor say?"

"They think he stopped taking his medicine. They also think he was drinking. Frank is furious." She stopped. "Honey Lee, what in the name of God is this all about. Why are you calling me?"

Honey Lee ignored the question. "Is he going to be all right?"

"They say he could be if he takes his medicine." Mary paused to think, "You know I didn't think too much about the fight with Jimmy, but maybe that and Jimmy's leaving was too much for him."

"Does Jimmy know?"

"Honey, are you crying?"

"No, I have a little cold. I'll let you get some sleep. Good-bye." She put the phone down knowing Mary must think her crazy. But she cared only about Danny. She ran upstairs and dressed hurriedly. She wouldn't waste one minute getting to the hospital. She would lie if she had to to get in to see him. She pulled out her dark skirt and the red sweater he had said made her look like Carmen. She wanted to make herself as beautiful as she could. She would make him smile, make him want to get well again for her.

Nana Murphy was surprised to see Honey Lee up, dressed, and putting on her coat so early. Honey Lee lied telling her that the librarian had asked her to come in early to help catalogue new acquisitions.

"Have you had a bite of anything?"

"No, Nana, but I've got to go."

"You'll melt away at the rate you're going."

She ran all the way to the station leaving her books, her gloves and hat behind. She hoped to make the seven o'clock train and find out when she got to Boston how to get to the hospital. She just made the train, which was much more crowded than the one she usually took. She sat in a seat by the window hoping no one would sit beside her, but she was soon joined by a middle-aged man carrying a copy of the *Lowell Sun*. Holding the front section out to her, he asked her if she would like to read it while he caught up on sports news. She took the paper and thanked him. The front page news was about the thousands of displaced people still wandering all over Europe trying to get home, trying to find relatives, children seeking their parents and parents their children. The man put the sports section down, so she handed him the front section. He asked if she were finished, and she told him she had read enough. "It makes me sad to read about all those lost people."

"You'd think they'd be settled by now, wouldn't you? It's a real shame." Changing the subject he asked, "What takes you into Boston?"

"School. I go to BU." She wished she hadn't given him the paper back.

"BU? I didn't know they had girls there."

"They do." He was a decent, friendly man, but she wished he'd go back to his paper.

"Maybe I'm thinking of BC. No girls there, are there?"

"I don't think so."

"You Catholic?" he asked.

"Yes." Isn't everyone in Lowell, she thought.

"What parish?" The inevitable question. Geography in Lowell was parish.

"The Immaculate."

"I'm Saint Michael's, over on Christian Hill. You know the hill?"

"Yes, I visited friends there recently. Jack and Miriam Williams. They live on Third Street."

"Two blocks down from us. I know both of their fathers."

Why had she forgotten her books and given the paper back. Either one would have stopped his flood of questions. There was nothing to do but to endure the conversation until they got to the North Station. When they got there, she called out, "I'm late for class," got off the train, and ran as fast as she could to get the subway car to Park Street, where she got directions to the hospital. Since the hospital was technically part of the Navy Base, she was stopped at the entrance by a guard who asked what her business was. The guard was sympathetic and directed her saying he hoped her husband was going to be all right. Husband. Well why not? That would get her in. When she entered the hospital, she asked where she could find her husband, Daniel Jackson. She kept her hands in her coat pocket to hide the absence of a wedding ring. A young man in uniform told her to go to the nurses' station on the third floor. She stopped beside the elevator. She had no idea what she was going to say to Danny. She prayed for the right words. There was no way to plan this meeting. She would have to trust herself. She went up to the third floor to the nurses' station where three nurses in white uniforms with military insignia on their caps stood at the station talking among themselves. When Honey Lee announced herself as Danny's wife, they were surprised. They told her that they didn't know he was married.

"You must be sick with worry, honey," a red-haired nurse said. "I'll take you to him. He looks a lot worse than he is. He's going to get better."

"Thank God."

The nurse led her into a large dimly lit room with beds lined up on both sides for at least thirty men, some sleeping, some eating, others curious about the new visitor. She heard a few soft whistles but ignored them. The nurse stopped at the tenth bed on the right side of the room.

"Danny, Danny. Wake up. Your wife is here."

He was lying on his back with his eyes closed. His hair had been slicked back. He never wore it like that. He was pale and still.

"Let me fix your pillow so you can sit up a little," the nurse said.

He said nothing when the nurse bent over him. Slowly he opened his eyes. Honey Lee gasped when she saw how empty they looked and how his face twisted in pain when the nurse moved his pillow. Then he recognized her.

"Honey?"

Honey turned to the nurse and thanked her, willing her to leave them alone.

"Oh, Danny. What happened? What happened to you?"

"Why are you here?" he asked. His voice was weak but not so weak that she could miss its coldness. When she didn't answer, he asked again. "Why are you here Honey Lee?"

She answered by repeating her own question. "Danny what happened? Why are you here like this?"

When he turned away without answering Honey Lee sat down on the metal chair beside the bed and waited. She reached out to put a hand on his shoulder but changed her mind. She folded her hands and bent her head. The man in the next bed called out, "Hey, Jackson, that's no way to treat a beautiful visitor. Are you sick in the head too?"

Danny ignored him and Honey Lee. Determined not to let the men in the ward see her cry, she shook her head, turned her face to the wall, and wiped tears from her eyes.

"Danny, I'm sorry. I'm so sorry. Please look at me."

At last he turned and looked directly at her still saying nothing. Again she started to reach out to him, but sensing his anger, she pulled her hand back. He stared at her without speaking or moving. Even his eyes were still and unblinking.

"Won't you say anything?" She pleaded.

"Sure," he said. "You are so damned beautiful. How's that?"

"Awful," she whispered.

"I need to sleep now. Thanks for coming."

He was trying to make her angry enough to leave, but she sat still looking at him and trying not to reach out to touch him. She knew he would not let her.

"I'm not leaving, Danny."

"Who told you I was here?" He asked after a long pause during which he stared at the ceiling.

"Miriam Williams."

"Miriam? Williams? Who the hell is she?"

"Miriam from the Blue Moon, whose wedding we went to."

"Lowell sure is a small town. No secrets there."

"Then I called Mary and Frank. You sent them away? Why? They're worried about you."

He looked directly at her for the first time and spoke slowly pausing between each phrase, "I sent them away. Because I didn't want to see them. I'm asking you to go away. Because I don't want to see you. I'm asking you again to go. Now. Leave me alone."

Although stung by his words, she said, "I'm not leaving Danny."

"Well that's a change."

"Don't, Danny."

She bent her head to the bed beside him. She found his hand and moved it to her head. It rested lifeless on her hair. She turned so that it rested on her cheek. Still he didn't move or speak even though her tears wet his hand.

"Danny, I've been so miserable. Forgive me. Please forgive me. I can't be away from you. Don't send me away." His index finger moved under her eye wiping at a tear. She reached for his hand with both of hers and held it kissing his fingers. "You have to get well and come home. I can't live without you. When I heard you were here I was terrified. You have to get well. If anything happened to you I would be lost forever."

She raised her eyes pleading.

He shook his head slowly and smiled. "Honey, you made your choice, and my being here doesn't change anything. I'm sick, but you didn't cause it and promises won't cure it. So do us both a favor and go home." He pulled his hand away from hers and turned over in his bed.

"I won't go. I was wrong. You're more important to me than anyone or any thing in the world."

Still not facing her, he said, "Honey Lee. I am not here because you jilted me. There is no such thing as a "we." Go back to Lowell. When I get out of here I'm gone."

"I'll follow you. I'll find you no matter where you go."

"I want you out of here." His voice had risen, and she could feel the eyes of strangers on her back.

"If you send me away, I'll sit by that fence out there," she said pointing, "every day until they let you out. Then I'll go wherever you go."

Just then a nurse who had been watching at the door came up behind Honey Lee.

"I think Mr. Jackson needs to rest now. Maybe you can come back later."

"Thanks," Danny said to the nurse. "This visit is tiring me. Good-by, Honey Lee."

She stood up and bent over to kiss him on the forehead.

"For now, I'll go. But I'll keep coming back until I get what I want." She turned and walked quickly out of the ward to the elevators.

"Mrs. Jackson, Mrs. Jackson, wait please." The red-haired nurse had followed her out of the room.

"He's weak, very weak right now. And he's been down. Give him a few days to get stronger, and you'll be fine, both of you."

"Thank you," Honey Lee said. "Is he really going to be all right?"

"Yes, but he has to take care of himself."

"He will. I'll make him."

When she got off the elevator downstairs, she found a bench and sat down. She took long, deep breaths trying to calm herself. *I'll make him change his mind if it's the last thing I do.*

CHAPTER 32

▼

Honey Lee left the hospital assured and determined. She walked briskly out through the gate to the trolley stop. At Park Square she took the Green Line up Commonwealth to Boston University. First she went to the library, apologized for being late and told the librarian she had to quit her job. When he told her she needed to give more notice, she agreed to work another week. Up in the stacks she found a dolly full of books for her to shelve. She continued shelving the books until four o'clock; then she went directly to the Dean's office to ask about procedures for withdrawing from the college. A student working at the counter gave her a form to fill out. She carefully entered her name and address, her student number, her birth date, the classes in which she was enrolled and the effective date of her withdrawal. The last line asked, "Reason for Withdrawing." Without hesitating, she wrote, "Getting Married," and handed the form back to the student who stamped it and made a copy for Honey Lee.

She took her usual train back to Lowell, ate dinner with her grandmother, took her books she no longer needed to the kitchen and sat staring at them. She would leave and return to Lowell at the same times she had since classes began. She would go directly to the hospital and stay either by his bed or in the hall until it was time to work at the library. She would carry her books with her so it would appear that she was still in school and so she would have something to do while she waited.

On Tuesday, she arrived at the hospital at nine-thirty. When she got off the elevator, the nurse who had spoken to her the day before came out from behind the desk.

"I hoped you would give him a few more days, dear." She held a clipboard against her chest. Honey Lee wondered if it held Danny's chart. "He told me not to let you in. I'm sorry." She was sympathetic and spoke soothingly.

"All right," Honey Lee said. She was prepared to wait. "I won't go in. But tell him I came, will you, please?"

"Sure, hon. You have to be patient with these guys. Their minds need as much healing as their bodies." They walked together to the elevator.

"I know. I can be patient. I will. But I'll come every day. I just want him to be told. Sooner or later he'll see me."

She took the elevator down to the first floor and found the bench she had sat on the day before. She sat to read. Just being in the same building with him was enough for the present. At three o'clock, she walked to the trolley stop and went up to the campus. Day followed day in the same pattern. She went to the nurses' station.

"Can I see him today?"

"No, dear, not yet."

"You tell him I came and that I'll be sitting downstairs until three o'clock."

The nurses were beginning to feel so bad for her that they talked to her about Danny. They told her what he ate, how much he had walked that day, how often he talked, how much sleep he had gotten. One day, the nurse she knew best, the red-haired one, walked her to the elevator and went down with her to the first floor.

"I know you're not his wife." There was no blame or criticism in her voice. "I knew you weren't from the beginning. You are in his dreams though. I knew your name before I saw you. I don't know what's going on with you two, but I'm betting that everything will work out."

Apparently he had called out for her in his sleep. "Thank you so much for that." Honey Lee impulsively hugged her. "He's stubborn. But so am I."

"He's beginning to weaken, honey." She laughed at the fit between her term of affection and Honey Lee's name. "I can tell. Every day, he asks without words, "Is she here? and I nod and, without words, say, 'Yes, she's here.' Yesterday, he just shook his head as if he couldn't believe you and almost smiled. You're pretty clever, and it's working."

She hadn't quite figured out how to manage weekends. All she knew was that she would go to the hospital every day even if she had to lie to her grandmother. On Saturday when she told Nana that she had to work all day at the library, Nana expressed concern. "Isn't it a bit too much working you're doing day after day? And on a Saturday, too." Nana was, as usual, fussing with love.

"They really need me, Nana." The lie tasted bitter in her mouth.

"Well, then I'll make you a lunch." She went to the pantry to get food for sandwiches.

"I'm so much trouble for you," Honey Lee said watching her grandmother spread butter on the thick white bread.

"Be off with you. What else would I be doing, then?"

As soon as she had said the word trouble, Honey Lee thought of the real trouble she was about to bring down on Nana. It couldn't be helped.

She took a later train and took her time getting to the hospital. She walked from North Station, stopping occasionally for directions but guided by her own sense of direction. At the hospital there was a different guard on duty and she had to identify herself and state her business again. She enjoyed saying that she was Mrs. Jackson visiting her husband at the hospital. It didn't feel like a lie. In her heart and mind she was Danny's. Soon the law, if not the church, would make it official.

Different nurses were on duty for the weekend, but they knew who she was immediately. "Honey Lee?" one of them asked coming out from behind the nurses' station.

"Yes, I'm here to see Danny Jackson."

"Not today, dear." The nurse shook her head and patted Honey Lee's arm.

"He won't see me," she said fully prepared for the refusal.

"No, but we'll tell him you're here."

"Is he still in the same bed?"

"Uh huh."

"Could I just look in, just to see him? I won't let him see me. I just want to see—to be sure he's all right." She was begging and she didn't care.

"We can't," one of the other nurses said. "He has a right to refuse visits. There's nothing we can do."

"I know. I'm sorry I asked. Don't forget to tell him I'm here," she said and went down to the lobby to wait.

She went to the bench she now considered hers and opened *Pere Goriot*, prepared to spend the next few hours reading, waiting, hoping.

"Honey Lee Murphy," Frank Jackson all but shouted her name, his voice like a wrathful preacher's. "What in God's name are you doing here? You call Mary at the crack of dawn, come here day after day. What in hell's going on?" Her heart thumping, she stood up. Her hands hung loosely by her sides, her mouth an open circle of surprise. "Honey, I'm sorry. I didn't mean to scare you." He opened his arms and drew her toward him.

When he released her, she asked, "Have you seen him lately? How is he? Is he getting better? Did he tell you I was here?"

Frank held both hands up, his palms facing her. "Whoa, Honey Lee. One question at a time. Me first. Then you."

"I'm sorry," she said. "Sure, your turn."

"Honey Child, what is this vigil you're keeping here?" He shook his head slowly from side to side, bewildered. "I thought you and Jimmy—"

"They didn't tell you?"

"Who, for crying out loud."

"Jimmy? Danny?"

"Tell me what?" He was impatient.

"I've been dating Danny. Jimmy found out. They fought."

"Sweet Jesus, Honey," he said. "This is crazy, just crazy. He can't get serious with you. He's—He's—"

She put up her hand to stop him, then took a deep breath and slowly released it. A few feet away, a man with a pail and a mop swabbed at the floor and watched them until Frank cleared his throat.

"Frank, I know about the divorce." She was calm now. "He told me."

He pounded one fist into the other hand. "No wonder Jimmy tried to beat the hell out of him. I'd like to do it myself."

"Frank, I'm going to marry him."

"Sweetheart, you can't. There's no future for you and him."

"That's what I thought, too. I sent him away twice. I'll never do it again, Frank. Never."

"You can't do that just because he's sick," he tried to reason with her. The man with the mop was watching them again. Frank glared at him and he moved on down the hall.

"That's what he thinks. But before I heard he was sick, I knew I couldn't live without him. God knows I tried to stay away from him, but I can't."

Frank led her to the bench to sit down. "But why him, for God's sake? Jimmy worships the ground you walk on. Mary and I always thought you two would end up together."

She shrugged her shoulders. There was no explaining why or how. She asked, "How is he, Frank?"

"Good. He loves it out there." He was talking about Jimmy. She wondered if he had deliberately misunderstood her question. "Says he'll probably never come back. Or did you mean Danny?"

"I wanted to talk to Jimmy, but what could I have said?"

"Let me drive you home after I see him. Come to the house. Talk to Mary. Maybe she can talk sense into you."

"You're angry."

"No, Honey child. I feel sorry for you. Danny should have let you be. Haven't you lived in Lowell long enough to know—" he sighed then continued, "Lowell is a church town, and the biggest church of them all is the Immaculate."

"Frank, I know all that, and I don't even know if he'll take me back. If he doesn't, I won't be able to bear it. Talk to him for me. Please."

"Maybe," he said. "Maybe after you and Mary have a long talk. But he won't listen to me. He never has. And he doesn't talk much either. I don't even know his wife's name let alone what went bad for them. You know what, Honey Lee? I don't even want to see him."

"Please go up. I need to know how he is, Frank."

He got up and went to the elevator. He pushed the up button so hard she wondered that his finger didn't break. She wanted to follow him up and into Danny's room, but she sat with the closed book on her lap. When the elevator door opened a few minutes later, she didn't even look up until Frank said, "Big mistake. I said I saw you, told him he could at least have the decency to see you, and he kicked me out. Let's go."

As they walked to the parking lot, Frank took her arm holding it so tight it hurt. Scowling, he said, "Damn fool. He's trying to kick everyone out of his life."

"He had a terrible war, Frank." She was quick to defend him.

"We all did, Honey Lee. Big deal. Did poor Danny tell you about his terrible war?"

"Stop it." She spoke sharply and pulled her arm out of his grip. "No, he didn't tell me. My grandmother did."

"Did she know about his marriage?"

"No. She was worried because he was a veteran, and sick, and older than me. She would have tied me up in my room if she'd known."

"She should have." When they reached the car, he opened the door for her and then got in himself. "So what did you plan to do about her when you married Danny?"

"I don't know, Frank. I don't know."

He turned on the radio and fell silent for the rest of the drive. When they got to Billerica Center, Honey Lee asked if he was sure it was all right for them to drop in on Mary without notice.

"She'd love to see you. Just a week ago she told me you two talked about getting together."

Honey Lee's stomach was churning. She would have to go through the whole thing with Mary, a strict Catholic who spent hours every week at Saint Andrew's Church praying and taking care of the altar linens as her mother had done before her. When they arrived, Frank called out, "Look who I've brought with me."

"Hi, Mary," Honey Lee said.

"Honey, great! I was hoping you'd come soon, and here you are. How's your grandmother?" She put her arms around Honey Lee and held her. "Come in, come in." She led Honey Lee into the warm living room.

"Frank, get Honey Lee something to drink."

"No, thanks. I'm fine."

"I'm going to make tea. You two are going to need it. You and Honey Lee need to talk," Frank said. He went to the kitchen to put the kettle on.

Mary looked more closely at Honey Lee. She pointed to the couch and said, "Sit down." They both sat. "It's about Danny, isn't it?" Mary asked.

"Um hmm."

"I knew it. I knew it when you called. What have you gotten yourself into?"

"Don't say it like that, Mary." Any hope that Mary would understand and be sympathetic vanished.

"Have you been dating him? Has he made promises to you?"

Honey Lee sighed. Frank called to them to come into the kitchen where he had set out the tea and cups and saucers. Steam rose from the kettle on the stove. "I'm going out, Mary." He was halfway to the door before Mary could say anything. Clearly he didn't want to be part of the discussion.

As soon as they were seated, Mary asked, "Well, has he? Made promises?"

"No. I did. Twice. And went back on them twice."

"You should have done it once. He's no good."

Honey Lee had never seen this coldness in Mary before. She busied herself stirring sugar into her tea. "Mary, I know about the marriage," she said.

Mary was shocked. "And still you went out with him?"

"At first I didn't know. Then he told me."

"He should never have gone near you. I wish Jimmy hadn't brought you to that dinner. I told Frank I didn't like the way he talked to you that night, but I never dreamed it would come to this."

"Mary, he tried to end it. He told me he'd go away."

Mary sniffed. "A little late for that I'd say."

"I told him I'd marry him. Then I changed my mind when my Nana got sick."

"So now you think you made him sick and you owe it to him to keep your promise. That's stupid, Honey Lee."

"That's not it. That's not what it's like."

"Then what is it like?" Mary snapped. "You do know what's at stake here, right?"

"Yes." Honey tried to sound strong, but Mary's contempt and anger made it difficult.

"Honey Lee, he can't marry you or anyone else. You know church law. Just how did you think you were going to get married?"

"We didn't know how. Danny was going into Boston to find out. Then my grandmother got sick—"

"She'd be a lot sicker if she knew what you were up to. You know that, don't you?"

"Yes, I know."

"And why Boston for heaven's sake?" Mary continued pushing.

"Boston. So no one would know either of us."

"I'll tell you what it will be like. A Justice of the Peace in a musty old office. No one but you and him and two people you round up to be witnesses. No church wedding. No Mass and Communion, not just that day but as long as you are together. And no respect anywhere in Lowell. You know how this city is."

"Stop," Honey Lee cried out. "I know all this. I hate it. But I love him. I need him. Try to understand, won't you?"

"I could kill him," Mary said. And then understanding dawned, "Oh, my God. That's why he and Jimmy quarreled, isn't it? He drove his little brother off."

Honey Lee prayed for Frank's return. There would be no help or support from Mary and none from Frank. But still she felt strong in her choice. "Mary, promise me one thing?"

"What?"

"Don't tell anyone. I have to find the best way of telling Nana Murphy. She has to hear it from me."

"God help her," Mary said and blessed herself. "I promise, but I'm going to pray that you come to your senses. For God's sake, Honey Lee think."

Frank finally came back. And Honey Lee said good-bye to Mary. She knew she would never see her again. On the way home, Frank said that if she was determined to go to the hospital the next day he would take her in if Mary wasn't going with him. "She'd have a fit if she thought I encouraged you." When he pulled up in front of the house, he leaned across and kissed her on the forehead.

"I don't know what to wish for. Danny would be lucky to have a good woman like you, and God knows he needs one. But Honey Lee, think carefully about what you're doing. Promise me that."

"I will Frank, I will. Thank you.

CHAPTER 33

▼

When Honey Lee opened the back door, she smelled the familiar odors of Saturday night supper—molasses, onions, pork and beans. She had come to love the ritual meals at Nana's house, unfailingly beans and hot dogs on Saturday, creamed salt cod on Friday, and beef pot roast on Sunday. The predictability of the meals was comforting. She stood in the doorway watching her grandmother at the stove—her crisp, flowered apron covering her housedress. When Honey Lee said her name, Nana Murphy looked up and smiled at her granddaughter.

"I'm glad you're early today. We'll have an early supper and a nice quiet night together. I've missed you these past weeks."

Honey set the table with the blue and white dishes that Nana had said that her father loved. He had always insisted that one dish was special, different from all of the others. Honey Lee had studied all the plates since Nana had told her about the special one, but she had never found it. The kettle for tea was already steaming. Honey Lee poured the hot water into the teapot and took it to the table. Nana brought the bean pot and the hot dogs. They sat down together, Nana asked for blessings on the food and on each of them in words Honey Lee had heard hundreds of times before. Her awareness of what she stood to lose made every bite she took, every word they spoke, and everything they did seem wonderful. She vowed to give as much of the time she had left to her grandmother and to treasure every minute of it. She was overwhelmed by love for her grandmother.

On Sunday, using another pretext for not going to Mass with her grandmother, Honey Lee went to the French church downtown for Mass and then went to the Square, where Frank had promised to meet her if he could. Several people she knew waved and called out to her or stopped to chat, some from the parish, some from school. Twice girls she didn't recognize called out, "Hello Colonel Murphy." Girl Officer days seemed so far away that she turned around to see who they were talking to. Twelve-thirty came and went and there was no sign of Frank. She walked toward the station. Fewer trains ran on Sunday, and the first one she could make would not get her to the hospital until four o'clock. If she took it, she would be too late getting back to Lowell to have dinner with Aunt Kitty, Uncle Peter, and young Peter, who were coming on a rare visit. She ought to be there. She could go to Chelsea and wait on the outside chance that Danny might see her and miss the special occasion dinner. Or she could stay in Lowell and go home to help with dinner and perhaps miss the one day that Danny agreed to see her. She was tired of choices with downsides. It would be wonderful to make a simple, comfortable choice. She decided not to go to the hospital. Since Frank had not picked her up, Mary had most likely gone in with him. She wasn't ready to see Mary again.

She was restless and didn't want to go right home so she decided to go to the movies so she could be alone and invisible. She bought a ticket and went into the dark theater. She paid little attention to the film, and halfway through it, she got up and left taking a roundabout way back to Concord Street. She got home just in time to set the table before her aunt and uncle came. They ate a delicious dinner in the dining room in honor of Uncle Peter. He said very little, but he managed for the first time since he had come home, to sit through the meal without jumping up and leaving the room. Honey had become more curious about Uncle Peter since she started dating Danny. But he was impenetrable. He answered questions only occasionally and then in monosyllables. She hoped that this dinner was a step toward returning to normal. Neither Aunt Kitty nor Nana Murphy had mentioned Danny since the terrible night they had ambushed her with the news about Danny that almost broke her heart.

After she and Nana had finished cleaning up after dinner, Honey Lee brought out her books and sat at the kitchen table. Nana sat in her rocker beside the stove with her sewing basket and a box of woolen scraps beside her. She was working on another braided rug using wool her cousin had brought her from the Talbot Mills in Billerica. When the rug she was working on got bigger, she would need to work it on the table where Honey Lee usually sat. Honey Lee had seen her grandmother make several rugs. One covered almost the entire floor in the living room. Another smaller one, which she had helped Nana make, was by the bed in her room. By ten o'clock both Honey Lee and Nana Murphy were ready for bed. Honey Lee could hardly wait for morning.

At the hospital the next day, she was happy to see the weekday nurses back on duty. Her favorite nurse, whose name she had learned was Edna, greeted her warmly. "Good morning, Honey Lee. I hear you didn't come yesterday."

"I'm glad you keep track of me even if he doesn't."

"Oh, but he does," Edna said smiling. "I heard that he noticed that you weren't here."

Honey Lee's face flushed with pleasure. Excited, she asked, "He asked for me?"

"Not in so many words. But they told us he said something like, 'I suppose she's here again,' and was surprised when they said you weren't."

"Disappointed?" she wanting all the details.

"Sweetie, I wasn't there. I've told you all I know," Edna said. "I'll go and tell him you're here." She hurried off down the corridor. Honey Lee watched her back and listened to the squish of her soft rubber-soled shoes. She went into the ward and came out again quickly shaking her head. Honey Lee nodded, shrugged her shoulders, and took the elevator down to the lobby. She sat on her bench and began to read. After about ten minutes, she heard the elevator door open and close, and then heard slow shuffling steps. She held her breath, kept her eyes on her book, prayed, "Dear God, let it be him." It was. He stood before her, unsmiling. "Honey Lee," he said, "what do you think you're doing?"

She raised her eyes and met his. She wanted more than anything to stand up and hold and kiss him, but she sat still.

"What do you want?" His voice held no warmth.

"You know what I want." He wore a loose robe over green hospital pajamas. His hair had grown long. It curled over the back of his robe. He kept pushing the hair in front away from his eyes. He looked better, less pale. Wonderful. She felt she couldn't bear to sit another minute. "How are you Danny? Are you better?"

"I'm fine."

She put her hand on his arm and moved to give him room to sit beside her. He sat, but on the edge of the bench as far away from her as he could. "Sit down beside me, Danny. And talk to me. Please talk to me. Thank you for coming down. It's been lonely." Her hunger for his touch became a prayer, "Dear God, let him please touch me to show me he loves me."

"You're a patient woman," he said, his voice still flat.

"I am. And stubborn. I told you I'd keep coming until you leave. Then wherever you go I'll follow." She put all of her reserve and strength into her words, willing him to understand that this time there would be no going back. "I won't let you go."

He put his elbows on his knees and rested his head in his hands, but his voice was no longer flat. Thank God he was feeling something. "Honey we've done this before. It's exhausting. I can't do it again." Honey reached over and started to rub his shoulders gently.

She whispered over and over, "Danny, I love you. I was wrong. I love you."

He raised his head and looked at her. "You are so beautiful. I wanted you so much."

"You still want me," she said. Urgent. Demanding. "Tell me you do."

He shook his head slowly. Panicking, she read the gesture as a no. "I do," he paused. "But I don't trust you."

"You can, Danny. You can. I want to marry you. I'll marry you as soon as I can. I'd marry you right here on this bench this minute if I could."

He groaned and said, "And if she gets sick again?"

"I would help her if I could. But you would be first, always first. Let me go right now to find out what we need to do. To do what we should have done weeks ago."

"No." He stood up. "Don't go." He took her in his arms and kissed her forehead. "Don't." Then her eyes. "Just stay here with me. I love you. I don't want you to go anywhere." He kissed her mouth. She felt him shudder as she held him. She sighed deeply, flooded with relief. She began to cry. "I was afraid you weren't coming back, and I was terrified."

"And I thought I had lost you forever," she said. "I thought I was lost, hopelessly lost. Danny, marry me. Tomorrow if we can." She held his upper arms, and when he didn't answer, she shook him. "Tell me you will."

"I will. I will. But not tomorrow. Not in a hospital. When I'm well. I won't let you marry a sick man."

She delighted in the strength with which he spoke until she realized what the words might mean. "What does that mean?" she asked. "How long? I don't want to wait."

"Honey, it won't be long. I'm better. The doctor will tell you. Come see him with me now."

"Just hold me a little longer," she said looking up at him. She could hardly bear looking into his intense dark eyes, but she couldn't not look. She traced his eyebrows and his lips with her fingers. "You are wonderful. I've never ever seen anything more beautiful. And you're mine. Thank God."

They separated enough to walk to the elevators holding hands. When they got off together, the nurses clapped and cheered.

Honey blushed and said, "Isn't it wonderful?"

"More than wonderful," Danny said putting his arm around her and kissing the top of her head. He led her into the ward and called out.

"Listen up, guys. This magnificent woman is going to marry me."

The men whistled, clapped, and shouted. Finding herself the center of so much attention, she became uneasy. She thanked them and put slight pressure on Danny's arm to signal her discomfort. As they turned and walked out, she heard the men talking about her.

"She's a tall drink of water, that one."

"Not water, you jerk, champagne."

"Where can I get one of those? Oh, God, tell me where?"

The laughter followed them as Danny led her past the nurses' station and down the long corridor. They passed two other wards before they came to a series of frosted glass doors with names painted in black. Danny paused outside of a door marked Lieutenant Commander, John Thompson, M.D. "He was on the first ship I was ever on. You'll like him." He knocked on the door.

"Come in." The voice was pleasantly friendly.

Danny opened the door, and they both walked into a sparsely furnished room with a desk, two straight-back chairs, a filing cabinet, and a sink. No pictures. No rugs. The man seated at the desk in hospital whites was looking at a file, taking notes. When he looked up and saw Honey Lee, he stood up and with a slight Southern drawl said, "Good morning, ma'am." And good morning to you, Jackson. Good to see you up and around. Keep it up. Go outside, get some fresh air, build up your appetite, and maybe we might even take you back into the Navy."

"Thank you, sir, but no thank you. I've had enough Navy." He turned to Honey Lee and said, "Sweetheart, this is Doctor Thompson. Doctor, this is Honey Lee Murphy."

"You have to be a Southerner with a name like that." The doctor said coming around the desk to take her hand.

"I used to be. But now I'm pure New England on my father's side and in my heart."

"You can't take the South out of a woman," he joked. "What can I do for you, Jackson?"

"Miss Murphy, Honey Lee, has agreed to marry me. I need to know about my release date."

"You keep up what you're doing and you'll be out in a matter of weeks."

"Weeks?" Honey Lee asked. "How many weeks, sir?"

"Well, I'd say two, maybe three, to be really sure."

"Great," Danny said, but Honey Lee was not happy. How could she wait weeks?

"Sir," Danny said, "do you know how we'd go about getting married in Massachusetts?"

"One of you must have a priest or minister who can help you with that," the doctor said.

"No, sir. We can't use a priest."

"Oh?" He looked puzzled, but didn't question them. "I do know you need birth certificates and certificates of former marriages and divorces if there are any. If you're both from Massachusetts, you can get those at the state house. You'll need a blood test, which I can do for you, right here, any time if you want."

"I'd love to take the first step today," Honey Lee said. "Could you do it right now?"

"Yes, ma'am, I can and I will." He smiled at her and went to the small sink to wash his hands. He drew the blood then told them he would give them the report in two days. He congratulated them as they left.

When they left the office, Honey Lee was surprised to see that Danny walked slowly and was having trouble breathing. "Are you all right?"

"Yes. But I need to lie down. Sorry." His forehead was beaded with sweat.

He leaned against her as they made their way back to the ward. When they approached the nurses' station, one of the nurses came and put Danny's arm over her shoulder so he could lean on her. When they entered the ward, the men sang, "Here comes the bride." Danny smiled and waved, but when they got to his bed, he sat down, exhausted. He lay down and closed his eyes. She watched him struggle to get his breathing back to normal.

When he was quiet she said, "We're going too fast. I'm making you get sick."

"No." He smiled up at her. "It's happiness. I'm not used to it. I can't believe what you just did."

"I love you," she said. "Rest, now." When she leaned down to kiss him, he raised his hand to her face.

"I love you, Honey Lee Murphy," he said and closed his eyes.

She sat until his breathing was regular and then tiptoed from the room. She went to the nurses' station and told them about the plans. "Isn't it wonderful? We're getting married as soon as he's well." They nodded and smiled with her. She told them that Danny was asleep and that she was going to the state house to get the papers they needed.

Too impatient to wait for a trolley, she practically ran to Beacon Hill. The gilded dome of the state house glistened in the sunlight. She had never been in the beautiful building before. She was directed to one of the lower floors to Records. It wasn't until she stood at the counter facing an unsmiling woman that she realized there would be no birth certificate for her here in this building. The clerk behind the desk looked bored and tired. When Honey Lee told her she didn't know the exact date of Danny's birth, she said, "Well what do you expect me to do?"

"Well, he's twenty-six years old and he was born in Lowell and his mother's name was Mary. Isn't that enough?"

"That's not a lot of help, Miss. Jackson's not an uncommon name. An exact date would be helpful."

"Please try. It's really important."

The woman frowned, left the counter, and came back in five minutes. "You're in luck. Only one Daniel Jackson born in the appropriate month. Do you need his marriage and divorce records too?"

Honey Lee gasped. She had completely forgotten. "Yes, please," she said. The woman left again and came back with more papers.

"Wait here. I'll have to type up copies and get a stamp so you might as well sit down." Honey Lee sat on a hard bench until the woman returned and handed her a white envelope. She said, "That's one dollar for each page."

Honey Lee handed her the money and took the papers. Another step closer. "Thank you," she said. "I hate to bother you, but could you tell me how I can get my own birth certificate? I was born in Atlanta."

"You write to the state house in Augusta or city hall in Atlanta. If you have the right date and name, it might take a week or two." She turned to someone in line behind Honey Lee and said, "Next?"

"Could I bother you for one more thing?"

"What now?"

"The address, the street address, of city hall in Atlanta?" Had she been less eager, she wouldn't have dared ask.

"Hold on," the woman said sighing deeply. She left and came back with a slip of paper. "That should do it."

"Thank you for everything." The woman finally smiled and wished Honey Lee luck. Remembering that she had passed a post office on her way to the State House, she went there and got a stamped envelope to write for her own birth certificate. She was tempted to look in the envelope to see Danny's birth certificate. She wanted to know his birthday. But she did not want to see the other papers, the ones that would put a name and a date to Danny's marriage.

When she got back to the hospital, she went up to the ward. One of the men put both of his hands on one side of his face and bent his head to signal that Danny was asleep. "I wouldn't wake him, dearie. He hasn't slept much since he got here."

Honey Lee thanked him and walked over to Danny's bed and sat down. She was happy that he was sleeping. It gave her time to watch him. With his hair falling over his forehead, he looked like a child with a bowl cut. She tried to find features that he shared with his brothers. The arch of his dark brows was his alone. He and Frank both had dark hair, but Danny's was really black and Frank kept his shorter. His mouth reminded her of Jimmy. She felt a pang when she thought of Jimmy, but pushed the thought away determined not to let anything spoil this day. She leaned back in her chair, smiling. She was content.

CHAPTER 34

▼

Nana believed that Honey Lee was taking classes and working at the library. It was both easy and difficult for Honey Lee to deceive her grandmother, easy because Nana Murphy trusted her completely and difficult because Honey Lee had no practice of deceit. But she could have continued the pretense calmly if Mr. Flynn had not called on Thursday. From the minute she came into the house that day, she knew something had changed. When Honey Lee went to the kitchen and called out, "Nana, I'm home," Nana did not respond as she usually did by calling out from wherever she was. She went into the back hall and called out, "Nana?"

Puzzled, she went into the living room. Her grandmother sat in her chair.

"Nana, are you all right?" she said leaning down to kiss her grandmother.

Nana did not return her kiss. "Yes, I'm fine," she said. "Mr. Flynn called looking for you. He sounds upset."

Honey Lee knew immediately that Mr. Flynn had learned that she had dropped out of school.

"Did he leave a message, Nana?"

"Just to call him." Her grandmother's unnatural reserve troubled her more than Mr. Flynn's call.

"I'll call h him now," Honey Lee said. Knowing it would be a difficult conversation, she willed her grandmother to leave the room.

Nana got up slowly and sighed. She said, "I'll be putting supper on." She walked toward the kitchen, turned, and said, "Come out when you're done, dear." Honey Lee watched her, worried.

Honey Lee sat down to think. She didn't know what to say to this kind man who had befriended her, whose son had wanted to marry her, and who had helped her get the scholarship to Boston University. The pure joy of the day with Danny was fading. Twice before she could bring herself to dial, she picked up the receiver and put it down. When she did dial, Mr. Flynn answered on the third ring. "Hello?"

"Mr. Flynn, it's Honey Murphy." She tried to steady her voice but it wavered. She put her hand over her heart and patted her chest as if to calm the furious beating.

"So it is. How are you Honey Lee?" His voice, cool and distant, chilled her.

"I'm fine thank you." She was anything but fine, cold to the bone even though she still had her coat on. She pulled the collar up around her ears.

"We need to talk, Honey Lee."

"About?" She played for time using the single word. She knew exactly what they needed to talk about and she would have to lie to him too.

"About Jack. About Boston University. About Honey Lee Murphy."

As she had guessed, he knew about both BU and about Jack. "Mr. Flynn. I'm so sorry. About everything. I should have called you, but I couldn't. I'm sorry."

"But why? BU was a great opportunity for you." There was no way she could explain to him. To tell the truth would unburden her immeasurably, but she couldn't.

"I had to."

"Had to." His voice changed. He asked again, "Had to?" When she didn't answer, he said, "Honey Lee, are you in trouble?"

"In trouble?" Yes, she supposed she was from his point of view. But then the tone of his voice when he asked and his peculiar emphasis on the word trouble registered. "You mean? Oh my God," She could hardly say the words, "you think I'm pregnant."

"Well?"

"No. How could you possibly think that?" She was stunned that he would believe this of her.

Mr. Flynn didn't speak right away, but finally he said, "It's the only thing that makes sense to me. If I'm wrong, I'm sorry."

"You are wrong, Mr. Flynn." Before he could reply, she said, "Good-bye, Mr. Flynn" and hung up. She sat staring at the phone. That's what everyone will think. Ellen and Jack and Jimmy and Frank and Mary. And Nana. Even Nana would believe that was why she had married Danny. She went slowly to the kitchen where Nana was setting the table. She went to the stove to help by taking the hash from the frying pan and putting it on a platter. Her grandmother poured water into the teapot and brought it to the table. They ate in complete silence for several minutes. Nana even skipped the blessing.

"Mr. Flynn is worried about you," Nana finally said.

"It was just a misunderstanding. We got it straightened out. He wishes I were still seeing his son," she lied.

"Such a nice boy. I wish you were seeing him too. I'm a little worried about you, too, if the truth be told." Nana was more than a little worried. Honey Lee could tell by the lines on her forehead and beside her mouth. And her eyes were troubled. She reached for her grandmother's hand and squeezed it.

"Please don't worry, Nana." She hated the dishonesty of her words.

"If you say I shouldn't, then I won't, dear."

At least Mr. Flynn had not told her grandmother about school, so Honey Lee could continue that fiction for a while longer. That was a relief. But Nana's trust burdened her. She couldn't keep up the pretense much longer. She would tell Danny they had to move more quickly. Soon after they had finished eating, she pleaded fatigue and went to her room.

When she went up to the ward the following day, Danny was dressed and sitting by the bed of another patient. He wore slacks and a sweater. He stood up and smiled when he saw Honey Lee and walked toward her with the long, free stride she had loved to watch and to match when they walked together. He was getting better; soon he'd be able to leave.

"You look beautiful," he said. "I keep forgetting how beautiful you are." He smoothed her hair back with both hands and kissed her once on each cheek.

"And you—you look ready to walk out of here. Healthy."

"You're medicine, Honey Lee. I'm better every day." She loved the sound of her name in his mouth.

They walked out of the ward together and went down on the elevator. The January thaw had set in. It was pleasantly warm. Danny led Honey Lee toward the outside door. "Is it all right for you to go out?" she asked, worried.

"Sure."

They followed a path that led around the building. Honey told him about the telephone call without mentioning Mr. Flynn's guess about her reason for leaving school. But she was urgent about her discomfort with her grandmother. "I hate deceiving her, Danny. I can't go on doing it."

He stopped and turned to face her. "You could tell her the truth." The edge of the old anger crept into his voice. "That you dropped out of school. That you are going to marry me."

She gasped. "I can't do that, Danny. On the day I tell her, I will leave her house for good."

"Are you afraid she'll change your mind?" She was saddened by his lack of trust in her,

"Of course not." She returned anger for anger. "And if you don't believe that, I don't know what I can do to convince you. The only way I can do this is to marry you and then tell her and then leave. I can't stay in her house after that. She wouldn't be able to let me. That's how it is with her about the church and about marriage. That's how it was with me until I loved you. How it is with everyone we know."

"I don't get it. Why are they like that?" He looked like a young boy puzzled by a confusing world. They were standing on the path near the top of the hill. A stiff breeze had come up.

"Danny, have you ever met a divorced person?"

"Sure," he said. "Lots."

"Lots," she said mocking him. "In Lowell?"

He scratched his head. "No. In the Navy. A lot like me divorced while they were overseas."

"I never did until I met you, and we both know why not. People in our world don't divorce. Divorced people are freaks in our neighborhood. There was a woman who lived somewhere in the parish that I kept hearing people whisper about because she had a daughter but no husband. I never saw her. And I heard whispers about divorce ever since I moved here. What about your own mother? Did she ever consider divorcing your father? Jimmy told me she wouldn't even listen to Father Finn when he said she should at least get a separation. That's the way it is."

"You're right. My mother wouldn't have done it. I would have been shocked if she had."

"Danny, I've made a choice for myself. But if I marry you and stay in Lowell, she will bear the shame of it. I won't do that to her."

"All right. We'll wait until I get out of here."

"But I can't go on lying. I hate it."

"Sweetheart, I don't want to marry you in a hospital. What kind of a wedding would that be?"

"The best kind we can have, Danny. We're never going to have a church, a priest, a blessing, and a family celebration. We both know that."

"Damn it all, Honey, I want more than that for you." He walked several steps away from her thinking. When he turned back he said, "I'll get out this week no matter what they say. Then we marry."

"You can't leave until you're well."

"I'm better. I'm fine."

"Not all better. I can hear your breathing. Sit down for a minute." She led him to a small stone bench and they sat down.

"Then be patient. Wait. Wait till I get out." He took her hands in his and feeling how cold they were, blew on them and closed his own hands over them.

"I'll try Danny."

The next day he told her that the doctor wouldn't let him leave the hospital before the middle of February. Honey Lee was desperate. "Look, Danny," she said holding an envelope out to him. "It came yesterday. We can marry now. We have everything we need." He took it from her and unfolded it.

"Your birth certificate," he said holding the thin sheet of paper in his hands.

"I had to tell Nana I needed it for school. Another lie. I can't keep doing this. I can't."

"Where would you live?"

"I could live in your apartment for a little while, couldn't I? I'd be your wife."

"Alone? People wondering who you are, why you're there. Tongues wagging and me nowhere around to help you." He shook his head "No. Let me try to work something out."

"I love you. I would marry you even if you were never able to leave this hospital and I had to pitch a tent outside." He begged her again to be patient and she promised to try.

Going back to Lowell, however, grew more and more difficult. Nana Murphy was over-solicitous as if she were an invalid. It pained her more and more to see the worry in her grandmother's face. She wanted to reach out and smooth the skin on her grandmother's forehead, erase the worry. She dreaded the day she would stand before Nana Murphy and give her news that was sure to break her heart.

On Friday, when she returned to the hospital, Danny was waiting at the downstairs door. He ran to her, put his arms around her, and kissed her. "I have the best news, darling. You won't believe it." He lifted her up and swung her around. "Doctor Thompson knows people. He gets things done. He's getting me a transfer to the hospital in Virginia. There's housing there, for you, for us, Veterans housing."

"When?" She was jubilant. It was going to happen. They were going to marry.

"Next week."

"Next week we marry? Here?" She pulled away from him and put her hands on his arms so she could see his face. She laughed out loud when she saw how happy he was.

"Yes."

"And we go together to Virginia?"

"That's the bad part. I have to go transport, and you can't go with me. Not even Thompson could pull that off. But you go on the same day on the train."

"When?" She tugged at his shirt. "When?"

"Tuesday." He handed her an envelope. "I want you to take this and go out and buy the most beautiful dress in the world." He put his hands on her shoulders. She looked up at him and held his gaze until her eyes filmed over.

"I'm so happy. I promise I will be a good wife to you."

"And I will spend the rest of my life making it up to you that we had to marry this way." They held on to each other rocking back and forth almost dancing in their excitement.

Honey Lee thought waiting would be easier once she knew exactly when it would end, but she was wrong. Once she knew, every hour seemed like a day. That night she went to the attic and found the suitcase that she had carried when she first arrived in Lowell. It was much smaller than she remembered, and she would have to put everything she would take away from Lowell in it. She carried the suitcase down to her room and put it under the bed. They had decided that she shouldn't come into Chelsea over the weekend. She had wanted to go in on Saturday, but Danny said, "No, dear. Spend those days with her. We have the rest of our lives."

Even though the two days were the last she would ever spend with Nana Murphy, she had to act as if they were ordinary days. On Saturday she planned to go down to the church as if for confession and then shop for Sunday dinner. She hoped that Aunt Kitty and her family would come to dinner so she could see them. She had to begin detaching slowly from the life she had built in Lowell.

Early on Saturday morning she got up and dressed warmly. Without planning it, she repeated the first walk she had ever taken in Lowell. On Perry Street, she stopped and stared at the piles of telephone poles which had been both playground and refuge for her. She climbed up on one of the middle piles and sat. It was the same pile she had hidden under after her father had died. How alone she had been when Jimmy found her and tried to comfort her. That was the first time she had heard of Danny Jackson, her friend's brother. Now she was all but married to him. And Jimmy. She would be Jimmy's sister-in-law even if she never saw him again. His face as it had looked the last times she saw him flashed in her mind, the fury in him as he rushed off to find Danny. What a sad good-bye for someone she had loved so much. She hoped he was happy and that one day they might be friends again. She jumped down and resumed her walk down to the church. She had never been to a wedding in the church but she had seen brides and grooms posing for pictures outside. It was a beautiful church for a wedding. She had believed that one day she would be married from that church, surrounded with her grandmother's family and friends.

She went around to the side and entered the lower church. She went up to the side altar and knelt. No words. She had no idea how to pray. With her head bowed, she waited. Then she silently prayed the words of the Act of Contrition. "Oh my God, I am heartily sorry for having offended you—" She stopped. She hadn't offended yet. Could she ask for forgiveness for what she was about to do? "I firmly resolve with the help of your grace to amend my life—" No, she could not say that prayer. She reached into her pocket and pulled out two quarters. She put the quarters into the moneybox and picked up the taper. She lit candles, one for Danny, a prayer that he would get completely well; one for Nana Murphy, a prayer that she would not be too grieved; one for Jimmy that he might forgive her and Danny; and the last for Ellen and Jack and all the Flynns, that God would bless and reward them for their goodness to her. Finally she found words for her own prayer.

"Forgive me Lord, God. I promise to be faithful and true in all my ways but this one. I am deeply sorry that having given my heart, I cannot take it away. Have mercy on me, I beg you. Amen."

She walked over to the school remembering with a smile how she and Jimmy and Ellen had battled for first place in eighth grade, how both of them had protected her when she went back to school after her father's death. They had been good friends to her; she couldn't imagine what she would have done without them. Ellen and her family were much on her mind as she walked up High Street. They had taken her in as one of the family, had shared their family homes and traditions with her. She and Danny would have to build their own traditions for the family they would become, a big family, she hoped.

CHAPTER 35

▼

On Monday, Honey Lee stopped at a small dress store on Dutton Street. She had passed it hundreds of times before but had never entered. She had often looked at expensive looking dresses in the window. For her wedding, no dress was too expensive. When she entered there was no one in sight in the store, but the bell on the door summoned a saleswoman dressed in a simple black dress.

"Good morning, Miss. Can I help you?" she said coming from the back of the store.

"Good morning. I'm looking for a dress for a very special occasion," Honey said relieved that she did not recognize the woman. Her relief was short lived.

"Aren't you the Murphy girl, the girl officer?" Honey Lee had forgotten that she had become a minor celebrity in Lowell. Well, it couldn't be helped.

"Yes. Can you help me find a special dress—for a dance?" She invented the dance to avoid questions.

"I knew your father," she said. "I was sorry to hear of his death."

At another time in her life Honey Lee would have pressed the woman for every detail the woman could remember about her father, but all she wanted today was a dress. "Thank you," Honey Lee said as she moved toward one of the racks to look at the dresses.

"Let me show you a few lovely dresses for your special dance," the woman said pulling out a filmy black dress with a long skirt and a bright red strapless gown. Honey Lee continued to run her hands over the other dresses on the rack stopping over a white wool dress with a scoop neck, long sleeves, and a full skirt. She pulled it from the rack.

"I think I'd like to try this one," she said.

"But, my dear, that's not a dress for a dance." The woman was trying to be motherly. "You could wear that to church."

"But I like it," Honey Lee said holding it up against her body. "I like it very much."

"Of course. It's lovely, but take the others in. Just try them. With your color the red would be just beautiful." The woman, holding the two dresses she had chosen, led Honey Lee toward the dressing room and hung the dresses on a hook just outside the curtained door. Honey Lee went into the dressing room carrying the white dress. She took off her coat and dress and taking the white dress from the hanger slid it over her head. Even if she had been blindfolded she would have chosen it for its softness.

Standing before the mirror, she smoothed the dress over her waist and ran her hands down the sides of the skirt which fell in folds almost to her ankles. Danny would love it. She knew he would. She took the dress off, dressed in her own clothes and came out of the dressing room.

"I'll take this one."

"Well, you certainly know your own mind," the woman said taking the dress from her and folding it. Honey Lee paid for the dress with the money Danny had given her and thanked the saleswoman.

She took the dress with her to the hospital for the nurses to hold until the next day. Word of the wedding had spread throughout the ward and beyond. The nurses and the men called out their congratulations. Honey Lee was lightheaded. She could hardly believe the wedding was going to take place the next day. Danny took her to see the chapel, a small dim room with seats for no more than twenty people and a plain altar with a simple cross. He told her that the judge would come to the chapel at eleven o'clock the next day. Honey Lee felt dizzy with the speed of it all. Danny told her he had been given an overnight pass and had made reservations for a wedding supper at the Copley Plaza in Boston. She hadn't dared to hope that they would spend their wedding night out of the hospital. She would have to tell another lie to Nana to explain an overnight in Boston. On Wednesday morning, she would begin to tell the truth. She would return to Lowell to pack and to confess to Nana Murphy. Danny had arranged for a sleeping berth on a nine-thirty train out of South Station on Wednesday night. She wished that she and Danny could have traveled together. They were hurtling toward new lives with dizzying speed. She felt giddy. But when Danny put his arms around her and told her how much he loved her, she knew she was doing the only thing she could do. And that they would be happy.

Leaving Danny was also getting harder. He walked her to the gate and said good-bye. She got to the train station just in time for the three-thirty train. She would be home in time for supper. On the train ride back to Lowell, her mind raced. It was her last trip home. When she came back to Lowell on Wednesday, her real home would be wherever Danny was. The visit to Concord Street would be just that, a visit.

When she got home, she held her grandmother a bit longer than she usually did. When later she said good night, she held her even longer. Nana Murphy commented on her loving ways, and she felt a wave of guilt and regret. How would she survive without her grandmother? How would her grandmother survive without her? How would she survive knowing what she had done? Nana Murphy would be certain that Honey Lee had put herself out of the embrace of the church forever. Honey Lee barely slept that night her head spinning, with joy and grief.

CHAPTER 36

▼

On her wedding day, she acted as if it were any old day. She ate breakfast with Nana, gave her a quick kiss good-bye, and walked out the door. Only when she got outside did she let herself think about the rest of the day. She ran the full length of Concord Street humming tunes from as many love songs as she could remember. On the train, she tried to imagine how the day might go. She thought of the one wedding she had ever been to, Jack and Marion's. Then she thought of the tiny chapel at the hospital and her simple white dress. Then she tried to picture Danny and herself together alone for the whole night. It was too much for her to imagine.

When she got to the hospital, Edna and another nurse named Mary met her at the downstairs door and led her to the nurses' break room on the first floor. It was bad luck, they said, for the groom to see the bride before the wedding. Someone had pressed her dress and hung it on one of the lockers. Honey Lee walked over and touched it. In her school bag, she had packed dress shoes, nylons, panties, a garter belt, a bra, and a new slip. She had chosen the slip with great care wanting it to feel like a wedding dress, elegant and elaborate. She had tried it on in the dressing room at Bon Marche. The lace bodice fit her perfectly ending just beneath her breast where the soft shimmering satin, cut on the bias, clung to her waist and hips before it fell almost to her ankles. She had blushed in the dressing room thinking of standing before Danny wearing it.

Still shy of undressing in front of others, she went into the small bathroom to change. She came out in the slip. Edna held the white dress for her. As it slid over her head and down onto her body she felt caressed by the soft wool. The nurses, who had thought the dress plain for a wedding, stared and said, "Oh." Honey Lee's face, flushed with excitement, glowed.

Mary went to a locker and brought out a dozen red roses. "Danny insisted on red," she said. "I told him they should be white."

Honey Lee held them to her face and smiled. They pinned a small white veil to her head with bobby pins "My sister's," Edna said.

Honey Lee turned and looked at herself in the mirror. She knew, as she had never known before, that she was beautiful. And she was glad.

Just before eleven o'clock, the doctor knocked on the door. "Time to go, ladies," he said.

Edna opened the door and Honey Lee came out into the hall.

"You are magnificent, my dear," the doctor said giving her his arm. They took the stairway to the second floor where the chapel was. Danny waited by the door of the chapel. Honey Lee put pressure on the doctor's arm. She wanted him to stop so she could watch Danny before he saw her, but Danny must have heard them because just then he turned. He walked toward her, his handsome face intensely serious.

"Honey Lee," he said. "Oh, Honey Lee." He stood before her and stared, then put his hand out to her. She took it and they walked into the chapel where the judge in a black robe waited at the altar. The small chapel was filled with men in pajamas and nurses in uniform. Doctor Thompson and the nurse, Mary, stood on either side of them to witness the vows. The judge read from a small book. "Dearly Beloved, We are gathered here…" The rest of the words were a blur until he said to Danny, "Daniel Jackson, do you take this woman, Honey Lee Murphy, to be your lawfully wedded wife to love and to honor in sickness and in health, for better or for worse, until death do you part?"

"I do," Danny said looking into Honey Lee's eyes.

In the same words, the judge asked Honey Lee if she accepted Danny as her husband. Clearly and firmly, she said, "I do." Honey Lee could hardly believe when the judge pronounced them man and wife that such a life-changing event could take place so quickly. She looked down at the thick gold band she had never seen before. It fit perfectly. How could he have known and when had he bought it?

Doctor Thompson drove Mary, Edna, and the newlyweds to the Copley Plaza Hotel for a wedding feast. The Doctor ordered champagne, and after the waiter had opened the bottle and poured glasses for each of them, he stood and held his glass up. "To Honey Lee and Danny, May the gods and all good spirits rain gifts down upon you. Health. Happiness. Children. And long life." Honey Lee's eyes filled as she touched her glass to Danny's. They drank—she from his cup and he from hers—and then they kissed. The others clapped. Honey Lee could hardly taste her food. She could not take her eyes from Danny. When they finished eating, the others left. They were alone as man and wife, amazed at the hugeness of what had taken place.

Danny led her to a couch in the lobby. He took her two hands in his and talked quietly. He began by telling her how he had come to know her before they had even met, how powerful his feelings were the first time he had met her, how he had despaired of ever being with her, how hard he had tried to stay away from her, and how ashamed he was of not telling her right away about his divorce, how he had believed that he could not live without her, and finally how sad he was that she, who deserved so much more, had had to pay such a high price to marry him. Honey Lee listened, never taking her eyes from his face. She nodded her understanding and held his hands more tightly when his feeling grew too strong for him. She told him that she knew having met, it was inevitable that they would come to this place in the way that they had, that she had no regrets, that she loved him so deeply that life without him was unthinkable.

It was she who said at last that they should go to their room. She wanted Danny without knowing what she wanted beyond holding him, kissing him, looking at him, and feeling his hands on her body. She was not afraid. They entered the room closing the door behind them. Danny took her in his arms and held her saying her name over and over. She pulled back enough to find his mouth. It seemed to her that ages and ages had passed since she had last kissed him. She would never have enough of him. She pulled away again and turned her back to him asking him to unzip her dress. He did. She dropped it to the floor and stood before him in her slip, her hands at her sides. He stared at her with such longing that she felt dizzy. She went closer to him and put his hands on her waist. His hands moved over the smooth satin on her body. With his fingertips he traced the lace at the top of her slip and the thin satin straps up to her shoulders and down her back. Then he drew her toward him and kissed again. She slid the straps of her slip down and let it fall to the floor.

A longing welled up in her from a place so deep she hadn't known it existed. It stopped her breath and weakened her knees.

"Are you all right, dear? Are you frightened?" Danny whispered.

She shook her head, unbuttoned his jacket and tugged at it. He let it fall to the floor on top of her dress.

"I want to see you, Danny Jackson," she said unbuttoning his shirt.

"I love you so, Honey Lee." His voice was hoarse. Deeper than she had ever heard it.

"I have always loved you," she said moving her hands over his chest and back exploring his body as she had so often explored his face. "You are wonderful," she cried, "too wonderful." Finally they lay together on the bed, he caressing her and whispering his love and longing. She had never dreamed her body had such power to want so blindly. When he finally came into her, she gasped, grateful for the sharp pain that marked her as his wife. His wife. Her eyes filled and overflowed.

Frightened, Danny asked, "Are you all right, dearest?"

"Yes. Yes. Now I am yours forever. She held him to herself shedding tears that washed away all sadness and longing. Everything she had ever wanted was here with her. He was her home.

CHAPTER 37

▼

In the morning they walked together to North Station. He waited with her for her train—sometimes holding her hand, sometimes folding her into his arms. She couldn't bear to spend a minute away from him, let alone a whole day. When her train was called, she told him she couldn't go, not yet. He nodded and they sat down and waited for the next train. She made him promise he would go right back to the hospital and do everything the doctors and nurses told him to do. He asked her to check to be sure she had her tickets for the train and the money he had given her. He promised he would be there to meet her when her train arrived in Virginia on Thursday. Nothing could prevent it. He begged her not to let her grandmother make her sad and sorry about what they had done. She said that of course she would be sad but never sorry. Reluctantly they went to the platform when the next train was announced. He walked with her and helped her up, then stood watching as the train pulled away. Looking at him standing alone, she thought her heart would break. It felt worse than any loss she had ever experienced, as if the other losses attached themselves to this parting. Never had Boston seemed so distant from Lowell.

On the train, when she was able to stop thinking about him, she practiced her meeting with Nana. She rehearsed and revised what she would say. But she could not find the right words to tell her grandmother what she had done. There was no way she could prepare her grandmother for another loss so like the one she had endured when her beloved Tommy had left and then married Savannah. This loss would be worse. Nana would know that her granddaughter was lost to her, to Almighty God Himself, and to the Holy Catholic Church. She walked up

Concord Street for the last time. She climbed the back steps slowly and entered the house.

"Nana, I'm home," she called out.

Her grandmother answered from the living room. "Darlin', I'm here. Come sit with me. I missed you. It's an empty place without you." Honey Lee paused in the hall to collect herself. She wiped her eyes and entered the living room where Nana Murphy sat, braiding thick strands of wool. She took a deep breath, embraced her grandmother, and sat on the footstool near her chair. She wanted to take her grandmother's hands in her own, but Nana's hands were busy.

"Am I a ghost that you're seeing and staring at so fiercely?"

"Nana, I've some news," Honey Lee said watching her grandmother's hands firmly holding the thick strands of red, white and gray wool she was blending into a smooth braid. Her grandmother looked up at her and dropped the braid to her lap.

"Darlin', is it such bad news?" she asked reaching out for her granddaughter's hand. Honey Lee held back tears as she took both of her grandmother's hands and raised them to her lips. "Nana, I love you so much."

"And don't I know that, dearie." Nana patted her head "Now what's the matter?"

"I've come home to get my things, Nana. I'm leaving."

"Leaving, is it?" Nana Murphy laughed. "And where would you be going all alone?"

"I've been lying to you, Nana. I hate lying to you. I won't do it anymore. I'm not at school, and I'm not working at the library." Although it was difficult, she looked directly at her grandmother.

"Honey Lee Murphy, what are you saying to me?" Nana's voice was high and thin. Her eyebrows raised, her mouth open.

"Yesterday, I married Danny Jackson. Last night was my wedding night." The words came out in a rush.

"But—without saying a word? Why in God's good name would you ever do such a thing without so much as a word to me?"

"Because Danny Jackson was once married—during the war."

"Then how could you be married to a man already married? It makes no sense."

"His—" she couldn't say the word wife. That word was hers. "She left him. Divorced him."

"Dear God in Heaven, child, what on earth were you thinking?"

Nana Murphy stood up and stiffly walked to the other side of the room as far from Honey Lee as she could. "It's a terrible, terrible thing you've done, a sacrilege."

"I know. But I had to."

"Had to? You, Honey Lee Jackson.?"

"Not that, Nana, not what you're thinking. I had to because I love him. That's why I'm leaving. I can't stay here."

Nana Murphy paced back and forth from the far end of the room to the hassock where Honey Lee sat.

"I couldn't help it, Nana. I tried. I really tried to stop seeing him, but then he got sick." This was going badly. She wished she hadn't said anything about being sick, but it was too late.

"You married him because he got sick? Is that any reason to break God's law?"

"It wasn't like that. I promised him before you got sick." She was crying now and the words were more like sobs than words. "Then I told him I couldn't. But it wasn't true. I knew I couldn't let him go. I tried, I really tried."

"Marriage is a sacrament in God's eyes binding until death. You know that, Honey Lee Murphy." Nana was pleading, searching for a way to undo the terrible thing Honey Lee had done.

"I do. And I told Father Finn I wouldn't see Danny again, but then I saw him and I knew that I had to marry him."

Nana Murphy came back to her chair. Honey reached out to her, but she shook her head and sat down without looking at her granddaughter. She rested her head on the back of the chair, closed her eyes and folded her hands in supplication. Honey waited. She heard her grandmother breathing quickly, struggling against tears.

"I'm so sorry, Nana." Honey wanted to take her grandmother into her arms to give and get comfort, but she didn't dare. Finally through tears, her grandmother spoke.

"I won't let you do this. I can't. You are not married. It can be undone."

"No, it can't. In my heart and with my body I married Danny. I love him. I need him. He needs me. He's a good man, Nana."

"No. A good man would not have done this. He would know how wrong it is. What it would cost you. Daniel Jackson is not a good man."

"Nana, don't. It's done. I knew if I told you, you'd try to stop me. So I did it without telling you. I'm going today to Virginia to be with him."

The sound of Nana's crying was unbearable. Honey Lee tried to touch her, but she got up, put her hands up, palms forward, and moved away as if Honey Lee were a dangerous enemy.

"No, don't touch me. I can't bear it. To lose you, too. It's too cruel. You were the answer to all my prayers for forgiveness for what I did to your father. And now it's happening again."

"Nana. Please sit with me. Help me to say good-bye."

"I can't. I cannot," Nana Murphy said and rose from her chair. She walked slowly from the room making a sound Honey Lee had never heard before. She wondered if the sound was keening. Honey heard her climbing the stairs; then she heard the soft creak of the floor above her as her grandmother walked to her room. Honey Lee moved from the hassock to her grandmother's chair. For over an hour she waited hoping her grandmother would come down. But she heard nothing. She climbed the stairs and went to her room. Her grandmother's door was closed. She pulled her suitcase from under the bed and packed. She went to the attic stairs and found two large paper bags which she filled with the clothes, books and pictures she had to leave behind. When the dresser drawers and the closet were empty, she looked around at the room she had lived in for five years, the room her father before her had used until he left home for good. She carried her suitcase down the stairs and left the house.

She turned to look up at her grandmother's windows. The dark green shades were pulled down to the bottom of the window. Wiping her eyes, Honey Lee began to retrace the steps that had brought her to her grandmother's house. She passed the terrible house in which the Jacksons had lived—Danny, Frank, Jimmy and the one who never came back. She walked by the church, resisting an impulse to go in for a visit and down through the Square to the train station. As she waited for the train, she remembered how forbidding her grandmother had seemed at first. Then how terribly much she had come to love her. More than she had ever loved her own mother.

The train was almost empty. She was glad. She closed her eyes and prayed. She prayed for her grandmother, for forgiveness for herself and Danny, and in thanksgiving for all the blessings she had found in Lowell. She took a taxi across Boston to the South Station remembering the crossing in the other direction four years before. This time the break was more final, more painful. She entered South Station and looked up at the clock under which she had sat alone waiting for her mother to find the luggage. She sat on the same bench waiting for the south-heading train that would take her to another new life.

978-0-595-35918-9
0-595-35918-3

Printed in the United States
109169LV00004B/83/A